THE LINEUP

THE LINEUP

20 Provocative Women Writers

Edited by Richard Thomas
Foreword by Alissa Nutting

Black
Lawrence
Press

Black Lawrence Press

www.blacklawrence.com

Executive Editor: Diane Goettel
Cover and book design: Amy Freels
Cover image: "Untitled (With Deer Skulls)" by Jennifer Moore

Copyright © Richard Thomas 2015
ISBN: 978-1-62557-915-7

Published 2015 by Black Lawrence Press.
Printed in the United States.

"Writing is…being able to take something whole and fiercely alive that exists inside you in some unknowable combination of thought, feeling, physicality, and spirit, and to then store it like a genie in tense, tiny black symbols on a calm white page. If the wrong reader comes across the words, they will remain just words. But for the right readers, your vision blooms off the page and is absorbed into their minds like smoke, where it will re-form, whole and alive, fully adapted to its new environment."
—Mary Gaitskill

"My belief is that art should not be comforting; for comfort, we have mass entertainment and one another. Art should provoke, disturb, arouse our emotions, expand our sympathies in directions we may not anticipate and may not even wish."
—Joyce Carol Oates

"Don't let the bastards grind you down."
—Margaret Atwood

Contents

Foreword

Alissa Nutting

I'll always remember the first hate letter I read while breast-feeding. Actually, it was a hate email, nestled between listserv mailings and bizarre SPAM offers (*"increase ur ejaculate 400%!!!!"*) that to a sleep-deprived new parent seemed too fascinating to delete without at least a cursory read-through. My daughter was just a few months old, and I'd finally reached a point of exhaustion that broke into the realm of the hallucinatory: paint often appeared to be moving on the walls, and if I stared at anything for more than a few seconds, its surface took on a sheer overlay of what appeared to be magnified, moving bacterial life. It was almost fun, though the repeating soundtrack of a screaming baby did somewhat harsh the trippy mellow these visuals might have provided in a different context. But one activity that seemed to mesh well with late-night feedings was to scroll through my email inbox, moving from one to another in a way that defied the filtering process and made the context of each one a surprise—photo-laden messages from friends kaleidoscoped into colorful HTML coupon offers from pizza delivery chains; these images burned away into the black and white ash of text-heavy editorial and professional emails, only to be followed by the rising phoenix of a newsletter mailing with an embedded lo-fi GIF that I might stare at for seconds or hours.

Then, suddenly, the hate email.

I am very much a learner and a student in this universe, but I do feel qualified to dole out this small piece of acquired wisdom: if it's possible for you to avoid publishing a darkly obscene comic novel about a female pedophile while you're also in the throes of postpartum depression and insomnia, maybe you should avoid it.

This is not to say that now, from a place of much greater balance and safety than I felt at the time, that I regret these events happened to coincide. It became one of the most defining periods of my life. The lessons I learned, particularly in the work of personal boundaries and emotional perspective, now seem a very fair trade in exchange for my trauma. Public scrutiny, much like the pain of birth, much like the early months of motherhood, had been something I'd told myself I was adequately prepared for. Before all three of these experiences, I'd felt certain that I'd had the mental infrastructure to endure whatever might happen. I was sure I would not succumb to paralyzing levels of distress.

I was incorrect in all three cases. With all three, at times the pain was much greater than my pride wants to publicly admit. Much greater than I felt I could take, wanted to take, and had imagined taking.

On that early morning when I came across the email, the light of my laptop's screen illuminating my naked chest and my daughter's closed eye and working mouth, I did not delete it without hesitation. I read it multiple times. The things it was saying about me, about the severity of my multiple defects of character, echoed loudly off of the core insecurities that likely steered me toward provocative writing and art in the first place, and in that moment I believed every word some stranger who'd never met me (and who hadn't actually read my novel *Tampa* that they were so offended by) had to say. I remember having to fight the urge to forcibly unlatch my daughter from my body: I felt like a poison well, like I was such a corrupt source that drinking my milk could cause her harm. When I came across other such letters during other feedings, this thought often returned. For a while I stopped looking at email during feedings, and then I stopped looking at email altogether—for a while. I turned entirely to provocative fiction and poetry, as I do during all my most desperate times.

During this period, I remember having a phone conversation with a friend who kept asking me the question of *why*. She was being supportive, but she was also understandably confused about the pain I was experiencing given my agency in the process. I'd chosen to write and publish the book, after all. "I just don't see why you'd willingly do that to yourself," she kept saying. I was lucky to have an enormous amount of support, both for me as a person and for the book, but at first I had a lot of difficulty hearing and feeling it—what actually echoed most in my brain at the time were not the sharp words of strangers but of friends, people who truly love me and could not reconcile the person they knew with the novel I'd written. "I think you're very talented," they'd often begin, kindly attempting to soften the coming blow. "But why in the hell would you write a book like *that*?"

Choice has always been an interesting concept to me in terms of art and writing. While I arguably choose the books I read, the films I watch, the subjects I write about, my instinct for and obsession with extremity has always felt preassigned. As a child, I remember secretly catching the first glimpse of a horror movie on my grandmother's cable television while she was doing dishes—I'd changed the channel from cartoons not sure what I was seeking exactly, but when I came to the horror movie I knew I'd found it. I had the sensation of transgressing in triplicate: what I was seeing was inappropriate on a moral level, plus it was inappropriate for my age, plus I knew that as a young girl I was not supposed to be drawn to things that were gross or gory.

As I grew and came to further understand the social prescriptions for my gender, extreme art became more and more of a sanctuary from these limitations. I saw a culture that said active sexuality, obscenity, and violence were male territories and expressions of power that were not open to women. Encountering and producing provocative art and writing—art that produced feelings of reverence, surprise, and disgust inside of me—was the way I could see beyond the limitations of the gendered social instructions I received on a daily basis. It freed me from them. That feeling of freedom is vital to my desire to be alive in the world. I understand that if I stop writing things that feel off-limits to me, if I stop reading and viewing things that feel off-limits to me, that freedom will atrophy. It is not a muscle society wants me to strengthen; it's not a space the mainstream feels should be accessible, particularly to women.

This is why the books I write will most likely always be books "like *that*," always gleaming with vulgarity, always unsettling. As a female author, I feel like vulgarity is a tree in my forest that the mainstream wants to chop down and harvest. So I've climbed it; I've taken up residence inside of it to prevent their saws from running. Obscenity is a natural artistic resource, and I will not let the status quo lay claim to it and haul it away to fuel its own historical purposes.

It might sound silly to say that raunchy, grotesque, and disturbing literature is what invariably keeps me going, but it's true. There's a politeness and an order to daily life that I often experience as deceitful, so much so that it can feel crazy at times. Provocative writing and art is a restorative form of honesty. For many like myself, it's one that is vital to sanity. I do not believe I could survive without it.

This is my "why"—why I have to write what I do and either adapt to endure the consequences that come alongside it (this is my preference) or mitigate the consequences through pseudonyms or by continuing to write but ceasing to publish. I'm extremely privileged in that the censure I've received is hardly worth mentioning compared to the consequences others have faced for their writing. I want to acknowledge and thank the provocative female writers who have been ostracized and threatened to the point of having to leave their homes, communities or countries. Who have lost their jobs or families. Who have been jailed, tortured, executed. Let us continue to thank and acknowledge these authors by reading and supporting provocative writing by women authors, particularly women authors whom various forms of intersectional oppression, such as transmisogyny and misogynoir, seek to keep silent. Our freedom and survival truly depend on actively fighting and dismantling the abusive frameworks that will acknowledge or tolerate the provocative writing of women of certain races, sexualities, gender identities, gender expressions, and social categories while excluding or repudiating the provocative writing of women of other races, sexualities, gender identities, gender expressions, etc.

I also want to acknowledge that my introduction to this anthology, and the anthology's final table of contents, are changes from the initial manuscript. While I feel it's my place to introduce the current anthology rather than to comment on these internet-searchable events, I do feel it's important for me to acknowledge and express gratitude for the provocative fiction of all the authors who were a part of this anthology at any point. My feelings surrounding the decision to write this introduction are congruent in many ways with my feelings surrounding the decision to craft pieces of provocative fiction: I worried about what others would think of me if I did write it vs. if I didn't; I worried what I'd think about myself if I did write it vs. if I didn't; I thought about the places where those categories were similar and where they differed.

Ultimately, in thinking about what I'd write for this introduction, I had an epiphany I feel very excited to share: the thing I love most about a great story of provocative fiction is that despite being drawn to it, despite feeling enriched by it, it's impossible to feel completely good about. It contains at least one thing that is chilling and repellant that the power of the text forces us to move through despite our reservations. We cannot escape the piece without confronting fear or abjection. I need provocative fiction because it helps me remember I cannot ever fully protect myself. It centers my attention in all the very places I try to avoid. My former professor Dave Hickey once said, "Art is what tells you things are not going to be okay." I hope you find in this collection a story that does indeed affirm for you this agonizing truth—how things are not alright—in a way that is profoundly unsettling, yes, but also helps this actuality feel a bit less lonely. I know I found many.

Alissa Nutting
March 9, 2015
Cleveland, Ohio

Introduction

Richard Thomas

If you just got done reading the foreword by Alissa Nutting, please feel free to skip ahead to the stories. If you would like to read my brief thoughts on this collection, then do continue.

When I think of the word *provocative*, there are certain images and connotations that come to mind, and yes, some of them have to do with sex. This collection is not about sexuality, although there certainly are some arousing moments. This collection is about taking risks, about getting strong reactions. That's how I think of the word provocative—provoking, defiant, edgy and enticing. Every story in here provoked a significant reaction from me. For some it was about loss, the sadness that overwhelms you—that pain and void created by absence and death. For others it was about the lengths we go to as human beings in order to fit in, to be accepted, and to belong. And for a few others it was the humor and self-deprecation that arises out of youth, failure and the things we do for love.

Yes, part of the reason I started thinking about putting together an anthology like this was because of the articles I've read over the past few years about the lack of recognition for women in literature—be it anthologies, magazines, awards, or even photo shoots. I am not rescuing anybody here, there are no white horses, these women do not need my support in order to succeed—they are already succeeding.

What I can definitely say about these authors is that each and every one of them has influenced my life as a reader, a writer, a teacher, an editor and a person. Some, I've known for years—having read tons of their stories, and many (or all) of their novels. Others are relatively new to me. But as I read more and more or their stories in literary journals and genre magazines, I started to create a list of names, people I wanted to seek out, to read more— voices to keep an eye on. I've met many of these writers in person at various conferences, have done readings with a few of them, or just applauded from the audience here in Chicago. For several years now this book has been coming together, the release date so far in the future that I thought it might never get here. And while all of that was happening, book contracts were being signed, film rights were being sold, collections came out, and more stories were published. It gives me such a thrill to see all of these authors succeeding, because I know how great they really are, how powerful their work is, and how important it is to read them.

I hope you enjoy this anthology—this has been a labor of love. These are some of my favorite stories, by some of my favorite authors. When people ask me for a good story to read, I often point to the ones in this book. When they ask me for a new collection or novel, you'll frequently hear these authors named. My bookshelves are filled with their titles, and I'll be reading them all for as long as they continue to publish. I'm honored to be a part of this project, and thanks to the generous support of Diane Goettel at Black Lawrence Press, this bound collection of provocative work is all in one place. I hope these stories stay with you, and that you are as inspired and touched as I was by their words.

Richard Thomas
July 29, 2014
Chicago, Illinois

Parts

Holly Goddard Jones

I had a daughter. When she was eleven, my husband and I took her to Spring Acres, the local pool park, for swimming lessons. She wore a purple bathing suit, the bikini I allowed over Art's grumbled protests, and she bounced on the diving board a little, and leaped, and cannon-balled right into the deep end. The splash of blue-tinted water made a fragile shell around her, gorgeous, and then she went under. She was fearless. There was that moment a mother feels when the heart pauses and the throat goes dry, that fear of—or desire for, maybe—the moment of crisis, when everything changes and you have to change, too, to make sense of it all. That's a strange word: *desire*. But it's there. When your wheels catch water on a rainy day and your brakes are suddenly useless, the pedal under your foot mush; when you're a few swats away from spanking your child too hard, and the coldness in your heart both terrifies and delights you. It's unexplainable, that desire, and perhaps it should also go unacknowledged, but I've since decided that the desire is useful, not shameful. Because it keeps you sane when the worst happens. And the worst does happen.

I felt that moment, and then she broke the surface of the water, and we caught our breaths together. Art, beside me, never looked up from his medical journal—the luxury of fatherhood.

I like to keep her here: young and alive, so many years away from the horror of that night in the dorm room. Her innocence and mine. She caught her breath that humid July afternoon, and I swear, it was just like the moment of her birth: the intake of air, the shriek of delight and fear. She waved to me from across the water, and I waved back, and we were laughing together. Felicia.

*

She was murdered eight years later, in the fall semester of her sophomore year of college. The boy who killed her, who got away with it, was named Simon Wells, and they'd met a few days earlier at a keg party on State Street. He'd made a pass at her, but she went home that night with his friend instead. The story came out at trial, and the boy she went home with, Marty, was the one who did most of the telling. The police put the rest together. It went something like this: the boys went to Felicia's dorm room—"to see if she wanted to party," Marty said. They smoked pot together, talked for a while, and then Felicia and Marty had fooled around some, kissing and "second base stuff," not wanting to make Simon uncomfortable. "He's a lonely guy," Marty had testified. "I felt sorry for him." After that, Marty claims that Simon "got crazy jealous," pushing him out of the way and forcing himself on Felicia. When she started to scream, Simon covered her mouth for a moment with a pillow—a novelty pillow, rainbow-striped, fish-shaped, that I'd bought for her myself—and when she screamed again, he covered her face again, and she was dead when he removed it the second time. Or seemed to be, Marty had admitted. She wasn't moving. Didn't seem to be breathing. It had happened so fast—he hadn't known that Simon could hurt her that way, or he would have done something, he would have risked his own life to save her. It had happened so fast.

"Then Simon sent me to get the car started," Marty said on the stand. "I didn't know what he was going to do. I wasn't thinking too straight by then."

So many holes in that. So much to doubt. But I want to believe that Marty had told the truth because Felicia had deemed him good, or at least good enough to sleep with. I've spent the five years since Felicia's death trying to reconcile the girl I knew, the daughter I'd made it my life's business to love, with the secrets that reveal themselves in death. You either make allowances or you lose the person a second time, and that's just the way of things.

When Marty left the dorm room, Simon set about covering up his crime. He sprayed Felicia down with a can of air freshener, wove a comforter around the room's two sprinklers, closed the windows and locked them. He tossed the emptied can on the bed, good as a bomb, and then he lit a match, set her on fire, and ran out of the room, pulling the door shut behind him. The doors at Keough Hall are solid oak, and they lock automatically. The first campus police officer to arrive after the fire alarm sounded secured the perimeter but didn't open Felicia's door. He waited for the fire department to arrive, and by the time they were able to break in, the room was a black and steaming husk, and Felicia, who shouldn't have still been breathing, was.

In another lifetime—the life before my marriage and even my courtship, the life before motherhood, when I still had interests and ambitions and hopes that existed outside of my daughter—I was an English major at a good university. And as every English major must, I took a survey on Shakespeare, whom I regarded with a kind of automatic, passionless appreciation. It was all too big for me, too grand, the fall of kings and death of lovers and old men raising their fists against thunderstorms and God. I believed in Shakespeare's goodness the way I believed in God's goodness: hypothetically, trusting the opinions of the majority over my own disinterest. I hadn't known any tragedy in those days. I had no real reasons for faith or for doubt.

The play I liked that semester was the one I wasn't supposed to like, *Titus Andronicus*. The professor presented it to us as a curiosity and sometimes as a joke. "Shakespeare does *Texas Chainsaw Massacre*," he'd said, affecting seriousness. He would read passages aloud with a melodramatic warble, working us like a stand-up comic, sounding, I would think later, almost desperate, as if the only way to excuse the play, to restore Shakespeare for us, was to shout the disdain that he'd rather keep private. What bothered me was that the play affected me more deeply than I could admit during final examinations, when I dutifully penned into my bluebook that it was "easily dismissible, though noteworthy as a testing ground for themes Shakespeare would later put to better use." Here is the sketch of things: There is a great Roman general, Titus, who gets on the wrong side of a powerful woman named Tamora, who becomes Empress. Titus has many sons, and most of them die during the play, but the important thing for you to know is that he has a daughter, Lavinia. Lavinia is raped by Tamora's sons, who then cut out her tongue and cut off her hands so that she can't tell anyone who'd committed the crime. Lavinia doesn't die, but she spends the rest of the play miming and weeping silently, and then Titus himself slays her at the end, along with a stage full of others.

That was the image I couldn't shake: Lavinia, led onstage by her torturers, robbed of her tongue and her hands. The outrageousness of it. The cruelty.

I hadn't thought about that play in my daughter's lifetime, all those good years of health and plenty. I'd had no reason to. We were, as families go, successful. When Felicia chose the local state college over Vanderbilt, Art's and my alma mater, Art had groused—but he wrote the tuition and housing checks without so much as a blink, and he drove the half-hour to campus at least once a week for a surprise visit, which she nearly always welcomed. She was a good girl. She'd loved her father. And Felicia, the mere fact of her existence, had continually fixed anything that threatened to break between Art and me. We were better together, united in loving her, than we could have been apart. It wasn't a perfect life, but I can look back on it now and know that it was as close to one as Art and I had deserved.

Then it was gone. Suddenly I was sitting at her bedside, listening to the hitch and hiss of the respirator, backing away every few moments to allow the doctors and nurses to change the bedding, which she frequently wet—the fluids poured out of her as quickly as they were pumped in by IV—and her dressings, which served as her skin. She was so swollen and bandaged that she was unknowable, her dark blonde hair burned almost completely away, the wisps clinging to her forehead as brittle and dark as curlicues of graphite. The room's heat was cranked up as high as it would go, almost 100 degrees, because—an irony, one of so many—her scorched skin couldn't retain any heat. The doctors and nurses wore hand towels around their necks. Art was stripped down to his sleeveless undershirt.

I passed out at one point, came to in a room down the hall, and vowed that I would never be so weak again, that I wouldn't leave her. I returned to find Art pacing the hallway outside her door, rubbing his face briskly with both hands. He'd been crying. Of course we both had. But I could tell he was upset about something new.

"They're going to amputate her hands," he said. He wouldn't have known how to soften his words. "She isn't stable enough to go to the operating room, so they're trying to sterilize her room. They're going to work on her right here."

I had stared at him, still lightheaded. It didn't make any sense.

"She can't live like this," he said, his voice high and choked. "It isn't possible. It isn't right."

I didn't know then what Felicia had suffered before the fire. It was six in the morning, about five hours since we'd gotten the call, and we didn't know that she was the victim of anything but an awful accident; it hadn't even occurred to me to wonder. Later that day Marty Stevenson would walk into his 11:30 section of American History fifteen minutes late, stumble on his way to a desk at the back of the room, and erupt into a fit of hysterics, scaring some of his classmates so badly that a handful fled the room, dialing 911 on their cells. That's when the truth, however distorted and partial, started to emerge. By the time the campus police chief came to the hospital to tell me and Art about Marty's confession, Felicia's hands and one of her ears were gone. It had come off into the doctor's hand like overripe fruit.

It was then that I thought of Lavinia. My daughter lay mute in her hospital bed, unaware of what she'd lost during her unconsciousness. She was swollen all over, bandaged into anonymity, her arms lopped and wrapped and strangely dear, resting on her stomach like paws. "You should touch her," a nurse told me, folding back the thermal blanket at the bottom of the bed. I watched her carefully peel down a stocking, revealing a foot that was peach and smooth and barely blemished, the toenails painted bright blue. Can you see it? That perfect small foot, the round, almost chubby toes, the cheerful, bright nail polish. I took it in my hands, pressed my cheek against it. I kissed each toe, the way I'd done when she was a baby. I whispered into the delicate arch.

Art couldn't do it. Here he was: a man, a father, a doctor. He'd given Felicia his high forehead and his hands. He'd given her his name. But when I backed away from her foot and beckoned him, he pinched his lips together almost prudishly and shook his head: a hard snap, left-right. The way a child refuses vegetables. Disgusted. Frightened. Absolutely determined. And that was when I began to understand that our marriage wouldn't survive this, even if Felicia could. He was already pulling away from her, wishing her dead, wanting to stop her agony and start his grieving. He didn't want to be father to a creature as destroyed and defeated as this one was, but I, in my selfishness, was determined to hang on to every last bit of her, even if she turned to ashes in my embrace. Titus had killed Lavinia because he couldn't bear to see her live with her shame. To me, Art's turning away from his daughter's foot was the harsher act, because it was rooted not in love, or in selfishness, but in weakness.

Felicia died three days later.

*

You know more than any mother should know, Art told me in the weeks after her death.

And he was right. I worked part-time at the library, a job I'd picked up after Felicia went to college, and I'd spend slow mornings on the public computer doing searches on the Internet, reading articles in the newspaper, scanning the blogs. *Simon is creepy, I know him from class, he totally did it,* I read on one page and felt the bitter thrill of absolute surety. *It's so sad but she fucked them both and this is the kind of shit that happens,* I read on another, and the thrill turned to fury and shame, and I don't think it's an exaggeration to say that I, too, could have been a murderer if I'd known who so thoughtlessly and cowardly posted that. I was breaking down, my sleeping hours only distinguishable from the waking hours by my dreams, which made my grief somehow more articulate. Over and over again, Felicia jumped into the swimming pool at Spring Acres. Over and over again, she failed to resurface. And the dream-me would think, looking at the still water, that it would be wrong to jump in after her because water puts out fires. That's when I'd usually wake up.

This is the kind of shit that happens. I started searching her bedroom, going through the items she'd left behind after moving into the dorms: the cheap jewelry box with the little spinning ballerina inside it, her Cabbage Patch doll with the yarn hair, the band posters she'd put up during high school. I looked under her mattress. I pushed aside clean underwear and balled-up socks, finding only a lavender sachet and a cracked plastic egg, the kind pantyhose used to come in, with a single stocking inside, twisted like a dead thing. She'd taken her secret self to college, and the artifacts of that life went up in flames with her. I was left with dolls and old yearbooks and the clothes I'd purchased for her, the life I'd allowed her while she lived under my roof, the remnants of a Felicia I had known and understood.

I'm good at finding that dark matter in the white space, and I'm maybe too good at living there, wallowing in it. I think things

I shouldn't think: that Felicia awakened after the fire started and screamed for me; that Simon and Marty laughed when they reunited at the car, high-fived and lit cigarettes with the same lighter, or book of matches, that had started the fire. I wonder about the times Art was with her alone, when she was a child. Had he hit her? Had he touched her? Art is a decent man, and he wouldn't have done either of those things, but some nights—when the last of the wine is gone and I can feel Felicia all around me, through me, even, like my pulse—everything I should know for sure doesn't seem so certain anymore, and I think about calling Art, at his new house across town, where he sleeps next to his new wife: Did you love her? Did you love me?

*

He just wanted to move on, Art told me as I was packing my suitcases on the day I left; he wanted to remember what happiness felt like. I wasn't thinking then: where I'd go, how I'd pay for it. And I should have felt *something* when he handed me that stack of crisp twenties—everything in his wallet—with assurances that I could also go on using the credit card for as long as I needed. Something other than embarrassment, or gratefulness; it was my money too. But I took what he gave me and tucked it into my purse, and I murmured something like *thanks* in a voice I didn't recognize.

"Don't mention it," he said, leaning over to pick up my bags for me. The bigger person, the big man. Our daughter had been dead for five months, and the trial hadn't started yet. "Where will you go?"

I didn't know. My parents were both dead, and my sister lived in Ohio. I had friends in town—women who resembled friends, at least—but most were also hospital wives, and few were good for more than the occasional light lunch at the country club. When Felicia died, none of them called me, but they all sent flower arrangements: gigantic bouquets that collectively cost more than my first car had. "A hotel, I guess."

"Take a room at the Washington House," he said. "I'd feel more at ease."

I nodded.

He put the bags back down and came forward, then put his arms around me. I let him. I tried to hold myself stiff at first, but I needed his touch—Christ, I always had—and he melted me, that silly old phrase I hate, the stuff of Hallmark cards and easy listening love songs.

"You don't have to leave," he said.

I inhaled the good smell of his neck, the Old Spice he still wore because his father always had. There were reasons for loving him, I know that even now.

"I'll call tomorrow," I said into his neck.

He backed away and picked my bags up again. Gentlemanly to the last, but I should have recognized how easy my leaving was—too easy. Twenty-two year marriages don't end like this, I thought as he loaded the car and kissed me, as I turned over the engine and pulled out of our drive. They don't simply flat-line. Not if there was life in them to start with.

*

He's a gynecologist, one of only two who still practice in Roma, which has a history of attracting the doctors fleeing malpractice suits and driving away the ones with real skill. But Art, who could have had a more glittery life than the one he chose, is good. Very good. His clients are loyal, all ages, and even now, the divorce four years done, one will approach me occasionally, recognizing me from the old family portrait he still keeps in his office. Crazy, but true. And she'll say, "What a good, good man he is. So understanding." I usually nod and agree and leave it at that. There are all kinds of understanding, I could tell her—all kinds of goodness—but what would it matter?

We both agreed, from the start of the marriage, that I'd be better off seeing another doctor, when the need arose. Another decision that came perhaps too easily, but it worked for us. When Felicia was sixteen, and she approached me about birth control, I took her to my doctor in Bowling Green—quietly—to get her examination and prescription. Art and I could function like that when she was still around, with these compact lives that were separate and whole and in no way intersecting. In mine: Felicia's sex life, which I considered myself *with it* enough to understand and even support a bit; my housekeeping and little trivial errands and my books, devoured more often than not with a glass or two of wine. In his: the monthly trips to Nashville with Beau Markham and Robert Zipes, the anesthesiologist and the surgeon—business trips, he called them, though we both knew that I knew better. I'd accepted that they probably played golf and drank to drunkenness; and perhaps they'd gone to strip clubs, too, though I never considered, or allowed myself to consider, the degrees of betrayal beyond that.

His work was in that life, too. One evening at dinner, when Felicia was an eight-year-old playing over at a neighbor's house, a question—perhaps the most obvious question—occurred to me for the first time, and I put down my salad fork, the look on my face apparently bizarre enough that Art paused mid-sentence. "Do you ever get aroused at work?" I said.

"No," he told me, mildly enough that I believed him. In bed that night, though—at least an hour or more after I had slipped off into sleep—he shook my shoulder. "Every now and then," he whispered, and I knew what he was talking about right away. "Once in a blue moon. And it shocks me."

"When does it happen?"

I turned around but couldn't see his face because his back was to the window, casting him in shadow.

"Sometimes during a breast exam. Most of the time just before the exam starts, and I can see a slice of her skin where the paper jacket gapes open."

"What about when you—" I couldn't finish.

"Do a pelvic?" His shadow shook. "Never. I may as well be kneading bread dough."

My stomach lurched. "Jesus."

"You think I'm some kind of pervert, don't you?" he said.

"No," I told him. I think that I meant it.

"Because it's common enough." He rolled onto his back and sighed. "It's a big joke in med school. But it happens less and less with time, anyway."

"You get used to it," I said.

"Something like that."

I pulled the covers tighter around me. "Do you worry about my doctor?" I asked him.

He was yawning. "Huh?"

"Dr. Nickell," I said. "Do you worry he's getting a boner when he touches my boob?"

"No," Art said, laughing. "It's real rare, hon. Ninety-nine percent of the time they're just parts to us."

"Parts," I said.

He patted my arm. "Yeah. Like Picasso: a breast here, a leg there. When you get hard, it usually doesn't even make sense. It doesn't have to be a beautiful woman or even a young one, just some-one who hits your senses the right way."

"Thanks a lot," I said.

"I like your parts," he told me, pulling the waistband of my pajama bottoms down so that he could slip his hand between my legs. He moved against me. "This," he said lowly. "This is what does it for me."

Bread dough, I kept thinking. But we had sex anyway.

*

I knew when Art called three weeks ago that he had news for me, probably bad. He only calls for moments like these, and he always prefaces his announcements with, "I wanted you to know first." Like it's a gift he's offering me, a neat little package of despair: *Dana, I'm selling the house. Dana, I met a woman. Dana, we're getting married.*

"Dana, Stephanie's pregnant," he said. "We're having a baby."

All I could make clear was this: Felicia would be twenty-four. While Art blathered on, that thought cycled in my head, first in words, then in images: the graduation she never attended, the boy-friend—the *one*—she never met, never had a chance to bring home. Some days I wonder if my life would be different—how my life would be different—if Felicia had been in a car accident, or had cancer, if she'd gone some way that wasn't so goddamned grotesque. Can you quantify hurt?

"She's about midway through her second trimester," Art said, and that snapped me back in a hurry. Stephanie. She works at the

Chamber of Commerce, and I always see her picture in the local paper: cutting a ribbon at some new business nobody wants to see in this town—Blockbuster or Burger King, nonsense like that—hosting a Rotary luncheon, "kicking up her heels"—the *News Leader's* words—at the Tobacco Festival Street Dance and Tamale Hour. She's thirty-five, and though those twelve years between us burn sometimes, I'm thankful that he didn't choose someone Felicia's age. He could have, too. He's more attractive now than he ever was: tan, fit, the kind of man who wears his middle age like a Rolex, a sign of his good breeding and achievement. I carry my middle age around like an ulcer.

"Twenty weeks or so," he finished.

"Pretty far along," was all I said.

"Well, she's starting to show." I could hear the television behind his words, and a sound like cabinets opening and closing, dishes being removed and stacked. I pictured Stephanie, apron tied neatly around her cute little pregnant bump, starting supper, giving Art concerned looks, marital shorthand: *Is she okay? Is she flipping out? Do you want one porkchop or two?* "But we wanted to keep it quiet for a while, make sure everything looks good. We're not in our twenties."

"You had an amnio," I said, knowing as I said it I was right. No Down's baby for Art.

"Well, sure." He cleared his throat.

"Congratulations," I said.

"I'd like her to know you," he said. "And so would Stephanie. We'd like you to be involved, I mean."

"A girl, then." I pinched the bridge of my nose, willing my tear ducts to behave. I thought about the Art in Felicia's face: her blue, wide-set eyes, her high forehead. And Art's hands, too: long, graceful fingers that she'd applied toward no particular talent or vocation, surgery or piano-playing or any of the old clichés. When she was a little girl, and my hair was still long—down to my waist, almost—she'd loved brushing it with my big wooden paddle brush, long strokes that lulled her toward nap-time better than rocking or warm milk ever had. With Art gone to work, we'd lie in the big master bed together, drowsing, and sometimes she'd reach over and pat my face with her still-chubby little fingers: *Mama,* she'd say. Like a blessing.

"Yep, a little girl," Art told me.

"Why do you think I'd want to know your child, Art?" I said. "I mean, did it cross your mind that the situation might be a little awkward for all of us?"

"Because she's Felicia's sister," he said.

That's the thing about Art right there: how on the one hand he can be so *good*—so damned noble, even—and on the other, a monster. Who would I be to this child? Aunt Dana? The babysitter?

"I don't think it's a good idea," I said.

In the background on his end of the line, a hot cooking sizzle—supper almost done. My own stomach, unbelievably, growled; I decided that I'd drive down to Hardee's for a burger, bring it home and eat it with one—or a few—glasses of the good red wine that I bring back from my occasional trips to Nashville. I've gained about twenty pounds since Felicia's death, and when my I saw my sister last Christmas, she had the audacity to tell me that I was "hiding from men"—as though my greatest trouble after the death of my daughter was figuring out how to date again. As if a man were any sort of solution.

"It's an open offer," Art said. "Indefinitely, okay?"

We said our goodbyes and hung up. Indefinitely: the word almost made me smile. This offer of his—made to assuage his guilt about an old wife, an old *life*—would be forgotten in a few weeks,

dead as Felicia. There would be baby showers and first kicks, a nursery to decorate, cigars—the good Cubans—to ship in and pass among
his friends. I would see his child only by accident, and probably
more often than I'd like: Roma's a small town. In a few years she
would start coming to the library, and when I'd lead Story Hour or
one of the Summer Reading Program sessions, maybe she would be
one of the small faces looking up at me. Maybe? Christ, it was likely.
There was only one library, and if he was as demanding a father as
he used to be—he'd wanted Felicia to be every bit as driven and successful as himself, though he'd regarded my own modest smarts, my
own lack of worldly ambition, as natural—Art would have her there.
Come hell or high water.

I dug my car keys out the basket I keep by the back door, pulled
my light jacket off a hook, and checked my purse for cash: eight dollars. I wouldn't be gone long. At Art's house, they would be sitting
down to eat dinner, the relief palpable between them, perhaps even
confessed out loud: "Thank God we have each other."

*

I will never have another child. This is a truth I settled with
long ago, because I was forty-two when Felicia died, and by the time
the idea of a new baby presented itself as a kind of solution—*yes, I could
just have another*—Art was gone, and my own body was changing, going
bad on me the way a woman's body will inevitably do. I'm not a modern woman the way my daughter was: Felicia, whose confident sexuality had fascinated and even impressed me a little, naive as I had
been at her age; who saw college as a step in a logical progression;
who'd never taken for granted that she could choose her own path
in life, take her time, treat dating as recreation and not husband-

hunting. I'm not a modern woman, but I can't help raging a little
at the unfairness of the situation—Art's ability to simply move on,
to replace our daughter with a new child as easily as he'd replaced
our old Toyota Camry with a Cadillac Escalade. Upgrading. I find
myself thinking more and more of that day when I left him: I'd
thought that I was leaving him, that I'd taken decisive action, but I
see now that Art ushered me out the marriage just as he ushered me
out of the house that afternoon.

Some nights, all of the things I know for sure—should be able
to count on, like gravity and oxygen and sunrise—lose their power
over me. I know who killed Felicia. I caught his eye a half-dozen
times in the courtroom and simply understood, felt the guilt baking
off of him like a fever, settling on me sick and damp and poisoned.
I know that much. But some nights, it's Art I want to see destroyed,
see broken. I want him to feel at least as bad as I do now, to know
loneliness—a woman's loneliness, the way it feels to be childless and
manless with nothing else to define you or drive you.

We met when we were in college at Vanderbilt. I was a sophomore, Art just starting his first year in med school. And the first
time we had sex—my first time ever—was in my dorm room, when
my roommate was gone for the weekend, visiting family. We locked
the outer door, turned the radio up loud, so no one in the hallway
could hear. I don't remember what was playing, but I remember the
scratchiness of the sound, and of my blankets; the coolness of the
concrete block wall that my left arm kept brushing as we kissed, the
bed was so small. There was the usual pain and blood, and when he
finished I cried, because I felt trashy, because I wondered what my
daddy would think. My daddy, who'd sold off twenty acres of good
farmland to make up the costs that my scholarship didn't cover.

Sex is always violent. Even consensual sex, or *lovemaking* as the hospital wives would always put it, prudish and vulgar all at once. I'm not saying that I hated sex—I didn't—or that Art was somehow rougher than other men, because he wasn't really rough at all. That night in my dorm, when I started to cry, he held me close, patted my hair, whispered in my ear that we never had to do it again if I didn't want. What happened to Felicia, the way our marriage disintegrated: none of that takes away from his essential decency, as much as I sometimes want it to. I don't know if Art is a good man, but sometimes a decent one is all you can hope for.

*

Two days after Art's phone call, I got in my car to drive to Felicia's grave and ended up in Bowling Green instead, sitting in front of the Wells Brothers Furniture Company. Simon's car—a newer black Corvette than the one I'd seen him enter and exit a half-dozen times during Felicia's trial—was parked on the store's side lot, angled across two spaces so that the doors wouldn't get dinged. He'd done that at the courthouse, too, and on the hottest days—this would have been late July—he'd prop a metallic visor up in the windshield. I could often see it in the lot from the courtroom: a wink of light in the distance, like a faraway ocean or a mirage.

His trial lasted two weeks, and the jury deliberations lasted two and a half hours: acquittal on all nine counts. No physical evidence linked him to Felicia's room, which was scorched, then flooded when the sprinkler system finally engaged—no sperm, no fingerprints, no sign of him on the Keough Hall security tapes, though the girl helming the front desk admitted that it wouldn't be hard to sneak by her—and the investigation got botched by a team of campus investigators who'd never handled anything more complex than noise violations, DUIs, and the occasional stolen bike or book bag. Simon cried alibi as soon as the police dragged him off, but the campus detective began interrogating him without investigating it, a point the defense hammered over and over again at trial. He was at his mother and father's house, his father said on the stand—definitely home at three a.m., when the dorm's fire alarm went off. Everyone was awake, his father insisted: a happy family sitting at the table, having a middle-of-the-night heart-to-heart about Simon's career anxieties. He was, after all, a 23-year-old college sophomore positioned to inherit a regional furniture chain of more than thirty stores.

His friend, Marty, is in prison. He pleaded guilty to voluntary manslaughter a year before the trial in exchange for a recommended sentence of twenty to life. His testimony was supposed to cinch Simon's conviction, but he ended up doing more harm than good: Simon's slick defense attorneys pinned Marty on a handful of piddling inconsistencies in his testimony, confused him on the stand, made him look like a fool and a liar. I don't feel sorry for him. But the hate, which has become so much a presence in my life that I may as well call it a part of myself, like my eyes or my hands, is for Simon. A useless sort of hate, though, one that I haven't the courage or even ambition to hone into a weapon. But I like the idea of revenge—big revenge, the kind Shakespeare wrote about. In *Titus Andronicus*, Titus kills his daughters' rapists and serves them to their mother in a meat pie. Crude, silly—that's what my professor had told us, anyway. But satisfying, too. We live, I've heard, in a civilized country, in a civilized time. Our movies are violent but our laws are just. The system will serve us. And I put faith in that, because I'm a middle-aged woman, most of my life a homemaker, and I couldn't even bring myself to give Felicia spankings when she deserved them. What was I supposed to do when the system failed me? What, if not destroy what was left of my own life instead of my daughter's murderers?

I knew that Simon worked the flagship store most evenings. He was on Bowling Green's local news less than a year ago, red Wells Brothers polo tucked into neatly pressed khakis, hair streaked blond but still trimmed short: a solid, All-American male. The segment showed clips of him unloading stock next to his dad, muscles well-defined as he lifted plastic-wrapped couches and recliners from the back of a semi; in another shot, he counted out change for a customer, and said, in a lull between the reporter's voiceover, "You have a nice day, now." The interview was sympathetic. The reporter mentioned that Simon's car had been vandalized, that he was accosted one night outside a bar. "I'm just trying to lead a good life and put this behind me," Simon had said. "I don't bear any grudges." The goddamn nerve.

I'd never gone inside Wells Brothers, even before Felicia's death. They didn't carry the kind of furniture I would have put in my home—not then, at least, when I was still a doctor's wife. I'd driven by once before Felicia started college, thinking that I might find a cheap bookshelf small enough to fit in her dorm room. They were closed, though, and I ended up buying one at Target instead.

I went inside. The showroom smelled cool and plastic, not rich with the earthiness of hard woods and leather. Theirs was the cheap stuff, just short of disposable: pressboard entertainment cabinets and laminated kitchen tables, overstuffed vinyl recliners in burgundy, green, and brown. Ceramic vases and lamps cluttered glass-topped end tables, the vases filled with dusty stalks of eucalyptus, that medicinal scent I've always hated, like cut grass and anise.

It was early evening on a Wednesday and quiet; a couple was on the far end of the showroom looking at the dining room tables, but the store was empty otherwise. The furniture was arranged into little areas meant to mimic rooms in a house: couches with chairs and coffee tables, kitchen tables set for dinner with placemats and plates. I wondered if Simon had designed some of these arrangements and knew that he must have. It was fitting: this man who understood nothing about the fragile construction of a family, piecing together bad fictions out of bad furniture.

The double doors between the stockroom and showroom swung open, and Simon came out. He saw me, started toward me.

I stood where I was and waited for the step that would bring him close enough to feel suspicion, then the step that would make him certain: I waited for him to understand that the mother of the girl he killed was finally confronting him, doing the thing she'd been too scared and weak to do during the trial. So many days I'd sat in that courtroom, Art next to me but careful not to let his arm or leg brush mine, watching this young man pass in his crisp, navy blue suit. So many times I'd caught his gaze, seen something inside him that I knew his own parents had been able to deny, or ignore: the combination of weakness and meanness, self-hatred and vanity. I'd known better than even Simon what a dangerous mixture those traits were, how they could—in the wrong circumstances—drive an otherwise average boy to commit the act of a psychotic. I knew all of that, but I couldn't do anything about it.

He stopped, less than a yard away. "Can I help you, ma'am?"

We made eye contact. I waited. In a moment, I was sure, he'd react: his body would become tense or his hand would start trembling; he'd say something like, "Why are you here?" or "I swear, I didn't do it." I had envisioned this meeting a thousand different times and ways—considered the dialogue that would follow—but this was the part I had always accepted as a given: he'd see me and he'd *know*.

"Ma'am?" he said. He rubbed the back of his neck, and I noticed for the first time how much fuller his face was now, three years after the trial—a detail that hadn't come through over the television. I could see that he was anxious, but only because he was confronted with a situation he didn't immediately know how to handle. Humor the crazy woman? Call the guys in the little white coats?

I looked at the floor. "I'm browsing," I said.

"Oh, okay." He nodded. "Make yourself at home, just holler if you need anything. We'll be running a special on Leatherlook through Memorial Day, so keep that in mind."

"I will," I said.

He backed away, smiling carefully. Before he turned—before he struck out across the showroom floor toward the couple in the dining area—I thought I saw something in his face. I went back to my car knowing that I was probably kidding myself, that *my* face meant no more to him than Felicia's life had. He'd moved on, like everyone else. Everyone but me.

I think that there are moments in a life when you have to leave a part of yourself behind to function—like molting. Felicia's birth was the first such moment for me: in the weeks after my labor I understood that my body wasn't the only thing that would always be different, that my soul had changed, too. Some loss there, but the gains were greater. When she died, I had to molt again, but I did it badly, and never really finished the job, because I get up mornings feeling like a mother, still, and I go to bed nights mourning my daughter all over again. If the anger is a part of me, Felicia's loss is a kind of amputation, and I haven't yet figured out how to function without her.

I left Simon's store that night understanding what a small thing a life is—how quickly it comes and goes, how even the bereaved, like my ex-husband, can evolve and adapt and find new ways to get by. I drove home thinking about Art's baby. Intoxicating to imagine this new child, this sister of Felicia's. She is a miracle and a curse: half of Art and none of me.

*

The library is never a loud place, but its energy changes. During the spring, before the middle school lets out and all of the buses begin their afternoon run, the light falls through the windows differently and the books almost seem to sigh, scattering dust particles around in swirls. I sit at the front desk reading a novel or magazine, and the big grandfather clock in the front entrance—the one the city purchased the year of Roma's bicentennial—counts off the new hour with low, spring-like thrums, a brassy, ancient sound. We don't have the world's oldest or most charming building. They made a lot of "improvements" in the 80's: dropped the ceiling, installed cold fluorescent lighting. Five years ago they covered the hardwood floors with wall-to-wall blue Berber carpeting—to minimize noise and retain the heat, the head librarian, Nita, said, but now the children's sneakers smack against the nubby plastic runners that criss-cross the floor at all angles, and I get tripped up at least once a day. A graying woman in cardigan sweaters and khaki skirts and neat leather loafers: the stereotypical old maid librarian, or getting there.

Yesterday, Stephanie arrived in that silent hour before the afternoon rush. Soon, the girls and boys would tear in, and as oddly respectful as they are in this place—the only place besides church, perhaps, that holds such sway over a child—the very walls vibrate when they're here. Until they start to drift off home for dinner, I'm captivated, and that short period of my day is when I can leave Felicia behind me for a little while. I love watching them sit at the tables, kicking their heels against the chair rungs, chins tucked into palms. They turn the pages of books so carefully, the little ones.

That silence right before is when I'm at my most vulnerable. It's physical—the emptiness around me, and within me, a kind of husked out, cried out place that's almost a pleasure because it's numb. And that's how Stephanie found me: sitting in my familiar chair with the worn-in seat cushion, printing a pile of overdue slips for mailing, sleeping with my eyes open.

"I hoped you'd be here," she said.

What do you say about a woman like Stephanie? She's attractive, but I was more attractive at 35; smart—that much is obvious by speaking to her—but not especially deep or sensitive, not *soulful*, which is what Art used to say he loved about me: *How much you care about everything. How you feel so much, all the time.* Polite, not necessarily kind. She is the woman who marries men like Art, who is able to understand, with a savvy that borders on calculation, that her modest charms have more value because she's the new model.

But she's also one of those women who seem more real in pregnancy. And it hurt me to see her that way—brown, nicely trimmed hair a bit more mussed than usual; the way her badly cut sailor blouse pulled tight around her middle but sagged under her arms, making her both sad and kind of lovely, too. I could glimpse, for a moment, what a person might love about her, and that was the worst, meanest kind of irony.

"Good to see you," I said, the lie so obvious and empty that I think we were both embarrassed by it.

"You, too." She gripped the edge of the front desk before me. Her fingernails were painted a smooth, even coral. "I've been wanting to talk to you for a while."

The library was so quiet. The only patron was an older man—one of those retirees who comes by daily and stays for hours—and he was off in the back corner, tucked away with the paperback mysteries and true crime books. One afternoon, this old man, Jimmy, his name is, stood right where Stephanie was standing, for hours, it seemed like, telling me about one of the books he was reading: *The Red Light Murders*. I let him. The victims were young women, he explained, wannabe starlets and prostitutes living in the bad part of Los Angeles, circa 1925. Killer filleted them like fish, took their eyes for trophies. And the author had proven, through new DNA technologies and old documents found on his family's country estate, that his own grandfather was the likely murderer. "Helluva thing," Jimmy had said, tapping the book's cover. "Just goes to show." He said that a few times as he talked—*just goes to show*—but he never finished the sentence, never told me *what* it showed, what kind of sense you can find in ugly death.

"How are you?" I said to Stephanie. I found myself motioning toward her stomach and felt ridiculous.

"Good," she said. I was glad that she didn't lay her hands of each side of her belly and smile serenely, like women on TV always do—like I had even done on a few occasions during my pregnancy, as if I were carrying around the secrets to the universe: me, the Goddess Mother, the first woman to ever create life. "I'm comfortable right now. My mother keeps telling me that I'll be suffering come July. And the humidity's always so bad mid-summer."

"I wouldn't worry so much," I said. "I enjoyed my pregnancy, right up until those last couple of days."

"Oh, I'm enjoying it," Stephanie said quickly. "I'm just dreading the heat."

The grandfather clock chimed the half hour, and my arms broke out in chill-bumps. I wasn't ready for a sermon from Stephanie, who appeared so full of good intentions that she might've been hauling them around instead of Art's baby. I knew what she was going to say to me, could've scripted it out for her on the back of the check-out cards we don't use anymore but keep around for scrap paper: *This means a lot to Art. Think it over, okay?*

"Stephanie," I said. "Why are you here?"

"I wanted to let you know that I'm with you," she said. "You know, thinking that you and the baby getting close would be a bad idea. Or weird, at least."

"Yeah, weird," I said, nodding. I wasn't quite processing what she was saying. I looked down at her round middle, how the red bow on the front her blouse drooped, one length of ribbon hanging much lower than the other.

"Art cares a lot. He can't see too far ahead sometimes, though."

I nodded again, but only because that's what she expected. The whole time we were married, Art was *always* looking ahead: to the next car, the next promotion, the next big vacation.

"He's not thinking of this baby as a person yet." She touched her stomach then. "He's just seeing her as this way of getting a little bit of Felicia back. You can't put that kind of burden on a child. She has her own life to live out."

"If you're lucky," I said. Unfair, probably, but I felt justified when I saw the look on her face: pitying, that look, and so certain. *Not me. Not my baby.* As if reason governs these things, or desire.

"I guess that's in God's hands," she said. I could see that she believed it—believed in this God of hers, his big hands in the sky. Fitting, really. Reduce God to his hands, his parts—big male hands that could hit or hurt on whim: like Simon's, like Marty's. Like Art's, for Christ's sake, those long, lovely fingers that he gave our daughter, that had touched me on too many nights to count, that had handed me those crisp twenties on a day that now felt like a million years ago. I pictured God as a pair of hands.

"I understand what you're saying," I told her.

She adjusted her purse strap and smiled. "He still loves you, Dana. Just like he still loves Felicia. That's okay, you know? I knew what I was getting into with him. I knew that he came with..." She hesitated.

"What?" I said, waiting for her to say "baggage." Stephanie looked like the kind of woman who'd spout pop psychology of the Dr. Phil variety.

She shook her head, all that nicely trimmed hair. "Ghosts."

I didn't want to cry—not in front of her, not at all. So I kept my face still.

She came around the desk, took my hand, and pressed it to the side of her stomach, where the curve started to recede into the sharp angle of her hipbone. The skin there was tight, dense but yielding, and the intimacy of the touch was infuriating and unfair: a shameful miscalculation, and I think she knew it as soon as she took my hand. I could smell her perfume—something light and floral—and beneath it, a sour note of perspiration. There was a flutter beneath my fingers, so familiar that for a second I couldn't breathe. "I'm sorry," she whispered. Outside, the air brakes of a school bus whistled, then hissed. I drew my hand away.

*

Two years ago, a couple of months after marrying Stephanie, Art showed up to my house with a box of Felicia's things, scavenged from his basement, and a bottle of Jim Beam. *I couldn't do this alone*, he told me, and so we went through the items together, trying to decide what to keep and what to give away, realizing that we had to hold on to all of it. We sat side by side on my sofa, and we flipped through the pages of yellowing photo albums, laughing over pictures of ourselves—young, thin, tan before tanning was taboo—crying over pictures of our daughter, taking swigs from the bottle and beginning the business of sleeping together before either of us would have acknowledged the possibility. There was that moment before we decided to go the bedroom when we both knew that everything could change again, and probably for the worse—but desire's a funny thing, the only way you can cope sometimes, and we didn't pause long.

We collided in the dark, clumsy, out of practice; it had been years since we'd touched, and I was conscious of the ways my body had changed since the last time we'd had sex. And when was that? I have no clear memory of a *last time*, just a vague sense that it happened before we got the call about Felicia—days, a couple or a dozen—and that it didn't happen after her death, despite a few half-hearted, disastrous attempts. Art was careful, even reverent. And though I never once harbored hope that he'd come back to me, there was a moment—when he placed his ear to my heart and listened, and I felt it quicken beneath his warmth, traitorous as always—that I believed, despite everything, if I gave enough of myself I could have them back again. That wanting it badly enough could make a difference.

Skinny Girls' Constitution and Bylaws

Tina May Hall

We will know each other by the way our watches slip from our wrists, the bruises on our knees, our winged shoulder blades tenting silk dresses.

We eat; we eat. We eat like wild boars, like wolves, like cyclists in training. We love the bloody shreds that cling to the T. We suck the gob of marrow that floats to the top of the soup. We gnaw the chicken down to splinters.

Everything is bone, bone, bone.

Her brother holds Polly to the candle to read her, the way one would a stolen envelope. Numbers float like seaweed under her skin. She is a mathematical genius. She has teeth like the keys of an adding machine. She tells her brother that his birth date plus his wedding day plus the day of his death add up to 243. He drops her so quickly the flame is blown out.

They call us witches. They look away from us in the bright light. The lavender crisps in the fields. The rain will not come.

Querida is the only one of us who once was fat. Her mother cooked with lard and made pink pastries on the weekends. But when she was thirteen, Querida got her period and a fever in the same week. She burned and burned. The priests said masses over her. Her bed was lit by a hundred candles. Her mother held a wet cloth to her brow for fifteen months while bees died in the space between the window and screen. And when she rose up, Querida was a blade of grass, sweet as spit, forehead blanched and thighs withered. We ask her what it was like and pinch her waist, but she only smiles. We love our secrets; anything hidden is so dear to us, we who are always on display.

When we run, our knees are castanets.

Thirteen of us, a baker's dozen. Pasteboard box of meringues, sweet and brittle. Thirteen horses wheeling at the fence. Thirteen water-striders, all legs and surface tension.

Bianca's job is to fasten ties around men's necks all day long. She has mastered the Windsor, the half-Windsor and the Four-In-Hand. She is practicing the Cross Knot. The Double-Simple is best for short men. Only a few wear bowties. Most prefer silk to polyester. Cotton is a daring choice. Bianca's fingers move quick as crickets. Many of her clients don't even realize she is there. The worst part is the collars. They are always too narrow or wide, too dingy or floppy. Bianca takes home the collars of the men she likes best and stiffens them herself with sugar and egg whites and mineral water, boiled down to a paste, painted on with a dove's feather, dried by her own breath.

We will gestate plump happy babies in the bone cage of our pelvis.

When we lift our arms to the moon, there is a sound like branches scraping.

Lizzie stops a car with her bare hand, standing in the middle of the road over the body of the dead squirrel. The car just kisses the skin of her palm as it drifts to rest, like a boat easing into dock. Beneath the wishbone of her legs, the squirrel shudders. The moon falls right out of the sky. Fur springs up to cover wounds, its tail traces an "S" on the asphalt.

We chant Plath at school assemblies. "One year in every ten, peel off the napkin, I eat men, I eat men," as we shake our pom-poms and swivel our hips, left, right, all around, a race track, a snake eating its tail, the eternal ouroboros. Our classmates love it, throw carnations at us, send us candy grams and risqué text messages, dream of us all weekend long.

We will donate cells drawn from the doorknob of our spines, the needle a key turning us.

At eight, Francie is the youngest of us. We feed her the choicest bits, the organ meat and the toenails, the nose cartilage. She is pretty as a stream, kind as a blizzard, graceful as a schooner a thousand feet underwater. She plays goalie on the hockey team and roars like a lion when she has a bad dream. She will not sleep alone; her fears are our fears. Her knuckles dig into our necks at night; her mouth touches ours when we least expect it. Little ghost, how often we have closed the door on you, how often you have tunneled through.

We will not stick our heads in ovens. We will not throw ourselves from bridges, nor weight our pockets, nor disturb our veins.

Nessa is the mean one, the one who deals with telemarketers and credit card bills. She never holds the door for anyone, puts the empty milk carton back in the fridge, tells people their pets are ugly and ill-behaved. In her spare time, she climbs, her feet wedged into the too-small shoes, her fingers caked with chalk. Once, she fell sixty feet and dangled there, hanging from the rope and a leaf-bladed piton, the last of three, the only one to hold. She broke all of her fingers that time, trying to find a way up or down. In the end, she swears she used her teeth to unclip the carabiners and release herself from the granite face, into the air, where she floated, hollow as a feather, lightning cracking around her, knowing what was coming, the morphine and its weird itch, the feeling of her tibia stitching itself back together, the forever lumpiness of her ribs, the first drops of rain, heavy as lead on her skin.

We will grow up to be doctors and stockbrokers and video store clerks. We will wear our hair like crowns and snort through flared nostrils.

Martine is 115 years old and still flat-chested. In her cold blue heart, three little men live. By night, they write love poems and keep her awake with their sighing. By day, they smoke cigarettes and discuss Nietzsche. Finally, they lick clean the last can of duck fat, cough up their black lungs, and wither into tiny skeletons, whose splintery outlines Martine can feel if she presses hard enough.

We pass each other notes in the hollows of our collarbones.

In the snow, Audrey is invisible. Her pink cheeks drain to white, her eyes pale, her skin turns waxy. She is the corpse-bride running after the soccer ball. She is the one who chirps, "We're late again," and hands round lunch in paper bags and builds scale replicas of Chartres out of the ice she scrapes from the windshield. Inside, Audrey is always the first to be seen. She is all roses and oranges and zebra stripes. She jingles when she walks—it is her molars rattling.

There is no noose that can hold us.

Fiona writes romance novels on her cell phone during lunch hour. All of her heroines are named Fiona, and her heroes are prone to swooning. Her publisher pays her in pounds and thinks she is a little old grandmother in County Cork. She writes, "Mark clapped the back of his hand to his forehead and said, 'I am overcome.'" And, "Frank sank gracefully onto the divan." And, "Steve reached out blindly as the world went grey."

Underwater, we are transparent.

Our mothers won't let us sit on their laps.

Colleen is deaf. We broke all of our grandmothers' rose-decaled plates proving it. We speak to her in signs and spell out the unusual words. *Filament, Frangipani, Balzac.* She sings us to sleep with her stony voice. She wakes at dawn to bake saffron buns with fat raisins poking out like roaches. In public, we must be careful. The sight of our fingers spelling causes heart attacks and car accidents. Mostly, we wait to talk in the dark, in bathroom stalls and movie theaters, broom closets and basements, our hands pressed into her hand, our knuckles kissing.

We fit six across the backseat and shiver together, arms and legs wrapped like eels around each other.

Olivia, Ophelia and Odette are identical triplets. They have red hair that has never been cut. They sleep on piles of it, bind it up in knots and rolls for the daytime, let it unfurl like bolts of silk after dark. They sing in unison, their clear voices making a chord. They tap dance and juggle knives. They do a ventriloquist act at the burlesque theater downtown. Between the strippers, the triplets appear, holding three dolls with long red hair. They are perfectly synchronized; they never falter. Their lips don't move. Once in a while, a chartreuse feather floats down from the catwalk or the light shifts and the stage glitters with loosened sequins. For the finale, they sit perfectly still, until the audience forgets which are the dolls and which the girls and breaks into spontaneous applause.

We will grow up to be spelunkers, ballerinas and landscape architects.

In fairy tales, we are the last to be eaten.

They call us late bloomers, daddy long-legs, frigid. They call us by each other's names and names we've never known and seat us in the back row of the plane, not realizing that it is our prayers which are keeping us from going down in a scream of burning metal. They call us *sweetheart* in the dark, never guessing we are all around them, so many of us packed in tight. That old game, we think. Breast, hip, thigh. *Sardines*, it was called, and the goal was to stay hidden.

We wash in teacups. We chart the stars on our scapula, make telescopes of thumb and forefinger. We cut our nails short as boys', the better to scratch at the chiggers embedded in our shins. We know our blood is sweet to drink; we know our bones are irresistible.

Lifelike

Ethel Rohan

When UPS delivered the first baby doll, Sandy clapped and shrieked. The newborn replica, dressed in a powder-blue onesie, came fitted with a heartbeat, glossed nails, ginger human hair, and mottled, veined skin. The doll so realistic Rob drew back, his scalp crawling.

"Isn't he darling?" Sandy asked.

Rob refused to touch the doll or to help choose its name. Sandy sat up most of the night with the doll, and decided on Pearce.

After breakfast, she phoned her employer, cited a family matter, and asked for a week's leave. Rob swallowed hard on his lump of bagel.

Sandy rang off and met his hard stare. "What?"

Over the next several weeks, she crammed the guest bedroom with these lifelike babies and their white wicker bassinets. Rob's rants and ultimatums went ignored. The evening she announced

she had quit her job to stay home full-time with the babies, Rob fell
dumbstruck. She lifted up one of the pink adorned dolls and cooed.

*

Rob suggested they go out to dinner. She needed to get away
from the house, he pressed, and those dolls. She refused. A movie,
he tried again. She loved movies. They could watch something at
home, she countered. They weren't a couple any more, he argued,
the dolls everything to her now. She'd stopped seeing her friends.
The phone hardly rang. They argued on and on, but she wouldn't
leave the house, not without her babies.

At the paper company, Rob worked late into the evenings.
They needed the extra income now that Sandy was unemployed and
splurging on more dolls and their accessories. So many dolls that
they'd overflowed into the second guest bedroom.

Sandy hadn't even noticed that the tropical fish had died.

He asked her again to go out. She refused again, and cradled
the yellow clad doll. He stormed out to Malarky's, a local tavern he'd
started to frequent. He sipped ice-cold beers and listened to country
music on the jukebox, gabbed with the half-deaf bartender.

He closed the bar and returned home to find Dollsville in
darkness, except for the jaundiced glow through the far bedroom
window courtesy of *The Cow Jumped over the Moon* themed lamp. He
trudged inside and paused outside the yellowed bedroom, its door
ajar. Sandy sang soft and low, *Daddy's going to buy you a mocking bird.*

She sat on the rocking chair with her back to him, only the
doll's bald head visible in the crook of her arm. He moved deeper
into the room and watched, disbelieving. Sandy's bloodied finger

moved in a circular motion over the doll's naked chest, smearing it red. He made some exclamation.

Sandy moved out of the chair, the doll clutched to her breasts. She backed away from him, blood trickling down her hand. He spotted the kitchen paring knife under her chair, realized she'd nicked herself.

He said, "Tell me you know they're not real?"

She shook her head and glared.

He reached for the doll. "You better see to that finger."

Her eyes filled. "She won't settle."

He paused, then, "Let me try." He eased the doll away from her and resisted the urge to throw it across the room.

"Maybe she could sleep with us tonight?" she asked.

He looked into his wife's pale, startled face and saw the mixture of fear and hope. He nodded. Her smile almost made his legs buckle.

Throughout the night, he jerked awake, imagining he could hear crying. He checked first on his wife and then on the doll between them.

See You Later, Fry-O-Lator

Monica Drake

The morning of my sixteenth birthday, I, Mademoiselle Icicle, used one sharp fingernail to etch a cartoon birthday cake in ice that blanketed my boudoir. Ice coated the inside of my bedroom window so completely the window was like TV without reception, opaque as a velvet curtain. I scratched a dash of candles on the cake, phallic and listing, and gave each candle-cock a paisley flame. The flames were a school of sperm. *Fuck me,* I wrote backwards, a message to anybody out in the snow—like there'd be anyone in the pitch-dark winter fields, where it was all apple trees and pine. I scratched a happy face. A happy face was the same from either side of the glass, speaking the same language from in the house or out.

When I pressed my hand to the ice and held it, the ice welcomed my skin. My hand left a print. I was the Ice Queen.

I'd gone to bed fifteen and woke up sixteen. My parents left during the night. Only the refrigerator breathed, wheezing and asthmatic. Ours was a stucco ranch house designed for Southern California, with picture windows like giant eyes meant to gaze over a beach, now blinded by a Midwestern blizzard. From inside, each ceiling-high window showed the dark slice of a snowdrift like an ant farm, a science fair experiment. The experiment was a question: How to be a house when you're not equipped? The roof leaked, the walls weren't insulated. The architect was insane, a homesick transplant.

But I wasn't an ill-equipped house. I was ice. Cold was immaterial. Who needs insulation? Who needs shoes, boots, a winter coat?

I opened the side door and our dog, Charlie, brought a rage of snow in. She dragged a bad front leg. The snow was specked with blood where Charlie'd been waiting. Ever since a car accident on the old highway, she chewed her leg like she was caught in an invisible trap.

In the shadows, my parents' footprints broke the snowdrift just beyond the door. A layer of new snow had settled where they walked. They'd turned back at least once. Turned in circles. Debating? Fighting? Maybe. Shadows of a snow angel in the yard was me the day before, when I was still fifteen, playing in the snow like some kind of kid. Farther off, a couch-shaped drift really was our old couch underneath, put out to air last spring. All summer at night I'd sat on the couch and read magazines while crickets sang. While my parents sang in the house, fighting, swearing, boozing it up.

If I were a savage I could read the tracks of my parents' path. *Savage Ice Queen: The Movie.* I could stand in packed snow barefoot. And I was in the snow barefoot, nightgown ruffle blowing against my ankles. Cold is only cold at first, before it fades to numb. I bent down, tucked my knees inside the nightgown to keep a thin line of flannel between damp snow and the heat of private corners, and looked for evidence. My parents had left, and not in a straight line. One but not the other of our two cars gone meant they left together.

That's so obvious! I looked for more subtle clues. The second car, the Old Car, was a sedan-shaped drift, a match for the snow-upholstered couch. But why did I worry where my parents went? I had what I needed: a house, a car, a job. A dog. Pretty much, the American dream. I'd overslept, missed the school bus, but a learner's permit's good as a driver's license when you come from an ice cave miles outside town.

I bundled my nightgown and lifted it. *Savage Ice Queen, pees in the wild.* Steam cut through the snow between my feet; the bright yellow stain made a hole in the ice crystals. The air filled with the muffled scent of the Vitamin B I took to turn around a split-end problem. My own heat was warmer as it rushed out; warm air brushed my ankles, and tiny drops splattered. It was the chemistry of urine over ice, body heat transferring. My own experiment.

*

Ryan, the stoner, sat closest to the door and tried to trip me as I slid into Chemistry late. Blank faces turned toward the late-opening door, not like they cared, but just asking *Who? Who comes so late?*

Me. Cheeks flushed, still hot from digging the car out of our long drive. Hair wet with melted snow. Mrs. Hapkewitz was behind her teaching counter like the host of a cooking show, with a Bunsen burner and metal tongs. Her elbows jutted out as she swung a test tube back and forth over the burner's blue flame. Lisa, a paper-thin slip of anorexic weightlessness, was passed out in the back row. I saw Ryan's outstretched foot but kicked it on purpose anyway, letting my waffle boot slap the side of his waffle boot, orange laces kissing. Snow fell on the slick linoleum off the frozen leg of my jeans. Mrs. Hapkewitz gave me a quick eyeball. Ryan smiled, with only one side of his mouth. I sat next to Rachel Swoops.

If I were a gas, I'd be Helium light, settling into my seat. My muscles burned from shoveling.

"Einstein's new trick," Rachel whispered.

"What's it supposed to do?" I hissed back, peeled off my coat, then pulled down the sleeves of a sweater to cover my wrist where the skin was marked with pink lines, burns from the grid of a fry rack from my job at Huff Burger. They called me *fry rack* at school. *Fry Girl, Grease monkey, ha!*

Rachel shrugged.

"Girls," Mrs. Hapkewitz said. Her voice broke the crazy way her voice always did, singing up and down even in a single word. "Pay attention." She added something to a beaker, one liquid into another, the first yellow as my Vitamin B. She held the beaker at her eye level, in front of her nose, and went cross-eyed, all frowning and squinted.

She'll need Botox, Rachel wrote on her notebook, and pushed the notebook my way.

Scientists invented Botox, I wrote back.

"What this *should* have done..." Mrs. Hapkewitz said. I couldn't help it. I laughed. I loved it when she said that. Every time, every experiment. They never worked, and I liked it that way.

"Justine, please." She started again, "It should've turned to a greenish gas. I'm not sure what's gone wrong..." And I couldn't control it. Why did I like this? It was like being tickled, seeing science fail, the parts not adding up. Mrs. Hapkewitz, pure optimism, shook her head like even small failure was unbelievable. I giggled, hoped she wouldn't notice, tried not to laugh and snorted instead.

Rachel, already close to flunking, acted like she didn't know me, with a hand to the side of her face. Mrs. Hapkewitz said, "Justine, enough," like it was a command for a dog.

But she wouldn't send me out. What I knew, and what she knew, is that I did my homework. I memorized Avogadro's number, the calculation of a mole. I had the periodic table taped inside my locker. In a room full of dyslexic anorexics, stoners and party girls, I was our Nobel Prize candidate. I pulled the sleeves of my sweater down, stretching the knit to cover the burns. *Fry-O-Lator* it said in the pink graphics of a burn scar, in backward cursive along the inside of my arm.

After Chemistry was lunch. Ryan saw my keys. "Driving now, fry girl?" He soft-punched my arm, my sleeve, where fry rack tattoos lay hidden below.

I nodded. Rachel looked surprised, more used to me late-night sneaking the car.

"Cool," Ryan said. And it was.

*

After school, before work, when I let Charlie out she stopped to nose the frozen yellow piss in the snow—mine. There was no sign of my folks, nothing about my birthday, still only the one set of tracks leaving the house now mingled with mine both coming and going. A splintered chair in the bushes looked run over. My parents were like lupus, MS or rosacea, the body attacking itself, a leg trying to divorce the hip, the brain. I was a free radical, bumping up between them. It was already getting dark out, a winter day short as school.

I brought my Huff Burger uniform into the kitchen, closed the kitchen doors and turned on the oven full blast. But heat didn't matter. I could change clothes in a blizzard.

The uniform was a brown polyester shirt that zipped up the back and wide, flared pants. The shirt had a built-in bra, a swerve in the striped fabric where my body was supposed to fill gaps, and fill in some kind of fantasy for the boss, like there was a formula between hips, waist and boobs: if one, then the other. My shirt stayed loose in empty points. I ran a fast line of concealer along tiny red dots gathered under my eyes, spots left from grease snapping in Huff Burger air.

The old car, musty and vinyl, had a dash cracked as dried mud. I headed down our long dirt drive and the car's tires slid into the grooves made by my parents like I was some kind of trolley running over old tracks. I pulled onto the highway. The car danced a slow glide sideways, front wheels grabbing for asphalt. I could slam on the brakes and the car would swing in a circle. Rachel Swoops and I practiced driving and sliding, cutting cookies, at the school parking lot at night, inside the metal cocoon of that old Plymouth; we wore spilled whiskey like perfume as the tires drew circles over the iced macadam.

The only problem with the Plymouth was rust holes in the floor. I could see the road. Slush hit my ankles with the kiss of icy spit.

*

"You're on fry rack," Jeff, the manager, said, before I even had my coat off. He ran a finger over his mustache.

I said, "I'm cashier."

He crunched up a paper bag and threw a long shot to an overflowing trashcan. Missed, hit the rim. "Nope. Rack."

The schedule was posted on the wall between the walk-in freezer and stacks of buns. I didn't want anywhere near fry rack. Rack was the worst, torture, a beginner's station, plus it was all grease and quick moves. Plus, I worked it way too often. Up front,

Dana leaned against the register, guarding her spot. Her hair was a curling pom-pom out the back of her hat, with no split ends. The boob gaps in her uniform weren't gaps, like she was proof of the if-hips-then-boobs equation. Jeff said, "Had a complaint about you last time. A secret customer said you weren't smiling."

A "secret customer" meant a company spy. They wrote up these little reports. Like I'd smile more now, written up? *There's ways to make a girl smile.* That's what I wanted to say, with Ice Queen sophistication: the hard crack of an ice coating over snow, the sweet taste of deadly sap in a Poison Sumac icicle.

He threw a fifteen-pound bag of onion rings at me. I caught the bag, white plastic slippery with frozen grease. *The Ice Queen never fumbles.*

"Ten minutes, dinner rush." He went to code Dana into the computerized register's system. Dana smiled, gave an eyelash flutter and tugged at a gold floating heart on a thin chain around her neck.

A low whisper gargled out, "You know they're screwing each other." The voice came from around the corner, behind the grilling machine, behind Burger Assembly. That corner was a house of mirrors with warped steel boxes in every direction, and in that corner, from everywhere, I saw skin and uniform and hair, and it was a grunt named Karen putting burgers on the conveyer belt. She was huge, a parade float, her tiny face lost in circles of fat. I hadn't worked with Karen in a month, but heard the rumors: she had to trade up uniform sizes three times. I'd traded down twice, shrinking, contracting with the winter's cold. Karen wheezed, and slammed a handful of frozen meat patties against the steel edge of a machine to break the stack apart. Her sausage fingers were huge, taut and red, reflected back in the fun house mirrors a dozen times or more.

What Karen didn't get is, if you don't eat, your stomach turns into a hard knot instead of an empty space; it turns into an answer instead of a question.

I put my hat on, got in place.

Heat came off the deep fry oil. A few steps over, cold rose from the drinks station ice. The two made a sickening corridor, hot and cold struggling to mix, and not in the gentle way of tornado weather but more like a house fire in winter. There was an orange heat lamp, glaring and bright, and a white light over the ice. In metal cursive script, on the side of each fry basket, it said *Fry-O-Lator*, *Fry-O-Lator*, *Fry-O-Lator*, with the TM of a registered trademark.

"We're closing tonight," Karen said, breathing hard, lips squished in her new face. "You and me."

Closing meant locking up at 2:30 in the morning, cleaning, and getting off the clock by three. The company didn't pay for work after three no matter what, so closing with Karen was good—she was a robot.

I put a basket of rings down and two baskets of fries. Grease snapped at my arms, a biting dog. My job was to tear open the big white bags, take two steps sideways, grab a new metal basket, fill the basket to the marker and sink the whole thing in grease. Fries have to be hot and ready. When a timer beeps, that means the fries are done, and then a rack rises automatically up from the grease. My job was to jump for it. One second is all management allows between when the timer rings and when fries are dumped under the heat lamp. All night long the floor mats grow slick, then slicker with splattered fat.

The beep started, I reached for the basket handle, dumped fries in the bin under the orange heat lamp, and let salt snow down over their hot skins.

On a fast break, I stood in back near the manager's office and called home. I traced a finger over my scarred arm and imagined quitting: *See you later, Fry-O-Lator. Ta da!* My arm was so scarred it had started to look plaid. On the schedule on the wall my name had been crossed out, Dana's name added for all the register shifts. I could see, through the narrow space between the burger counter and the shelves, Dana and Jeff trap flies in the microwave. Dana laughed, a flash of white teeth. The trick with the fly is, they don't have enough water in their bodies. Microwave a fly and nothing happens. A fly is its own kind of superhero.

On the other end of the phone line, in our snow covered ice cave, the phone rang. My mother's voice came on, apologizing: "Sorry, we're not in right now, but if you'll leave a message..."

"Mom?" I asked the answering machine. "Dad? You there?"

On the way back to my station I slid a chicken sandwich in my uniform pocket. The sandwich was dead, meaning cold and under the lamp too long. My dad, if he came home, would take the sandwich apart like a mechanical thing and warm it in pieces, balanced on a knife over a burner.

*

The dinner rush trickled in, then hit; the lobby jammed with kids and old people and some football game that'd just gotten out, and the orange heat lamp at the fry station made my eyes so dry they went blurry.

I poured fries into little paper bags, moving fast, orders in and orders out. A ribbon of white paper pumped out at my station. Fry Rack was a dance, both arms swinging: scoop fries, grab the salt, drop the little paper bags of fries into the bigger paper bags, tear the order off the roll and drop that in the bag too.

Dana's register jammed, or maybe she needed change. I don't know, but Jeff was up there, keys in hand. He reached around her hips. One hand to either side. His mouth to her neck. She turned, giggled. The crowd pressed against the counter. Dana smiled, a hand on her ass. Where was our company spy? I didn't lose pace.

Deep in the rhythm, another fry timer sounded its steady bleat. I turned, dropped the aluminum fry scoop into its rack, hit the timer-off switch, grabbed for the handle on the fries as they rose from the grease, turned halfway back around, and boom! Jeff cut past me, all managerial, in my way, his body in front of my body.

"We need at least three baskets down. Two rings. The orders are backing..." He grabbed fries from the bins, shoved fries in his mouth. As he skated past, his knee hit my knee, foot to my ankle—on purpose? He ducked sideways, and kept going. Both hands full, I skidded on the spot between the big black floor mats, where grease layered over the fake tile floor. I slipped, swung an arm to grab for anything solid, slid into the mechanized basket as it rose, and with a hiss there it was, a pink brand rising around my fingers, with no time to look. Orders came in fast. Jeff was gone, back to counting receipts or browsing porn or whatever he did in his office. I put my burned hand to the ice trough in the drinks station. Held a round cube. The metal basket had left the kiss of a hot, pink grid, *y-O-Lato* seared backward across my palm.

*

Late that night, I took the trash out to the locked dumpster. The dumpster was surrounded by a brick fort, with a locked metal gate in front, like Huff Burger trash was pure gold. In winter, in town, the streetlights reflected against snow and kept the night from ever being as dark as it was outside of town, out where I lived, in the fields. Under the streetlights, the night stayed a glowing blue. In that blue-white light, I looked behind the brick walls around the dumpster, checked for crazies, then moved with Ice Queen stealth over frozen asphalt.

Karen locked up. Our cars were last in the lot. She drove a rust eaten clunker, small and squashed. My car, twice as big and twice as old, had seats inviting as a sofa, but the lock was frozen and wouldn't take the key. Karen scraped her windows while her rollerskate-mobile warmed up. I warmed my key in one hand, blowing hot breath on it. I had to force the key, first in, then side-to-side. Karen got in her car, and the car dropped lower under her weight.

When I turned the key in my ignition, nothing happened. No heater, no engine, no radio. The Plymouth clicked. I gave it a minute. Karen took off, wet tracks in the snow. I tried again. The lot was empty now, except for me and my car, and then snow, new drifts over old, and the black spots of exhaust and salt that marked patches of ice and gravel.

I reached under the dash, popped the hood, opened the door. Soon as I did, one car came spinning down the highway. The hum of chains against gravel and ice carried from faraway. Headlights moved toward me. I closed the door again, ducked low. The car edged past, tossing slush like damp confetti in a sad parade of one. The taillights moved into the distance, red and warm, then finally gone. When I opened the door, a night wind cut through the wide, flapping legs of my uniform.

I knocked snow off the Plymouth's hood, lifted the hood and looked inside, until I heard another car coming. Then I got back in and locked the door.

The car moved past. It skidded to a stop. There was the high-pitched whine of a car in reverse. The driver pulled into the lot backwards, tried to brake, and the car slid until he'd passed me again. I looked in the rearview.

Slowly, the car pulled forward, inch by inch, until we were driver's side window to driver's side window. There was one man inside. His was an old car, a Nova to my Satellite. He rolled his window down. I wiped condensation away from my window, and peered through the cleared space.

The man pointed down, then turned his hand in circles: *Roll down the window.* I shook my head, behind fogged glass. A Plymouth Satellite is a comforting wall of metal. Except for the holes in the floor. Tiny planets of new snow glittered in the wind.

"Car trouble?" he shouted. White teeth, a dark stocking cap.

"No," I yelled back.

He said, "Pop the hood," and gestured with his gloved hand, thumb pointing at the night sky. A strand of yarn splayed from his frayed glove. It was just him and me, dark gloves, stocking caps, a long stretch of empty highway. And I was the Ice Queen. I'd sit there all night, stay in my car, wait for him to leave and hike along the road on my own. *Ice Queen patience. Superhuman endurance.*

Then what?

He said, "I'm good with cars."

I could walk all night and into the day. I could go home, to an empty cave.

A Huff Burger bag blew along the side of the freeway. The bag was light, as though underdressed for the cold, and moved fast as a lost kid running to someplace like home. I could do anything. I could stand up to burns, to cold, to this freaky stranger, if that's what he was.

If I were Dana, I'd have a cell phone. I'd have a house, and parents in it. I'd have boobs.

The man got out of his car. He put his gloves on my fender. "You'll freeze, out here," he said. What did he know? I was already a sheet of ice, a frozen branch, a twig. I could freeze in my own house, if I wanted to. The man's eyes darted down the road.

I was an icy slip of nothing. I was invincible.

I reached low, pulled the t-bar to unlatch the hood. I stayed in my car, watched him rustle through his trunk. He connected jumper cables, started his engine.

He called out, "Give it a try."

I turned my key. *Click.* He walked around to stand outside my window. *Click.* He disappeared behind the hood again. Like he knew what he was doing. A fine ruse.

I could see his hands working, through the gap between the hood and the car body, his skin grey white as it reflected one lone parking lot light overhead. It wouldn't be hard to steal my carburetor. "This cold weather," he yelled out. "Need all your Cold Cranking Amps."

He scraped corrosion from the battery, cleaned the connections with a screwdriver. His hands were chapped, a cut across one knuckle. A cotton glove blew off the fender. He didn't see it go.

"Try again," he called, and stepped to the side. He rubbed his hands together, blew on his fingers.

That glove would be one of the world's small mysteries, resting alongside the highway frozen into the slush, snowed over until spring. People would wonder: *why take one glove off here?* The man would puzzle over where the glove had gone, left with only one of the pair.

The glove would be like my parents, gone without reason.

I turned the key. He shook his head. He pulled off his stocking cap and wiped his hands on it. His face was flushed, dark hair blowing forward.

I had a pen in the car, and I put the pen in my coat pocket. I'd stab the man in the eyes if I had to. That was my plan. Armed with the pen, I got out of the Plymouth, walked across the snow, and picked up the man's glove where it lay in slush. I put the glove back on the fender with its mate. Mystery solved.

"Thanks," he said.

I fingered the pen. Kept my eyes on him.

He reached for the gloves, pushed them down into his pocket, and started scraping terminals again. "I don't know. Might be electrical." His breath was a white cloud. He wiped his nose on his hat.

I said, "The battery's almost new," and watched my own breath cloud, then fade.

Beyond the smell of exhaust, there was something else in the air. Cinnamon, or vanilla. His pant legs flapped in the wind. Polyester. They were navy blue, with a paler blue stripe. I asked, "You in a marching band?"

He looked over my way, then went back to chipping at corrosion on the battery terminals. He said, "You look cold."

Cold? I said, "I can stand in snow barefoot." Savage, and proud of it. "I can reach into hot grease with my bare hands."

He laughed, and shook his head. "Nobody should have to stand in snow barefoot..." He hit something inside the car with the side of a wrench. Tapping. "...or reach into hot grease. Try it again. Might be your starter."

I didn't move to start the car. But in my pocket, I let go of the pen. I took my hand out, and opened my palm to show the brand, the geometry of a fry rack grid against the constellation of grease-splatter burns. The backwards cursive, *y-O-Lato*, was blistered and raised, the burn still new.

He leaned in close, squinted to see under the flickering street-light, and said, "Jesus!"

The strange thing was, for a minute, just as he said it, I saw my hand as though it wasn't my hand at all but was somebody else's, a red and raw thing, like my dog Charlie's leg. He said, "What's that about?"

I nodded at Huff Burger. Closed my hand. The skin was stiff and hot. I put my hand back in my coat pocket, and then it was mine again, but not like it mattered—just skin and bones, immaterial.

"Listen, you need a ride somewhere?" His car sat waiting. There were no other cars on the road. Everything was icy and muffled.

"I'll walk."

"To where?" He looked up and down the road. "You smell like French fries."

Fry girl.

"It smells good."

I smelled something sweeter. "Smells like doughnuts, to me." The air smelled sweet as a bakery. But I hadn't eaten in hours, in days, all week. An Ice Queen doesn't eat. Even an anorexic can't compete with ice.

I needed food the way a fly needed water: barely.

"Panda Pastries," he said, and nodded down the highway. Far down, there was a giant, revolving doughnut-bellied panda sign. Sweet, frying dough. Perfume. Sugar. I said, "Never smelled it from here, before."

He pointed at his car, took the few steps, opened his car door and showed boxes, pink and marbled with grease stains. He pulled one box out and had to use two hands because the box was that heavy. He sat it on the hood of his car. When he opened the lid, I saw a field of crullers and maple bars, powdered sugar coated cake doughnuts, chocolate filled, and éclairs. There were oversized fritters and coiled springs of glazed dough, bars and doughnut holes. He said, "Have what you want," like he thought he was offering me the world or something.

I stayed back. Kicked the snow. I said. "Is this like, 'Hey little girl, want some candy'?"

He shrugged. "My own personal embarrassment of riches. I take'em back to the dorm." His blue striped pants, I saw now, weren't real clothes. It was Panda Pastries gear. "They call me 'Nuts Man'," he laughed. "Cause I provide. Go ahead, dig in."

I didn't need food. The doughnuts smelled so sweet! But what did I need with sweet? Then I saw, in one low corner of Mr. Nuts Man's greasy box, a cupcake. It was a white cupcake with blue and red letters across the top, and a scatter of sugared dots like confetti. *Happy Birthday*, the cupcake said.

"Whose birthday is it?"

"Nobody's," he said, and shrugged. "We just make'em up."

It wasn't my birthday anymore, either. It was after midnight. I flicked a finger at the box, like that crap was only for suckers. Fatsos and softies. That cupcake was a trap, laid in my path. This guy was a softie. The Ice Queen lived on cold air. I breathed in. But even the air now was sweeter than before. I said, "And you don't mind?"

"Mind? No way, have all you want." He leaned against his car.

"I mean, you don't mind being called 'Nuts Man'?" And for some reason, as I said it, my eyes welled up. My throat was tight. I choked, reached a hand to my neck.

"You okay?" he said.

I said, "That smell!" I coughed. "Maybe I'm allergic." My voice broke, my eyes clouded. Even my hands started shaking. Could I be allergic to a smell? It was the smell of a kitchen. An oven used for more than heat.

He ducked down and looked up, as though to see my eyes. "You're too cold. Let me walk you to a pay phone."

A payphone. I shook my head. Who would I call at three-thirty in the morning? Rachel Swoops? Her parents would kill me, think I was on drugs. My parents, who knows? Mrs. Hapkewitz at least would understand the failed science of a dead car, a late night. My lips felt fat, but I wouldn't cry now. "No need," I said, and I held my own hand, one linked in the other.

He said, "Troy," and he held out his hand. I unclasped my hands, and reached out.

"Justine," I said. His hands were so cold, at least as cold as mine, and somehow that was almost a comfort.

Troy drove me home. I held a pink baker's box on my lap. The car filled with the smell of burgers, fries and doughnuts. In matching polyester, our coats and winter boots, we passed through suburbs crowded to either side of the highway.

"Keep going," I said.

When we got to my house outside town, there were no cars in our long drive.

Troy pointed, "That drift looks like a couch."

Still nervous, I asked anyway, "Want to come in?"

He shut off the engine, followed me around to the side-door. "You have a dog." He meant the frozen spot of yellow snow. My morning experiment, a lifetime before.

"We do," I said. And as I turned to look for Charlie, one hand out with a key for the door, I slipped on ice and slid, the fry-rack dance, and the world swam underfoot. I grabbed Troy's shoulder, he put a hand to my side, steady again. When I caught my balance, I pushed open the door to the house and we moved from dark to darker, from the night sky to our cave.

"Your parents don't believe in furniture." He kept his coat on.

I shrugged. "We used to have more."

The dog was inside. "She's hurt," Troy said. Her shoulder was damp where she chewed, where she looked for metal pins buried deep in her bone.

"Ages ago," I said.

He said, "But she's bleeding."

I shrugged. "Self-inflicted."

Charlie followed us into the kitchen. I closed the doors, and turned on the stove. We had a table and chairs. A ceiling light. I poured brandy from a bottle up above the sink, one short glass for me and one for Troy. My parents' brandy was a bribe; I didn't want him to leave.

I said, "You're in college?"

He nodded, looked in the fridge. "There's nothing here," he said, like he'd never been in an ice cave before.

"There's milk," I said. "And beer. And this." I pulled the cold chicken sandwich out of my coat pocket, dropped it on the table. It had started to snow again outside, big damp flakes that covered our tracks. Troy moved for the front door. I said, "Where are you going? It's a storm."

He went out, just like that, and then I was alone in the house again. I felt like a five-year-old afraid to go to sleep, and at the same time like a grown up with a house all my own, but neither way felt nice or right or settled. I picked up a little rag rug, off the floor, and gave it a shake. Dirt fell. I put the rug over my lap like a blanket, waited for the sound of an engine, or the lights of Troy's beams against the snow on our driveway.

Fast enough, the screen door rattled open. Troy stomped snow off his boots. He slid one big, pink box onto our wobbly kitchen table, opened the lid and flashed a world of crullers, éclairs, cake doughnuts and fritters. That cupcake, my own little birthday, sat in one corner all dressed up with nobody to sing.

Early morning, I showed Troy to my parents' room. Their floor was carpeted with dirty clothes and towels. Cold candles dripped hardened wax onto saucers. A chest of drawers had the drawers out, the bottom of one drawer splintered like somebody had stepped right through it.

"Sure they won't come back?" Troy lifted a book off the blankets and touched the worn sheets.

"I doubt it." The air smelled greasy and sweet. It was *Fry Girl and 'Nuts Man, Episode One.* He started to unlace his boots. He slid one boot off, to show a black sock. The mattress had two indentations, two dips or gullies—the shape of two people, sleeping side by side. Troy, when he slept, would roll into one like an old habit. I ran my hand along the other. And this was a new story: me, sixteen, older than I'd ever been, with a warm man soon to be sleeping in my parents' bed.

He asked, "What if they do?"

I said, "Wake me."

The Creepy Girl Story

Janet Mitchell

The day the daughter is dressed in new everything, the father brings home the kids: Kid boy. Kid girl. Shoulder-size, of cement. Blind kids with open mouths and big cheeks. Chink twins imported from China.

"I had to," the father says, cradling a kid in each arm. "In all good conscience I couldn't leave them sitting as cute as kids, among Saint Francis, a porcupine, and a gladiator with half a helmet for a head."

"I have a new blouse," the daughter says.

"What to name them?"

"I have a new skirt."

"Sue Yen and Michael Yang."

"I have new shoe-zees."

"I will scrub you up."

"I have new toes."

How to describe the father?

He is a man of legs, loosening his tie and looking out over his garden. A garden of grass stretching back to pussy willows along the fence heaped with honeysuckle, and evergreens coming down towards him, a forest of his own making with white pines, a few birches, a magnolia tree and a Chinese dogwood. There are flowering shrubs and flowers too: rhododendrons, azaleas, forsythias, lilacs and zinnias encircling a stone bench and a bath for birds, all wound up with ivy the father regrets ever having asked Mr. Watson to plant as fill.

The father is a man who sleeps on his back, with his legs crossed at his ankles and his hands crossed over his heart.

He is a man with a pipe in his mouth, a shovel in his hand, and packs of seeds in his pockets.

It is the season to plant.

Down in the cellar, gathering steel wool and rags, filling a bucket with water, not too hot, not too cold, the father does not see that Mr. Watson's new men, Larry and Bill, are not doing what they are being paid to do. Larry is not digging out dirt to make holes for the new shrubs Bill has been bringing round back from the truck. Larry has jammed the shovel into the dirt, Bill has pushed the shrub over, and they have walked over to look through the sliding glass door at the daughter.

The daughter, she smiles. She pulls her new blouse over her head and shakes her curls once she is free of it. Her fingers unsnap the front of her new bra. She moves the thin straps over her shoulders, down her arms and off her wrists. She shakes her newly grown titties.

Larry lets his hair out of its ponytail. He runs his fingers through, smoothing the sides, pulling it tighter and tying it back up again with the rubber band he's been holding in his mouth.

The daughter lifts her skirt and looks down at her lacey panties. A hand slides underneath, and her fingers pull at the hair there.

Bill goes down on one knee. He keeps his chin up, his eyes on the daughter.

She opens her mouth. She turns her back to them.

He fishes out the fresh pack of cigs he's been keeping between his sock and his skin. He slaps the bottom of the pack against the palm of his hand.

The daughter bends slowly low. Her skirt goes slowly higher. She reaches back and puts her hands up underneath her skirt. Her panties are coming down. At her knees, she keeps them. She looks at Bill and Larry, their upside down faces slack and worn.

The sound of the cellar doors being opened from within.

Larry and Bill look away from the daughter to see the cellar doors, the left and the right, opened and placed flat against the brick of the patio. The father's head is surely soon to be rising.

The daughter turns around and presses her body against the sliding glass door.

Larry and Bill walk back to where they had been working. Larry picks up the shovel, which has fallen over. Bill squats by the shrub, takes out his knife and cuts the burlap bag from around the roots. Larry shovels in, throws the dirt, shovels in. Bill re-adjusts himself.

The daughter moves back and looks at the faint mists some of her has left on the glass, slowly fading away.

The father is on his knees on the brick patio. Before him sit Sue Yen and Michael Yang. His long sleeves are cuffed up to his elbows. His tie is gone. His hands are scrubbing their little faces first with steel wool, then with soap and rag. He whispers for them to be patient for he has the dirt of four thousand years to clean off of them. He kisses Sue Yen's cheeks, rubs Michael Yang's nose. "My babies," he says, "my sweetest darlings." He rises, in need of more water.

The daughter stands naked in front of the father's closet. All his clothes hang there, waiting for him to come in and put them on. She reaches out her arms, rushes in and hugs the clothes to her.

Bill unwraps the pack of cigs, throws the wrapper onto the burlap bag to be picked up later and first offers Larry. He's already got the head of the lighter popped back, and Bill lights two. Shit man. Shit. Shit yeah. They hold the cigs to their mouths as though joints.

The daughter dresses. She puts one arm, then the other into the shirt with the pearl buttons. She takes the silk tie he had been wearing when he came home and places it under the collar. She wraps the tie over itself and knots it large and square. She slips on the herringbone jacket, the cashmere socks, the heavy loafers with the tassels.

But before the clothes, the daughter takes out a pair of the father's shorts and puts them on. She holds the waistband tight, cinched in with one hand and the other, she balls her fist and shoves it down front.

She never puts on the trousers.

The father paints Michael Yang a fire-face dragon and Sue Yen dogwood flowers across their Japanese kimonos. The fire-face dragon looks too fierce for such a small boy, but the dogwood flowers are so delicate they look as though they have not been painted on at all, but are actual dogwood flowers, that have been shaken down by the wind to fall as they would fall, as they did fall, as they have fallen on the kimono and in the hair of the small girl.

The father takes a rag and dries off his hands, his forearms. He stands, calling, "Larry, Bill," and walks up the steps leading from the patio into the garden. He sees them finish their smoke, toss the butts onto the burlap bag Bill ties and slings over his shoulder. Larry walks toward the father, and Bill catches up after he's tossed the trash into the metal can.

The father puts a hand on Larry's shoulder and walks him over to the stone bench and the bath for birds. He wants the birdbath moved and the children put in its place by the time he gets back with some sealant.

Larry and Bill nod, say they understand, and would like to do as he says, but they'll have to wait for Mr. Watson to move the birdbath. Last guy moved one about the same size threw out a disc.

"Over there then," the father says, pointing to the Chinese dogwood. "And get rid of this ivy."

The daughter hears the father's car, pulling out. The single honk of his horn, which means he won't be long.

She hurries to pull on her little girl's dress: all cotton, with a bib top and puffy sleeves, a flouncy ruffle at the bottom that swirls wide when she twirls. She brushes her curls and clips a ribbon in.

Larry moves Sue Yen and Michael Yang. He pulls up the dandelions he hadn't seen before. He shows them to Bill, says they'll spray later. Bill hacks away at the ivy. He gathers up the cuttings in his hands and shoves them into the bag Larry holds open for him.

The daughter presses herself up against the sliding glass door and watches them.

Larry turns his head over his shoulder, and then Bill turns his.

She has her eyes on them.

They set out walking toward her.

She unlatches the sliding glass door.

They slide across the door, wipe their feet, and step on in.

She lies long.

They are on her, over her, in her, all at once.

They smell of sweated dirt, of smoke, of summer.

They leave her as they found her. Though now she is bleeding, and they are sucking on their fingers. They knock on the sliding glass door as they go. She takes their hairs out of her mouth. She puts her fingers inside of her and feels it. She is more than wet. She feels herself stiffening.

The daughter is still lying there when the father comes home with the sealant. He hoists her up to lean her against his shoulder and carries her into the garden. He walks past the flowering shrubs, the rhododendrons, the azaleas, the forsythias, the lilacs and the zinnias and sees the ivy has been cut to his satisfaction. He walks over to the Chinese dogwood, thinking he must remember to tell Mr. Watson that Gaudio Brothers is having a sale on wrought-iron gates and that he should pick up some lavender while he's out there. The Chinese kids should have something good to smell. He stands the daughter behind Sue Yen and Michael Yang. Even close, he can tell she's not right. He steps back and looks at her. No, she'll never do. She's much too tall. He lies the daughter gently down into the grass. He takes out the sealant and rubs it on Sue Yen and Michael Yang. They glisten. He tells them not to worry, they won't be wet long, and if he can think of where it was he went to, to find this girl, he'll go back and get her mate. She must have been part of a pair. Funny, though, he can't think of what he looked like. Always get the pair, they are easier to arrange.

This Is How It Starts

Shannon Cain

There is a boy and there is a girl. Jane sees the girl on Tuesdays and Fridays and she sees the boy on Wednesdays and Saturdays. The other three nights she sleeps by herself in her big, firm bed.

She gathers the dogs each morning at 6 o'clock. This requires both the boy and the girl to leave her apartment and refrain from preparing any breakfast. Given the chance, the boy would make eggs benedict. The girl would make cheese omelets. On Jane's mornings alone, she eats cold cereal with sugar.

The girl is fond of her strap-on. The boy is fond of cunnilingus. This is satisfying to Jane. Plus, Jane can say this to the girl: "It would be nice if your dick were bigger." Jane would not make this statement to the boy, though it may be slightly true.

Jane goes to art school in the afternoons and walks dogs six mornings a week and again at night. She realizes this is a cliché, the student dog-walker, but such is her life and she can't help it. She lives in an apartment that has been occupied since 1948 by a member of her immediate family. In New York, you treat rent control like an heirloom.

Outside her window there are identical brick buildings surrounding a courtyard with mature elms and a well-maintained playground. Jane grew up on those swings. Twenty five thousand people in a half-mile radius live in apartments identical to Jane's, with their metal kitchen cabinets and square pedestal sinks in the bathrooms. She is comforted by this sameness, and by her place inside it. Eight years ago, Jane's mother moved to Boca Raton in a nest emptying role-reversal, as per family tradition. Unless Jane produces a child, the corporation that owns the buildings will quadruple the rent when she moves out. Her mother takes for granted that Jane will prevent this from happening. So, she supposes, does Jane.

*

The girl often gets lost in the maze of buildings when she comes to see Jane. She calls from her cell phone. "I'm at a fountain," she says. Sometimes there's no landmark other than a mound of daffodils. Jane comes down to find her.

The girl is a doctor. The boy is a lawyer. If they were married to one another they'd have kids who resent their ambition. They'd live in Upper Montclair and commute to Manhattan. The boy, in fact, does live in Upper Montclair. The boy is someone's father but the girl isn't anyone's mother. Jane is not necessarily reminded of her own mother when she looks at the girl, but nevertheless the girl frowns in a disapproving way from time to time that makes Jane feel like lying to her.

Jane calls the girl at the hospital and says she'd like to play nurse. The girl is a feminist and reminds Jane that patriarchal power trips do not turn her on. Jane takes the number six train uptown and waits for the girl in her office, and when the girl's shift is over Jane crawls under her desk and performs some oral tricks she learned from the boy.

In his law office on East 52nd Street the boy represents children with chronic health conditions caused by lousy medical treatment. He specializes in vaccination cases. His clients are mostly babies who got autism from their diphtheria shot. Jane doesn't know how he can bear to spend so much of his day with heartbroken people.

The girl is shorter than Jane and has beautiful breasts. They are small and oval, with very pink nipples. A tuft of turquoise hair sprouts from the left side of her head, and her ears have many piercings. Her eyeglass frames came from the 26th Street flea market. In the emergency room where she works, teenage patients tell her their secrets. It is not uncommon, she tells Jane, for adults to ask for a different doctor. Despite Jane's status as an art student and its accompanying expectation of hipness, she cannot match the girl's effortless bohemian chic.

The boy is tall. He has two children, a son and a daughter. They attend a private Montessori school on the Upper West Side. His daughter plays in a junior symphony: the oboe, which is unusual for a child of eight. His son plays soccer, which is not unusual for a child of any age. Jane goes to Upper Montclair on Sunday afternoons to watch the boy's son run around the field with other four year-olds. The boy's enthusiasm for his son's team is endearing. When the boy spots his ex-wife at the game, he puts his arm around Jane's shoulders.

In her big firm bed, the boy is huge, a two hundred and forty pound sandbag. Jane likes the feel of his heaviness; likes to know she can handle the weight of his body without gasping for air. On Fridays, the girl, who is considerate about such things, brings paraphernalia in different sizes. She is a hundred pounds lighter than the boy.

The girl and the boy know about one another. Jane sometimes considers introducing them. The next part of this fantasy involves Jane floating a proposal that they both occupy her bed, maybe on Thursdays and Sundays. Jane knows the girl would not go for this. The boy, it goes nearly without saying, would.

The boy surprises Jane with expensive tickets to see a famous lesbian comedian. The show is on a Wednesday, which is the girl's night. Jane calls the girl.

"I need to reschedule," Jane says.

"This is how it starts," the girl says.

*

Jane's apartment has two bedrooms. In New York this is sometimes more space than entire families occupy. In the spare bedroom she makes her art. She paints on panes of glass purchased at the hardware store. The paintings are meant to be viewed from the back, through the smooth surface of the glass. To accomplish this she must paint her foregrounds first, top layers before bottom. She must put the blush on a cheek before she paints the cheek. Sometimes she sits for an hour, looking out the window at her slivered view of the East River, planning her layers.

*

Jane has always been this way with boys and girls. She likes boys for their size and for their crudeness, the way they bumble through life thinking all the while they're in control. She loves girls for their strength but mostly for their skill in the sack. She doesn't like the way that girls talk so much, the way they sit and talk cross-legged and shirtless on the couch or sit and talk in the recliner by the window or sit and talk on the bed, straddling Jane.

The girl is a talker. Often when the talking mood strikes the girl, her lips are pink and maybe still slightly puffy from her vigorous interaction with Jane's. Jane makes sounds to signify she's listening.

*

Jane's mother calls from her duplex in Florida. She wants Jane to find a photo of her grandfather she believes is located in a cardboard box in the hall closet. Jane conducts the search holding the phone with her shoulder. Dust stirs.

"The house next door finally sold," her mother says, "to a couple of women."

"I'm not finding it, Ma," Jane says.

"Don't make me come look for it myself!"

In her retirement Jane's mother has become a smart aleck.

"I hope you aren't harassing them," Jane says.

"They told me they're cousins. Such bullshit. Seventy-year-old cousins buying a house together? What do they think, I'm Anita Bryant?"

"The picture isn't here," Jane says, and sneezes. "They're afraid. Bring them a cake."

"God bless. With a frosting yoni, how about."

*

Jane is the only dog walker in the eleven thousand identical apartments outside her window. Her mother started the business when Jane was seven years old. The complex has an economy of its own, a closed system, of which Jane is a part. Hardware stores nearby sell fans that go neatly in the small horizontal windows, shelves that fit in the dead space between the coat closet and the front door, replacement kitchen cabinet knobs. Jane does the math: there are one hundred ninety eight thousand cabinet knobs in her complex.

Jane has twenty-five dog-walking clients. She takes the first group at six a.m. and the next at eight. She repeats the pattern at four p.m. and again at six. The dogs are grateful. The humans are in fact technically her clients, but she knows she works for the animals. She picks up the dogs' warm shit only because they can't do it for themselves.

"Let me come to work with you," the boy says. His kids are at their mother's house. It's a sunny Saturday and the boy's lips are still slippery from his adventure down below and she feels in no position to deny him. They get dressed and fetch the dogs.

In each building's lobby, he holds the leashes while she runs upstairs to collect more clients. This makes the work go faster. "I'll leave the law," he says, "and be your doggie boy." His hair stands up in back, pillow-mussed. The bill of his baseball cap is frayed, the cardboard showing through. His T-shirt says *Vito's Pork Shop*. He hasn't yet shaved.

"No you won't," Jane says.

"Dare me." He pants a little, sticking out the tip of his tongue.

"The pay is lousy, my friend," Jane says. She takes the leashes from his hand and pushes past him, to the next building.

The boy walks behind her, all the dogs at her side. There is silence, during which she assumes his thoughts have moved on to football or food. But at the next doorway he says, "Lousy pay is why they invented rent control." His eyes flicker upwards, in the direction of her apartment.

In evolutionary terms, her job at this moment is to encourage him. Her girl instinct is clear about this. She is supposed to say something to spark further comments regarding shared domesticity. "Really," she says. "I thought it had to do with immigration, or urban blight. Or something." She hands him the leashes. "An incontinent poodle awaits."

*

To make her art, Jane is required to know everything about the image before she starts painting. She cannot paint a table then put an orange on it later. She must paint the orange first, and then form the table around it. She enjoys the puzzle of this technique. Her teacher frowns at her work. He says if she insists on preventing the painting from emerging of its own accord, her art will have no depth. He cannot see that flatness is the entire point. She will probably fail his class.

*

The girl does not appreciate animals. This is unusual for a lesbian. She plants her bare feet in Jane's kitchen and prepares a vegetable upside down cake with organic carrots and fresh dill and basil. Jane drinks wine at the dinette table left behind when her grandmother moved to Phoenix in 1981 and watches the girl through the kitchen doorway. The fluorescent lighting makes the girl's short blonde hair glow like the wood fairy in a picture book belonging to the boy's oboe-playing daughter.

The girl scoffs at Jane's paltry collection of spices.

"I've survived so far with no sage in my life," Jane replies.

The girl removes her blouse and finishes her cookery performing an impersonation of Emeril on ecstasy, topless. Jane pours more wine for the girl and holds the glass to her lips. She is wildly attracted to feminine women with an edge.

*

"I love you," says the boy.

"I love you," says the girl.

*

The boy has purchased a society-building computer game for his daughter. The child constructs a virtual room with no doors and places her avatar inside. The avatar pees in the corner. She grows depressed and lonely. After two weeks she curls up and dies. The boy makes an appointment with a child psychologist, who advises him to ask his daughter how much she really enjoys the oboe. As he tells this story to Jane, he cries.

The girl has deeply green eyes. She asks Jane to leave the boy. She says this, and then is silent. Against this self-assuredness the boy doesn't stand a chance. Lying in the girl's arms, Jane should be thinking about what to say next, but she ponders instead the unfair advantage of girls over boys. Their adaptable body parts and their ability to say what they mean. She falls into a bewildered silence.

*

In the subway car the boy sits with his knees spread apart. Jane compensates by pressing her legs together, sideways. Other men on the train sit this way, too. She points it out to the boy. "It's a physical thing," he says into her ear. "One mustn't constrict the package." Also the boy has a loud voice. He doesn't mean to occupy all that aural space, but it happens. Often she feels a great need to tell him to pipe down, especially in restaurants.

She calls the girl at the hospital to cancel their Tuesday. "I'm sick," Jane says. "I think it's the flu."

"Drink fluids," the girl says. Being a girl and a doctor, she knows a lie.

"I'll see you next week," Jane says.

The girl doesn't say anything more. The girl is figuring her out.

*

Jane's clothing accumulates on the floor around her bed. At six a.m., she roots through the pile for her jeans and a t-shirt. There is a faint smell of dog shit. She collects the dirty pants and shirts and piles them into the wicker laundry basket that has lived in the hall closet since before she was born. When members of her family abandon the apartment, they buy new household items upon arrival in their retirement communities. She imagines her grandmother breezily pushing a modern lightweight iron over her housedresses. Serving poolside cocktails in tropical drinkware made of plastic. Objects in Jane's kitchen have vintage value: a mirrored toaster shaped like an egg, a set of Flintstones jelly-jar glasses, a pale yellow Fiesta Ware butter dish.

The laundry room in the basement is empty. She pushes quarters into the slots and starts a load. When Jane was twelve her mother sent her downstairs to bring up the whites and she walked in to find a man she recognized from the elevator fucking a woman who wasn't his wife. The woman sat on the washer containing the bed sheets Jane had come to collect. It made a vibrating, spin-cycle racket. With great earnestness the man pumped away, his pants around his ankles. The woman's blouse was off her shoulder, her skirt bunched around her waist. Her head was thrown back, an unselfconscious expression on her face. Jane stayed rooted to the cement floor, looking at the woman. "Run along, now, honey," the woman said to her, and smiled. She panted slightly, as if she'd been running. She didn't cover herself or jump off the washer. Jane smiled back and went outside and sat on the swings.

She leaves her laundry to its cycles and collects her clients from their sleepy owners. She walks them through the silent green grounds between the red brick buildings. There is so little sky in the city.

It is part of her routine to leave the kitchen light on so she can find her window from outside. She notices the harshness of the fluorescent bulb, and the way that her window stands apart from the others. She's supposed to walk the dogs briskly, give them some exercise. She is aware that some of the owners watch from their windows. She sits on a bench outside the playground where in the third grade she kissed Sissy Hirshfeld. It was St. Patrick's Day, and Sissy had a four-leaf clover painted on her cheek. Sissy's brother, Donny, whose Valentine to Jane had a picture of Minnie and Mickey Mouse holding hands, watched them.

*

Jane is painting a pair of women on barstools. One wears red sneakers. She hasn't done the background yet, but when she does it will be an outdoor scene, with a river flowing behind them and dark clouds in the distance. The woman being watched has heavy-lidded eyes, which Jane didn't intend. She was going for a detached gaze, but has ended up making her look sleepy. She works on the figure in red sneakers, who seems to have lost interest in participating in the scene. She looks like she'd rather go for a naked run along the beach. Jane stares at the picture for thirty-eight minutes. She finds a pair of pliers in the drawer and using the handle cracks the glass neatly in half with one firm tap. The two heads look out at her. One is distracted, the other just tired.

*

The boy buys Jane a puppy. It is inordinately cute. "What am I supposed to do with this?" Jane says.

The boy is crestfallen. "How can you deny this face?" he says, cradling the dog. "She's purebred. She's smart."

"I have plenty of animals in my life already," she says.

"But you love dogs," he tells her.

"Other people's," she says, and kisses him. He's just come from work; his tie is loosened. She pets the short hair at the back of his neck. He puts the dog down and carries Jane to the kitchen, where he plops her on the counter and removes her jeans. Over his shoulder Jane watches the puppy sniff around the closet door, where she keeps leashes and poop bags. The puppy whines and scratches at the floor. The boy moans. Jane thinks about the girl.

*

At two o'clock in the morning Jane's doorbell rings. The boy is sound asleep in Jane's big firm bed.

"How did you get into the building?" Jane asks the girl.

"I fucked the doorman," the girl says.

"There is no doorman," Jane says.

"I have something for you," the girl says, grinning seductively. "In here." She brandishes a leather backpack, and eyes the closed bedroom door.

"You're a little bit drunk, aren't you?" Jane says.

From inside the bathroom the puppy scratches. Jane lets him out and he bounds over to the girl, butt wiggling. The girl doesn't bend over. "What's this?"

"I'm not keeping it," Jane says.

"It's cute," the girl says. "Maybe I'll take it home."

"You hate animals."

"I'm starting to come around. What's it called?"

"A golden retriever."

"I know that much. What's its name?"

"Untitled," Jane says. "You don't want this dog."

"Why not?" the girl says. She hasn't touched it. "It's growing on me already."

"For one," Jane says, "it's a boy dog."

"And for two?"

"For two." Jane pauses. "I haven't decided whether to keep it yet."

"I thought so," the girl says.

They sit together on the couch. It's a small couch, upholstered in horses and carriages and ladies in hoop skirts. Their knees are touching. The puppy slinks to the corner. The girl puts her hands over her face and cries. Jane hadn't expected this.

"You aren't sick," the girl says. She takes her damp hands from her face and puts them on either side of Jane's neck. "Your glands aren't even swollen." Her voice is louder than usual.

"I'm sorry," Jane says.

The girl looks at her through red eyes. The girl begins to talk. In her speech there are references to needs, to respect, to truth. She talks for nine minutes. The clock on the VCR is just over the girl's shoulder. The girl curls and uncurls the strap on her backpack. She winds down with a mention of survival, then intimacy. Jane watches her face, which is beautiful.

There is a pause, during which Jane does what she always does when the girl finishes talking. She searches for something relevant to say, some piece of information, something that will not require her to form a sentence containing any of the words the girl has just used. She looks for a small fact, a clarification. What she ends up with is this: "The dog was a gift."

"Ah," the girl says.

"I'm giving it back," Jane says.

"Don't," the girl says. "Give it to me." She glances at the bedroom door. "I dare you."

"As I said. You don't want this dog."

Outside, a window across the courtyard goes dark.

"Right," the girl says, and leaves.

*

"I'm going back to my wife," the boy says. They are sitting at the dinette table. Normally he would be gone by the end of her first dog shift but today she comes home to eggs on the table.

She pushes her plate away. "This is my great grandmother's china. It's antique."

"It was on the top shelf," he says. He gestures vaguely toward the kitchen.

"Don't tell me," Jane says. "It's for the sake of the children."

"Right, that's about right."

"Yeah. You owe it to them."

"No need to get bitchy, Jane. I needed to do this,"—he gestures to the space between them—"to figure myself out."

"Glad to be of service."

The boy stands, picks up the puppy. "You never really wanted him."

"No," she finally says. The dog licks his plate. "Give it to the kids."

"Jill is allergic."

"Jill. Christ. What's your mother's name? June?"

"Alright, then." He puts the puppy down and takes their plates to the kitchen. "Say what you will. I deserve it, I guess."

It's a trick of the modern boy, Jane thinks. Show us the best of yourself on the way out the door.

"So the dog was a consolation prize."

He stands in the kitchen doorway. "I get it," he says. "You're pissed."

She stands up and removes her pants. "I'm getting in the shower." She moves toward the bathroom. With her back to him she takes off her shirt, then her underwear. She does not turn to face him. "Do the dishes before you leave. Chip a plate and I'm giving my grandmother your phone number."

She sits on the bathroom floor, which is chilly against her naked skin. It is tiled with ceramic octagons the size of a quarter. They need regrouting. Oyster crackers, she thinks they're called. While she waits for him to leave she does the math: in the bathrooms of her apartment complex there are three-point-two million ceramic oyster crackers.

*

She must turn in something for art class, which won't do much good for her grade but will at least represent having taken a stand against professorial interference. In her newest painting, a woman in a black cocktail dress sits on a large empty box in the middle of a prairie. She is barefoot. The prairie grasses are long, and bent by the wind. In the distance are fat white clouds. The woman's head is thrown back, taking in the sun. Her legs hang over the side of the box, whose black interior is the only stillness around.

*

Jane rents a storage room roughly the size of her kitchen in a twelve-story building near the docks on the west side. The location is inconvenient, is probably for the best. The hallways are carpeted, and lined with padlocked doors. The view from the stairwell window is magnificent. She wonders how many years it will take for the owners to install plumbing and rent the units as studio apartments.

She calls a moving company, which sends two large men to her apartment. They take away her grandmother's table, the couch, the boxes in the closet. She wraps the jelly glasses and the china in newspaper and packs them in a wooden crate. The men haul it all away, wordlessly. Vacated by her mother's needlepoint, the walls are spotted with clean squares. Jane's footsteps echo. She puts her mattress in the middle of the bedroom floor and hangs her art in the living room windows. Through the painted glass, the light throws deformed images against the bare parquet tiles. The colors are muddier than she'd expected.

*

After two weeks the girl hasn't called. Jane is pregnant. She calls her mother, who is pragmatic about such things.

"You're not ready," her mother says. "Live a little, I say. I'm sending money. I'm doing it now." Jane can hear her mother licking the envelope. "Don't go to the place in Queens, whatever you do. Helen from 4C went there and the nurses were bitchy."

Jane sits on the kitchen counter with the phone to her ear and is silent. Her mother talks, filling up space, which is good.

"Call the doctor," her mother says.

At first Jane doesn't know what she means. There's a silence. "She isn't in the picture anymore, Ma."

"I'm walking to the mailbox with this check," her mother says.

"How about you bring it here yourself?" Jane says.

Jane is pretty sure her mother is crying. "Tell the doctor you need her, is my advice. She'll come along, she'll drive you home afterwards, feed you soup." Jane hears her mother's footsteps on the gravel driveway. She pictures an open sky, and palm trees.

Mereá

Nancy Hightower

The first thing that retreats before you is its name. Mereá, the city of winding caves. The city underneath the sand.

"She'll take you, Señor. She'll take you and make you forget, just like she took your wife," the abuelo says to him, his face crinkled like old cabbage. He gestures to Gil to withdraw his gaze from the two faint lights in the horizon. "We are in Carnival now," the old man continues, taking Gil by the arm back to chaos of the city streets. "Venga. See the dancers." Skeletons shimmy their way around bodies barely covered in bright tops, short skirts, loose shorts. He watches, fascinated by the rhythmic jounce of those bodies thrusting in and out in perfect time to the drummers.

It had been the same scene when his wife disappeared a year ago.

They had camped out in the desert that night, away from the din of the city, he and his wife and the guides they had paid to show them the giant dunes of the Sechura Desert. "I'm going for a walk," she had said, one hand holding her hair up while she wiped away a trickle of sweat from the curve of her neck, her deep-green dress clinging lightly to her thighs. *Let me come with you,* he had thought but not said. It was too soon for romantic walks. And so he had let her go—to gaze at the stars, to wonder why they had come to this desert when his firm was busy and she was still recovering; to weep a little where he could not see, where he could not wipe away her tears the moment they began to course down her cheeks—he let her go, with only a flashlight and compass should she lose her way among the dunes.

When she hadn't come back within the hour, he began to worry, paced the camp until the guides said they would look for her. They returned three hours later, shaking their heads. *Her tracks double back on themselves,* they said, heads bowed apologetically, *then disappear. She is not here, Señor Gil.* Shifty looks exchanged. *Come, let us go back to the city.*

A month he had stayed there, hiring two private investigators to search the grimy barrios for any clue of where she might have been taken (the city, despite being a tourist destination, was known to have an active slave trade). *Perhaps she met another man,* one of the detectives suggested. Gil explained once again there was no other man, there was no argument she had stormed away from. She had simply wanted to take a walk (and weep till her eyes were dry, but he left out that part).

"You mustn't keep looking for her, señor," the abuelo brings him back into the present moment with a touch on his arm.

"My wife?" Gil sighs, not understanding the lack of compassion he sees in the old man's watery blue eyes, the whites yellowed like old milk. "One of the guides said to come back here a year later—to the day. He was specific about that. Said I might have a slim shot in hell of finding her—."

"Beh, your wife," the man spits, with naked disdain this time. "It is Mereá that you must find. If you find her, if *she* lets you find her, then you might find your love—if Mereá lets you remember how."

*

Tonight, he finds the approximate location of their old camp, and as dusk shades into indigo, he goes for a walk, just as his wife had done. The air begins to chill, and all he sees are stars and sand, no strange cave or hole into which his wife might have wandered. He cries out his wife's name several times, imagining her face as he last saw it: a sad smile, the tears already making her eyes seem glassy and distant. *I'll see you in a few minutes,* she had promised.

At last he grows tired, lays himself down on the desert floor and stares up at the sky. The world tilts before him; he feels as if he could drop straight through the stars and land on the other side. Slowly he closes his eyes, settles his breathing to take long, slow draughts of air. *Slow your breath almost to the point of dying, then Mereá will come, will let your feet slide in between her eyes and find the first step,* the old man had told him. There's no wind, no noise. In that stillness, at last the two lights appear, one on each side of his feet. *Slide between her eyes.* He inches forward on his back, feels the ground suddenly slope downward. Within a moment, the eyes are aligned with his head. As he descends into the dark opening, his foot lands on a stone step. Legend has it that some nights there are twenty steps leading down into the heart of Mereá; other nights there are thirty. Or one hundred. *There are some who descend forever,* another warned him. He is able to make it to the ground floor in two hours, stepping down sideways since the steps are narrow and not of equal distance from each other. Little else they told him about the city beneath the sand, whether from fear or ignorance he couldn't say. He knew only that his wife must surely be there if this is where she disappeared.

The stairs finally get wider as he comes upon a small plaza, walled, and sees that all paths lead out into different catacombs that snake their way throughout the city. There is no one around to ask for directions, but he swears he sees the back of someone just disappearing into the tunnel on his left. *Hello hello,* he calls after them, but the city does not have good acoustics, and his voice sounds as if it comes from far away. The tunnel is too dark, but still he enters, shuffling forward like an old man until his eyes adjust to a dim light. There are no lamps along the walls or floor or ceiling—nothing to account for the soft glow that barely lights his way.

"Is anyone here?" His voice is almost hoarse, as if he hadn't used it in a week.

There's no answer, except for a deep, whirring noise that rumbles from somewhere behind the walls. He follows the dimly lit path, comes out soon enough into a murky atrium with vast underground lakes—no plants, only an old chairlift that creaks and hums. Gil watches for a while as chair by chair passes him, then lets himself be scooped up into a seat. *Mereá, she is fickle, that one,* the old man had said, when Gil told him his plans. *Let her lead you where she will. Otherwise, you'll not find your wife, nor yourself, after a while.* Now Gil is lifted high over underground lakes, some so large they seem like small oceans at midnight, the outlines of iridescent blue-green waves against perpetual twilight. The sound of water mingles with music, a slow, haunting song rising above the crash of waves. His eyes grow heavy as the chair dips and climbs. Despite Gil's efforts to remain awake and vigilant, he is gently rocked into a deep slumber.

A jerk on the chairlift wakes him up, and he remembers his wife, or tries to; already the image of her grows fuzzy—auburn hair and cherry mouth. No, small pink lips and blue-gray eyes. The sad smile as she said goodbye. On the other side of the lakes he now sees a carnival, neon lights obscenely blinking on the rides. People are walking throughout it, and so he jumps off at a small landing area and runs to its entrance. A few people are in line for the Ferris wheel ten yards ahead. He tries shouting to them, asks if they have seen his wife, but no one turns around. He feels a small pull on his sleeve.

"Don't believe everything the old woman says, for she's bored and makes up lies." It is a young boy with auburn hair, red freckles sporadically placed on his face, blue-grey eyes. He could have been their son, if they'd had children.

"Have you seen this woman…" he begins as he pulls out a picture of his wife, but the little boy shakes his head and takes his hand.

"Follow me," he whispers and walks away to the right, through a mass of people that seem to be suddenly everywhere. The little hand is wrenched from his, and he finds himself pushing through the stiff, silent bodies just as he had back in New York. Where did the boy go? He finally spots him, twenty feet away and heading towards the roller coaster.

"Here," he says, stepping into the car.

"My wife?"

"One ride. Then I'll show you."

He gets in beside the boy. There are only three other people in the roller coaster, on the far end. The boy turns to him and smiles, a strange, boyish smile that holds no joy. The coaster begins to creak upwards, and the boy quickly grabs the bar in front of them. The fall is almost a sheer drop, and he yells out curses and obscenities as his legs and ass come high off the seat. By time they hit the second hill, the boy is thrown into Gil's lap. When their run is finished, he looks to the back of the coaster. Only two people are in the car where there had been three.

"It sometimes happens," the boy whispers in his ear.

His stomach keeps flipping over, a nausea he hadn't felt since that night so long ago. The endless wait in the hospital. "My wife?"

"She's not here, I can tell you that much."

"Then what was the point of me riding?" he asks as they got out.

The boy shrugs. "I'm lonely," he answers and points to the Ferris wheel. "That is the only way out of the carnival, if she lets you," he says, and then waves goodbye. It was the time of carnival when his wife disappeared, but this place was static, grotesque even, with its rides that wanted him.

The Ferris wheel doesn't turn very quickly, but neither does it stop to let people on or off. The seats swivel around and face the other side, where the exit to the carnival is, but that is a matter of chance, apparently. Some people, Gil notices, take only one turn on the ride and then leave. Others are on for longer and look as if they are about to be sick.

"That woman in the blue dress has been on for a month now," a voice crackles. He turns and sees an old woman sitting on a chair. She is small and humpbacked, with thinning grey hair still streaked with brown and parted in the middle. This must be the old woman who lies (at least, according to the boy). But does it matter now?

"Hop on. She's the only way out, but she likes the men, so hope she doesn't take a fancy to you."

That women often took a liking to him was nothing new. "I must find my wife," he explains. He tells her how no one will talk to him, how he needs to find his wife before she starts to believe he has given up trying. Auburn hair, thin, pink lips, almost as tall as he. Surely someone must have seen her?

The woman doesn't answer, merely looks wide-eyed at him, grinning with a gaze as blank as a baby's, the white of one eye creeping up into milky blue. He turns away from that strange face and moves on to the Ferris wheel. This ride, with cherry-red lights on its spokes, only takes one person at a time. He sits down as a chair wheels in and a bar lowers itself to sit across his lap. The ride brings him high up over the city. Cerulean lakes ripple over to the right, and a small mountain stands forlornly to the left, gray and jagged. In between is thick fog, the rest of the city hidden. He supposes there has to be a city. There can't just be this carnival and the mountain.

The wheel seems to double in size as it turns; an hour goes by (or is it longer?) before Gil is at the very top. Indeed, he is high up, sees that the roof of the city is less than a foot away. He reaches out his hand, gently caresses what feels like soft flesh. He could swear he feels a delicious shudder in reaction to his touch before he is pulled downward. As he gets close to the ground, he tries lifting the bar, but it doesn't release its clasp. Three more revolutions, and he begins to think that perhaps she wants to keep him there for a while, warming her seat and rocking the chair. But on the fourth spin, his chair wheels around and he is facing the opposite direction. She is letting him go. He jumps out and takes a few steps, but then stops and looks back at the wheel. *Thanks for the ride.*

He walks over to a bench that sits on a little hill, a stone path that leads from it out to a series of buildings about half a mile ahead. He tries to find the mountain to get his bearings straight.

It isn't there.

"Come tomorrow and look again. Perhaps you will see it, rising up out of the surrounding snow." It's the old woman again, by his side once more.

"I don't have the time for your lies."

She cackles at that. "What is time? You dream it up just to divide your life into bite-size pieces, waiting to be devoured." A slight lick of thin red lips, tongue gliding over thoughtfully. "You must forget those nights; know that she certainly has. Go to the mountain. Near the peak is an inn that could hold the entire city of Mereá if it wanted to, but it hates crowds. The double doors open at a simple command to avoid your touch." She lays a withered hand lightly on his arm. "Sign yourself in, and take the back stairs up to where the rooms usually are. There's the room with a bed in the air. Don't stay there—it belongs to the little boy."

Gil stares hard at her eyes, silently pleading. "Who is he?"

The old woman sighs and withdraws her hand. "Does it matter? This is Mereá. You came here wanting to remember and to forget; you cannot have both. And the mountain calls you, but not now." Without another word, she hobbles back in the direction of the carnival.

Where is he supposed to go for the night? If night even comes. There is no sun in this place, only dim street lights that glow a dirty kind of yellow or dusty orange. A few moments of vermilion. But they never go out altogether or seem to change in intensity, only color. He could have been here for only a few hours, perhaps days. His watch has stopped.

He travels down different streets, tries to find a place to sleep. One building resembles a bank, but the teller is in the wrong place. She sits there right up against the store window and waves at him while counting money; on the other side is a wall with no door. There is no way for a customer to reach her. Next to the bank is a building that has Clothing Store in big gold blocks on the front. Hanging off the lower part of the E is a dress. Deep forest green. Slim cut, slightly off the shoulders. He recognizes it at once. Not a dress his wife wore often, but she had chosen it for that dinner party in April, when she had dared to kiss him, grazed his arm with a caress after so many weeks of nothing. He stares at the dress. It's never the thing itself, like language and time, but what it represents. He tugs at the hanger on the giant E until he can pull the dress away. Quickly picking it up, he searches for a way to enter the store, thinking that someone must have seen her. He walks all the way around the building to discover there are no windows or doors. *No exit,* Gil thinks ruefully, and makes his way back to the bench. The mountain is back, its peak capped with snow this time.

He could not have spent the entire night running. But there the mountain sits, with a trail that snakes its way up to the peak, dotted by inns, lights glowing in the windows. He reaches the base in a few minutes and begins the long trek up, until hours later, he meets the lodge. He remembers not to knock on its doors (since it did not desire his touch, like the carnival did). But the old woman hadn't told him the command to open them, so he just stands there, waiting. He dimly remembers another lodge where he had stayed with...who was it? His wife? No, the brunette, with lips as full and red as cherries. The doors slightly part. His fingertips graze the glossy wood as he pushes it further, just enough to let him in. He walks into a desolate lobby, calling out for help. No answer. He wants to find the little boy again. Perhaps the boy could remember his name for him; already, the sound of it was beginning to grow faint in his mind.

He wanders up and down hallways, climbs the stairs to the second floor where the walls are painted a bright yellow, the doors blood red; obscene colors, so bright. His hand finally tries a door, finds it unlocked. He quietly enters a suite with small shoes lined up along the wall and the bed suspended in mid air. Two spiral staircases coil up to it on either side. This must be the boy's room.

No one answers as he called out his wife's name. Then he cries out the name of his lover, the brunette—the one he had gone to after so many weeks, no months, without touch or kiss, without the scent of a woman's neck to lull him into sleep. He goes out and keeps walking down the hall, turns into a foyer that is actually a balcony overlooking the main room of the chalet. Another giant bed—with a mass of blue-green pillows and maroon, satin sheets—fills the entire balcony. It must be a feather mattress, to have it so plump and ready to sink one's body into. Yet it is the emotion felt inside the expanse of these walls that cradles him, like a place called home. Not the home he once knew with its windows shut partway, the screen broken, and paint scraped off the porch. Not the home where his parents had scolded him for being late to dinner or planted kisses on his cheek at bedtime. Nor the home he had lived in for ten years with his wife. Not even that.

This room brings him to *before*. A word placed on the tip of the tongue prior to one's first cry, the ache to see and sound it out with eyes closed. *Rest here. Do not try to leave, since it's almost impossible to find it again,* the walls whisper. Certainly he hadn't felt that way last year when they had slept in separate bedrooms. He had once gone to a room such as this to meet the brunette with the cherry mouth, who didn't release her clasp even when he had accidentally cried out his wife's name in such pleasure. But still that did not bring him *home*. Not even later, at the party where his wife had finally laid her pink lips on his with that sweet, lingering kiss, which promised something more than the empty hours they had been sharing since early spring. Something more than what they had lost that night in the hospital. He steps out onto the bed and wobbles his way across the mattress to the edge of the balcony. A flash of green from below as he sees his wife walking across the room, raising her hand in greeting to someone just beyond the lobby door. "Stop, I'm here," he yells, scrambling across the balcony bed; it is like running on the ocean, his feet sinking in every step. Finally, he reaches the door, thinks he can catch her now that he is free to run. But the hallway goes on longer than it should, and sometimes leads to doors that refuse to open. When he reaches the back stairs and runs down to the lobby, he finds only the old woman, white hair streaked with brown and lips too red in a face so withered. "You lost the dress," she clucks. "Always losing what you say you want the most."

No exit. "Where is she, dammit?"

The old woman leans back now and closes her eyes. "Alright, if you want to play it that way. Go through the city to the auditorium. Many mornings, I've seen the entire audience sitting there, staring at an empty stage. Some people have gone in only to find themselves already there, performing. If you find her there, you'll be able to leave. Isn't that what you most want?"

"Yes." But the word comes out slowly (hadn't she tried to get him to stay before by lying?). The trek down the mountain is surprisingly quick, and within a few hours, he finds a path that narrows into a street that curves down and inward with sharp corners. Thick air forms a sugared canopy over the entire area. Shops and restaurants on the right blend into onyx walls, sometimes smaller than he remembers them being at first glance, some not there when only moments before they were. He searches for her there, looks for the curly, brown ringlets that framed her face. No wait; that was the other woman. The one his wife found him with that night he tried to break it off. He wants his wife. Auburn hair, blue-gray eyes. He stays there for days, wandering amid the stores. He hopes the donut shop is there today instead of the flower stand with its array of tropical orchids: Tigrillo, Creeping Goodyera, Snake Mouth. Sizzling meat was heard and smelled by everyone just two days ago, but the store from which its aroma emanated now only sells watches that tell time between the hours of twelve and six. Three women are standing outside it, chanting *buy time when you can, no matter how broken it is, and always listen for food.*

Black-light lamps line the streets outside the cafes. The dim, purple glow makes everyone a beacon, a belly-full of ghosts who glide from store to store. Hunger is but an excuse to keep moving along the walls. Their voices hum a dull murmur, no words to give him information on where to go or how to get back. Mereá. Once discovered, the rules change. She grows with you. Unhinges her mouth to devour whatever memories you have, contracts the direction of her roads so you are always returning to the choices you didn't make.

The last shop is darker than the rest. He goes in, finds an arcade with games that don't work anymore. People stand in front of the screens, trying to move through flashing scenes they once remembered to be true. He walks to one game with his name on the top in flashing lights. His gaze is fixed on the character who is lost in a dark city, looking for his wife. His hands take the controls to guide the person through all the shops, mazes, and changing terrain, but he soon realizes they don't work. The character moves on its own accord, and he watches as it gets lost among a myriad of rooms in some kind of inn, meeting a woman there. Always the wrong one.

He leaves the game, walks all the way to the back of the arcade. The boy is waiting for him there, eyes now red and tearstained from having to wait for so long. Together, they walk hand in hand through the octagon, for weeks, perhaps, until one day, a door opens up and they find themselves looking into the auditorium. The boy looks up at him. "You said you'd visit someday, remember?" As they enter, he wonders how one can remember anything in this place with so much movement. They take a seat in the back row, where it is the darkest. A man sits on stage, between two women whose backs are turned towards him. On the left, the woman with auburn hair cascading over her shoulders absentmindedly holds a toy fire truck in her hand. She never turns around, despite his cries of *I'm sorry.* The cherry-mouthed brunette just stands beside a window, waiting for him to visit.

"Whom did he chose?" the boy asks in wide-eyed wonder. Gil merely shakes his head, entranced by the moment of indecision. Of never knowing. For twenty years, he has been sitting there, watching himself on the stage. He can't recall the sky, much less the sun. For who would come out of that strange womb, once allowed back in?

Shot Girls

Kim Chinquee

When Dot and Rache turned twenty-one, they thought they were invincible. They'd thought that way before, but somehow being twenty-one gave them an edge, as if it were some feat like running a marathon or hiking barefoot across the world. They were twins. They didn't dress the same, but they didn't try to look different, either. Dot's hair was always longer because it grew so fast. They shared a wardrobe, which they kept in one big walk-in closet, with outfits in sizes three and four, and forty pairs of shoes lined neatly on the carpet.

They were still in college, and after their birthday they'd gotten jobs at a dance club called "The Heap." Dot was the "shot girl," and Rache was a bartender, although she wanted to be the shot girl too, but Dot got the job because she could sell a little more with the way she sometimes flaunted, though she wasn't proud of it. It was just the way she was. Rache was more reserved, but wanted to be like Dot. Sometimes, they envied one another. At the bar, guys would ask about them being twins, and Rache was stuck behind the bar, while the guys followed Dot on her rounds, going from table to table carrying racks of test tubes filled with drinks with sexy names—Blow Jobs, Screaming Orgasms, Watermelon Screws. Since the shot girl could wear what she wanted, Dot wore short skirts and skimpy tops. When it got late, she carried the tray above her head, getting fondled along the way, which came with the job. Sometimes she wished she were the bartender, just so she wouldn't always feel invaded, and she pictured herself with Rache's job, using the counter as her barrier, her Great Wall.

One day they walked to a tattoo shop by their apartment. The smell of the place reminded Dot of laundry detergent, and it made Rachel think of the freshener in their mother's blue Toyota. They wanted identical tattoos, so Rache told that to the tattoo artist, the guy with his name, Frank, tattooed on his cheek.

He looked at them with their same blue eyes and thin dark hair, but he didn't say anything about it because he was too anxious to show them his tattoos. He took off his shirt, exposing the wispy vines and circles that wound around his chest and biceps, and a big red dragon that was spread across his middle. "It's horimono," he said. "Japanese tattoo art."

"We don't want to go that far," Rache said.

Dot sneezed and Rache said, "Bless you."

Since tattoos seemed so mainstream to them, they wanted something different and unique, yet something that would make them more alike, so they chose the Japanese character for friendship.

Afterwards they went home and freshened up before they had to go to work, feeling proud of what they'd done. Dot closed the blinds, looking down at the passing headlights, wishing she had enough money saved for her own car, and Rache flipped the TV to CNN, to

a broadcast about Diana's death which wasn't new. People were crying on the screen, and Rache wondered what was wrong with them.
Dot went to the end of the hallway to look in the full-length mirror,
straightening it before unzipping her jeans so she could see her new
tattoo. While she removed the gauze, Rache asked what she was doing,
then went to see her tattoo in the mirror, too. They stood hip-to-hip,
matching up their tattoos as if they were coded birthmarks. They compared their new tattoos, and each thought the other's looked better.

"Yours is darker," Rache said.

"I think it's inflamed," Dot said, touching it.

"I'm really glad we did this," Rache said.

"Me too," Dot said, putting her arm over Rache's shoulder.

They stood there for a while, looking at their reflections in the
mirror, telling each other they made a perfect team.

*

That night, before going to work, they went to see their grandfather, who had had a stroke a month before. The left side of his face
hung lower than the right, and he slurred his speech a bit. He'd lost
weight, and stayed in bed a lot, although when Rache and Dot came
to visit him, his face lit up and he tried to look like he was healthy.
Since the stroke, he'd been staying with their mother, who worked
as a medical assistant, and lived in a small brick ranch, where Dot
and Rache had lived until their birthday.

They walked in without knocking. Their mother was sitting in
a chair beside the table, reading last week's Sunday comics, sipping
on a cup of coffee, still wearing her blue scrubs.

"There's a fresh pot if you want some," she said, looking up.
Then she went back to reading and the girls sat across from each

other at the table, trying not to lean back on the chairs since their tattoo sites were stinging. They'd decided they weren't going to tell their mother about what they'd done that day.

"Grandpa still alive?" Rache said.

Their mother looked up quickly, saying, "Jesus, Rachel, don't be saying things like that."

"I'm kidding," Rache said.

"How is he?" Dot said.

"You could stay with him every now and then. I can't afford the help."

"We're in college, Mom," Rache said.

"We could come between a couple classes," Dot said.

"We're all he's got," their mother said, curling up the corners of her paper.

They went into his room, where he was lying in the bed, clicking the remote, switching the show to *Lawrence Welk*. "Your grandma liked this guy," he said.

He was in his king size, which the twins' mother had moved over in a U-Haul, with all his other stuff. Now he had the twins' old room, traces of them still left behind, the picture of them in their cheerleading uniforms, extending their arms to make a crooked W for the West Side Wolverines. The Boys 2 Men poster was taped up behind the bed, and a Brad Pitt centerfold was tacked to one side of the door. The TV was on the white dresser that they'd used since they were babies, that held their small pink socks and training pants and frilly Sunday dresses, although recently it held their pastel bras and skimpy shorts and bright bikinis.

They sat on either side of him, and he smiled, the left half of his thin lips slightly paralyzed, which made his smile crooked.

"How are my twin girls?" he said, slower than he used to, yet there was vigor in his voice, and it was as clear as an adolescent's whistle.

He put his arms around them as they crawled in like they did when they were younger and stayed with him, when they'd wake up early in the morning, smelling the coffee, scrambled eggs, and bacon that their grandmother had made, and they'd get under his sheets and rouse him in his sleep, staring closely at his face, at the sleep still in his eyes, at the curl at the corner of his lips that made him look like he was smiling, which made them wonder what he had been dreaming. He was always warm under the covers, and as they woke him and he spoke, they could smell the newness of his breath, that was sort of sweet, and they watched the wrinkles forming under his green eyes as he smiled and welcomed them in his arms, into his waking world.

Now they still loved to cuddle under his soft covers, feeling the warmth of his aging body, and they felt like they were ten again, their grandmother scurrying in the kitchen, banging pots and pans, and right now, as he watched *Lawrence Welk*, Dot thought she remembered the melody that the band was playing, and not just that but some tender moment, although she couldn't recall exactly what it was. It was familiar to Rache too, but to her, everything about the show brought the same reaction, and she didn't cherish the memory quite like Dot, who had more affection for her grandfather.

They talked to their grandfather for a while longer, telling him about their jobs, about their school, explaining to him they had to find a major. He didn't understand since he hadn't even graduated high school. He'd been a welder most of his life. He was proud of them.

*

At the bar, Rache made the shots, and Dot wasn't on till nine, so she sat there smoking cigarettes. Rache looked at her sister, envying her perfect body, although Rache's was identical to Dot's, except she had longer arms, and she had on a pair of jeans and a sweatshirt that said "The Heap" in crooked golden letters. Dot shivered, and asked Rache if she could have a cup of coffee.

"Wear something for a change," Rache said, pouring the French Roast, then going back to funneling Baileys into narrow tubes.

"Have you ever seen a shot girl with long sleeves?" Dot said, flicking her lighter off and on. "I'm supposed to show my skin. It's my job."

"You can always bartend."

Dot lit a cigarette. "Maybe I'll call Frank."

"You're not afraid of anything."

"Nu-uh," Dot said.

"I wish I was the shot girl," Rache said, putting the whipped cream inside the silver compact fridge.

"No, you don't," Dot said. "You don't want this slutty job."

Later the place got packed, and Rache ran around behind the counter, spilling drinks over her long sleeves. Dot got burned in the face with a slender cigarette that a tall thin woman waved around, and then a big-necked guy in a Giants' sweatshirt grabbed Dot's ass. Dot pretended that she liked it, and asked him, "What's up, soldier? You want a body shot? I have a new tattoo."

He asked her where it was and she said, "In my panties," then he dropped a hundred in her glass and told her she could show it to him later.

At shut down, Rache had her sleeves up, wiping up the counters with a soppy rag while Dot sat at the bar. "We should find new jobs," Rache said.

"Some guy dropped a hundred in my glass. He wants to see the new tattoo."

"No shit? Jesus," Rache said. She was jealous. "Keep that up, and you'll be rich."

"Maybe we can apply for scholarships," Dot said. "Or maybe Mom will help us."

"Think again," Rache said.

"I guess it isn't all that bad," Dot said.

"Yeah, you're right," Rache said, picking up a broken bottle from a sticky tray. "It can be sort of fun."

Outside, the hundred-dollar guy was leaning up against the brick, toeing pebbles with his boot.

"That's the guy," Dot said. "You can go ahead."

"You'll be OK?" Rache said.

"I'm good at this. I'm a sleaze, remember?"

When Rache got to the corner, Dot turned to the guy. "What's up?" she said.

"You want to see my truck?"

"Yeah, OK," Dot said. She knew she shouldn't be going to some guy's car alone this late at night, but he looked innocent enough, and she knew she was a tease, and then she thought about the hundred dollars, figuring she must owe him something.

After they got to his truck, she pulled up her skirt and slid her panties down an inch, as if she were showing her driver's license to the Wal-Mart clerk while buying Camel Lights. "There it is," she said.

He lit a cigarette. "My wife left me last week. I'm real young, separated. I don't want a relationship, just sex." He had nothing else to lose.

Dot had heard all that before, "no relationship, just sex, no relationship, just sex," as if it were some recording she'd heard so many times, a scratch on her favorite jazz CD, that kept replaying in her sleep, and she'd gotten used to it, knew when it was coming and didn't even think to fix it. Now she felt obligated.

Dot looked at the moving shadows that the flailing branches made. The streetlights shone past them, through the tinted windows of the truck. He kept looking out the window, then at her, then down at the floor, and Dot thought he was going to cry. She thought he needed cheering up, so she leaned over and unzipped his pants. When she was done, he took her home.

Rache was sitting on the sofa, watching a rerun of *Three's Company*, picking peanuts out of a jar of Skippy with a fork. She had been worrying about her sister, and feeling lonely and left out, when Dot walked in, dropping her purse and keys on the table by the door.

"How was the guy?" Rache said. The air conditioner hummed, sending a blast of cold across the room.

"Just like all the others," Dot said. "Don't worry. You didn't miss anything exciting."

*

The next night, he came back. He waited afterwards, leaning against the building, playing with a stick. Rache and Dot walked out together, and Rache leaned in toward Dot, telling her to ask if he had friends to set her up with.

When Rache walked away, Dot went up to him. The moon was full and bright, shining on his curly hair.

In the car he said she didn't look old enough to be working at a bar, and she said he didn't care how old she was, and he admitted that was true. He said he felt sort of revengeful towards his wife, that the younger Dot was the better. He laughed to himself a little bit, then leaned over, kissing her. They took off all their clothes. His skin was hairless, smooth, like a sports car that had just been shined with Turtle Wax. After everything was over, Dot said, "I'm eighteen," pulling down her skirt and putting on her panties.

He rolled down the window and lit a cigarette. She watched him blow smoke out the narrow shallow gap. She looked at him, noticing his satisfaction. She didn't want to let him go.

When Dot got home, Rache was waiting, worried, anxious, just like always, and she asked Dot how it went, and Dot said it was great, that Doug was a super guy, and that they'd had sex in the parking lot.

"Oh," Rache said. "Really?"

*

Rache and Dot rummaged through the kitchen at their mother's, trying to find the chocolate cookies. "Shit," Dot said, looking into the black and white cow jar. "I bet Mom's boyfriend ate them all."

They made sandwiches with white bread, Miracle Whip, and fresh tomatoes from their mother's garden, and they left their knives sitting in the sink, then went to see their grandfather, who was lying in his bed. He was sleeping, and the TV was still on. It was MTV. They sat on the floor next to their dresser, close to one another, their backs leaning up against the wall. "He's not going to make it, is he?" Rache said.

His chest rose and fell and as he exhaled, his breath escaped through the gap in his front teeth, making a small whistle. It reminded Dot of a toy Santa they had when they were younger that whistled in his sleep. "Looks like Santa," Dot said.

"I'm serious," Rache said. She was almost crying.

"He's only eighty-one," Dot said. "Grandpa Brunner died at 102."

They sat there, eating their sandwiches, then wiping off their lips with their paper towels, and they decided to let him sleep, so they left him a note, telling him how much they loved him.

*

For a couple weeks Doug waited for Dot, and she started staying at his motel room. He teased her, saying she was cheap, since she did anything he asked. She wanted him to be her boyfriend, yet she was content with having sex, figuring soon enough he'd divorce his wife, and realize how good she was to him. Rache felt left out, and she resented her sister for always putting her guys first. When Rache *did* see Dot, she asked if Doug had a friend for Rache to possibly go out with, but Dot said she could do much better.

One morning after Doug had brought Dot home, Rache and Dot sat on the checkered sofa at their apartment holding bowls of Raisin Bran, smelling the brewing coffee that had started automatically.

"So what if his friends aren't decent," Rache said, stirring her spoon, mixing up the sugar, scooping out a clump of raisins. "You always get the fun."

"I'm a slut," Dot said. "You don't want to be like me. It can be fun at first, but after a while, all you are is cheap. You can lose control."

"Well, I want some fun. I've only been with Roger, and that was only high school. How many guys have you been with? Twenty-something, right?"

"I lost count," Dot said. She got up and went into the kitchen, almost tripping over a stack of books. She set her bowl on the Formica, and she poured two cups of coffee, adding cream and sugar to Rache's purple cup.

*

A few nights later, after the bar was closed, Rache and Dot put on their leather jackets and stepped out, seeing Doug leaning up against the building in the alley.

"It's set," he said. "I have a friend for Rache."

"Not a loser, huh?" Dot said, reaching in her purse and pulling out her pack of smokes.

"Dot, stop it," Rache said, nudging her.

"She'll like him enough," he said.

Dot lit her cigarette. He said, "Come with me." After they walked to his truck, Rache slid in the tiny seat in back, anxious and excited, and Dot got in the front.

As he drove, Dot looked out the window, at the glowing lights, at the letters on the billboards, at the cars that they passed by.

"She's sexy," he said to Dot. "Just like you."

"Be nice to her," Dot said. "She's not a whore."

"I still want some action," Rache said, leaning forward. She was smiling, bright-eyed. She grabbed Dot's cigarette and took a drag.

"Don't worry," he said. "You'll get your share."

He drove to the Days Inn and stopped the truck. His room looked the same as always, shoes scattered on the floor, Ruffles bags and beer cans sitting on the table, and the TV was still on. He grabbed the ice bucket and said he'd be back, and then he left the room.

"I can't wait," Rache said, going to the mirror and touching up her eye shadow.

"Jesus," Dot said. "It's nothing special. You can get sex anywhere." She sat on the bed and Rache sat on a chair beside the table, toying with an empty beer can.

When Doug came back, he put ice in plastic cups and opened a Coke and poured it before adding shots of Jack. "My friend is coming in a minute," he said, giving Dot a drink, then Rache.

Dot took a sip right away, then slammed the rest, and Rache sipped slowly, saying she didn't want to be drunk when she met his friend. Doug opened a nightstand drawer and took out a joint and lit it, then sucked on it and handed it to Dot.

"Where you from?" Rache said.

"Nowhere special," he said.

"He's separated," Dot said, sucking in the joint.

"Yeah, I'm married," he said. "Dot takes care of me." He laughed.

"Like a Virgin" was playing on MTV. It was some Madonna marathon, and Dot started dancing on the mattress, moving in sync with the music, undoing the top button of her shirt, sliding a hand up and down her curves, balling up her other hand, putting it to her lips as if it were a mike. Doug told her she was crazy.

Rache sucked on the joint, then got on the bed and moved in front of Doug as if she were a stripper. "Where's my tip?" she said.

Another song came on and Rache poured herself more Jack. Dot felt dizzy and got down, leaning into Doug as he spun her around. "Hey," she said. "You spike these drinks, or what?"

He laughed and then she laughed and then they started kissing.

"Hey," Rache said. "When's my guy getting here?"

"Pretty soon," he said.

Dot plopped down on the bed. She felt funny, like things were fuzzy and she figured it was the joint, and she thought it worked rather quickly compared to the other stuff she'd done. It all belonged to Doug.

Rache was getting drunk. She took another hit, then laughed, and she grabbed Doug, dancing close to him.

Dot tried to get up, but she could barely move, so she lay back on the bed. She felt paralyzed. Then everything was black.

Doug's friend finally arrived, and Rache danced between the guys like a sandwich. She said she wanted to have a little fun. They talked to each other and to her, calling her a piece of trash, and Rache, said "Yeah, I am. Come and get me, hotshot." They kissed her, took off her clothes and she got on the bed and danced around, feeling like an exotic dancer, holding a beer in her right hand, raising it to the beat of the song on MTV.

*

Dot woke up first. She didn't know how long she'd been asleep. Could've been seconds, minutes, hours. It almost seemed like days. The place reeked of sweat and cigarettes and booze. She noticed her shirt was unbuttoned all the way, her skirt hiked up past her thighs. She pulled on her skirt's hem and as she buttoned her pearl buttons, she looked over on the floor, and saw Doug sleeping, and Rache lying next to him, naked, her hands tied behind her back, and a thick gold rope around her neck. On the second bed was a guy sleeping on his back, one leg hanging, his left toe touching the red carpet. He was snoring, but just so slightly that if she hadn't seen him, she probably wouldn't have noticed because of the racket coming from the air conditioner. His hair was long and stringy and his chest was hairless just like Doug's.

When Rache finally woke up, she could barely open her eyes. Her whole body hurt, and she didn't know where she was until she saw her sister, and then things started coming back to her. Dot untied her. "What happened here?"

"Holy hell," Rache said.

"Jesus," Dot said.

Dot helped Rache get dressed, lifting her shirt over her head, pulling up her jeans, then they sat around the table, on the plaid cushions of the wooden chairs. The morning light shone through the thick green curtains that were held together with shiny metal rods, and the TV was still on, its volume low, and there was some program on CNN, a pulled-together lady with bright lipstick.

The whole place smelled and looked like sex, like a porno movie that had gone on too long, gotten out of hand, the director and producer and the crew joining in even after the camera had gone off. Polaroids sat on the dirty table, snippets of ash floating all around them. In some of the photos, Dot was lying naked on the bed, her arms and legs sprawled out, Doug lying next to her, his hands between her thighs. In the other photos, Rache was naked, lying with her hands tied, and Doug's friend was on top of her, his back to the camera, his head turned with a half-grin on his face. Another was of Rache on her knees, Doug's jeans down past his hips, her legs and hands tied with that golden rope. Her bunched eyebrows and widened mouth that took him in made her look like she was screaming. Dot sifted through the pictures, tossed them across to Rache. "Jesus," Dot said. "We need to call the cops."

Rache shoved the pictures in her purse. "No way." She started a cigarette. "Some friends you have," she said.

"I'm a slut," Dot said. "We all know that."

Dot picked up Doug's Levi's from the floor and rummaged through his pockets. She took his wallet, cigarettes and keys. Then she found the other guy's gray shorts by his feet and felt his pockets, but all of them were empty.

"Over there," Rache said, pointing to the nightstand that was filled with empty cups, and wet from melted ice cubes.

Dot picked up his wallet, letting the water drip. She looked at his driver's license. "His name is Len," she said. "What a stupid name. Guy's only twenty-one."

"You're not going to steal it, are you?"

"Like they didn't steal from you?"

"I said I was fine," Rache said.

Dot got the Jack, went for the beer, then grabbed their clothes and put them in the bathtub and soaked everything with booze. She opened the dresser drawers and dumped the catsup and the mustard that she'd gotten from the fridge on all of Doug's belongings. She hiked up her skirt and pulled down her panties and urinated on the bed where Len was sleeping. She wiped her crotch with a faded pillowcase that looked a shade of yellow.

"You're such a freak," Rache said.

"Serves him right," Dot said.

Rache turned off the TV, and Dot stuffed all the wallets and keys inside her purse. She messed up the sheets, and wrote on a piece of Days Inn paper, "This isn't over," and left it on the bed.

"I'm telling you," Rache said. "It wasn't all that bad."

They opened up the door, and the new sunlight was dim, but it made their eyes hurt. Rache and Dot looked back, then sat on the lawn next to the pool and Rache leaned against a tree. They just sat there for a while, staring at the uneven rays reflecting off the water, at the dirty edges of the pool, at the blades of grass drifting off in numerous directions. "I guess we better go," Dot said. And then they got up, and walked arm-in-arm for a couple blocks, and they knew they were close to home, but too far to walk in the state they were both in. So they walked to an Exxon station and Dot called a cab, and they waited on the curb in silence, just sitting feeling the warm sunrise, watching cars pass by, ones driven by people who looked as if they were on their way to work.

"We have to call the cops," Dot said.

"No," Rache said. "No cops. What's the difference between Doug fucking me and fucking you? Same with the other guy? You would have done it too."

"I asked for sex with Doug," Dot said.

"So did I," Rache said.

"Not like that," Dot said.

Rache told her she was fine, that everything was fine.

They got tired of waiting for the cab, so they got up and strolled along the sidewalk. Trash lay on the curb, McDonald's bags, and broken beer cans, a pack of crumpled cigarettes. A loud truck zoomed by and the driver honked its horn. The sun was hot, but the air was still a little chilly. Small clouds wandered overhead.

They walked along the edge of the Bay, streetlights glowing down, sunrise peeking up. Birds were singing over the drum of the distant train that came through town at the same time every morning. Dot took the wallets from her purse and counted all the money, about a hundred dollars, and she gave Rachel half. Dot handed Len's wallet to Rache and took Doug's credit cards and tossed them in the water, one by one, but all they did was float. Dot looked at the pictures in Doug's wallet, one of him and his pretty brunette wife, and she crumpled it and tossed it overhand just like a baseball.

"Look at this," Rache said. She handed Dot a picture of a young girl in a purple swimsuit sitting on a swing. There were four snapshots, each with different poses. "That's odd," Rache said. She put the pictures in her purse, and then removed the photos from last night and filtered through them, one by one.

"I wonder if he'll come back," Rache said.

"He never will," Dot said, tossing Doug's wallet in the water, watching it splash slightly as it sunk.

"He's going to need his wallet," Rache said. She studied the picture of her on her knees in front of Doug. She handed it to Dot.

Dot stared at it, looking at Rache's face. Dot almost started crying. She took Rache's pictures and threw them in the water. She watched them as they turned with the small wind that made the water stir.

"I guess that was pretty awful," Rache said.

"Are you kidding? It was horrible. A nightmare," Dot said. "Let's not do that again."

She remembered how they used to dare each other to jump into the Bay, how they'd feed the seagulls tiny breadcrumbs, letting the birds get so close they pecked the girls' bare feet. Now Dot stared at the falling moon's reflection on the water, and she thought she saw a figure, like a girl, floating on the bay, moving in a quiet motion with the gentle chilling waves. It was Rache, it was just the way she pictured things ending up, Rache floating in the Bay, shining in the watery light.

They sat on a bench and rested, watching a small boat slither by, sending a slight wave in the water. A bird landed on a wooden stump, perching its beak upward, turning its petite head at a slender angle. Then it spread its wings and flew away.

"I know why Grandpa loves you more," Rache said. "You've always been the brave one."

"That's not true," Dot said. She heard a splash coming from the water, a fish jumping like the jack-in-the-box they had when they were kids. "Remember that time we went fishing in the lake? And you and Grandpa did the breast stroke? Racing across while I stayed in the boat? I was scared to death. And then you won, so he bought you extra ice cream. I was so upset. I hated going fishing." She looked at her sister. The air was getting hot.

Rache put her arm around Dot, feeling her lean arms, feeling the strength in all their smallness. She said, "We are *so* alike."

Like Falling Down and Laughing

Jessica Hollander

The students in my first class at Stewart Wade High gathered on metal bleachers. In almost-adult clothes, they held leather bags and waxy-bright books; they were skinny but tall. Stretched little kids. The gym smelled of rubber. In Michigan I had taught Advanced Junior Lit, but here in Chapel Hill, Brant and I were forced to take what jobs were available. I explained that the kids were responsible for locking up their clothes.

"Someone wants my gym shorts, he can have them," a boy said.

"You'll have to work out in your underwear," I told him.

"You'd make us do that?" a girl asked.

"Just watch your stuff."

Since they hadn't brought exercise clothes the first day, I had my students walk the perimeter of the room in their socks for twenty minutes. They moved sluggishly. I encouraged them to talk to each other. "Walk and talk!"

I ran back and forth across the center of the room, clapping a few times for the different groups, creating energy. I shouted optional subjects each time they completed a lap: "Pets!" "Favorite Games!" "Assets of Education!"

The kids wearing sandals had to sit on the bleachers and watch. I tried to ignore them. I tried to ignore how the landscape of my body had changed since college. Cellulite had gathered. Excess hung over the elastic of my gym shorts. Brant and I hadn't had sex since the move: we feigned exhaustion or distraction; we looked away when the other was changing, like we suspected our loss in quality employment had taken a toll on our bodies and we were afraid to see the cost.

One student, Ingrid, had her ears pierced all the way up. She had hoops and sparkly studs and little silver crosses. When she saw me looking at them, she said, "One for every breakup." She walked beside a girl with a parrot tattoo arched around her shoulder. These bodies were poised for rebellion.

*

Brant had wanted to move to Chapel Hill to be near his mother. In the past, she'd occasionally overnighted baked goods to us; the postage cost so much we could've bought five loaves of bread or a month's worth of cookies. But when we lost our jobs three months ago, his mother sent one of her Concern Packages every other day. Brant felt bad about the postage to the extent that I met the mailman in the hall and ripped off the stickers. "Add it up," Brant said. "She should be spending that on pillows and those hats with flowers pinned into them. She should live propped on pillows, wearing a series of fancy hats." He insisted we live near his mother for more convenient delivery.

The day we moved into our new apartment, Brant's mother brought us a doormat printed with three rows of ladybugs. Their bodies touched on all sides, except the word WELCOME interrupted the middle row. She wore turquoise jewelry and a cardigan embroidered with baby penguins. Since her husband died, she was crazy about grandbabies. When with us, she followed strollers around museums and insisted we sit near the loudest screaming infants in restaurants.

Her eyes watered when she stepped into our apartment, looked at the scuffed floors, the walls with odd smears and holes. Boxes outlined the rooms; shoes trailed from paper bags; our furniture was gathered in haphazard clumps. In the kitchen, the metal cabinets had corroded: big chunks were missing. We had nowhere to put our cleaning supplies. The garbage sat in the middle of the living room.

Brant didn't look at her. "Welcome to our fake life." He pulled stuffing from boxes. He threw Styrofoam peanuts and newspaper balls gently at me.

It was a parade. Pieces clung to my chest and shoulders and hair. I smiled because this wasn't really our life. This was a moment we stepped off track with plans to arrange things perfectly before stepping back on.

One of the silk carnations pinned to his mother's straw hat drooped over the brim. She gripped the welcome mat with both hands in one corner. It kept slipping. It hung angled over her legs.

I bent down and examined the mat. "We're not really in a welcoming state."

"You'll be glad for the color coming home," she whispered, positioning it in the hall.

*

Until last spring, we'd been saving. Brant and I graduated with education degrees and were career-counseled into jobs teaching English at different high schools. We moved out of student housing to a suburban apartment complex manicured with small, round bushes against the buildings, trim green grass, and plots of marigolds and pansies in the medians of the parking lots. We put money away each month. We accumulated an eclectic mix of furniture, one piece at a time. We talked about going off birth control.

But we did not have tenure. At the end of our third year teaching, when we lost our jobs, our luckier colleagues gave us bottles of wine and In Sympathy cards with orchids on the front or delicate birds against a pink-gray dusk. Like we had died. We went home to our grown-up apartment, drank wine, and lay frowning on the couch, our legs tangled together. We had furniture all around us. The walls were white and covered with odd prints and paintings we'd bought on art walks.

"You can't lock in a thing like adulthood," I said.

Brant reached for the bottle of red wine and knocked it over. The wine soaked into the white carpet.

He kicked my legs getting up and stumbled toward the kitchen, where I assumed he'd get a towel. Instead he came back with a steak knife and began sawing away at the couch arm's upholstery. "Our life's over here," he said.

I tried to pull him off. "We can take things with us."

He struggled against me and went on sawing. Threads and thin strips of fabric fluttered to the ground, and I looked around for a way to stop him. I unbuttoned my shirt and threw it at him. He kept sawing, but he glanced at me as I took off my bra and clumsily unzipped my skirt. My head pounded from all the movement. He dropped the knife and helped me with the tights.

*

My students only liked the kicking part of kickball. They ran full speed at the giant red ball, and they got it in the air. But they jogged slowly toward the bases. They swung meekly at pop-ups, short-armed throws to first base.

"Hustle it up!" I called. Teaching gym felt a lot like taking care of people. I developed a shouting voice. I tried to get them excited about physical fitness.

Ingrid hung around sometimes at the end of class. She told me about her boyfriend, David, who was in my third period. "He thinks you're hot." She helped carry the bases to the supply closet. I had a free period next and didn't trust leaving things out.

"He digs curly hair," she said. "I do too, clearly."

David had dark curly hair. He had a tongue ring and a wry smile, and he played bass. I was flattered that these kids liked me. In high school I wore combat boots and limp flowery skirts and thickly lined my eyes. Now, I wore no makeup. I wore tennis shoes and cotton shorts and pulled my hair back in a clump.

"He asks about you," I told Ingrid. "He wants to know how you scored, and then he tries to beat you."

Ingrid nodded. "You have to find ways to prove you're better. Or else why bother sleeping together." She dropped the bases in the closet, and I locked the door. I wasn't surprised these kids were having sex. I watched her walk across the gym.

*

Our ladybug doormat sat in the hall outside our apartment—
we were the only tenants who had one. Sometimes Brant and I came
home and found the mat in front of a different door. Where did we
live? We didn't know if people moved it as some kind of prank or if
they were overcome with jealousy. We never asked, just pulled the
mat back in front of our place, number 39, then went in quickly
and locked the door.

Since Brant couldn't find a job, he was forced to substitute
when positions came available. "I'm working with six-year-olds," he
said. We ate Indian takeout in the kitchen, ripping naan to pieces.
"I introduce them to letters. Meet Mr. *C is for cinnamon and also for carrot.*
Mr. *Ch is for choke.* We sound out the words."

He pulled at the stretched neck of his T-shirt. He had short
blond hair and a trim goatee. He was capable of looking like someone who knew something, but every day he came home, threw his
loafers at the wall, and put on these old torn T-shirts he had worn
in college. The sleeves reached his elbows.

"Those kids are still developing," I said. "You're teaching
them how to be humans."

Brant picked up a steak knife and carved into our Ethan Allen
table. It was a beautiful table. I tried not to look.

"I want to know what they think," he said. "I ask them if they
like a sentence, one of those subject-verb-whatevers—*Jane walks away*—
and they just stare at me. They don't even know what it means."

"Your mother's crazy about kids," I reminded him.

"She's the real deal," he said. "She's in a place to love everyone."
He worked the knife deep into the wood. "You should see what these

kids bring to Share Circle. Pearls and Rolexes and stuffed animals so big they're like extra students with their own necklaces and watches."

Brant's carving resembled a heart; he ran the blade over and over the perimeter. I put the leftovers in the fridge and watered the spider plant I'd bought at the grocery.

"I don't approve of that accumulation," Brant told me.

"Your mother's right. We might as well have some color in our non-life."

*

A couple weeks later, Ingrid came to my office. She had a fierce expression. "I can't stop digging them." She showed me her thumb-nails jammed beneath the nails of her middle fingers. The creases filled with blood.

I took her hands and flattened her fingers against my palms.

"You only own yourself," I said.

"There's no more room on my ears," she told me. "And I refuse to get a tongue ring. I don't want to give him that."

When David came to third period, he waved, and I ignored him. It was unprofessional to hold a grudge. He stretched near me on the court. "Hey Alison, I guess you heard. It's the crash of the year." He gave me a smile like there was a conspiracy.

"Is there something funny about it?"

"Well, it's life." He watched a pretty girl enter the gym in her street clothes. She had long black hair she never pulled back, and she wore unnervingly bright clothes. She had three friends who followed her around.

This was the second day in a row the girl had come to class in jeans and a large V-neck and necklaces to her navel. She climbed onto the bleachers without saying anything. Other girls watched.

"Get on the court!" I yelled to her. I had the basketballs out; kids were working on their jump shots.

She put her arms around her stomach and rocked forward. Two girls walked toward the bleachers to see about her, and one of them paused and whispered to me, "She gets wicked cramps."

I sent the girls back to the court and climbed the bleachers myself. I'd seen this before: bodies used as an excuse. I had a male gym teacher in middle school that let pale, anxious-looking girls out of class with no questions asked.

"Exercise helps those kinds of cramps," I told the girl.

"I can't today." She frowned. She rocked forward and let out little moans. She was beautiful in a way that bored and exhausted me.

On the court, the balls stopped bouncing. Several students stood watching us.

"Is she alright?" David asked.

I didn't even look at him.

"Go to the nurse," I told the girl. "If you can't participate, don't bother coming at all."

*

Once more, the welcome mat was gone. Brant and I had gone to a Chinese restaurant with Brant's mother and let her pay for us. I'd given my fortune cookie to Brant, and he'd scowled when he read the slip of paper. He ripped it to pieces and threw it on my plate. "That one's yours," he said.

We searched our hall for the doormat. We went to the first floor; we went to the second. At the end of the second-floor hall Brant punched one of the small, clouded windows overlooking an alley. The glass shattered in long shards that further shattered on the carpet.

I ran toward him, expecting doors to fling open, sirens, a
night in the jail wait-room. A dozen small cuts covered from his
knuckles to near his elbow.

"I loved that mat," he said. "It was so nice of my mom." One-
handed, he unbuttoned his shirt.

I helped him. It was the first move I'd made toward him in
weeks. Lately, at night, Brant always wanted to have a hand on me.
On my stomach, locked under my arm, resting on my hip. He had
read somewhere that skin-on-skin contact increased your happiness, and he was willing to try it. To me, it felt like possession. Like
if my body belonged to him then he had two bodies, and this made
him stronger.

No doors opened. We tied the shirt around Brant's bloody
hand and finally found the mat on the fourth floor, in front of the
last door of the hall. Brant pounded on the door with his left hand,
but nobody answered.

"It's nice to know you can get things back." He made a show stepping on the word WELCOME, and he grinned as though this could
be turned into a joke we could share. "Thank you," he told the mat.

Inside our apartment, he took off a loafer and handed it to
me. In college, Brant had worn sneakers so ragged you could see his
toes, and while we talked once at a party, someone pulled off Brant's
sneaker and ran away with it. "That's an important shoe," he'd told
me. By the time we left, his sock was beer-soaked, and he refused to
sully the shoe we'd finally found in the oven. I carried the sneaker
for him, like a purse, dirty laces slung over my shoulder. That was
the first night we slept together.

I held his brown loafer in our leaf-cluttered entryway, and dirt
crumbled into my hand. Usually he threw his shoes into the middle

of the room, and I had to leave them or put them away. The loafer was a sad thing to me. I lined it next to mine by the wall and locked the bathroom door while I showered.

Afterward, I tripped over a winter boot in the hallway. Shoes were scattered around the floors and the furniture; he'd gotten into the seasonal shoes and the event shoes, and there were flip-flops and never-worn Kenneth Coles and the three-inch sage heels I hadn't seen since my aunt's wedding. In the kitchen I found the floor blood-streaked and littered with bits of leather and Brant's brown loafer destroyed on the cutting board. I reorganized as best I could, though shoes were hidden in appliances and beneath couch pillows. I found two in the hall, but still several went missing, so some pairs were no longer paired.

Later, when I climbed into bed, I brushed my foot against Brant's shoe, the one he'd left on. I couldn't tell if he was sleeping or pretending. I reached for his hand, the one not wrapped in bloody gauze and discoloring the sheets. He took my hand and squeezed it.

*

For several weeks after the breakup, Ingrid came to class glowering. She swung a bat so hard it flew from her hands toward a group of girls, who ducked, shielding their faces. When she failed to break seven minutes for the mile, she punched the side of the bleachers and broke one of her fingers. I told her to go to the nurse, and she stared at me until her friend with the parrot tattoo led her away.

She sometimes stopped by my office in her free period. I had a toaster on my desk; I bought strawberry Pop Tarts because I knew she loved them. She showed me a tiny X she'd scratched into her forearm with a paperclip.

"That isn't a great form of expression," I told her. "Maybe you could find another distraction."

"It's not a distraction." She had her feet propped on my desk; she wore tight black pants that zipped at the bottoms. Between bites of Pop-Tart she leaned forward with her lighter and flickered flames at the frayed bottoms. Her ankles reddened. "I know what I'm doing."

"How can you know something like that?"

"It's not hard to have a plan. It's the only thing that matters." She dropped her legs and crawled onto the desk toward me. Her lips were red and swollen as though chewed-on. She kissed my jawbone near the ear, and then she kissed me on the lips. It happened so quickly I didn't move until she pulled back and offered me a bite of her Pop-Tart.

The pastry broke as I took a piece of it; red and white crumbs littered my desk. I narrowed my eyes like I knew what she was talking about.

"This is good," I said. "I thought it would be too sweet."

We had a moment when I imagined our expressions looked exactly the same.

*

One evening, Brant's yuppie friends from high school came over and repositioned the furniture. They yelled and laughed about teenage exploits: smoking Romeo y Julietas in the woods, wearing big-legged jeans, raising hell at the Mothers' Bake-off.

"Welcome," I said and then excused myself to the bedroom, where I shut the door and got under the covers to watch reruns of shows I'd loved in High School: *Roseanne, Home Improvement, Beverly Hills 90210*. I couldn't think about Ingrid. I thought about the rest of them. My students' apathy was so thick their eyes were constantly out of focus. I couldn't get them excited. They blinked at me several seconds after I gave instructions. I hated that pretty girl with her times-of-the-months that occurred several times a month but who didn't look so sick after class talking to David.

When Brant's friends left, I heard them in the hall congratulating themselves about something. Brant came in and turned off the television. He swayed in front of it, looking at me.

"I wish I could go in reverse," he said. "There's this space when you're smart enough and young enough to cook things up."

"My students run so slow," I mumbled, half asleep.

He stumbled around, taking off his khakis. "You want to have sex?"

"I can't this week," I said. "My period's an ice machine."

He climbed into bed, pulled the covers away from me, and bunched them up around him. "Let your students go slow. There's nothing good on the other side."

*

I did not often wish for a simpler time. My girl students traded body secrets like currency, whispering of homemade tattoos and arms slashed with safety pins and vomiting and fucking on foosball tables. The pretty girl and her friends lay moaning on locker-room benches. I found them once in their underwear in a shower stall, sniffing markers.

Ingrid's self-destruction diminished; she regained her regal posture and wore sleeves covering her markings; she pierced the thin end of her eyebrow. Every day now she came to my office and closed the door, and she kissed me.

Sometimes she sat on my lap or crawled across my desk or took hold of my hair and pulled me that way from my seat. I was careful not to initiate. I imagined myself a doll, willing to accept inflictions the girl needed to inflict. It was a type of therapy.

After we kissed for a while, Ingrid was nice. She made Pop Tarts and held my legs in her lap, petting my shins. She told me about David's obsession with her body: how he'd smoothed her hair and traced her birthmarks and sniffed her armpit. "When we started fighting, I didn't let him touch me. Not even the filthy pads of my toes."

"I never saw it like that," I said. "I never saw pushing Brant away as a punishment." When I wanted Brant to pay attention to me, I used to take off my clothes.

*

Some nights I came home and found the furniture turned upside down, the undersides hacked at. Some nights I found the kitchen full of white smoke and Brant lying beneath the blaring fire alarm with his eyes closed. Some nights he stabbed a knife into his bedside table, and I listened to the dull thuds, no longer caring about this furniture I once wouldn't allow a glass of water to sit upon. Brant made me nervous, but I understood the destruction. These things he did I did too, only differently.

The night I came home to an empty apartment, I knew Brant was at his mother's. I pretended to sleep when he returned late at night, when he removed his shoes and placed them on my stomach and arm. He talked while he undressed: about the hot-air balloon mobile hanging from his bedroom ceiling, about the cartoon movies his mother kept above the television. I couldn't move. I tried to keep the shoes balanced.

After a few evenings of him gone, I drove to his mother's place and saw his red Oldsmobile half on the curb, the front wheels twisted toward the house. I wanted to go inside. I wanted to bring Brant home and hand him a knife and tell him it was better. But I couldn't stand to see the sadness I knew he unloaded onto his mother.

When Brant got home that night, he put his shoes on my stomach. "I'm thinking of moving in with my mother."

In the silence that followed, I sensed him watching me. I turned onto my side and let the shoes fall to the floor. He shook me a few times after that, but I didn't open my eyes.

*

Every day before lunch, Ingrid came to my office, and we walked together to the cafeteria. In the high-ceilinged room not so different from the gymnasium, the periphery lunch tables were empty. Everyone squeezed around the few tables in the center; they packed in so many chairs some tables had a double circumference. No one was willing to sit alone.

I'd become friendly with Angela, a fifty-something woman who taught printmaking and had Ingrid and her friend with the parrot tattoo in one of her classes. Ingrid and I found Angela and the friend in the faculty corner. I sat next to Ingrid, brushing her arm.

"You have to make it through high school," Angela told the girl with the parrot tattoo. "Everyone's wrapped up in the culture or rebelling against the culture. It all spins around that."

"You know, there's more culture outside," the girl said. "There's culture all over the place." She and Ingrid shared sushi rolls they'd brought in little Japanese boxes with sticks of bamboo drawn across the tops.

"My boyfriend moved out," I told them, suddenly proud to have had this happen to me. "He calls from his mother's. He says soon, when he's ready, we'll get hitched."

"Sounds like an asshole I'd fall for," said Ingrid's friend. She was quick with the chopsticks from the box to her mouth. She sucked on a piece of ginger.

"He says I'd be a good mother," I said. "Like his."

"Do not marry him," Ingrid said.

"It's common for twenty-somethings to move back with their parents," Angela said. "Fuck society, they think. It's easier to have your parents love you."

Some nights I heard scratching on my door and in the morning found hacked strips of wood covering the mat. It didn't make sense given Brant still had a key. I never chain-locked the door, pretending instead that he would come home any minute.

*

I told myself it was a phase, more of this non-life business. Something we could laugh about eventually, like with the doormat, like *Mr. Ch is for Choke*. Like losing your balance is funny. You sit on the floor for a while, and then you get up.

I went to Brant's mother's. I had this idea I could laugh at Brant now, and he would laugh too, and the ridiculousness could be over.

His mother answered the door with a floury ball of dough in her hands.

"He's in a fragile state," she said. The thin muscles of her arms bulged as she worked her fingers through the dough. Watching her made me almost want to move in, too. She had a carefully put-together house, with floral trim lining the walls and a big cherry cabinet to hide coats and shoes. The carpet had fresh vacuum lines; a sprinkler sputtered arcs around the backyard.

I found Brant lying in bed. On the floor around him, he'd built up a Lego town: blue, red, and yellow houses with their angled roofs in steps. But G.I. Joe dolls were stationed outside each door, like they were taking over. Little Lego people posed mid-walk. They had broad-smiling, idiot faces.

"I'm still working," he told me. "Eventually we'll have enough money to buy a house and have kids, and then we'll have the real deal. We'll move right over."

"I thought you hated kids. And their poor understanding of sentence structure."

He blinked at me. He focused on my mouth, like he couldn't understand it. "This is a lovely place. Here we're supposed to love each other."

"This isn't our place," I said.

"This is how you get me." He lifted his hands above his stomach and made an explosion noise.

I drove from his mother's to the grocery and bought three spider plants. At home, I pulled the welcome mat inside the apartment and laid it on the floor, like the apartment was the outside and the world was a place to feel comfortable in. Plants and furniture surrounded me. With a steak knife I hacked away at the couch. I tried to laugh. I laughed.

*

Again, the pretty girl came to third period in her street clothes and sat on the bleachers with her arms around her waist.

"Get on the court!" I yelled. My students were stretching. I would line them up for relays today; I had five blue batons. I was trying for camaraderie.

"I can't!" the girl said, sobbing.

I took her into my office. The nurse had given me some ibuprofen for times-of-the-month. I handed her the bottle. "Your classroom decorum grade includes originality," I told her. "I pulled this crap in *my* gym class."

After a few minutes, the girl walked onto the floor in her gym clothes, her face tear-streaked. She'd pulled back her hair. She slumped toward the rest of us.

When the race began, the kids cheered, and with those around them cheering, everyone tried to out-scream the others. The pretty girl ran anchor in her group, and she ran her heart out. I saw the pain on her face. When she finished in second place, she threw the baton on the ground and leaned against the wall. David jogged over and put his hand on her back.

She moaned.

Another girl put her head between her knees and said she felt sick. Then another and another, until I had five girls moaning that they were going to vomit all over the floor. And I started feeling nauseated too, watching them writhe around. I wanted to hold my legs to my chest and whine like I was going to die.

Instead, I sent them to the nurse. Once they were gone, I lined up those who remained, and we had another race. This time I watched from the bleachers. They cheered themselves on.

*

A week later, in the cafeteria, I spotted Brant at the popular boys' table. He was still substituting, but he didn't sit with the substitutes. He didn't sit with David at the Goth table, or with the hipsters, druggies, or thugs. With his combed hair, his Ralph Lauren sports jacket, he managed to look like he belonged with that cable-knit group of boat-owners, a group that would make his mother proud.

He slouched hungrily forward. The other boys leaned toward him, and Brant's deep laugh spread across the room.

I touched Ingrid's wrist. "That used to be my boyfriend."

Beneath our table, Ingrid had her hand on my leg. Together, with two paperclips, we'd carved a heart on my thigh. Every day now I shaved and slathered my legs with lotion, and it burned.

"Not bad," Ingrid said. "He reminds me of someone I used to be in love with."

I experienced a tiny movement of pride. It was another life. He used to hold my hand and feel happy.

Blooms

Kathy Fish

Dan the neuropsychologist wants to test Nona's personality. Nona is Dan's research assistant. They work together in a large university hospital. Every day he asks her to talk about her boyfriend. This, she resists. She feels it would be untoward, like presenting a case at Grand Rounds. The neuropsychologist wants details and supporting arguments, some factual account. She hasn't the energy for it.

Nona observes Dan's pale green eyes widen whenever he speaks to their boss, the department chair. His speech becomes formal and direct. The department chair closes his eyes as if he's listening through headphones. Nona is not personally qualified to speak to the department chair.

She's in the conference room reading a paperback when Dan enters. His face resembles a self-portrait of Van Gogh. He gives her the personality inventory and a #2 pencil and sits on the rug like a kindergartner. He laughs and hangs his head in his hands and sighs deeply.

He says, "Nona, my daughters—do you know how much I love them?"

"A lot. What are their names again?"

"Thomas and Greg. We chose not to burden them with societal norms and expectations."

Nona knew this, she just wanted to hear it again. Later, she'll climb under the quilts with Bill, her boyfriend and whisper this into his ear, hoping to make him laugh.

*

This afternoon, she's scheduled to test Patient RD. She sees him over a period of three days every six months. His actual name is Ray Dripps, but in the textbooks he's referred to as RD. In neuropsychology circles, RD is considered a celebrity. He got sick after riding the Screaming Terror at Busch Gardens when he was fifteen. He vomited all over his friend's Camaro, then went home and slept for twenty-four hours. He woke up with a spectacular headache.

RD's chief problem is that he perseverates. He's incapable of changing mental sets. He carries a flashlight and flicks it on and off. When Nona administers the neuropsychological exams, she asks him a number of questions, to which he answers, "I don't give a rat's ass." His photo, in the medical journals, shows a man with a mild, expressionless face and one hand raised, palm out, as if he's taking an oath.

She plays a card-sorting game with him in which the rules constantly change. RD has a genius IQ yet this game confounds him. She tells him, "It's okay, really. This game is tough. It's exactly like life, my man."

"Yes, thank you," he says and bursts into tears. He leans over and kisses her knee. In his chart, she writes *emotionally labile*.

The exam room is roughly the size of a walk-in closet. There are no windows. Nona is not allowed to dress it up. Bill gave her one of those glass-sipping birds when she got the job, but she can't have it in here. It sits next to the coffee maker in the conference room. It swings forward and sips from a mug. The sipping bird wears a top hat and a bow tie. Nona thinks the patients might enjoy it.

She feels boxy inside her clothes today. She feels unwieldy and outsized, like a hedgehog, in her lab coat. In reality, she's very thin. She's a minnow. RD is peevish and uncooperative. She finishes the game and forgoes the other standardized tests, the memory tests, the language batteries. She needs to run out her time with him, so instead she writes her grocery list. Her boyfriend's needs are simple: chicken pot pies and baking potatoes and Quaker Oat Squares. Gold's medicated powder. Minted dental floss. Also, he drinks one whole gallon of milk per day. She writes it all down. Out of the corner of her eye, she notices that RD is rubbing his crotch, looking at her legs. They really need the sipping bird in here.

*

After work, Nona takes the Ride-On bus to Hy-Vee and buys the food and walks home with two bags in each hand and her purse slung across her chest. She wears a pea coat and a stocking cap. She and Bill live in a log cabin duplex at the top of Dodge Street behind Home Town Dairy. A line of refrigerator trucks are parked, motors running, all night, but she's never seen them go anywhere. Also, she's never seen any cows. Where are the cows? Ahead, the side of the duplex that she and Bill share is dark like an eye with a patch.

She lets herself in and turns on the lights. The bookcase in the center separates the living room and the bedroom. Bill's a lump on the waterbed, which takes up every last inch of the room. She has to crawl along the edge of it to get to the bathroom door. Bill rises and falls on a wave.

"I'm unwell," she says, turning on the fluorescent light over the bathroom sink. She splashes her face with water, scoops some into her mouth.

Bill shifts under the quilts. "I read today," he says. "The Biophysics of Archery and the Archer."

Nona crawls onto the bed and pulls the quilts away from his face. "Liar."

"It was fascinating."

The man who lives on the other side of the duplex nailed a target to the cottonwood tree and practices archery every day. Even in December, he's out there practicing. For a while, they referred to him as William Tell. This was when every morning Nona and Bill left the log duplex together to get coffee, to go to their jobs, when they rode in the rusted Vega together and laughed about their neighbor. When Bill was himself.

"Do you know," Nona says, "there's a bucket beside the secretary's desk full of formaldehyde? Do you know what's inside it, floating around in all that preservative?" She runs her fingers along Bill's brow to his cheekbone. "Can you guess?"

"I hate guessing."

"This will amuse you. Guaranteed."

Bill groans and rolls over, away from her.

"Hey. Come on, we were talking."

On the other side of the duplex, she hears music. Something old and familiar that her brother used to play. Three Dog Night. She smells onions and tomatoes cooking. The neighbor man belts out, "Joy to the world," then, "shit."

Nona rolls off the bed. "I'll fix you something."

She pierces a potato and the frozen crust of a pot pie with a fork and puts them both in the tiny oven. She pulls the personality inventory from her bag and sits in front of the oven with a blanket over her legs.

I like to torture small animals. T or F?

It's entirely too easy to guess what they're after. Nona considers answering the questions to make Dan the neuropsychologist think she's a paranoid schizophrenic. Or suffering from some rare, yet elegant psychosexual disorder. Dan has a wife named Chris. Thomas and Greg are very little. Dan put his hand on Nona's shoulder once, in the exam room. He rubbed her collarbone with his thumb.

The wall clock sounds like raindrops on tin and on the other side of the duplex, the archer whoops and says, "God damn." Bill struggles out of the bed. Nona hears him peeing.

Sometimes I feel I am the Christ. True.

Bill comes and warms his palms by the oven.

Nona says, "Hey, this is weird. Everything's amplified. Even my own voice, right now. I think I'm running a fever, but I'm so cold."

"That's odd."

"Have you guessed?"

"What?"

"In the bucket. Okay, I'll tell you. It's a human brain." She nods. "There's a brain in a bucket by the secretary's desk. A mop bucket."

"Oh Christ, that's awful." Bill crumples onto the sofa. "That's horrific. Why on earth did you tell me that?"

Bill's belly is a drum on his lap. She'd like to thunk it with her index finger, hear it reverberate. It's one bowlful of melancholy he's got there. Six months ago, she hurt him by sleeping with another man. But Bill's funk had been in place long before she had drinks with the graduate student and ended up not coming home that night. Nona tells herself this, but she is not absolutely sure it is the case.

So every night she tries to fix this one horrible mistake. To show him. See? She's not going anywhere! See how she makes dinner and tells interesting stories?

*

Everything in the town before the first snow is colored an expectant silver-gray. The hospitals and clinics, the lecture halls, and dormitories huddle, watchful like old men. Nona sold the Vega and now she takes the Ride-On bus with the college students. When the bus passes over the bridge, she closes her eyes. The river churns beneath her, the color of nickels. Every morning, there is the collective breath of the students, fermented and sweet. And the blind man who sits directly behind the driver, who runs his fingers through his hair and licks them.

At the office, Dan and the secretary are leaning in, looking at the brain. The bucket sits on the secretary's desk. The reception area smells like Nona's high school science lab.

"It's smaller than I expected," the secretary says.

"Everybody says that," Dan tells her. "The seat of consciousness is not much bigger than a grapefruit. Nona—wow. Did you sleep at all last night?"

"How'd she die?" the secretary asks.

"Hanged herself." Dan touches the brain with his index finger.

The secretary nods. "It's kind of cheerful the way it bobs around like that. It reminds me of Christmas. I'm sorry, but it's true."

Nona pulls off her pea coat and replaces it with her lab coat. She'd tested this patient over a period of twelve months. The woman had a stroke and suffered from word deafness. She believed everyone around her had begun to speak in code. She presented with generalized anxiety disorder and paranoia. Nona thought this was a pretty reasonable response. In testing sessions, she passed the woman notes: *Trust me. I am your friend.*

"Here," Nona says. She gives Dan the personality test. "Finished."

"Why didn't you stay home this morning? You didn't want to stay home? You should see yourself. We're not supposed to bring germs into this place."

"I'm fine. I'll be fine."

"No, you should go."

"Nope. Staying."

There's a stain on Dan's white shirt. Nona wonders if it's the same one he wore yesterday.

"Let Bob take care of you. You know, for a change."

"Bill."

The secretary lifts the handle of the bucket. Some of the formaldehyde splashes over the edge onto her skirt. She sets the bucket on the floor and covers it with a towel. "Probably the smell is what's making you sick," she says. "It's getting to me, too."

"I thought someone from neurobiology would have picked it up by now. Why do we still have it?" Nona asks.

The secretary shrugs. Dan walks off waving the personality test. "I'll have your results this afternoon. Oh the mysteries of Nona!"

*

RD's bored with the memory tests. He aces them anyway. Nona says, "Remember those six words I gave you earlier? Do you remember them? RD, what were those six words?"

"I don't give a rat's ass."

"Wrong," she says.

In a pocket in the back of RD's chart are copies of his brain scans. CAT scans, MRIs, and PET scans. Nona takes them out. She doesn't usually. She's not supposed to.

"You want to see these?" She holds them up to the light. He takes them from her.

"Those look like flowers," RD says. "Like blooms."

Dan and the department chair are talking right outside the door. The department chair is from Lisbon. He presents with authority at Grand Rounds. He shows the scans on an overhead projector and points to the focal lesions that explain everything. Much can be learned about brain function from those who are damaged. They are our expeditionary guides. If Dan and the department chair come in now Nona will probably get into trouble.

"Are you giving them your brain, RD? You know, when you die?"

"Peonies. Maybe they look like peony blooms. No. Chrysanthemums."

RD examines the scans. He lifts them to his face, one by one. "Chrysanthemums are the favored flower for homecoming corsages. Chrysanthemums are an autumn blooming flower, that's why. Of course, peonies are always covered with ants."

"You shouldn't. They cut your head open with a saw. It's horrific."

Outside the door, Dan stops talking when the department chair sneezes, then sneezes twice more.

"I'd better put these away now," Nona says. RD's looking at his PET scan, tracing the fluted edges of his cortex. He won't give it to her.

"Gray blooms," he says.

"You can change your mind. Even if you signed something. It's okay to change your mind." But this is not his strong point.

He's about to cry. He's shoving the scan into the pocket of his chart and his hands are trembling. It's gone quiet outside the examination room.

"Hey now," Nona says. "Don't, don't." She means to pat RD's hand, but raises her fingertips to touch his broad, shining forehead, the skin that covers his skull.

*

Bill calls at lunchtime.

"I just wanted to hear your voice."

"You've had a rough morning?"

"Yeah." He starts to say something else, but he doesn't. He doesn't love her. Why does he stay? She experiences a sudden, blinding desire to go home and kick his ass. The Home Town Dairy cows live quite placidly on a farm, of course. Many miles away.

*

Dan's passing out flyers to the staff as they leave for the day. He and his band are playing tonight at The Mill. Mostly covers of

John Prine. It is their first gig, but he's acting confident. The Mill
specializes in spaghetti with a choice of sauces. It's very cheap.

"You have to come," he tells Nona.

"Who's John Prine?"

Dan stares at her. "Okay, that's it. You really have to come."
He pulls Nona into the conference room, pours coffee.

"Shouldn't you be going?"

He looks at his watch. "I have some time. Anyway," he says.
"This?" He's got a printout of her test results. They sit down.

"I'm weary, Dan. I'm not kidding."

"It's bogus anyway. Somebody did a little horsing around."

"Just get to know people the normal way why don't you."

The secretary pops in to unplug the coffee maker and say
good-bye. "You don't look a bit better," she says to Nona. "In case
you didn't know, it's snowing."

They hear her go around flicking off the lights. On the white
board, the department chair has drawn a crude representation of a
diseased amygdala. It looks like an almond.

Dan's tapping his pencil on the table. "Come and hear us play
tonight."

Nona's whole body aches. "I just want to go home."

*

On their first date, Bill took Nona to hear a string quartet in
the music department. They were both still students. After, they
bought hot dogs from a street vendor and sat eating them on the
stone wall surrounding her dormitory, swinging their legs like
children. She asked him if he was having a good time. You're the
best thing I know, he said. You're the best thing I'll ever know. She

laughed, loving the wide-open admiration in Bill's eyes and said, well, maybe wait and see first.

Nona takes her Tupperware bowl out of the mini fridge in the conference room. It is a good-sized bowl. The leftover salad inside is covered in fur. The bowl takes some scrubbing before it's clean. She runs the water until it's scalding and rinses the bowl four times. She lifts it to her nose and smells it, then dries it with a paper towel.

The hallway is dim. She has to feel around for the light switch in the reception area. She kneels down and pulls the towel away from the bucket and winces from the smell. Carefully, she dips the Tupperware bowl into the formaldehyde. The brain bobs away slightly at first, then swims in with the liquid streaming into the bowl.

*

The Ride On bus arrives late and empty. Nona takes a seat and places the bowl on her lap. The contents slosh around like soup. She wraps her arms around the bowl and holds it to her chest. She is shivering.

The driver looks at her in the rearview mirror and says, "Long day, huh?"

Nona looks out at the steady, slow falling snow. She wishes the bus weren't lit inside. It lumbers across the bridge and past the university buildings. A couple of students are pelting each other with snowballs outside a bar. Nona hears a thin stream of Christmas carols from the driver's radio. She grips the bowl tighter. The bus continues up Dodge Street to the dairy and her stop.

The duplex is bright on both sides tonight. She can see it through the snow. She's sure Bill is there, right now, awake and smiling and ready to receive her. As the bus draws nearer to the stop, Nona believes she can make out Bill's form through the snow and clouds of exhaust from the Home Town Dairy trucks. He is standing out there without a coat. It is as if he knows. Nona stands up. The motion of the bus sends her forward. She has to grab onto a seat back, catch her balance. But he's there, she's certain that's him, standing under the light.

The bus stops.

"Okay, Miss, you take it easy now," the driver says. But she is already down the steps and out, ankle deep in snow.

The bus pulls away from the curb. Nona wants to run, but she might slip. That must be Bill waiting for her. She calls out to him, but the snow swallows her voice. She is breathless to tell him. I have quit my job. I have stolen the brain. And together, we can bury it.

Jagannath

Karin Tidbeck

Another child was born in the great Mother, excreted from the tube protruding from the Nursery ceiling. It landed with a wet thud on the organic bedding underneath. Papa shuffled over to the birthing tube and picked the baby up in his wizened hands. He stuck two fingers in the baby's mouth to clear the cavity of oil and mucus, and then slapped its bottom. The baby gave a faint cry.

"Ah," said Papa. "She lives." He counted fingers and toes with a satisfied nod. "Your name will be Rak," he told the baby.

Papa tucked her into one of the little niches in the wall where babies of varying sizes were nestled. Cables and flesh moved slightly, accommodating the baby's shape. A teat extended itself from the niche, grazing her cheek; Rak automatically turned and sucked at it. Papa patted the soft little head, sniffing at the hairless scalp. The metallic scent of Mother's innards still clung to it. A tiny flailing hand closed around one of his fingers.

"Good grip. You'll be a good worker," mumbled Papa.

*

Rak's early memories were of rocking movement, of Papa's voice whispering to her as she sucked her sustenance, the background gurgle of Mother's abdominal walls. Later, she was let down from the niche to the older children, a handful of plump bodies walking bow-legged on the undulating floor, bathed in the soft light from luminescent growths in the wall and ceiling. They slept in a pile, jostling bodies slick in the damp heat and the comforting rich smell of raw oil and blood.

Papa gathered them around his feet to tell them stories.

"What is Mother?" Papa would say. "She took us up when our world failed. She is our protection and our home. We are her helpers and beloved children." Papa held up a finger, peering at them with eyes almost lost in the wrinkles of his face. "We make sure Her machinery runs smoothly. Without us, She cannot live. We only live if Mother lives."

Rak learned that she was a female, a worker, destined to be big and strong. She would help drive the peristaltic engine in Mother's belly, or work the locomotion of Her legs. Only one of the children, Ziz, was male. He was smaller than the others, with spindly limbs and bulging eyes in a domed head. Ziz would eventually go to the Ovary and fertilize Mother's eggs. Then he would take his place in Mother's head as pilot.

"Why can't we go to Mother's head?" said Rak.

"It's not for you," said Papa. "Only males can do that. That's the order of things: females work the engines and pistons so that Mother can move forward. For that, you are big and strong. Males fertilize Mother's eggs and guide her. They need to be small and smart. Look at Ziz." Papa indicated the boy's thin arms. "He will never have the strength you have. He would never survive in the Belly. And you, Rak, will be too big to go to Mother's head."

*

Every now and then, Papa would open the Nursery door and talk to someone outside. Then he would collect the biggest of the children, give it a tight hug and then usher it out the door. The children never came back. They had begun work. Soon after, a new baby would be excreted from the tube.

When Rak was big enough, Papa opened the Nursery's sphincter door. On the other side stood a hulking female. She dwarfed Papa, muscles rolling under a layer of firm blubber.

"This is Hap, your caretaker," said Papa.

Hap held out an enormous hand.

"You'll come with me now," she said.

Rak followed her new caretaker through a series of corridors connected by openings that dilated at a touch. Dull metal cabling veined the smooth pink flesh underfoot and around them. The tunnel was lit here and there by luminous growths, similar to the Nursery, but the light more reddish. The air became progressively warmer and thicker, gaining an undertone of something unfamiliar that stuck to the roof of Rak's mouth. Gurgling and humming noises reverberated through the walls, becoming stronger as they walked.

"I'm hungry," said Rak.

Hap scraped at the wall, stringy goop sloughing off into her hand.

"Here," she said. "This is what you'll eat now. It's Mother's food for us. You can eat it whenever you like."

It tasted thick and sweet sliding down her throat. After a few swallows Rak was pleasantly full. She was licking her lips as they entered the Belly.

It was much bigger than the Nursery, criss-crossed by bulging pipes of flesh looping through and around the chamber. Six workers were evenly spaced out in the chamber. They were kneading the flesh or straining at great valves set into the tubes. The light was a stronger yellow here.

"This is the Belly," said Hap. "We move the food Mother eats through her entrails."

"Where does it go?" asked Rak.

Hap pointed to the far end of the chamber, where the bulges were smaller.

"Mother absorbs it. Turns it into food for us."

Rak nodded. "And that?" She pointed at the small apertures dotting the walls.

Hap walked over to the closest one and poked it. It dilated, and Rak was looking into a tube running left to right along the inside of the wall. A low grunting sound came from somewhere inside. A sinewy worker crawled past, filling up the space from wall to wall. She didn't pause to look at the open aperture.

"That's a Leg worker," said Hap. She let the aperture close and stretched.

"Do they ever come out?" said Rak.

"Only when they're going to die. So we can put them in the engine. Now. No more talking. You start over there." Hap steered Rak toward the end of the chamber. "Easy work."

*

Rak grew, putting on muscle and fat. She was one of twelve workers in the Belly. They worked and slept in shifts. One worked until one was tired, then ate, and then curled up in the sleeping niche next to whoever was there. Rak learned work songs to sing in time with the kneading Mother's intestines, the turning of the valves. The eldest worker, an enormous female called Poi, usually led the chorus. They sung stories of how Mother saved their people. They sang of the parts of Her glorious body, the movement of Her myriad legs.

"What is outside Mother?" Rak asked once, curled up next to Hap, wrapped in the scent of sweat and oil.

"The horrible place that Mother saved us from," mumbled Hap. "Go to sleep."

"Have you seen it?"

Hap scoffed. "No, and I don't want to. Neither do you. Now quiet."

Rak closed her eyes, thinking of what kind of world might be outside Mother's body, but could only imagine darkness. The thought made a chill run down her back. She crept closer to Hap, nestling against her back.

*

The workload was never constant. It had to do with where Mother went and what she ate. Times of plenty meant hard work, the peristaltic engine swelling with food. But during those times, the females also ate well; the mucus coating Mother's walls grew thick and fragrant, and Rak would put on a good layer of fat. Then Mother would move on and the food become less plentiful, Her innards thinning out and the mucus drying and caking. The work-

ers would slow down, sleep more, and wait for a change. Regardless
of how much there was to eat, Rak still grew, until she looked up and
realized she was no longer so small compared to the others.

*

Poi died in her sleep. Rak woke up next to her cooling body,
confused that Poi wasn't breathing. Hap had to explain that she was
dead. Rak had never seen a dead person before. Poi just lay there,
her body marked from the lean time, folds of skin hanging from
her frame.

The workers carried Poi to a sphincter near the top of the
chamber, and dropped her into Mother's intestine. They took turns
kneading the body through Mother's flesh, the bulge becoming
smaller and smaller until Poi was consumed altogether.

"Go to the Nursery, Rak," said Hap. "Get a new worker."

Rak made her way up the tubes. It was her first time outside
the Belly since leaving the Nursery. The corridors looked just like
they had when Hap had led her through them long ago.

The Nursery looked much smaller. Rak towered in the opening, looking down at the tiny niches in the walls and the birthing
tube bending down from the ceiling. Papa sat on his cot, crumpled
and wrinkly. He stood up when Rak came in, barely reaching her
shoulder.

"Rak, is it?" he said. He reached up and patted her arm.
"You're big and strong. Good, good."

"I've come for a new worker, Papa," said Rak.

"Of course you have." Papa looked sideways, wringing his
hands.

"Where are the babies?" she said.

"There are none," Papa replied. He shook his head. "There haven't been any...viable children, for a long time."

"I don't understand," said Rak.

"I'm sorry, Rak." Papa shrank back against the wall. "I have no worker to give you." "What's happening, Papa? Why are there no babies?"

"I don't know. Maybe it is because of the lean times. But there have been lean times before, and there were babies then. And no visits from the Head, either. The Head would know. But no-one comes. I have been all alone." Papa reached out for Rak, stroking her arm. "All alone."

Rak looked down at his hand. It was dry and light. "Did you go to the Head and ask?"

Papa blinked. "I couldn't do that. My place is in the Nursery. Only the pilots go to the Head."

The birthing tube gurgled. Something landed on the bedding with a splat. Rak craned her neck to look.

"But look, there's a baby," she said.

The lumpy shape was raw and red. Stubby limbs stuck out here and there. The head was too big. There were no eyes or nose, just a misshapen mouth. As Rak and Papa stared in silence, it opened its mouth and wailed.

"I don't know what to do," whispered Papa. "All the time, they come out like this."

He gently gathered up the malformed thing, covering its mouth with a hand until it stopped breathing. Tears rolled down his lined cheeks.

"My poor babies," said Papa.

As Rak left, Papa rocked the lump in his arms, weeping.

*

Rak didn't return to the Belly. She went forward. The corridor quickly narrowed, forcing Rak to a slow crawl on all fours. The rumble and sway of Mother's movement, so different from the gentle roll of the Belly, pressed her against the walls. Eventually, the tunnel widened into a round chamber. At the opposite end sat a puckered opening. On her right, a large round metallic plate was set into the flesh of the wall, the bulges ringing it glowing brightly red. Rak crossed the chamber to the opening on the other side. She touched it, and it moved with a groaning noise.

It was a tiny space: a hammock wrapped in cabling and tubes in front of two circular panes. Rak sat down in the hammock. The seat flexed around her, moulding itself to her shape. The panes were streaked with mucus and oil, but she could faintly see light and movement on the other side. It made her eyes hurt. A tube snaked down from above, nudging her cheek. Rak automatically turned her head and opened her mouth. The tube thrust into her right nostril. Pain shot up between Rak's eyes. Her vision went dark. When it cleared, she let out a scream.

Above, a blinding point of light shone in an expanse of vibrant blue. Below, a blur of browns and yellows rolled past with alarming speed.

Who are you? a voice said. It was soft and heavy. *I was so lonely.*

"Hurts," Rak managed.

The colours and light muted, and the vision narrowed at the edges so that it seemed Rak was running through a tunnel. She unclenched her hands, breathing heavily.

Better?

Rak grunted.

You are seeing through my eyes. This is the outside world...But you are safe inside me, my child.

"Mother," said Rak.

Yes. I am your mother. Which of my children are you?

The voice was soothing, making it easier to breathe. "I'm Rak. From the Belly."

Rak, my child. I am so glad to meet you.

The scene outside rolled by: yellows and reds, and the blue mass above. Mother named the things for her. *Sky. Ground. Sun.* She named the sharp things scything out at the bottom of her vision: *mandibles,* and the frenetically moving shapes glimpsed at the edges: *legs.* The cold fear of the enormous outside gradually faded in the presence of that warm voice. An urge to urinate made Rak aware of her own body again, and her purpose there.

"Mother. Something is wrong," she said. "The babies are born wrong. We need your help."

Nutrient and DNA deficiency, Mother hummed. *I need food.*

"But you can move everywhere, Mother. Why are you not finding food?"

Guidance systems malfunction. Food sources in the current area are depleted.

"Can I help, Mother?"

The way ahead bent slightly to the right. Mother was running in a circle.

There is an obstruction in my mainframe. Please remove the obstruction.

Behind Rak, something clanged. The tube slithered out of her nostril and she could see the room around her again. She turned her head. Behind the hammock a hatch had opened in the ceiling, the lid hanging down, rungs lining the inside. The hammock let Rak go with a sucking noise and she climbed up the rungs.

Inside, gently lit in red, was Mother's brain: a small space surrounded by cables winding into flesh. A slow pulse beat through the
walls. Half-sitting against the wall was the emaciated body of a male.
Its head and right shoulder were resting on a tangle of delicate tubes,
bloated and stiff where they ran in under the dead male's body,
thin and atrophied on the other. Rak pulled at an arm. Mother
had started to absorb the corpse; it was partly fused to the wall. She
tugged harder, and the upper body finally tore away and fell sideways. There was a rushing sound as pressure in the tubes evened
out. The body was no longer in the way of any wires or tubes, that
Rak could see. She left it on the floor and climbed back down the
hatch. Back in the hammock, the tube snuck into her nostril, and
Mother's voice was in her head again.

Thank you, said Mother. *Obstruction has been removed. Guidance system
recalibrating.*

"It was Ziz, I think," said Rak. "He was dead."

Yes. He was performing maintenance when he expired.

"Aren't there any more pilots?"

You can be my pilot.

"But I'm female," Rak said.

*That is alright. Your brain gives me sufficient processing power for calculating a
new itinerary.*

"What?"

You don't have to do anything. Just sit here with me.

Rak watched as Mother changed course, climbing up the wall
of the canyon and up onto a soft yellow expanse: *grassland,* whispered.
The sky sat heavy and blue over the grass. Mother slowed down, her
mouthpieces scooping up plants from the ground.

Angular silhouettes stood against the horizon.

"What is that?" said Rak.

Cities, Mother replied. *Your ancestors used to live there. But then the cities died, and they came to me. We entered an agreement. You would keep me company, and in exchange I would protect you until the world was a better place.*

"Where are we going?"

Looking for a mate. I need fresh genetic material. My system is not completely self-sufficient.

"Oh." Rak's mouth fell open. "Are there...more of you?"

Of sorts. There are none like me, but I have cousins that roam the steppes. A sigh. *None of them are good company. Not like my children.*

*

Mother trundled over the grassland, eating and eating. Rak panicked the first time the sun disappeared, until Mother wrapped the hammock tight around her and told her to look up. Rak quieted at the sight of the glowing band laid across the sky. *Other suns,* Mother said, but Rak could not grasp it. She settled for thinking of it like lights in the ceiling of a great room.

They passed more of the cities: jagged spires and broken domes, bright surfaces criss-crossed with cracks and curling green. Occasionally flocks of other living creatures ran across the grass. Mother would name them all. Each time a new animal appeared, Rak asked if that was her mate. The answer was always no.

"Are you feeling better?" Rak said eventually.

No. A sighing sound. *I am sorry. My system is degraded past the point of repair.*

"What does that mean?"

Goodbye, my daughter. Please use the exit with green lights.

Something shot up Rak's nostril through the tube. A sting of pain blossomed inside her forehead, and she tore the tube out. A thin stream of blood trailed from her nose. She wiped at it with her arm. A shudder shook the hammock. The luminescence in the walls faded. It was suddenly very quiet.

"Mother?" Rak said into the gloom. Outside, something was different. She peered out through one of the eyes. The world wasn't moving.

"Mother!" Rak put the tube in her nose again, but it fell out and lay limp in her lap. She slid out of the hammock, standing up on stiff legs. The hatch to Mother's brain was still open. Rak pulled herself up into the little space. It was pitch dark and still. No pulse moved through the walls.

Rak left Mother's head and started down the long corridors, down toward the Nursery and the Belly. She scooped some mucus from the wall to eat, but it tasted rank. It was getting darker. Only the growths around the round plate between the Head and the rest of the body were still glowing brightly. They had changed to green.

*

In the Nursery, Papa was lying on his cot, chest rising and falling faintly.

"There you are," he said when Rak approached. "You were gone for so long."

"What happened?" said Rak.

Papa shook his head. "Nothing happened. Nothing at all."

"Mother isn't moving," said Rak. "I found Her head, and She talked to me, and I helped Her find Her way to food, but She says She can't be repaired, and now She's not moving. I don't know what to do."

Papa closed his eyes. "Our Mother is dead," he whispered. "And we will go with Her."

He turned away, spreading his arms against the wall, hugging the tangle of cabling and flesh. Rak left him there.

*

In the Belly, the air was thick and rancid. The peristaltic engine was still. Rak's feet slapping against the floor made a very loud noise. Around the chamber, workers were lying along the walls, half-melted into Mother's flesh. The Leg accesses along the walls were all open; here and there an arm or a head poked out. Hap lay close to the entrance, resting on her side. Her body was gaunt, the ribs fully visible through the skin. She had begun sinking into the floor; Rak could still see part of her face. Her eyes were half-closed, as if she were just very tired.

Rak backed out into the corridor, turning back toward the Head. The sphincters were all relaxing, sending the foul air from the Belly toward her, forcing her to crawl forward. The last of the luminescence faded. She crawled in darkness until she saw a green shimmer up ahead. The round plate was still there. It swung aside at her touch.

*

The air coming in was cold and sharp, painful on the skin, but fresh. Rak breathed in deep. The hot air from Mother's insides streamed out above her in a cloud. The sun hung low on the horizon, its light far more blinding than Mother's eyes had seen it. One hand in front of her eyes, Rak swung her legs out over the rim of the opening and cried out in surprise when her feet landed on grass. The myriad blades prickled the soles of her feet. She sat there, gripping at the grass with her toes, eyes squeezed shut. When the light was less painful, she opened her eyes a little and stood up.

The aperture opened out between two of Mother's jointed legs. They rested on the grass, each leg thicker around than Rak could reach with her arms. Beyond them, she could glimpse more legs to either side. She looked up. Behind her, the wall of Mother's body rose up, more than twice Rak's own height. Beyond the top there was sky, a blue nothing, not flat like seen through Mother's eyes but deep and endless. In front of her, the grassland, stretching on and on. Rak held on to the massive leg next to her. Her stomach clenched, and she bent over and spat bile. There was a hot lump in her chest that wouldn't go away. She spat again and kneeled on the grass.

"Mother," she whispered in the thin air. She leaned against the leg. It was cold and smooth. "Mother, please." She crawled in under Mother's legs, curling up against Her body, breathing in Her familiar musk. A sweet hint of rot lurked below. The knot in Rak's chest forced itself up through her throat in a howl.

Rak eventually fell asleep. She dreamed of legs sprouting from her sides, her body elongating and dividing into sections, taking a sinuous shape. She ran over the grass, legs in perfect unison, muscles and vertebrae stretching and becoming powerful. The sky was no longer terrible. Warm light caressed the length of her scales.

*

A pattering noise in the distance woke her up. Rak stretched and rubbed her eyes. Her cheeks were crusted with salt. She scratched at her side. An itching line of nubs ran along her ribs. Beside her, Mother's body no longer smelled of musk; the smell of rot was stronger. She crawled out onto the grass and rose to her feet. The sky had darkened, and a pale orb hung in the void, painting the landscape in stark grey and white. Mother lay quiet, stretched out into the distance. Rak saw now that Mother's carapace was grey and pitted, some of the many legs cracked or missing.

In the bleak light, a long shape on many legs approached. When it came close, Rak saw it was much smaller than Mother— perhaps three or four times Rak's length. She stood very still. The other paused a few feet away. It reared up, fore body and legs waving back and forth. Its mandibles clattered. Something about its movement caused a warm stirring in Rak's belly. After a while, it turned around, depositing a gelatinous sac on the ground. It slowly backed away.

Rak approached the sac. It was the size of her head. Inside, a host of little shapes wriggled around. Her belly rumbled. The other departed, mandibles clattering, as Rak ripped the sac open with her teeth. The wriggling little things were tangy on her tongue. She swallowed them whole.

She ate until she was sated, then crouched down on the ground, scratching at her sides. Her arms and legs tingled. She had a growing urge to run and stretch her muscles; to run and never stop.

A Galloping Infection

Paula Bomer

After they carried his wife's body out of the two bedroom house
they'd been renting all week at The Golf Club of Key West, after the
police had left, James Ordway thought many things, quickly, all in
a row, and imagined them as a list on a piece of paper.

He no longer would have to disappoint her. He, who'd never
committed adultery in the eight years of his marriage, could fuck
new women. He no longer had to glimpse her aging, sagging, naked
body in the bright morning light. He no longer had to worry about
how her bitter, tired and nasty behavior would affect their two sons.
He no longer had to listen to her speak insecurely and incorrectly
and childishly in front of people who made her nervous, in other
words, just about everyone she didn't know very well (her trailer
park childhood in Illinois never fully left her). He wouldn't have to
look at the dark roots growing in on the top of her head, her brassy
dyed hair rough and desperate looking. He could get rid of her two
annoying cats, whose litter box disgusted him, and to whom he

was allergic. He never again had to deal with her truly hateful and grasping sisters. And although he deeply appreciated her dinners at night, he'd never have to eat them again, which filled him with relief. Why? If he appreciated them, why did he also feel relief at not eating her regular meals? His mind wandered from the list...how relief and appreciation? That strange force of nature, ambivalence.

He supposed he was trying to cheer himself up. He was, and always had been, an optimist. Or, as Kelly had put it, in denial.

Somewhere she'd read that people who suffered depression were too realistic. They saw things too clearly. This was not James's problem. But it had been hers. She tried taking Paxil for a while, but remarked she preferred reality, depressing or not. "And anyway," she told him, when she announced she was over taking Paxil, "I'm only unhappy because our marriage sucks. Nothing is wrong with me. I don't have a chemical problem. You're just a shitty husband."

Now, that was true, and James had always known it to be true, but he comforted himself with the fact that he wasn't the shittiest husband out there. No, that award would go to one of the husbands of Kelly's "friends", or acquaintances rather, the women she dealt with in her daily life of taking the boys to school and lessons and the playground. Perhaps Carl, her friend Gigi's husband would be the poster boy for the world's shittiest husband. Carl traveled two weeks out of the month, and when he was home, he went out every night. Gigi had confessed to Kelly she thought her husband might be having an affair. Drunkenly, one night during a ladies night out, Gigi said to Kelly that she and Carl hadn't had sex in three years.

"And so I said, what are you going to do about it?" Kelly related to James that night, smoking a cigarette on their back porch in Brooklyn. "I mean, no marriage is perfect. But three years? And she acts like it's no big deal. I said, aren't you going to see a therapist? She laughed at me. Really. Like trying to fix your marriage was some kind of joke. She doesn't feel any responsibility to even *try* to make it a better marriage." James had been watching ESPN when she arrived home that night, drunk and wanting to gossip. Kelly had dragged him away from a great basketball game to tell him about Gigi and Carl. At the time he thought, hypocrite. As if your marriage were so perfect.

But then there came a point, a few years ago, when their marriage seemed kind of perfect, if not only or especially in comparison to everyone else they knew. The miseries people had! No sex, no money, women still married to their own mothers not their husbands. Six hours of TV a day. Women eating two entire Entenmann's cakes in one sitting in front of Kelly, as if this were normal. Women hating their sons and loving their daughters. Eventually, Kelly stopped trying to make friends, and James couldn't really blame her. But he did anyway. He wasn't convinced that feeling better than others was the best they could do. Of course, he did nothing about it. And they had problems as well, but nothing dramatic. Kelly drank and smoked. This was their biggest problem, according to James. She rarely behaved out of control. But she'd get woozy and quiet, or worse, talkative and boring at night. James was their biggest problem, according to Kelly. His coldness. The way he just ignored his wife and kids when he didn't like what they had to say. The times where he didn't seem connected to the family at all, just like some floating big man in the house, who co-habited with the rest of them. This, according to Kelly, is what exhausted her, made her bitter and bitchy. When confronted by her, James just ignored her.

"See? See?" she said, as he stared into a magazine or walked slowly into another room. "And you wonder why I drink? You're not here. Hello! You don't even care."

Anyway, now she was dead. Now, their two boys sat watching cartoons. Will's stern face was swollen and blotchy, but he was pretty focused on the screen. Jamie, their three-year-old, didn't quite get what had happened, but it would sink in as the days went by. James walked into the narrow room, toward his sons. They'd never rented here before. Kelly had found the house online and was more or less happy with it. That was a relief for James. The last thing he wanted was her ruining another vacation by bitching the whole time about what exactly wasn't perfect about their plans. Fucking control freak.

James stood there for a moment, watching his boys watch TV. Then he went back to the front of the house, thinking he'd sit out on the front steps. He sat down and the Florida sun shone hotly on him. Two gray-haired, pink and yellow shirted golfers walked by and stared at him. Had they seen the ambulance? The police car? Probably. Maybe he should go inside and hide. Shamefully. Or respectfully. Maybe he should keep making phone calls. Turning his face toward the sun, he decided not to do anything for a moment. He decided to stay right there. It was a strange development, the Golf Club. Everyone hid in their cars or in their little, uniform houses. The quiet was eerie, really, not comforting. It was not the quiet of, say, the country. It was the quiet of a highly developed area where many of the houses were empty most of the time, being second homes, and the people who were there kept to themselves. As if hiding something.

Everyone has something to hide, thought James.

She was sick before they left. Every winter, she got a terrible sinus infection. This time, she also had a bronchial infection. He

came home from work the day before they left for Florida and she
was lying on the couch, a box of tissues in her lap and a pile of dirty
tissues next to her. "I'm sick. Really sick. They X-rayed my lungs
and I don't have pneumonia but I have a bronchial infection and a
sinus infection, like always. The doctor said I can't smoke. That my
lungs are a mess. I'm scared."

And here was the thing. Every year she got sick and she got
scared, and she cut back on the cigarettes and booze for awhile, but
as soon as she started to feel better, she went back to her old ways. A
bottle of wine at night, followed by five or ten or more cigarettes. It
was one thing when they first met ten years ago. Then, for whatever
reason, James found it sexy. European or something. For a while
now, since the kids arrived actually, he'd found it disgusting. On
the plane, she ordered a glass of wine.

"I thought you were on antibiotics? You're not supposed to
drink while taking antibiotics," he said to her.

"I'm not taking the antibiotics," she said. "It would ruin my
vacation."

Indeed. From the first night of their arrival. she coughed and
gagged up stuff, spitting it into tissue papers. Then she'd look into
the tissue. God, to have to see her peering into her foul tissues! Like
looking into her own asshole. The rage was so intense that he'd...walk
away. Nasty, nasty woman. He noticed bottles of Advil and aspirin
and all sorts of pain relievers and decongestants and cough medicine
around the rental house. After a day at the beach and in town walking
around—they'd had beautiful weather, divinely sunny and moist and
warm but not hot, not stifling—she'd asked him to stop by Walgreen's.
"My head is still killing me," she'd said, and he returned with a white
paper bag of more drugs and new boxes of tissue.

At night, after the kids were asleep, her eyes were glassier than usual. Now, Kelly's eyes were often a bit glassy. That happens to people who drink a bottle of wine a day. And she was flushed, but again, people who drink red wine were often flushed at night. And of course, they had spent a good part of the day in the sun, which gave them all a flush. And so. And so James thought, how was he to know.

But he did kind of know. Slowly knowing something. The idea occurred to him. The idea that Kelly was really sick, that something was really wrong.

The night before she died, he emptied the garbage pail in the upstairs bedroom where they slept. He carried it downstairs, annoyed and disgusted—why didn't she bring her foul snot-rags down to the kitchen garbage herself? Pig, he thought. The kitchen lights were on brightly and Kelly lay in the living room alcove, visible to him, coughing and lying there in front of the television, a blanket over her despite the heat—and as he dumped the tissues into the garbage, he looked down at what he dumped out.

Why? Why does one look at a loved one's snot and filth? Just normal curiosity? The desire to hate? The desire to know?

The dirty tissues, dripping black and red, sent up a strong, acrid scent as they tumbled into the kitchen garbage. Blood and... blood and what? James looked away. What else was he to do? He looked away with disgust. Shaking the foulness off with a quick shake of the head.

He had not always been disgusted by Kelly and he wasn't sure when it started, but he had been disgusted by her, with her, on and off now for some time, because they lived together, because they were growing older together.

The night before she died, they lay sleeping next to each other, not closely though, because of the king size bed. They had watched a mundane drama next to each other on the couch earlier. It ran late, and they were tired. When they went up to bed, James fell asleep immediately. Hours later, in the quiet dark of the middle of night, she woke him. Wheezing, gasping, her eyes bulging with fear. "Something's wrong, James. Something's wrong..."

"What? What...?" He was barely awake.

"I can't breathe. My heart." She started coughing so loudly. He shushed her, automatically. "Shhhh, don't wake the kids." He was so tired. He just wanted to sleep.

Then she put a hand on his shoulder, a hot, fierce hand. "You don't know what they want from me. You can't see them. You don't see anything. You don't see." Is that what she said? How could he really remember, after all that had happened since then? He carefully removed her pinching fingers from his shoulder and fell asleep.

The next morning, she appeared fine. Making coffee, and then sitting on the couch with the kids in front of the cartoons.

"Hey, do you want to go see a doctor here?"

"No," she answered right away, without looking up from the cartoons.

He went and sat next to her. She looked awful underneath her browned skin. No suntan could hide the truth of her inner life, her sickness. Her face was a mass of hanging flesh. Her hair seemed to barely cover her scalp. He smelled toothpaste and suntan lotion and something else. The something else was not a good smell and it pushed him up and away from her and back into the kitchen to get a coffee.

*

He had, at one point, truly loved this woman. People do change. It is not true that people don't change. The only thing is that they almost always change for the worse. Occasionally some miserable ugly person blossoms into a happier self later in life. But Kelly had not been miserable or ugly. And perhaps she had only one way to go. It's that she went that way so quickly, so effortlessly, that James barely noticed it happening. Before he could do anything, before it registered with him, Kelly had turned into a lonely, bored outcast who had no pleasure in life. Her face and body lost all joy, all hope, all generosity. Her dead spirit took over her very body.

Once, when they were in their early twenties and newly engaged, they had drinks at the Plaza Hotel in Manhattan. Afterward, they took a carriage ride around Central Park. Their drinks had been insanely expensive, the ride seemed silly and not worth it, and yet, and yet. And yet Kelly glowed with appreciation, with gratitude. Her head slightly bowed, her eyes wet with life and wonder. She was humble and small and happy to be alive, giving off a warmth that James soaked up as he wrapped his arm around her while they walked back to their apartment. He used to soak her up. Just being next to her, just letting his body *be* next to her body, this was where he got his strength in the past.

And now where was he to go for strength? It had been years since he sought it from her. There had been his work and his children. And he had let himself not be strong, he had let himself be exhausted.

The night she died, he'd seen her come back from the bathroom. Half asleep, deep in the night, he saw her. She wore a thin white nightgown and her arms were glowing red, slick with damp. She coughed so loudly that he sat up, the noise had startled him so. Her naked hands were held over her mouth and as she pulled them away from her shaking face, a dark wetness dripped from her fingers to the ground. "I'm dying. I think I'm dying and I'm scared", she said.

"We'll go to the doctor in the morning," James said quietly, "you'll be fine." Had he believed that? But no, James believed in nothing anymore. He just knew what to say when something was supposed to be said.

"I'm so scared," she said, rubbing her filthy hands up and down on her gown. Her voice was not her own anymore. James reasoned, there in the middle of the night, that she wasn't making sense because he didn't recognize her voice.

"Go to sleep. Just go to sleep."

As she approached the bed, a smell so poisonous came upon him that he quickly hid his face in his pillow and curled himself on the very edge of his side of the enormous mattress. There, like that, as far away from death as he could get himself without actually leaving his wife alone in the room, he slept next to her, as whatever was left inside of her stopped existing altogether. He did not feel shame in thinking about this. But he did feel wonder. How can we live so? Die so? It barely seemed possible that their lives could be so cheap. Could it be his wife died because she didn't live? Oh God, why didn't he do something? Why did he just let her be so sick? Why did she let herself get that way?

They were not brave people, not in the face of life, and now, clearly, not in the face of death. Soon, the chill of her death would come over him, he felt it in the distance of his own body. The sun in

Florida could only do so much to warm him. He would miss her in the way he would miss an arm that's been cut off. He'd be ashamed, as if something were physically wrong with him and this wrongness were obvious to the world. This would be his way to sorrow, through shame and humiliation, through the public recognition of his broken life.

The phone rang and it startled James. And, with the phone ringing (he would not answer it), he turned his head away from the street, into the house and saw his two children coming toward him, through the darkened narrow passage that was their rented home, their faces shadowed and hidden, featureless creatures, running toward him, toward where he sat outside in the sun. Fear gripped him. Why had they stopped watching TV? Oh, God, if they just would never stop watching TV, everything would be OK! They came at him, like monsters, red and burnt and huge-seeming from where he sat. He didn't want to meet them—not now, not yet.

They were just his children. But they would want to know things he couldn't tell them. They were coming. So fast, and soon, they would be on him like animals. Crawling all over him. He was not prepared, no he was not, and it didn't matter.

Stillborn

Karen Brown

They moved into the dead woman's house in August. First the woman's husband who had kept bees died, and then a year later the woman had followed. Diana heard this from the white-haired neighbor the first time they visited the property. The house was reached by a narrow, unpaved lane flanked by old beeches grown close together. At the end of the lane was Long Island Sound, a gray expanse, dotted on windy days with white caps. The house backed up to the salt marsh, and from the upstairs window Diana could see across the blowing grasses to a row of painted cottages like a colorful necklace. Their new address was Edge Lea. She was six months into her pregnancy, and the house, a rambling clapboard cottage, felt calm and empty. They'd wait until after the baby to paint the beadboard walls and redo the kitchen. For now they would simply take down the ramp leading up to the front door. In the end, it seemed the dead woman's husband had needed a wheelchair. The ramp was made of heavy pine planks that took a day's work to pull away. Diana's husband yanked at the rusted nails with a hammer, sweating and cursing, swatting at the bees bobbing about his head and shoulders.

Inside the house Diana found an empty Ponds Cold Cream container high up on the linen closet shelf. It was milk glass, the kind of thing she might have hidden small treasures in as a child. She set it on the window ledge above the sink. Diana was not the type to hum or sing aloud to herself, but she found it natural to do so here in the dead woman's house. Maybe it was the woman's spirit, she thought. She wasn't concerned or frightened by the thought of interference by the dead woman's spirit. She sang songs from old Broadway musicals like *Oklahoma* about a girl who can't say no, and songs from her elementary school music book, Señor Don Gato and that high red roof. Her husband came in from working outside with a bee sting on his forearm.

"You can't swat at them," she said. "Bees sting in defense."

He gave her one of his looks. His lip curled up. She loved that look, and loved provoking it. She took him under the chin and shook his face back and forth.

Her husband put his dirty hands on her stomach, distended and hard like a medicine ball. The baby shifted and pressed her little foot up. "Oh!" she said. "She's telling you to back off, buster."

Her husband smiled, hesitantly. "*Buster*?" he said.

"I don't know," she said. "I don't know where that came from."

"Your mother?" he said. "Did your mother ever say that word?"

"The movie," she said. "The last one we watched."

At night they sat on their new couch and watched Alfred Hitchcock movies, one after the other, and ate long sticks of licorice. She was annoyed. Her husband considered her mother cheap and uneducated. His fear that she would become a woman like her mother was something he'd never admit. "My mother would never say *buster*," she said. "Not seriously."

"Maybe she should. It's better than a lot of other words she's used," he said. He went to the sink to wash his hands. On her white shirt he'd left the imprints of his fingers.

By September the few summer people had gone. Diana decided to plant bulbs along the back of the house—daffodils and allium, hyacinth and crocus. It had grown cold at night, and the wind came off the salt marsh, rushed up the narrow lane from the Sound. The house groaned and rattled. The rows of trees grew bright, as if electrified. There was cold rain, and the leaves came down into the dead yard, pretty and wet. She bought the bulbs and began to dig with her trowel. She sang softly as she dug around with her trowel, uncovering a small bone, then another. *Femur, fibula, humerus, clavicle*. Tiny bones, delicate and dirt-stained. She stopped digging, the bones uncovered. I've dug too deep, she thought. She leaned onto the side of the house and pulled herself upright. The sky was dotted with swirling leaves. The marsh grass filled with wind. She stood for a long time looking down at the upturned earth, and her hand holding the trowel shook. Her husband was at work, teaching at the university. She went to the neighbor Mrs. Merrick's house and knocked. The old woman lived at the end of the lane in a wood-shingled cottage on a bluff overlooking the rocky shore. She came to the door, her white hair long and loose past her shoulders.

"What is it?" she asked, sharply. Diana imagined she thought it was the baby, and she didn't want to be burdened.

"Something in the garden," she said.

The two of them walked back down the gravel lane, and Diana pointed toward the spot. Mrs. Merrick went over and looked down. She had on leather shoes, plaid slacks, a wool sweater. The wind lifted the strands of her white hair. She bent lower and then stood up and looked back at Diana. "It's the stillborn," she said, flatly. Her face seemed deflated, the skin sagging around her mouth. She kicked the pile of dirt back over the spot with her shoe, and then she came over to Diana and took her arm. Diana allowed herself to be led back inside her own house. Mrs. Merrick boiled water for tea. Outside the sky was blue and white and riddled with leaves.

"What were you doing digging there?" the woman said. She searched through Diana's cabinets for cups, for the tea.

"I was just planting bulbs," she said.

"Those go in the front, not the back."

"How was I supposed to know?" Diana cried. She had her hands placed on the mound of her stomach.

Mrs. Merrick's face softened. She took out the good china cups and saucers. "Don't go worrying. It was years ago that baby was buried. Before you were born."

The dead woman whose house they lived in had given birth to four children. The stillborn baby was her third. "A wisp of a thing, not full term," Mrs. Merrick said. She blew on her tea. Her hair was still disordered from the wind. Diana stared at her teacup. Mrs. Merrick got a faraway look. "It wasn't unheard of. She had other babies to tend, and she knew there'd be more, and it was done. The husband took the shovel. Not sure how so much of the soil could have washed away, but that must be the reason you uncovered it. No stone or marker. Just up near the house there where you dug."

The woman took a loud sip of the tea. She eyed Diana. "Drink it."

Diana imagined she had stepped into a fairy tale. This was the witch, the tea spiked with henbane, the ground littered with dead children. Her baby did a spin—*back handspring*, her husband would have said. *Our little gymnast*, he called her. She reached for the tea, and her hand still shook.

"No marker? Nothing?"

Mrs. Merrick scoffed. "The baby never drew a breath. Now I hear in the hospitals they have special nurses, and grief counselors, and they let the parents and the family members hold the baby and put clothes on it. They bring in photographers and take pictures even."

Diana couldn't tell what Mrs. Merrick thought about all of these new developments, whether they were a waste of time, whether grief was something best dealt with alone.

"Was she sad?" Diana asked.

"Sure, I'm sure she was. Carried the baby for nearly seven months. Must have felt something—useless, tired, guilty. All sorts of things you feel."

Diana sipped the tea, uneasy. She kept seeing the bones.

"Your milk comes in and there's no child to nurse. You flatten out and there's always something that was supposed to be there, after all that—swollen feet, and various discomforts."

Mrs. Merrick put her cup noisily into the saucer. She stood up and placed both in the kitchen sink. She walked carefully, favoring one hip. Her plaid pants sagged in the rear. Diana watched her walk to the door. "You'll be fine," the woman said. She opened the kitchen door and the wind nearly grabbed it from her hand. She turned back.

"Bulbs go in the front of the house," she said. "Looks pretty. First thing you see when you come home."

And then she was gone.

Diana didn't tell her husband about the bones in the garden, or what would have been the garden, if she'd ever planted the bulbs, which she did not. She hid them in the crawl space under the porch in their little boxes. Her husband would have called the authorities, let them take the bones and examine them and launch an investigation. Mrs. Merrick would be contacted to give testimony, and Diana knew she'd be disgruntled, called upon to talk about something already over and done with. The dead woman's remaining children, scattered around the country with their own families, might not have known they had another sibling. Diana felt she had disturbed enough. Now when she saw Mrs. Merrick at the A&P the woman steered her shopping cart close and reached out and gave Diana's hand a squeeze. It was their secret.

In late October, the sun dull and low over the salt marsh, the marsh grass flattened from frost, Mrs. Merrick came to Diana's door. She carried a small wicker basket. Diana saw her from the window in the upstairs hall—the wind flapping her coat, her hair held back with a scarf like the kind the women in the Hitchcock films wore when they went for drives in convertibles. When Diana opened the door Mrs. Merrick stepped inside quickly, covertly, as if she were being followed. She smelled of cloves.

"I've baked you something," she said.

She set the basket down on the kitchen table and took out a loaf of pumpkin bread.

Diana thought of food carried in baskets, wolves watching from the woods. "Oh, how nice," she said. The baby was large and sluggish these days. Diana always felt as if she might topple over. Her back ached. She spent a lot of time trying to nap.

"I didn't wake you, did I?" Mrs. Merrick said. "I won't keep you."

Diana insisted she stay. "We'll have tea," she said. She went to the cabinet, but Mrs. Merrick told her to sit, and she'd get it ready. And like the last time, she set out the china cups and started the water to boil. She sat down at the table with Diana and scanned the kitchen, the room beyond.

"It seems so empty," she said. "Nice and neat, though."

"Did they have a lot of furniture?" Diana asked.

"Oh, too much," Mrs. Merrick said. "And then they had things on shelves and tabletops, stacked in corners. All sorts of odds and ends. Collecting dust."

The kettle boiled and she rose to pour the water into the teapot. "Once the children were grown and gone it seems the things took their place." She looked at Diana as she set the teapot on the table. "Things never take the place of people in my book, but for some they do."

"What sorts of things did they have?"

"Oh, books and magazines and knickknacks—collections of things—buttons, china, shells, even taxidermy creatures—chipmunks and birds and the like."

Diana thought again about the bones. Maybe they were just the bones of some little animal. She could have been wrong.

"Like the Nut Lady?" Diana asked. "Was it like that?"

The Nut Lady, Mrs. Tashjian, lived near Diana when she was a child. Her old house was the Nut Museum, and admission was one nut. Diana's mother would send her to the door with food—CorningWare dishes filled with casseroles—and Diana would duck beneath the over-grown trees and ring the bell, the casserole warm in her hands. The woman, stooped and bright-eyed, had a singsongy voice. Behind her the house was dark and somewhere were displays of her collection of nuts and nut art, and squirrels running up and down the grand staircase, and cobwebs, and damp plaster. Diana wouldn't go in, even though the woman asked her to. "My mother is waiting," she'd say, and point to her mother's car idling under the tree canopy. Later, after the woman was taken to the home, and the house was sold, and the trees were cut down, Diana always wished she had gone inside, just once.

"They were eccentric," Mrs. Merrick said. "Everyone has their own obsessions."

"Did you know them well? Did you know them when she had the baby?"

Mrs. Merrick looked at her over her teacup. Her eyes were the palest blue that Diana had ever seen, as if their color had washed away.

"I was a girl," she said. "About sixteen."

"Did you ever help her with the other children?" Diana asked.

Mrs. Merrick set her cup down carefully on the saucer. "Of course I was a help in those days. I cared for them all—Elizabeth and Matthew and Nancy. They were good babies. Good children."

"But she never considered a name? In all the time she carried her?"

Outside the wind picked up and a tree branch made a grating sound against the house.

"You should cut that back," Mrs. Merrick said. She stood up, supporting her weight with a hand on the tabletop. She took the basket. "Time I should go."

Diana walked her to the door. The baby moved, a slow roll from one side to the other. She pressed her hand there, and Mrs. Merrick watched her, her pale eyes impossible to read. She opened the door and the salt air blew through, flapping the appointment slips and advertisements stuck to the refrigerator.

"Iris," she said. She turned and looked at Diana. "That was the name she was thinking for her."

Like the bulb, Diana thought. She nodded. "It's pretty," she said.

"What name have you settled on?" Mrs. Merrick asked.

Diana smiled. "Oh, I like Madeleine," she said. "But my husband wants Katherine, for his grandmother."

Mrs. Merrick smiled. Her eyes flashed. "You carry her, you name her." She slipped her scarf over her head and tied the ends under her chin. Diana watched her walk down the lane toward her house. The Sound beyond was alive with little darting waves.

That night Diana told her husband she wanted the baby to be named Madeleine.

"I've thought it over," she said.

He looked at her askance over his laptop. "I thought we said we'd see if she looked like a Madeleine or a Katherine once she was here."

Diana lay out on the couch with her feet up. She put her hand on the mound of her stomach. "She's already *here*," she said. "And she seems to me to be a Madeleine."

Her husband gave her a look then. Not the look she liked, but one she'd never seen. She didn't know why she was insisting on a name, and she regretted it now that she saw his expression—one of betrayal, and confusion. *Who are you?* his face said.

In November she found the postcard. She'd been pulling out the drawers built into the wall of bookshelves. One held a matchbook from Hundred Acres, a restaurant that had been closed for years. She was curious about the dead woman. She admitted to herself that she was looking for something. The postcard depicted a painted image of the entrance to another private beach off of Shore Road, less than a mile away. The postage date was August 5, 1959, and it was addressed to Arlene Guernsey. *Wish you were here*, the message said. It was signed, *Charlie Warlie*, with a slanted, messy hand, in pencil. Diana held the postcard to the window to read it in the light. She knew the dead woman's name was Arlene, she'd seen it on the papers at the closing—Arlene Whitcomb Life Trust. Whitcomb was her married name. Her husband had been Roy. Mrs. Merrick had said it herself—"Oh, Roy was the most patient man," she'd said. "Patient and long-suffering." Diana had thought she meant *suffering* in the physical sense, but now she wondered if his wife had been cheating, and his *suffering* had been of another kind.

That afternoon Diana's husband called to tell her he was going to New York.

"I'm taking the train," he said.

Diana felt a little put out. She'd wanted to talk to him about Charlie Warlie and Arlene. She wanted company, and it was so close to her due date.

"Why are you going?" she said. "What if I go into labor?"

Her husband sighed. "The baby isn't due for a few weeks." He didn't explain why he was going, and Diana didn't ask. It was always something for school—meetings, and readings, and conferences. She was used to his traveling. It was something she wasn't supposed to question.

"Fine," she said. "I can always call Mrs. Merrick."

There was a silence on the line—a little pause. "Who?"

"Our neighbor," she said. "Down the lane."

"Oh, yes," he said. "Or your mother." Then he laughed, as if both of these solutions were nonsensical. "You just call the doctor and a cab. That will get you to the hospital in plenty of time."

"And what about you?" she asked.

"Of course you call me," he said. "I'll be there in plenty of time, too."

That night the wind and rain came at the house in gusts. Diana heard one of the shutters bang and then make a sound as if it'd been wrenched from the house. Blustery, she thought. She'd remembered yet another song from her childhood about a maiden singing in the valley below, and she sang it out loud into the dark room. The baby was moving, and she sang the song to her and imagined that when she was born she would remember it. Eerie, lilting melodies were always memory triggers in old movies. Then there was another sharp banging noise, and Diana felt suddenly cold. The baby stilled, as if listening with her. She didn't want to investigate the noise, but she felt she must. She eased herself to the end of the bed and stood. She felt a funny twisting feeling, a little cramp. "Oh," she thought. But it was nothing. The noise came again, and Diana leaned on the banister as she went downstairs. In the living room she could hear the noise, constant now, a sort of hurried, urgent knocking. She went to the kitchen door and peered out. The porch light illuminated a small patch of grass below the steps, and there was Mrs. Merrick turning away. She had on a dark slicker, but Diana saw her white head when the hood blew back. She saw her gnarled hands yank the hood back on. And then she was gone around the house. Diana didn't open the door and call for her. It was too strange, Mrs. Merrick being there at this hour in the storm. Diana went around to the front of the house and peered out of the living room window, and there was Mrs. Merrick heading back down the lane. She had a flashlight, and the light cast its narrow beam, filled with spikes of rain. The slicker blew around her like a dark orb.

*

Ava Merrick had long suffered her name. She had the dark hair, the lush mouth of Ava Gardner, and boys would always find some comparison, and girls always hated her. She'd taken Lizzie and Matthew down to dig clams. Mrs. Guernsey had been home with the baby. It helped that this was a small shore community, that the summer people left, always a blessing, that quiet stretch of fall and winter, into spring. It was late summer then, only a few families lingered—the Norths, the Skeltons. There were two boys about her age who went about together, and they appeared at the end of the beach and approached her.

"Ave Maria," one said. "It's Ava."

She ignored them, and continued to wade into the water, digging with her toes. Lizzie plopped a clam in the bucket, and a boy leaned over to look. Lizzie beamed at him. Matthew was more hesitant—a timid seven-year-old. He stood by his sister like a protector.

"You've got some," the boy said, the rakish one with sunbleached hair, Howard Skelton.

He grinned at the children, as if he were a nice boy. Ava knew he was not, that this was a ruse. Still, she ignored him.

"What about you?" he asked Ava. He waded over to her to look into her bucket. His fingers slid along the rim and then slid up along her waist.

Ava stepped away from his hand. His friend, Will North, laughed. Once Will had come upon her reading and sat down beside her in the sand and touched her breast, as if she were an item in a store to be perused. She didn't say anything about any of this to her father. Her mother was dead, and there were no women to confess to other than Mrs. Guernsey, and Mrs. Guernsey was busy, always busy with the children, the baby, the house, the garden. At night in her bed she would relive these incidents, and though her face burned with shame from the memories, she found she also got a sharp pleasure from them. When Mr. Guernsey, Roy, took her with the children to the movies in Niantic and placed his hand on her leg in the dark, Ava was prepared to feel both the shame and the pleasure.

He approached her one morning soon after on the beach. He was dressed in his work pants, his button-down shirt. His forehead was high, his hair thinning and fair. Ava had never seen him on the beach in the morning. She watched his leather soles slipping, and imagined his shoes filling with sand.

"Just the girl I've been looking for," he said. The wind and the water seemed to take his voice.

Ava looked up at him. "Is everything alright?"

Nancy had come down with a fever the day before, and they suspected bronchitis. Ava's childhood friend had died of pneumonia, and she'd sat with her holding her hot hand, the whole time thinking she'd get well. She was worrying about Nancy, her little flushed face and the cough, when Roy wrapped his long arm around her shoulders and steered her toward the path that wound up through the stones to her house. Ava feared the worst—Nancy taken to the hospital, the news broken to her by Mr. Guernsey in the kindest of ways. She'd be needed at the house to watch the children while they sat by Nancy's bedside. She was thinking about all of this when they came to the door of her house.

"It's Nancy, isn't it?" she said.

Roy Guernsey opened the door and led her inside. He was flushed, breathing heavily, and Ava had a moment of fear that he had gotten ill himself. But no, he had tugged her toward his chest and put his hands in her hair and then slid them down her back, pressing and kneading, his mouth moving to her neck and then, with an awful groan, to her mouth. Ava's father had gone to work. It was a workday, after all. Ava hadn't forgotten the movie theater, but she hadn't expected that what happened there would lead to this sort of violence. He'd dragged her down onto the floor. Her head hit the leg of the armchair, but he didn't notice. She heard his belt buckle fall to the floor beside her, felt the weight of him, and then his sharp entry—a knifelike searing. He panted and moaned and then made a sound like a high wail. All of it, even the pain, thrilled her. She'd watched his face the whole time—his eyes squeezed tight like Matthew's when she took out a splinter. His flyaway hair, the sheen of his pate, the long, dignified nose. Her body felt the heat of his, the damp between them becoming wet. He'd fumbled with her shirt, with the catch to her bra, and when it came free he'd sighed and nuzzled his mouth there like a baby. He'd tugged at her pants and slid his mouth down, and she'd watched the top of his head in surprise, the way it dipped and bobbed. Beyond the surprise she felt nothing the first time.

They lay in a heap of clothing on the living room floor. The light came in and the rushing sound of the tide hitting the rocks. He curled beside her and kissed her and said her name over and over, as if he were practicing it. He was like a small boy after, tender and sweet. She put her hand on his cheek, on the fine stubble of his chin that had made the skin around her mouth burn. She didn't remem-

ber what she said. Then he was up, telling her to dress, telling her
he would see her again soon.

"You understand what this means?" he said.

Ava had stared at him, buttoning her blouse. The house in
its disorder humiliated her—the clutter of her father's collections,
the pile of laundry on the sofa, the mess in the kitchen she'd not
yet cleaned up.

"We're lovers," he said. "Secret lovers."

When fall came, and school, Ava would babysit at the Guernsey's in the afternoons, and Roy would come in from work and
loosen his tie and pour a drink and watch her. She would pretend
nothing was different, but the children knew.

"Why is your face red?" Lizzie would ask. She'd put her two
hands on Ava's cheeks to feel for a fever. Ava would take the children
out on the windy beach, and Roy would come and walk along beside
her and whisper to her. "Stay home tomorrow," he'd say. "Tell your
father you're sick."

Ava had been a good student and hated missing school, but
she was also dutiful and desirous and she would pretend she had
a sore throat, or a headache, or women's trouble, and her father
would grudgingly leave her, and tell her to call Mrs. Guernsey for
anything. As soon as he left, Roy arrived. He'd yank off his shirt,
unbuckle his belt. They'd taken to using her bedroom at the front
of the house, where the sea seemed about to break in through the
windows, and the glass was salt-stained, and the gulls looped and
sang. Back then there weren't manuals or magazines that talked
about how to please men, but Ava knew now that she pleased him
by instinct, by watching his face, listening to the noises he made,
his body a map, a gridded space where she might place her mouth,

her hands. When she soothed the children to sleep she would slowly drag her fingernails up and down their backs, and Roy Guernsey shuddered and sighed when she did this to him, straddling his legs. She wouldn't say now that she loved Roy. They rarely talked about themselves, and she was aware that love had more to do with the sort of closeness that talking revealed, but at the time she knew nothing about that. He would send her little notes, folded into small squares he pressed into her hand when he saw her: *Tomorrow* the note might say. Sometimes: *Wednesday*.

One day after school Mrs. Guernsey stopped her in front of the house and asked her to come inside. She wore a stained apron, and her hair fell about her face, loosened from a soft bun. She looked drawn and thin, but still beautiful in a way that made Ava, with her rounded limbs and broad shoulders, feel awkward. Mrs. Guernsey took her into the kitchen and handed her a bottle of Lydia Pinkham's tablets.

"Your father says you've got women's issues?" she said.

Ava had seen the ads in the newspaper—accompanied by a woman's face in distress:

Too Worn-Out to go? Another date broken…Couldn't stay on her feet a minute longer! Lydia E. Pinkham's Vegetable Compound always relives cramps. Try it next month.

Or:

"Please Let me Alone!" Out of sorts…disagreeable! Lydia E. Pinkham's Vegetable Compound has helped so many women whose nerves are frayed by those dreadful "monthly" headaches.

She took the pill bottle, and looked at the label.

"Don't be embarrassed," Mrs. Guernsey said. "These will help."

Years later Ava learned that the tablets were taken by desperate barren women hoping to induce pregnancy. "A Baby in Every Bottle," Mrs. Pinkham claimed. She had never taken the pills; the bottle still sat in her medicine cabinet. When Mrs. Guernsey handed them to her she hadn't gotten her period for two months, and hadn't needed them. At first she'd seen it as a relief from the bloody pads. It was Roy who noticed her growing abdomen, whose terrified expression forced her to accept the truth. Still, he passed her the notes, and she met him. He moved his hands over her, enthralled. Everything felt better to her then—she became aroused at the sight of him at the door, and then aroused when he pressed the note into her hand, and then in the days in between she felt overcome and panicked with desire. The pregnancy caused her no trouble at all. She was a big-boned girl and wore loose dresses. She cut slits in her waistbands and wore sweaters and her father's heavy plaid coat in the winter. As the weather grew warmer she wore men's shirts she found at St. Anne's Nearly New shop. It was the style, anyway. She didn't worry about the baby coming. She assumed Roy would tell her what to do. She left it all up to him, despite the way his face became pinched and pale against her pillowcase when, after they were done and lay spent, she placed his hand on the baby moving inside of her.

Of course, she'd had cause to worry. She stood now at her kitchen window and tied a knot in the belt of her heavy sweater. She'd gotten a chill last night. The Sound was still dark, the sky gray from the storm. She couldn't say what sent her out in the rain to Diana's house. The house had been dark, Diana presumably asleep. Roy and Arlene were dead, there was nothing she could do now about the bones. She would bake a cottage pie to take over, her desire to be inside the house again after so long impossible to deny. She told herself it had nothing to do with Diana's baby. She peeled the potatoes, set them to boil.

Diana called her husband's cell and it went to his voice mail. She pressed her hand to her abdomen and heard herself make a sound like a cat's mewl. She tried to sing something, but she had forgotten the words, the melodies. Outside was bitter cold, the wind whipping up what looked like bits of ash, and she didn't want to leave the house. Arlene Guernsey, she determined, had met some man one summer and carried on with him behind her husband's back. She could see, from the date on the postcard that she'd already had her children, that she would have had to hire a babysitter to leave the house to meet him—maybe Mrs. Merrick, then a teenager. And there'd been a baby, one conceived from the illicit affair, and the baby was the stillborn, out there in the dirt along the house. Diana felt her pulse race at the thought—the baby hidden away, the hospital, the doctor, never consulted. She was sure Mrs. Merrick knew, and she was sure she would drag it out of her. It was only right that she heard the story of the bones on her property.

Her phone rang and it was her husband. "What is it? Why didn't you leave a message?"

"There was a storm," she said. "I thought the house would blow down."

"That house isn't going anywhere," he said. "It's been there for a hundred years."

"And I think I'm in labor," she said. She felt her abdomen tighten again, a long cramp. "I'm going over to Mrs. Merrick's."

"No," he said in what she often called his *stern father* voice. In the background she thought she heard something—a soft question, high-pitched. "Call the doctor. Call the cab."

"I need to ask her something," Diana said. "Who is that there?"

"What do you mean? I'm at a conference. Lots of people are here."

"I mean there with you, in the room."

"Lots of people are here in the room. It's a big room, Diana."

She could tell by the sound of his voice that it was a small room. And there it was, that soft voice again, a laugh. Perhaps it was the television, she thought, and she imagined him in a hotel room, and the television on, maybe an old movie.

"What are you watching?" she said. "Is it Leslie Caron? Oh, not *GiGi*!"

There was a silence, then the sound of rumpled hotel bed sheets. "Diana, I'm not sure what you're talking about. But if you're in labor, if you're *sure*, you need to call the doctor and the cab."

Suddenly she didn't want the doctor, or the cab. Mrs. Merrick knew how to deliver babies. She'd delivered the stillborn, she was sure of it now. If she was going to have her baby she would have it there, in the old house by the sea. She hung up the phone and put on her wool coat and her gloves. She went out the kitchen door and down the lane to the end of the road where Mrs. Merrick's house sat. The wind here was harsh, numbing her face. The tightening in her abdomen had increased. She went up to the front door and used the knocker—oxidized green, shaped like a horseshoe crab. Mrs. Merrick came immediately. She stared at Diana as if she didn't know who she was. Behind her Diana could see the room—shelves of small posed creatures with threadbare fur, canning jars filled with color-ful buttons, with marbles, with sea-washed glass. Diana was looking at the inside of the Guernsey's house, the way Mrs. Merrick had described it. She was suddenly fearful of being invited in, remem-bering her mother waiting in the car, and the Nut Lady asking her inside. Her mother had been the one who'd known all the words to the show tunes, who'd sung them to Diana as a child. They'd made the casseroles and driven them around to the elderly and unfortunate. Diana remembered the white Skylark with the cloth seats, the casseroles stacked in the back steaming up the interior, her mother flicking her ash out the cracked driver's side window.

Mrs. Merrick promptly shut the door, and in a moment came out in her coat, carrying a covered dish with two potholders. "I was just heading over to your house," she said, with no other explanation.

Diana looked back down the lane at her house. It seemed impossibly far. But she turned and the two of them headed in that direction, Mrs. Merrick's gait slow, rolling like a sailor, and Diana reeling from the pain of what must certainly be a contraction. The wind was at their backs, pushing them along.

"Early this year," Mrs. Merrick said, glancing up.

Diana saw that it was snowing—flakes shifting in the wind, settling on the gravel road, on her house's rooftop, on the mailboxes in front of the summer cottages. Inside her house Mrs. Merrick set the casserole on the counter. Diana had questions to ask her, but she couldn't now remember all of them. Her phone was ringing. Diana waved at it. "It's just my husband."

They sat down in their usual spots at the table. The wind rattled the windows.

"You've had a disagreement?" Mrs. Merrick said.

Diana said they had not. She felt incredibly sad, overwhelmed.

"Arlene Guernsey had a lover, didn't she?" she said.

Mrs. Merrick offered no response. She went to the cabinet. "Should we have tea?"

"I found the postcard. Good old Charlie Warlie. And she got pregnant, and the baby was Iris, wasn't it?"

Mrs. Merrick dropped a teacup into the sink. "Oh dear," she said. "I'm so sorry. It broke."

"Oh for fuck's sake, don't worry about those stupid cups," Diana said. She eased herself out of the chair and leaned on the table. She made a sound that didn't make sense. Her voice seemed unlike her own. She felt an icy rush down her legs and looked to see a puddle widening on the floor.

Mrs. Merrick looked, too. She rubbed her hands on her pants. "You're having your baby," she said. Her blue eyes were darker today, like the Sound. Diana felt she was being tugged along, unbidden, by the course of events.

"There was a girl he was seeing," she said, the shock of the moment compelling her to confess. "Some student. We thought we might make it work. But it won't work, will it?"

Mrs. Merrick said, "Go on and get in bed."

Diana pulled herself up the stairs by the banister. She could hear Mrs. Merrick rummaging around, opening cabinets. She hated her husband, hated his secrecy, his inconstancy. She hated the baby for being his. "I don't care what happens to it once it's out," she called to Mrs. Merrick. "You do whatever you think is best. Take it to the orphanage. Give it to the fairies."

Mrs. Merrick came to the doorway. "Now you're sounding foolish." But Diana saw her smile, a faint movement of her lips.

*

Ava's baby had come early, her water breaking like Diana's, and pooling on the floor of the kitchen while she scrambled eggs. She'd thrown down a towel and headed up the lane to the Guernsey's. She wasn't thinking clearly, but she wanted to let him know, and what other way was there? She had thought of clever methods—small notes like those he'd written, with the single word *Today*, or the message *It's time*, passed to one of the children and on to him, but in the shock of the moment they appeared to her what they really were— childish, silly. It was midday, a Saturday, and warm, the caretakers out with their buckets of oil paint, freshening up the cottages. She remembered that smell of the paint, would always associate it with that day. It was Arlene who came to the door, and Arlene who suddenly saw what was happening. Arlene with the pale skin, the soft unraveling bun, who sent the children off with her mother, who called Ava's father and said that Ava had gone along to help. They were going to Mystic Seaport and spending the night, she'd said. Her mother was oh-so-happy to have Ava's help, she told him.

At first, Roy did not come into the room where Arlene had taken her. Ava could hear his and Arlene's voices downstairs— Arlene's hushed and questioning, Roy's high-pitched with surprise.

"Who could it have been?" she heard Arlene ask.

"One of those summer boys, maybe the Skelton kid," Roy said. "They were always hanging around."

"She would have been further along," Arlene said.

"Some boy at school then," Roy said.

Ava knew she had made a mistake. Like the notes, the game of it all, the idea that he would accept the baby as his seemed a delusion. She remembered then the tender place where her head had hit the chair leg. She felt that, and more, as the baby forced its way out. Well into the night its head appeared and then slid back, appeared and slid back. Arlene was red with frustration, nearly crying, and Roy was there, his face marked with fear. Arlene had pressed Ava's legs back and ordered her to push. Ava had cried out and told Arlene to get Roy out of the room.

"Now's not the time for modesty," Arlene said. "I need help. Do you want a reputation? Is that what you're after? You're a bad girl, Ava, and you want everyone to know it?"

"I won't push until he goes," she said. "I won't do it."

His face had grown hideous to her, his hands, his long fingers, those of a monster. When the baby finally came Arlene had wrapped it up and handed it to Roy and he had finally left the room. Ava had cried, shrieking, until Arlene hissed at her to be quiet, and placed her hand over her mouth. The windows had been black, the sea sound very far away, like the sound inside the whelks she held to the children's ears. Ava had slept. The next day her breasts had been heavy, and there was no baby. Arlene had come in to tell her that Roy had taken it to some friends who'd always wanted a child.

"I know you'll be grateful for their kindness," Arlene said. "Later you'll have other children."

But Ava had known that she would not have any other children. "A girl," Arlene had said to Roy when the baby had finally slipped out onto the bed. Ava had opened her eyes, and witnessed the look that passed between them, one of complicity, and fury, and cold acceptance. She had, in the practical way that would be hers for the rest of her life, gone home to the house she shared with her father. She hadn't asked who the people were who had taken her baby, or where they lived. She had imagined, instead, the little girl growing up in a beautiful house with a rose trellis, and a swimming pool, and a bedroom decorated with music boxes and ballerinas, lavished with items a woman who'd yearned for a child for so long might be inclined to purchase. Ava wasn't asked back to the Guernsey's. The children came down to the beach and glanced longingly at Ava's house, but they never came close, and if she happened to come near them out walking they moved away, as if a punishment lay in store for them if they did not. Roy and Arlene had lived together in the house until their deaths, both of them stony, and unapproachable, even in their later years. Ava had watched Roy tend his bees, the gentle smoke, the white hood, the hives set up far from the house near the marsh. The bees traveled Edge Lea collecting pollen from Ava's delphinium, from her small-dwarfed apple tree, wanderers who always returned to this tall man hidden behind a mask. She'd remembered the way his head had bobbed below her waist, the way the hair on his crown caught the light. She watched him grow old, and infirm, with a sense of vindication and despair.

Ava had been bad, perhaps, but that time with Roy had been enough to sustain her for a lifetime. Until the bones had been revealed, pale and small in the dark earth, she had never thought she'd needed more than that. Her baby had been too early, small, and silent. Perhaps she had not lived, and they had spared Ava the truth. Perhaps she had lived only briefly, and they had done what they had to do out of necessity. She would not think anymore about the bones. She concentrated on Diana's baby, who roared out of the womb and wailed, whose limbs cycled and whose eyes met hers with the most daring of looks. "Naughty girl," Ava whispered, and despite the uncertain happiness, the possible misery of the world that awaited her, she placed her in Diana's arms.

The World of Barry

Stacey Levine

Barry was everywhere and so easy to marry, full of springtime which is always hope and trust.

The mountains face our living room window, their unsolicitous peaks white and blue; the neighborhood is silent because it was made that way. Barry sits in his armchair, reviewing cases; I steal to him, tilt the brown drink in his mug, pinch the little string overhanging his pocket and tug, pulling more, then more, coiling the cord upon the floor; so much came out of Barry, it is hard to say—

Barry was always familiar, his thick, low, syrupy voice of Boston and mud. Junior partners often exhibit great propulsion and charm; he barrels through the turreted streets downtown, smiling, punning, grabbing a drink, stopping to observe holidays, to pray. Our home is a flexible hinge between the grass ridge and the sky full of dark matter, those invisible forces that hibernate—

Barry often prefers the creamed chicken; our living room table is ruby granite and slate. He bought an oak mule chest and end tables layered with mosaic; at night in the bed I grow down, down, backward into the cement basement floor of my parents' home while Barry waits, still as a moth—

Like many people, I am an expert in following the rules of my own design, biting back the urge to question these or analyze. Today I tear past Barry's office desk and to the elevators in a rage; why can't he do better, stop laughing, read something beside torts, open his mind, pick up a raisin cake? I dash to the street where by chance my mother and father are driving past, waving gladly with their four hands, throwing popcorn, wearing argyle sweater vests, happy in general about life as it is lived—

Such episodes cause me to feel strange every day.

Barry's vehicle is as large as a small house, with lush, curving metal flanks of midnight green, exhaust pipe thick as a fireman's hose, its mouth pouring white volumes of fog and upon this mouth I must briefly affix my own mouth, in order to best appreciate life, I think, though Barry has never instructed me to do this, nor have TV broadcasts either; yet it is truer than god or the atmosphere—

Barry orders the roasted chicken; we have little to discuss; the newspaper describes a man fitted for a prosthetic face and arms—

Barry drives us home in silence; odors seem to fly from his body—lemon, vulture, brine, it is hard to say, the mingling of all our family's sweat and the opposite of this odor: sense. And Barry is not a bad man, as the dean of law once said; Barry swims agreeably beside my false self, scanning the face of the sky, its mineral dark; at each day's end we see our back door ajar, and lakes up high that we ignore—

All these complex mental processes to keep Barry out; and Barry is cheerful most often, needing no help from the journal club; soon the neighborhood annexation will begin; on so many evenings the chicken is luscious; afterward in town, the foolish clichés of the cinema help keep us silent, thoughtless, separate, and cold—

Barry was originally a chemist, as everyone has ever known; my father told me about Barry long ago when I was small, for I had never satisfied my parents' bodies nor was satisfied by theirs, and screamed unusually, struggling against dependence and the shame rising through it; Barry rarely wants to punish me, though I found ways to make him do it—

Barry's shape is different when he is with me than when he sits alone and reads; Barry wrestles over the idea that god may be cruel, and he implies I should consider this too. But my shape has grown defended and smooth, and I believe Barry's choice in furniture is poor, too: the chest with laurel leaf motif, the heavy cherrywood bookcases rising like vaults to our roof. Unbeknownst to Barry, I set a bowl of milk each day in the rafters to feed a family of sick mice—

Barry and I are very thirsty these days; dust from the warring earth flies through our throats; perhaps we are waiting for the world to mature, to catch up with us. The back side of god is too strange, too vulnerable to hold all of life, Barry worries aloud as he drives; I laugh, feigning anger in a spirit of play, though the danger of our games is what frightens Barry and me—

Barry is not poor or free. Our window holds the soft, alkaline mountain sky, the ribbony road to the old town; the house ticks in the animal dark; the kitchen knives are turned backward and I keep the chicken warm in a soft white sauce, molding it for Barry. In a lapse of self I lure the mice to the floor, pulling aside the kitchen door with the softness of children or breasts, and there they pour in a stream of fur, bathing in our home's warmth; the mice position themselves at the toilet to drink, and this begins to happen every night—

Barry prays for a way into the jumbled panels and panes of god while shifting lanes in his enormous car, and Barry's doubt gives him pain in the mind, foot, and spinal cord; he cares too much what god thinks, which is especially comic at sporting events. Soon, he will take a new case to court, but tonight, there is Barry, standing in the mirror, nude, post-coital worry the flavor of our room; and Barry will make an appointment soon for the urinalysis; there is the council meeting too, and in general, there is too much to do; I scuff across the tile in the far middle of the night, looking through the skylight to mother and father in their part of the sky—

The pepper crust chicken is pretty as a young bride; the fund-raiser begins at 6:45; there is the board meeting and the upcoming census, too; my cotton dress like a swab, the Earth held in place by a concerted tie, the sun that will someday break; at night I hold Barry's wrist in my fingers, feeling his absent-minded largesse, the heat of his vacant legs—

My parents hurry from Portage Bay, hoping not to miss the mountain view. Still buried in the bedspread, I see Barry's face, his thoughts straddling duty, succor, ice. We enjoy meals and sweets with enormous oral greed, and Barry favors dark bread, in fact; he is far too tall and big and often makes me laugh, has a hearty appetite for slaw, large genitals, and a voluminous smile; Barry most frequently enjoys the cream mustard chicken, and all in all, Barry has too much inside, too many preferences—

While I am running, Barry thinks deeply about the case. We live on Sky Island Drive, overlooking the parcels of valley land, and Barry and I must not care about preserving that place. He loads his golf clubs into the cargo area, slamming the tail gate; in the front seat I wear microplastic sunglasses, quiet, for Barry must not know that, at night, our house is alive with mice; Barry's shape makes my shape change, ballooning too far then coming back to me strange, so Barry and I are departing in the dinosaur way and will not outlast the sky and stars. Well, what could you say.

Push

Amina Gautier

The teacher's clothes hang off her. She is what the girl's mother calls a "Skinny Minnie." Even the girl's sister dresses better. She gets her clothing from Lerner's, which has not yet become New York & Company. When the sister is away at work, the girl slides the magazines out from her sister's hiding place and stares at the models, especially the two black ones. The women are lovely in a way the girl didn't know black women could be. Her mother is not beautiful, neither is her sister, though her sister probably could be if she tried a little harder.

When the teacher calls her back after releasing the class into the schoolyard, which is a parking lot for the teachers in the morning (they have to clear their cars out after lunch to make room for the kids to play at recess), the girl does not fully grasp that she has done something wrong. The teacher lets all the other kids go and then says, "Not you."

"Did you push Colleen down the last flight of steps on the way out of the building?" Mrs. Greenberg asks in such a way that the girl thinks it entirely possible she is merely curious. After all, the stairwells are painted a deep dark green, which makes it hard to see. The girl wears thick neon laces in her Adidas and she follows her laces down the stairwell, using them as a light to keep her from crashing into the kid in front of her, unless she wants to. Colleen's place is right in front of her. They are both five feet two inches, but the girl has more hair, which makes her seem taller, so Colleen gets to stand in front. This is size order. Nothing about it ever changes. The girl thinks that nothing ever will. All day long there is a small wooden chair to sit in, with one bolt missing and one edge torn away so that whenever the girl wears tights, which is only on picture day or when her mother forces her, she gets snagged to the chair. There is always the small metal desk with the fake wooden top. It doesn't lift the way the desks do in the old movies, where the kids come to school with lunch pails and apples and where the boys attach mirrors to the front of their shoes so that they can look up girls' skirts. (Okay, the part about the mirrors and the shoes isn't from a movie. The girl's mother's boyfriend has told this story more than once, claiming it was something he'd done in his boyhood days, and the girl believes him. She has seen a picture of her mother as a schoolgirl, with a bright clean face and mischievous eyes, and has come to think that the kids in her mother's day were probably all up to something. In any case, she likes the mother's boyfriend, whom she has been trained to call Uncle. He is her favorite of all of the mother's boyfriends she calls Uncle, and she is willing to believe anything of him.)

Back to the teacher and the question now, yes?

Yes.

The girl sometimes has trouble paying attention, but this happened at a time before kids started coming down with ADHD the way they used to come down with colds and flus. The girl goes undiagnosed, undrugged, and is merely scolded by parents and teachers to pay better attention.

See what I mean?

The girl decides that the truth is to be used only as a last resort. She says, "No, Mrs. Greenberg. I didn't push Colleen down the stairs."

"I have a perfectly good set of eyes," the teacher says. "I saw you do it."

"Okay," the girl says. Though she is willing to lie, she is equally willing to capitulate. It all depends on her mood and where it takes her.

"Okay?" the teacher says. "Is that all?"

"Okay, I pushed her," the girl says. "It was an accident." The two of them are still standing in the schoolyard, where kids loiter and teachers look out of place. There are games of jump rope, skelly, freeze tag, and double Dutch going on. The girl watches kids run and then stop as if paralyzed. One boy is tagged in midstride. He freezes with one arm pumped outward, teetering with one foot raised, waiting for someone to unfreeze him. The girl imagines herself joining in unannounced, heroically tagging the boy to unfreeze him, saving him from the clutches of a frozen life. By now, she truly believes that pushing Colleen was accidental. The girl lives by her whims.

"I don't believe you," the teacher says. "Follow me."

*

She follows the teacher back to their classroom on the fourth floor. The teacher mumbles as she unlocks the classroom door and turns on the lights. The chalkboards are clean. For the last half hour, kids begged for the chance to wash the boards. The girl has done this before, but only once. She remembers the privileged feeling of standing at the front of the classroom with a basin of warm water and a thick porous sponge at her disposal. First, she erased the boards, wiping away the day's spelling words, math problems, and penmanship lessons in the teacher's looping cursive. Then she dipped the sponge and squeezed it out. Starting at the top of the board, she'd pressed it against the hard slate and dragged it downward, the grayish green chalkboard turning gleaming, wet, black. After several vertical strokes took her to the edge of the board, she'd looked back and seen the board drying in streaks, swaths of water quickly evaporating as if she'd never been there at all.

The teacher waves her over, and even though the girl expects to be struck, she comes. These are the days when everyone has a pass to beat up kids—teachers and neighbors alike—the days when parents thank you for doing it and then bring their kids home and tear them up some more. The girl has seen the teacher yank a boy by the ear to push him into the corner. The teacher points to the nearest seat and says to the girl, "You will sit here for the next hour to think over what you have done. Open your composition book to a fresh page and record your reflections."

"What does that mean?" the girl asks. She is thinking of reflection like in the mirror and, anyway, the teacher lost her once she said the girl had to stay a whole hour. She is supposed to go straight home after school and wait in the apartment until her mother and sister get there. Although she usually lollygags playing in the schoolyard and buying candy in the bodega, she has never gone home an entire hour late.

"I want you to explain why you constantly pick on Colleen. You're nothing but a bully. Perhaps if you can see that in black and white, you'll stop tormenting the poor girl." The girl does not think of herself as mean or as a bully. She doesn't even dislike Colleen. It is just what they do. The girl doesn't think Colleen minds as much as Mrs. Greenberg seems to.

The teacher looks at her watch and slides out of her coat. "Since I am giving you an hour of my unpaid time, you had better make it good."

The pressure. The pressure. The girl has never been good at language arts. She prefers science and the solidity of the earth as she has come to know it; she can stare at the cutaways of the earth, revealing core, mantle, and crust for hours. When she finishes her workbook assignments before the allotted time runs out, she draws volcanoes, paying close attention to her rendering of ash clouds and magma chambers. She doesn't know what Mrs. Greenberg wants her to say, but she opens her notebook to a fresh page. Staring at the chalkboard, which looks lonely with no student, no teacher, no dust, and no words, the girl thinks that if she could write her thoughts all across it, she might be able to produce something beautiful.

The teacher hangs her coat on the back of her adult-sized chair, and the girl realizes that she is still wearing hers. She slips her arms out of the sleeves and drapes it over her shoulders, wearing it like a cape, like She-Ra, Princess of Power. Mrs. Greenberg carries her lesson plan to the boards at the front of the room (the ones at the back are covered with construction paper) and begins copying the next day's spelling words on the far left board. The girl thinks about copying the words now and getting a head start. When all the kids are present, Mrs. Greenberg has to leave the assignments up on each board until every kid has copied them, which can take a while because the kids have to be called up in shifts, the ones from the back rows and the ones with poor eyesight coming forward and crouching with their notebooks balanced on their knees as they get as close to the board as possible. Last year, the girl had twenty-eight classmates. This year, she has forty-four. Pretending to write what Mrs. Greenberg wants, the girl jots down the spelling words. The third word down is *cower*, the fifth word is *intimidate*. The girl stops copying when she realizes that the teacher is trying to make a point.

When Mrs. Greenberg writes at the chalkboard, it is easy to see just how poorly her clothes fit. The girl can see the extra material at the back of her suit jacket billowing out over her waist. The girl's sister works for a company that pays next to nothing, but her clothes fit better than the teacher's. Mrs. Greenberg's shoulder pads are not at the shoulders; they hang down over her biceps. The teacher's sleeves are too long. When her arms are down by her sides, her thumbs disappear, the cuffs swallowing them. The girl is feeling charitable, and so she decides that although the teacher is definitely to blame for her invisible thumbs, she should not be held responsible for the shoulder part. Anyone can see Mrs. Greenberg has weak shoulders.

The teacher's pantyhose are the old-fashioned kind, the kind with the little lines down the back of them, the kind the white women in those old black-and-white movies wear with the skirt suits whose hems fall way past their knees. The seams at the back of the teacher's pantyhose do not follow down her leg in a straight line. They curve around her calves, twisting all the way to the front. Mrs. Greenberg is bowlegged. Perhaps, the girl thinks, this is why her stockings are always crooked.

The stockings make her think of the movies Uncle always brings over. Every time he comes over, he brings a big black garbage bag stuffed full of dirty newspaper, and inside the bag there is always a VCR. He takes out the VCR and hooks it up to the big floor model television in the living room, where everyone can watch. He brings popcorn for the stove and puts in tapes of old movies, of films he said were made when he was little. The girl is a sucker for these movies. She likes Rosalind Russell. Maureen O'Hara. Doris Day. She will watch old movies until her eyes are dry. They sit on the plastic-covered couch, he and the girl and the sister and the mother, watching women telling men to put their lips together and blow, having a good time, until the mother crosses her arms and says,

"Thought I was the one you came to see."

*

Mrs. Greenberg speaks over her shoulder. "How are you making out?" she asks.

"I don't know what to write," the girl says.

Mrs. Greenberg turns from the chalkboard, which is half-filled with tomorrow's lessons. "Alright," she says. "Try this. How would you feel if the roles were reversed? What if it were you that was always being pushed or shoved or picked on? What if you were always Colleen's target? How would you like it then? What do you get out of torturing an innocent girl? Think about answering at least one of those questions and see if you come up with something to say."

The teacher raises her eyebrows, implying profundity. The girl remains unimpressed. It could never be the other way around. Colleen is not a leading lady. The girl likens her to the brunettes in the old movies, the ones who never get the guy. The girl is thinking of Ruth Hussey in *The Philadelphia Story* and Janice Rule in *Bell, Book, and Candle*. There is always a Katharine Hepburn or a Kim Novak to tempt the Jimmy Stewarts of the world. Colleen is the kind to get attention only by default.

*

Though she can hardly remember how it all began, the girl's first push truly was accidental. Mrs. Greenberg assembled the class in two rows by the coat closet, boys on the left and girls on the right. Colleen was in front of the girl, Abdul to her left. As they filed out of the classroom and down the hall to the far stairwell, the girl began to lag behind. She had spotted a small reddish stain in the center of Colleen's skirt. It bloomed brightly as if someone had cut her, as if she'd sat on a tube of paint. Entranced by the blooming, spreading stain—it had no edges, it looked like an inkblot, like something the girl's sister had shown her from an old college psychology textbook before she'd dropped out to make money—the girl lifted her feet mechanically, walking with legs made of wood, knowing Colleen knew things that the girl had yet to learn, wondering if she should follow Colleen more closely so that no one else might see (for surely the girl hadn't noticed the stain when they'd first lined up), when, closing the space between them, the girl stepped too close, right on the back of Colleen's LA Gear sneakers, making Colleen stumble and collide with the girl in front of her. The girl imagined them as a line of dominoes toppling from the one accidental push, but it did not happen like that. Colleen righted herself quickly, but not quick enough to fool Mrs. Greenberg, who walked alongside the class, keeping close to the middle, a vantage point that allowed her to survey the entire line. She cut her eyes at the girl, saying nothing, chalking it up to clumsiness, to an accident. An accident it had been that first time. After that, it simply felt too good to stop. First, there was the closeness of Colleen's body when the girl pushed her, stepping close enough to smell the grease against Colleen's scalp. Second, there was the Jean Naté that wafted from Colleen's collar. When the girl stepped against Colleen, she saw Colleen begging her mother for a splash of cologne from the yellow bottle in the hopes that wearing it would make someone finally notice her. Stepping against the back of Colleen's sneakers was stepping into her life, a life the girl guesses to be less complicated than her own. Colleen, the girl thinks, has a father and no unrelated uncles. When she goes home, someone is always waiting.

*

The hour draws near. For the past ten minutes, the girl and the teacher have been sitting quietly, trying not to look at each other.

The teacher begins to straighten up. "Did you find any answers?"

"I think so," the girl says, though her page is still blank. She takes up her number two pencil and presses the lead deep into the paper, attempting to copy the glamour of Mrs. Greenberg's cursive:

Dear Colleen,

I'm sorry I pushed you down the stairs today and all the other times. I would not like it if you did it back to me. I hope you don't do it, because pushing is wrong, and if you do it just because I did it, then we will both be wrong, which will add up to be more like -2 than 0.

She looks over her words, feeling no remorse, yet hoping this is what her teacher wants. She knows that this is not one of those times where the answer will become clear once she grows older, knows some questions are meant to go unanswered. Like why she has so many uncles if her mother is an only child. Like why Uncle cannot live with them. Or at least leave his VCR.

"If you have any last thoughts, you have five minutes to get them down," the teacher says.

What it really comes down to is the rightness of the push.

When they are going down the stairs and the girl pushes Colleen down the steps or forces her into the railing, the girl feels a part of something larger than herself. She believes, deep down, that Colleen expects it, in fact cannot live without it. On the rare occasions when the girl has not indulged in a minor act of violence, she has caught Colleen sneaking wounded glances at her. Though Mrs. Greenberg can never understand it, the girl knows that Colleen also lives for the skirmish. There were forty-five kids in Mrs. Greenberg's class. If it were not for the girl's attentive violence, Colleen would be a nobody. She'd go unnoticed and uncalled on by Mrs. Greenberg, lost in a sea of indistinguishable black kids in a public elementary school with an overcrowding problem. The girl draws a line through her apology and turns to a fresh page.

Dear Colleen,
You don't have to thank me.

They Make of You a Monster

Damien Angelica Walters

When the footsteps approach, Isabel scrambles to her feet. She staggers; spots of light dance in front of her eyes. Two days without food. Two days without water. She backs up until her spine presses against the stone wall. Tucks her hands behind her. She knows it won't make a difference.

She tells herself she won't scream.

The Healers, three women draped in robes of red, enter her cell. They don't say a word. She keeps silent when they grab her. Twists away from their grasp. Fights against them with all the strength she can summon, but it's not nearly enough.

Then they snap the first finger, the pinkie on her right hand. The pain is white. Blinding. Below the pain, a sensation of leaking. Emptying. Her cries echo off the stone, and from another cell, she hears shouting. One of the Healers laughs.

By the fifth finger, she doesn't have the strength to struggle anymore.

By the eighth, she can't even scream. Wavery moans slip from her lips. The greedy stone walls gobble them up and wait for more.

By the tenth, the world is grey, flickering in her vision like candleflame.

After the last snap fills the air, the Healers weave a spell to fuse her bones back together, to fill her up with something new. When they let her go, she crawls to the corner of her cell, holds her ruined hands to her chest, and sobs into the filthy straw.

*

Midday, a guard shoves a bowl of porridge through the bars of her cell. Her stomach rumbles, but she makes no move for the food. If she does not eat, will they force it down her throat, or will they allow her to starve? A pointless question, for she knows the answer.

The porridge is bland, with neither milk nor honey to give it flavor, but she eats it all. She does not want to die.

Not yet.

*

At night, a guard walks the passageway between the cells, his feet tapping a steady rhythm on the stone. He stops outside the bars of Isabel's cell, his face all sharp planes and angles, his clothing tainted with sorrow.

She pulls her knees up to her chin. What does he see? A young woman in a dirty dress or a monster in the making?

He runs his fingers along one of the metal bars, his skin safe behind leather gloves. All the guards wear them. For their protection.

"You knew it was forbidden," he says, his voice a blade.

She holds her tongue.

"You knew the risk, the penalty, yet you still did it. Does that make you brave or a fool?"

He walks away before she can take another breath. It is not her fault. What she is. She holds up her hands. What she *was*.

They've made her something else now.

*

They came for her two days after Ayleth fell. She doesn't know how they knew what she'd done. Perhaps someone was hiding nearby. Watching.

She pushes the thoughts away and thinks of Ayleth's dark hair, her green eyes, the way she laughed into the wind.

*

She feels it growing inside her, a darkness where before there was a spark of light. Their corruption.

If she had a knife, she would cut it out and leave it bleeding on the floor.

*

The guards bring in a girl whose face still holds tight to child-hood. Her fingertips leak thin grey trails of smoke. Her fire is spent. She does not fight against the guards' grips, does not cry. She is already broken.

They put her in the cell across from Isabel's.

The girl screams when the Healers come, and Isabel covers her ears. Had her own screams sounded so loud? So long? If her gift was fire, she would've set the straw in her own cell ablaze and burned herself alive.

*

Moonlight peeks between the bars of her cell's window, a window too high to reach, even if she stands on her toes. It does not matter, though; the only thing beyond her window is a rocky cliff facing the sea.

She closes her eyes, breathing in the stink of her own waste. The hopelessness of the stone walls. How many were in this cell before her? How many listened to the waves crashing against the rocks? And how long before they gave in?

*

She paces in her cell. The sun has turned the air thick and sticky, and the straw rustles with each step of her bare feet, scratching against her skin. They took away her shoes when they brought her here.

The guard in the passageway does not look in her direction. He does not look at any of them. He smells of roasted meat; her mouth waters.

The girl in the cell across from Isabel trembles, her teeth chatter, and ice crystals form on the straw beneath her. Is there even enough left of her inside to miss the warmth of her flames? She is too young, far too young, to be so defiled.

*

"Let me see your hands, little fool," the night guard says.

She turns away so he cannot see them. Her heart races. Will he kill her? It would be a kindness.

Instead, he walks away.

She doesn't know why he wants to see; nothing shows on the outside. She feels it inside, ugly and wrong.

*

They bring in an old woman. Her back is bent; her eyes, clouded with white. She cries for her children to save her, but no one will come except the Healers and the guards. Everyone knows that.

Isabel doesn't think it will take long for the old woman to give them what they want.

*

She dreams of drops of blood falling from the sky, of a field of knives littered with bones, and wakes drenched in sweat with a strange taste in her mouth of sour milk laced with ashes. Her old magic, her *real* magic, tasted of ripe raspberries.

*

The guards take away a woman with long dark hair. She walks with her back straight and her mouth set in a thin line; her eyes flash with defiance.

A door slams. After a time, muffled screams creep into the air and hang there for hours. When the guards bring the woman back, she smells of urine, vomit, the acrid tang of fear. She leaves a trail of blood on the stones, and the sight makes Isabel's stomach twist into knots.

*

The new king took the crown the year of her sixth summer.

"You must never," her mother said, time and again. Even at six, Isabel understood why. "Never, ever."

And she listened. Until Ayleth.

She thinks of Ayleth's broken body, the blood dripping from the corner of her mouth. What would happen if she touched her now? Would she be able to hold it in?

*

Finally, the guards come for her.

They bind her arms behind her back. Even with their gloves, they do not touch her hands. They lead her into a windowless room; the door shuts with a bang that vibrates in her teeth. The room smells of pain and sorrow. Of giving up. Giving in.

The man in the room smiles—a lie.

There is a table covered with a stained cloth, the fabric full of bumps and bulges. She does not want to see what the cloth is hiding.

"Will you serve your king?" the man asks.

She takes a deep breath. Doesn't answer.

She will not.

He does not remove the cloth from the table, he does not ask his question again, and the guards take her back to her cell.

*

Magic was not always forbidden. When Isabel was a small child, there were no Healers, and only criminals were locked away. The old king was loved by the people, not feared. He loved balls, grandeur, music. The new king does not care for music, save that born of screams. Only those sworn to his service are allowed to wield magic; even then, they are only allowed a magic that has been perverted. Inverted. Fire to ice. Healing to—

No. She will not think of that now. She cannot.

Rumors say the king acts in cruelty because he secretly wishes he was born female. If so, he might've held magic. Instead, he has only his cock and the kingdom to grip.

But the why doesn't matter. Not here.

*

She dreams of Ayleth running toward her. Though Isabel runs as fast as she can to get away, to keep her safe, Ayleth won't stop.

She wakes just before Ayleth touches her hand.

*

They take the young girl out and do not bring her back. When the night wind blows cold through the window, Isabel thinks perhaps it is the girl, making ice for the king's wine.

*

The new magic inside her hungers. For what, she doesn't know, doesn't want to know.

*

The guards take her to the stone room again. The table is uncovered, revealing knives, hooks, spikes, and something shaped like a metal pear, something that screams malevolence. Anguish. She feels the blood run from her face. Her fingers tremble.

"Will you serve your king?"

She swallows before answering. "No, I will not."

They laugh when they take her back. They know she will give in, eventually.

Or she will die.

*

She and Ayleth grew up in the same village, casting shy smiles
at each other until finally, Ayleth kissed her behind the baker's shop.
Their love was not as forbidden as magic; people pretended not to see.

The day Isabel broke her promise of never, they were foraging
for berries atop a wooded hill. In the distance, the spires of the cas-
tle gleamed in the sunlight. Ayleth paused with a handful of berries
and whispered, "I would like to burn it down with the king inside."

"Do not say such a thing," Isabel said, casting a glance over
her shoulder.

Ayleth shrugged. "There is no one to hear. Only us." She took a
step forward. A twig snapped. Leaves crackled. Her mouth dropped
open as her legs slipped out from under, and she tumbled down the side
of the hill, her shouts punctuated with thuds and thumps all the way.

Isabel raced down as fast as she could without falling herself.
At the bottom, she found Ayleth holding her belly, blood dripping
from the corner of her mouth. Isabel tried to help her stand, but
Ayleth shrieked and begged her to stop.

The village herbwoman would not be able to help. Not with
this. In spite of Ayleth's protests, Isabel grasped her hands and let
the magic out.

And the sensation...her mouth flooded with the sweetness of
berries, her fingertips tingled, and inside, it was as if butterflies
were dancing soft beneath her skin. She felt it leave her body like a
breeze through a window; as it flowed into her lover's, Ayleth's eyes
brightened, her mouth formed a circle of surprise, then laughter
bubbled up and out. They danced together like children, forgetting
for a moment that, as proscribed by the king, the magic was wrong.

*

The guards carry out a body, laughing all the while. Isabel sees long dark hair. Pale limbs streaked with the telltale lines of blood poisoning. A face with blank eyes where defiance once lived.

*

The night guard watches her through the bars. She meets his stare, hiding her hands in the folds of her dress. She fears what they've done to her, fears who they've made her become, but she is not her hands. She is not their monster. She will not let it change her.

Yet she fears it already has.

*

She stumbles as they push her into the room with the table. A skinny man with a ragged beard stands in the corner. His clothes are tattered. Shackles bind his bloodied ankles.

"Will you serve?" the man with the false smile asks.

"Never."

He nods at the guards. They hold her arms tight as they guide her toward the shackled man. The smell of his unwashed body makes her eyes sting.

"No, I will not do this. I will not."

But inside, the twisted magic says *yes*.

She struggles to break free. The guards shove her toward the man. She lifts her hands. A reflex. Not on purpose. When her skin touches his, when she realizes what she's done, it's too late. Pain radiates through her belly like claws and fangs tearing free. Her fingers clench, digging into the man's flesh. She tries to hold the magic in, but it will not stay. She cannot make it bend to her will. It rips free, an animal in search of prey, and leaves the taste of rage in its wake. A vile brew filled with bitterness.

The man's eyes widen. His mouth opens. His face contorts in pain. His body spasms.

He falls.

For one quick moment, a feeling of power, of possibility, rushes through her. Then she shoves it deep down inside, and shame floods her. One of the guards nudges the man with his foot. He does not move. The liar smiles.

"Do you see what you are?" he says.

She closes her eyes. She doesn't want to see; she doesn't want to know.

*

The night guard pauses in front of her cell again. Isabel wipes away her tears.

"They will take you from here when you agree. You will have meat, wine, clean clothes."

She shakes her head. She is not a monster. But she thinks of the man, the way it felt to take his life, and she shudders.

*

"Will you serve?"

"No," she whispers.

"You don't really want us to tear up your pretty flesh, do you?"

"I will not serve," she says between clenched teeth.

It is her turn to scream, to leave a trail of blood on the stones.

*

She dreams of the field of knives. Of Ayleth, her blood pouring from a wound Isabel can no longer heal, her arms outstretched. Isabel tells her no, but Ayleth doesn't listen. She grabs Isabel's hands and falls to the floor, her eyes open. Unseeing.

In her dream, Isabel laughs.

She wakes with a cry in her throat; her mangled body answers with a shriek of its own. She catches movement from the corner of her eye—the night guard, walking away.

*

Death came for her father in the shape of a lingering illness that caused his limbs to wither and his skin to turn grey. Her mother forbade her to help.

"I cannot lose you both," she said.

So Isabel held her magic in, no matter how hard it fluttered, yearning to help.

The twisted thing inside her now scrapes and pushes, burning to hurt.

*

The night guard taps the bars of her cell.

"What do you want?" she asks.

"Why do you fight?"

She doesn't answer. He would not understand.

"They're looking for your friend."

A whimper escapes before she can steal it back. Not Ayleth. Anything but that.

"Why do you care?" she whispers.

"The king's sister is next in line for the throne. She does not share her brother's penchant for cruelty. She would be a good queen, I think."

She looks up. He is staring at the window.

"The king is coming to the prison tomorrow. He is not happy with the progress of late." The guard steps close to the bars. Looks into her eyes. "He does not wear gloves," he says, his words so low that, save for the movement of his mouth, she might have imagined them.

The breath catches in her throat.

He gives her a small half-smile, the expression strange on such a harsh face. "You remind me of my sister." As he walks away, she steps back with her hands held between her breasts. Why would he tell her such a thing?

How long until they find Ayleth? How long until they force Isabel to watch while they press the blades against Ayleth's skin?

Her eyes burn with tears, and she covers her mouth to hold in the sound.

The waves crash upon the rocks. The wind blows in through the bars on the window. The cell fills with the smell of the sea.

She thinks of the girl who could make fire. The dark haired woman. The old woman crying for someone to save her. She thinks of all those living in fear, the ones they haven't found yet.

*

In the morning, she hears a strange coarse laugh. Heavy footsteps move down the hallway, and she steps close to the bars. Waits.

The metal is cold beneath her fingers. The footsteps move closer.

Will they kill her once the king is dead?

She looks at her hands, her weapons. Not perverted. Per-
fected. The monster inside her extends its claws.

Let them try, she thinks. Let them try.

Rondine al Nido

Claire Vaye Watkins

"Now I am become Death, the destroyer of worlds."
—*Bhagavad Gita*

She will be thirty when she walks out on a man who in the end,
she'll decide, didn't love her enough, though he in fact did love her,
but his love wrenched something inside him, and this caused him
to hurt her. She'll move to an apartment downtown and soon—very
soon, people will say, admiringly at times, skeptically at others—she
will have a date with a sensible man working as an attorney, the
profession of his father and brothers, in the office where she is a
typist. They will share a dinner, and the next weekend another, then
drinks, a mid-day walk through the upheaved brick sidewalks of her
neighborhood, a Sunday morning garden tour of his. On their fifth
date she will allow him to take her to bed.

Before they met, he'll have been a social worker and after they
make love he will tell her this and about the terrible things he'd seen
in that other life. He'll begin—At CPS, there was this woman. She
had this little girl. Beautiful. Two years old.—then stop and lean

down and put his lips to her hair. Do you really want to hear this? he'll ask, as though just remembering that she was listening. He'll feel her head nod where it rests on his chest and go on. About the Mexican woman who let her beautiful, bright two-year-old daughter starve to death in a motel room near the freeway. About the teenage boy, high on coke, who broke into the apartment next door and slit his neighbor's throat. About the man who worked at the snack bar at the Sparks Marina, who lured a retarded girl into the men's bathroom with a lemonade. About the father who made his son live under their porch in Sun Valley, about the hole the boy bored up through the floor so he could watch his stepmother brush her hair in the morning.

He will talk and she will listen. It will be as though she's finally found someone else willing to see the worst in the world. Someone who can't help but see it. For the first time in her life, she will feel understood. When he finishes one story she'll ask for another, then another, wanting to stack them like bricks, build walls of sorrow and inhumanity around the two of them, seal them up together. An uncontrollable feeling—like falling—will be growing in her: they could build a love like this.

Then, feigning lightness, she'll ask him to tell her about something he did, something terrible. When he was a boy, maybe. It will be late. Watery light from a waxing moon will catch the corner of the bed, setting the white sheets aglow. Two candles—the man's idea—will flicker feebly on the nightstand, drawing moths against the window screen. He will tell her about his younger brother and a firecracker and a neighbor's farm house in Chatsworth, of straw insulation and old dry wood that went up like *woosh* so fast it didn't seem fair, of running around to the front door and ringing the bell—she will find this curious, the bell—and helping the neighbor, an elderly woman, down the front steps. Now you show me yours, he'll say, and laugh. He will have a devastating laugh.

By then, there will be much to tell—too much. A pair of expensive tropical lizards she'd begged for then abandoned in a field to die when their care became tedious. Birthstone rings and a real gold bracelet plucked from a friend's jewelry box at a sleep over. Asking an ugly, wretched boy with circles of ringworm strung like little galaxies across his head to meet her for a kiss at the flagpole, laughing wildly when he showed. These she'll have been carrying since girlhood like very small stones in her pocket. The sensible man will be waiting. Who can say why we offer the parts of ourselves we do, and when.

*

Our girl is sixteen years old. Her palms press against the stinging metal of a heat rack. Her best friend Lena, a large-toothed girl from Minnesota, stands across from her, palms pressed against the rack, too. Their eyes are locked and a skin scent rises between them. This is their game, one of many. In the pocket of our girl's apron rests a stack of fleshy pepperoni, their edges curling in swelter. Behind her, the slat-mouthed pizza oven bellows steadily. A blackened sheet of parchment paper floats in a dish of hot grease. The grease has a name and as our girl tells the story this name will return to her along with the other details of this place which had until then left her—the flatulent smell from a newly opened bag of sausage, the flimsy yellowed plastic covering the computer keyboards and phone keypads, the serrated edge of a cardboard box slicing her index finger nearly to the bone. Naked in her own bed with a man for whom she feels too much too soon, our girl will recall the name of the grease—*Whirl, it was called*—and the then-exquisite possibility of searing off her fingerprints.

Lena, her friend, pulls finally her hands from the rack, shaking the sting from them. You win, she says.

Our girl waits a beat, gloating, then lifts her palms from the surface, lustrous with heat. She folds a pepperoni disk into her mouth. Let's go again, she says.

Soon, our girl is cut loose for the night by the manager, a brick-faced, wire-haired woman named Suzie. She goes to the back of the restaurant, to a bathroom constructed from sheetrock as an afterthought when the most recent developers converted the space from one large address capping the end of the frontage strip mall to three smaller, cheaper properties. On the plastic shelves in the bathroom are stocked fluorescent light bulbs and printer paper and a dozen two-gallon plastic tubs once used to store a cream sauce that the franchise no longer offers. She removes her hat, her apron, her once-white tennis shoes and ankle socks. She unpins her nametag from her patriotically colored collared shirt and pulls the shirt off over her head. Yellow granules of cornmeal sprinkle into her eyelashes and along the part of her hair. She steps out of her khaki pants stiff with dried doughwater and dark, unidentified oils. At a row of three metal sinks adjacent to the bathroom, two delivery boys wash dishes. One of the boys, a nineteen-year-old named Jeremy, has convinced himself that he loves our girl though she has already once declined an invitation to watch *Dawn of the Dead* in the single-wide trailer he has all to himself on his mother's boyfriend's property.

She stands before the mirror in her bra and underwear, listening to the hollow slow motion clangs at the triple sinks. She steps out of her underwear. Suzie bellows from up front and someone's non-marking sole screeches against the tile. In the sink, using the pink granulated soap from the dispenser, our girl scrubs the smell of herself from her panties. Later, the dampness leftover from this washing will remind her of the pizza parlor and of poor pathetic Jeremy the delivery boy, and other remnants of a life she already wishes she could forget.

She waits for Lena on the bench in front of the counter, watching carry out mothers waddle to and from their idling cars with their pizzas and their slippery, foil-wrapped cheesesticks. Six and a half hours ago, in the parking lot of the Wal-Mart across the highway, Kyle Peterson, a tenor sax in their school's jazz band and Lena's boyfriend of nearly a year, dumped her for the first chair flutist, a freshman girl a year younger than they and a thinner, looser version of Lena. Two hours later, our girl wiped mascara from under Lena's rubbed-raw eyes in the sheetrock bathroom and asked her friend whether she wanted to get the fuck out of this shit town. Two hours after that, after she was certain her mother and stepfather had left for their Friday Night Step Meeting, our girl dialed her own phone number. When she got the machine, she said, I'm going to Lena's after work to stay the night, and, I love you, which is what she always says after she lies to them. By the time Lena gets off they've each an uneventful adolescence worth of recklessness welling inside them and one of them has a driver's license and a like-new Dodge Neon and it's just the tip of summer, which means there are college boys from places like Chicago and Florida and New York City wandering the Strip, sixty miles away, boys who came to Las Vegas looking for girls willing to do the things she and Lena think they are willing to do.

At eight o'clock Lena changes out of her uniform and wets her
hair and underarms in the bathroom sink and then the two walk out
into the parking lot with their soiled uniforms balled under their
arms, their apron strings trailing along the asphalt, as though they
don't have to be back for tomorrow's dinner rush, as though they
don't have to be back ever again.

On the road all there is is the desert and night and the taillights of the cars ahead of them. The radio comes in and out. Once,
without taking her eyes off the road, Lena says, I should have done
it with him. I don't know why I didn't. Our girl says nothing. Only
nods. When Lena swings the Neon around the final curve of the
mountain range separating their town from Las Vegas they see light
sweeping across the valley floor like a blanket made of lights, like
light is a liquid and the city is a great glistening lake.

Lena sucks a little saliva from her over-large teeth and asks is
it okay if they turn the radio off. She has never driven in the city.
Our girl says, That's cool, because the radio is suddenly nothing
compared to the billboards and limos and rented convertibles and
speakers embedded in the sidewalks emitting their own music into
the air, and because she'll say anything to soothe Lena, to keep her
driving.

Our girl directs Lena to park on the top floor of the parking
garage at the New York New York. It is June, 2001. This is the Las
Vegas that has recently given up on becoming what they were calling
a family friendly vacation destination, so that the water slides and
roller coasters and ice skating rinks that were once part of the mega-
resorts have been torn down to make room for additional hotel towers, floor space and parking garages like this one. Lena pulls hard
on the parking brake, the way her mother taught her. She moved

from Minnesota freshman year when her mom was offered a job as the Nye County health nurse. Her parents have been divorced since before she can remember. She sees her father, an accountant, on Christmas and Easter and lives with him in St. Paul for five weeks during the summer. Lena doesn't know anything about what was once Wet 'n' Wild or MGM Grand Adventures. But our girl spent her birthdays and end-of-year field trips in these places and could be saddened by this, could consider it the demolition of her childhood. But thoughts like those will not come to her for years.

Lena has a tube of waterproof mascara and a peacock-blue eyeliner pencil in her purse. Our girl has vanilla bean body spray and kiwi strawberry lip gloss and gum in three different incarnations of mint. All these they trade in the front seat of the Neon until both are eyelined and fragrant and fresh-mouthed. From the parking structure they walk through the New York New York. The shops in the casino are facaded with half-scale fire escapes and newsstands and mailboxes with replica graffiti on the side. They sell Nathan's Famous hot dogs or tiny Statue of Liberty erasers and keychain taxicabs and all varieties of shot glasses.

Our girl leads the way. The floor is busy carpet or plastic cobble. Tacky, her mother would call it, dully. The ceiling is lit to suggest stars glittering at twilight, as is popular along the Strip at this time. A bulbous red glittered apple rotates above a stand of slots. Our girl ignores the directional signs, which point their followers down circuitous routes pitted with pocket bars and sports books. Once, Lena touches her lightly, thinking they've lost their way. Our girl says, Trust me, and Lena does.

Outside there is a breeze threading through the warm night and a jubilant honking of cars and all those billions of bulbs flashing in time, signaling to the girls that they are, at long last, alive. Across Las Vegas Boulevard is an enormous gold lion posing regally amid the mist of a fountain. The lion is the property's second; the original—a formidable open-mouthed beast forged in mid-roar— was replaced because it frightened some Chinese tourists and was considered bad luck by others. Down the expansive block is an unimpressive aging Camelot and beyond that a black glass pyramid the apex of which emits a thick rope of light supposedly visible from space. The girls set off in the opposite direction, toward an ever-expanding ancient Rome and, across the palm-lined, traffic-clogged boulevard, the Eiffel Tower where our girl's stepfather poured concrete during phase two. They cross a Brooklyn Bridge whose waters are strewn with coins and pass before the wood-toothed mouth of a grinning Coney clown that will be demolished long before either girl reveals the happenings of this night to anyone.

The weekend crowds are dense on the sidewalks and mostly foreign or Midwestern. This allows the girls to amuse themselves at intersections by grasping hands, stepping off the curb against a red light and glancing backwards to see the crowd follow in their wake, taxicabs honking wildly. They have a teenage sense of their surroundings: they wander unknowingly into the photos of strangers and twice Lena tramples the heel of a Japanese tourist walking in front of her. But they feel men and boys before they see them, poking each other in the ribs, perking for button ups and baseball caps and over-sized jerseys, whirling around at the sound of a skateboard.

Soon, propped on the rubber handrail of a down-bound outdoor escalator, our girl stares unblinkingly at a cluster of young men headed in the opposite direction. When they pass, Lena turns and waves to them, but our girl dismounts the escalator coolly and without turning, wielding the fearsome magnetism of ambivalence. When they reach the top, the young men turn and descend the escalator.

The young men outnumber the girls by two. Our girl likes the way the four of them form a slowly closing semi-circle around them. She likes, too, how they all look the same in their baggy jeans and pastel collared shirts. They are dressed as most boys their age or slightly older dress, as though the tops and bottoms of them were mismatched pieces from two separate puzzles, one marked boy and the other man. One of them introduces himself as Brad and another Tom and another Greg and the last Allen. Except for Allen, they say these names too often and like candies too large for their mouths— This is *Brad*. *Brad*, shake her hand. Don't be rude, *Brad*—and because of this it becomes clear to everyone that these are not their real names. Everyone except Lena, who waves and says, Nice to meet you.

The one who calls himself Tom suggests they walk up to the Bellagio to watch the fountain show. The girls glance at each other, raring, and say, Sure, as they do at the show when one young man— Greg, is it?—offers them a fountain cup whose orange soda has been clandestinely cut with vodka. Lena's mouth twists up as she releases the straw, but our girl urges the cup up to her again and Lena drinks more heartedly. They pass the cup back and forth. This is what they came for.

Soon, the industrial fountain spigots emerge from the glassy black surface of the water and somewhere strings begin to hum. The song is "Rondine al Nido," which pleases our girl not because she recognizes it as such—she doesn't—but because she wants Lena to experience the pure painful awe of the bright-lit Bellagio fountains and she believes this is best conveyed when those cannon blasts are paired with something classical, something like the agony of ill-fated love.

After the show, the boy who calls himself Greg turns to them. He is large with the over-expressed muscles that come from a university rec center, so unlike the aching, striated parts of a man who works for a living, as our girl's stepfather would say. Greg asks, How old are you guys?

Old enough, says Lena, and this makes our girl proud.

Greg laughs. We'll see about that.

The boys ask them more questions—where they live, where they go to school—and meanwhile one of them replenishes the fountain cup. Our girl lies up a city life for them: moves them into adjacent two-story houses near the Galleria Mall, skips them ahead to senior year and enrolls them in a school whose football team once came out and trounced their own.

They drink. They walk. The boys say they go to UCSB, though our girl will misremember it as UCSC so that in the coming years these boys and what they do to them will combine with far-off Santa Cruz, California and years later, lying beside the sensible man with the devastating laugh—the first man she will not see beyond—the boys will have the scent of damp redwood and the sharp angles of that region's mountain lions, which she once read about.

In her bed, the candles dimming behind her, she will say nothing of these associations. She will be barely aware of them. She'll tug the top sheet out from under her, touch absently her fingers to the dampness leftover between her legs and say, They had a room.

But the sensible man—being who he is—will find the angles in her face. The redwood wet will be in his throat when he asks her, You went there? Alone? But you were just a girl.

I had Lena, she'll say. My friend.

Because he'll know what's coming, this will only make it worse.

*

The boys lead the girls to their hotel, where entering once meant passing through the jaws of a fearsome gold lion and now means nothing. Warm with sugar and liquor, our girl wants badly to tell Lena this—about the original lion and the superstitious Chinese tourists—because Lena still lived in Minnesota when they tore down the first lion and tonight's lion is the only lion Lena has ever known. It seems, for an instant, that if Lena knew about the old lion that at last the miles between Minnesota and Nevada might fold like a sheet, that distance crumpling into closeness and they would tell each other everything, always.

But the time for telling passes. In its place is the sudden chemical smell of chlorine and a flash of the too-blue of the dye in the water encircling the statue and then the girls are met with a blast of air conditioning and stale cigarette smoke and the noise of the machines inside the MGM Grand.

The six of them make their way across the floor, toward the hotel's two towers. The boy called Tom lays his hand on the back of our girl's neck. As they pass a security guard standing beside a golden trashcan, she is possessed by the impulse to sink her fingers deep into the glittering black sand of the ashtray atop it, but she resists this. Behind her, Lena stumbles, rights herself, then stumbles again. The boy called Brad grips her upper arm. *Bitch be cool*, he says through his slick teeth.

Lena walks steadily for several steps then stops. She has felt his words, more than understood them. She says, *I have to pee.*

Our girl tells Tom, We'll be right back, and follows her friend to the ladies' room.

Lena locks herself in the handicapped stall at the far end of the bathroom and sits on the toilet without taking down her pants. Our girl goes into the stall beside Lena's and shuts the door. She sits on the toilet in the same way. A woman is washing her hands at the sink and the automatic faucet blasts in spurts. Lena breathes heavily through her mouth. The woman at the sink dries her hands partially and leaves.

Our girl reaches her hand underneath the wall dividing them. Lena considers the fingers extended toward her then laces her own between them. They say nothing for a long time, only hold hands under the stall. Lena begins to cry, softly. Aside from the dim noise of the casino making its way back to them, the wet efforts of Lena's nose and throat are the only sounds heard. This is a beautiful time for our girl.

I don't feel good, says Lena. I miss Kyle.

Are you going to throw up?

No, says Lena. Then, Yes. Our girl releases Lena's hand and leaves her stall, allowing the door to swing shut behind her. She gets on all fours, the tile cool against her palms, and crawls under the partition into Lena's big handicapped cube. Lena is on her knees leaning over the bowl, her purse on the floor beside her.

Our girl says, Here, reaching over to lift the toilet seat. As Lena begins to vomit, our girl gathers her friend's wavy hair in her hand and holds it. Get it out, she says. All out. Between purges Lena mumbles a pathetic string of words intelligible only to herself, but having certainly to do with Kyle.

Our girl fingers the soft baby hairs at Lena's nape and says, Shh.

Eventually, Lena lifts her head slightly. I think I'm ready to go home, she says.

As though the word has materialized them on her, our girl becomes instantly sensitive to the persisting dampness of her underwear. She sees the sheetrock bathroom in the back of the pizza parlor. Jeremy the delivery boy. Her stepfather. His long commute to jobsites in Vegas. The empty and near-empty potato chip bags swirling around the backseat of his car like deflated Mylar balloons. Then, her memory lurching from shape to shape, there is her mother, hands shaking, unable to sit through a meal without popping up to get him seconds or refill his glass with milk.

Lena heaves again. Our girl tucks Lena's hair into her shirt collar. She quickly removes her own shoes, her pants and then her still-damp underpants, all the while smelling the overpowering mother smell of nail polish remover and Oil of Olay and menthol cigarettes. She folds her panties in half and half again and tucks them in the paper-lined metal wastebasket meant for soiled feminine hygiene products and their wrappings.

Lena moans into the toilet bowl. I want to go home, she says.

Naked from the waist down, our girl stoops and fishes the car keys from Lena's purse.

No, you don't, she says, and begins redressing.

As the girls wash and reassemble themselves at the sinks their eyes meet in the mirror. Our girl nods and says, You're fine. Let's have a good time.

Lena smiles weakly. I'm fine, she repeats. They return to the casino.

*

In her bed, she'll go on. The room, she'll begin, remembering two queen-sized beds with thin synthetic quilted coverlets in mauves and gold. All the lights turned on. No, the light was from the TV. Beer from cans in a torn box sitting on its side at the bottom of a small black refrigerator. But the sensible man will interrupt her.

Was it all four of them?

No. And she'll see in his face relief the excess of which forces her to turn from him, to the window and the pinkening dawn. One of them left to get pancakes, she'll say. Allen. I gave him directions to IHOP.

Three, then, he'll say, his voice blank as a dead thing. And you two girls.

We started watching a movie. Something with Halle Berry. Lena said she'd almost done it once with her boyfriend in Minnesota. But.

Had she?

No. I told her she had to get it over with.

Had you?

Yes, she'll say. But not like that.

What did they do to you?

She will shake her head, a movement nearly imperceptible. It wasn't like that. Afterwards, mine asked for my phone number. Tom, I think. He said, I really like you. Or something.

Did he ever call you?

This question will surprise her, and she will have to pause, trying to remember. No, she'll say eventually. I gave him the wrong area code. They thought we lived in the city.

And your friend?

Lena. She passed out on the other bed. I thought maybe she was faking. I don't know why. During the movie the big one got on top of her. Brad. He took off her clothes. Her eyes were closed but she was mumbling something. I don't know what. The other one spread her out, kind of. The big one spit into his hand. I remember that. I was on the other bed, with mine.

Jesus.

The other one put his dick by her face. He hit her with it, softly. They called her names. Drunk cunt. Fuck rag.

Jesus Christ.

Here, she will stop. Are you sure you want to hear this? she'll ask. Though she won't be able to stop even if he asks her to. He'll nod, slowly.

Lena woke up, she'll say, during. She got out of the bed and stood by it. They didn't try to stop her. She was naked, looking at the floor around her. For her clothes, maybe. Or the keys. But then she stopped and just stood there, looking at me. Tom—or whatever—was already inside me. She was just standing there.

Now Lena is limp in the light from the hotel television, as though, underneath her splotchy skin, her bones are no longer adequately bound together. She stares at our girl from between the two beds, her naked body like a question she can't ask, a prayer she can't recall. Behind Lena, the two young men look to our girl. She forces herself to wonder what they want from her, though she knows. Permission. The big one is shirtless, with his pants splayed open. The other has removed his pants, though he still wears his collared shirt, buttoned up. His bare ass glows blue in the light from the TV and he holds his dick in his hand.

Once, before Lena got her license, the girls were waiting at the county clinic for Lena's mother to drive them home, and they found a file folder filled with pictures of diseased genitals mounted on heavy cardstock. Lena said her mother used them when she gave sex-ed talks at the high school. Our girl flipped through them. Lena giggled and looked away, saying the pictures were gross. Our girl went on. They *were* gross, but in a curious, enthralling way, like a topographical map of a place she would never visit. But then there was one photograph in which the photographer—or the doctor. *Who takes these pictures?* she had wondered suddenly. *A nurse, probably, or an intern*—had captured the patient's thumb and index finger where they held the penis. She could see the man's grooved thumbnail and a little rind of skin peeling back from the cuticle. It made her wish she weren't a woman.

In the hotel room, Lena reaches for her friend. She says her name. The boys look to her too, even the one called Tom, above her. Our girl takes Lena's hand.

It's okay, she says. We're having fun.

She urges her friend back to the bed, gently, as though pulling the last bit of something shameful and malignant out through the tips of Lena's limp fingers.

Afterwards, on the way down to the lobby, our girl watches her own face in the polished doors of the elevator, and then Lena's, puffed around the eyes and mouth, her hair clumped to one side where they'd poured something on her. Through the summer, the tight circles in which the girls circumnavigate the pizza parlor will overlap less and less every day. Sometimes our girl will be at the oven, watching Lena's back as she works the line and the heat will well up in her and she'll want to cry out. But what would she say? Sometimes, as she cuts a pizza, boiling grease cupped in a pepperoni will sputter up and burn the back of her hand, or her bare forearm. This will bring her some relief.

That summer, Lena will shrink and yellow. Her eyes will develop a milky film. Even her big teeth will seem to recede into their gums, as though the whole of her is gradually succumbing to the dimensions of their town, its unpaved streets, its irrigation ditches and fields of stinking alfalfa. The four walls of the pizza parlor, the low popcorned ceiling of her mother's manufactured home. When Jeremy the delivery boy shuffles back to the walk-in where Lena stocks the commissary and asks her to come over to watch his band practice, she'll say yes, her voice wet with inevitability and exhaustion. The master bedroom of his trailer will start to feel like her own. Jeremy's love for her will be an unquestioning and simple thing, with rising swells of covetousness. It will be this particular strain of love—that's what he'll call it—that makes him hit her for the first time, on the Fourth of July, on the darkened plot of packed dirt in front of a house party where she'd danced too closely with a friend of his. Our girl will watch this from the porch of the house, where a crowd will have gathered. She will do nothing.

By September, she and Lena will not even nod in the halls. When the assistant principal comes over the intercom first period and makes the announcement, our girl will try to make herself feel the things she is supposed to feel: Grief for dead people in buildings she didn't know existed, sorrow for a place she can't envision. Deadened, but afraid of the deadening, she will look across the classroom to Lena, hoping to inflict upon herself that sickly shame that the sight of her old friend now evokes, thinking it the least she could do. But Lena—standing humped beside her left-handed desk with her right hand over her heart, crying—will be barely recognizable. This will bring our girl a sturdy rising comfort, a swelling buoyancy: a person can change in an instant. This, almost solely, will take her away from here.

The loudspeaker will emit a disembodied human breath. Things will never be the same, it will say, as if she needs to be told this. As if she doesn't know the instability of a tall tower, a city's hunger for ruin. As if this weren't what she came for.

Pomp and Circumstances

Nina McConigley

The Shirley Basin seemed to be a big stretch of nothing that fell between Casper and Laramie. There was no cell-phone coverage and not many houses except a few small ranches slipped between strips of cottonwood-lined creeks and the bases of rising hills. The basin at one time had been a forest. Lush, tropical, a swamp. Now every summer and into fall, people combed the sagebrush and scrub for petrified wood, for a small piece of Eden preserved. The basin is so rich with uranium that ghost towns once filled with miners lap at the edges. Low prices and over-supply has all but cut short business. In the early nineties, black-footed ferrets were released here. Once thought extinct, these little bandits thrive, feeding off prairie dogs and roaming the plains at night.

Rajah and Chitra Sen are heading across the basin to a graduation in Laramie. Their eight-year-old son Hari lies sleeping in the back seat. The graduation is for Rajah's coworker's son, Luke Larson. Richard Larson is proud of his son, and has invited everyone in the office to attend the graduation. Rajah is the only one going. One, because he has never been to an American graduation and thinks it will good for Hari, and two, because he finds Richard Larson hard to say no to. For months, Richard Larson has insisted upon calling him "Senator." He has done this since he first saw Rajah's name on the thin wooden nameplate on his desk: RAJAH SEN. Now all the other engineers in the office, and even Bobbi the secretary, call Rajah "Senator." It is a nickname that sticks, that perseveres like a fossil.

It is Chitra who states the obvious. "Senator? Didn't you tell them you are already a King?"

Rajah says nothing. He is the only Indian in the office. Hari is the only Indian in his school. Chitra is one of three Indians in their house. They are one of maybe six Indian families in Casper. She, perhaps, has it the easiest.

The drive is a little less than two-and-a-half hours, and they have been silent for most of it. Rajah Sen thinks his wife is rude to the Larsons, as she had not wanted to come to the graduation. He thinks she is being difficult when it comes to making American friends. Rajah knows Chitra has been to the Larsons' house three times. One of those times, they went together. It was a holiday party. An event for which they were instructed to bring a "white elephant" gift. Chitra had selected a soapstone elephant from a shelf in their house. On its flanks, there was an inlay of garnet-colored stones. But at the party, they realized they were not to bring elephants at all. They had gone home with a plastic reindeer. When you lifted its tail, small chocolates dropped out of its behind. Hari had screamed with pleasure.

Chitra has told Rajah that she had been invited for tea at the Larsons' twice without him. With not just Richard Larson, but his

wife Nancy. A thin, tanned woman who has a knack for matching.
She has deep set eyes and wears a great deal of eyeliner. Chitra also
wears eyeliner. Kohl she has brought from Kolkatta. Chitra's eyes
look sleepy, the kohl making her exotic. Nancy just looks startled.
Both times the Larsons had her over, Rajah was out of town. Richard Larson had planned that. They actually drank coffee and not
tea. And the second time, Nancy Larson had baked. She had made
a stack of lemon bars so thickly sprinkled with powdered sugar that
Chitra looked as if talcum powder covered her sari. Talcum powder
did cover her skin, and made her smell of sandalwood.

Chitra has said little about the teas; except for she does not
want to go back to their house again. If there is an office function, she would rather stay home. Rajah is sure that Chitra has done
something to offend them. At the Christmas party, Chitra, who was
not used to wine, told outlandish stories of India. She told Richard
and Nancy Larson that hijras had danced at her and Rajah's wedding. That they were good luck. Rajah Sen saw Richard's face as she
explained them to him. Rajah is sure that at the last tea something
must have been said, as Richard too has not mentioned Chitra.

As they drive, Chitra thinks the snow fences look like abandoned snake skins in the grass. They curve and bend and then stop
abruptly. These wooden skeletons hold more than the skin of winter
snow. Along this stretch, some ranchers use the fences to create
large drifts in the basins. It gives them a ready supply of water in
the spring. It is still spring now, and the prairie is in a green-up.
Magpies lunge along the roadside, the smell of sagebrush is sweet.
Plodding red Hereford and black Angus populate patches of the
plains. They are loose stock, as this is open range. Up in the hills,
and on Elk Mountain which rises before them, snow still sits on the

peaks. A bit like Nancy Larson's lemon bars. Except underneath the peaks are rock and preserved things. Nancy's lemon bars, due to high-altitude baking and dry air, only stay good for a day.

When the Larsons first invite Chitra to tea, she was surprised to find Richard home. The invitation had come from Nancy alone. They live in a modest ranch house on the East side of Casper. Without all the holiday decorations, the house is spare. The living room contains a cloud-like couch, the tables all have ornate legs like curving columns. There are prints on the walls of Indian warriors wearing headdresses. There are the heads of deer watching them. Richard is a good hunter, and every fall fills their freezer with antelope, deer, and sometimes elk. Nancy brings Chitra a steaming cup of coffee. On the table is cream in a pitcher shaped like a cow. The cream comes out of its mouth. Their sugar bowl is from a different era. A small urn with hand-painted flowers rimming the bowl.

"Do you like Casper? Have you settled?" Nancy asked.

"Yes," said Chitra. And she meant it. Before they lived in Casper, they lived in Toronto for almost year. Before that, they were in India. Toronto exhausted her. It was full of other Bengalis, and every weekend they went to Indian party after Indian party. Parties where satellite TV blared cricket or Indian movies. Parties where all the wives would put on their best saris and jewelry. Chitra would spend hours preparing chachchari or parathas. Parties where endless cups of tea were drunk. The talk would always be of India, or of the best schools to send their children. Here in Casper, they know few other Indians, and in many ways, it is a relief. She can wear jeans and cotton tops, and when they are invited to any function, she simply goes to the bakery of the grocery store and buys donuts by the dozens, cookies with frosting the color of gods.

Richard Larson does not join them at first. He comes in after their coffee has been drunk, when Chitra is admiring Nancy's quilts, which she has spread across an overstuffed pink chair in the living room.

"So the Senator is in Riverton! Hope he's not gambling away your fortune!" Richard Larson laughs.

Chitra does not know of the casino there, but she laughs along.

Richard Larson takes a hard look at Chitra's sari. She had worn it because it felt polite. Because she was going visiting. It is a simple one. Blue rayon with a series of dancing birds on the border.

"I like your costume, your dress," he says. "I like the one you wore to the Christmas party." She is not sure if Richard Larson is flirting or stating a fact.

She had worn one of her wedding saris to the Christmas party. It was purple, silk, ornate with heavy gold work. It had been stiffly packed for months, and so starched she felt she couldn't walk properly.

"Thank you."

There was a quiet at the table. It was just past lunchtime. A clock in the kitchen ticked a little beat.

"These fabrics are very pretty," Chitra said. She pointed to the calicos and patterns of the quilts.

"Yes, Nancy has an eye for color."

And then Richard Larson asks her for something she could never tell Rajah. He asks if he can try on a sari.

*

By the time they hit Medicine Bow, Hari is awake and asking to stop. They bypass the Virginian Hotel, which means nothing to them, and instead go to a small gas station. The inside smells of smoke. They buy sweet coffee and chocolate, then get on the road again.

Rajah takes in the wind turbines outside Medicine Bow. The town is almost bordered by them, and driving into the place, they look like cartwheeling crosses marking some sacred space. He thinks he is clever to think this, and begins to tell Chitra his observation, but instead tells Hari.

"Do you see those crosses?"

Hari scans out the window of their Honda and says blankly, "They are wind turbines." His class has been learning about green energy at school. Turbines are the newest point of contention in Wyoming. Some say coal bed methane brings salty water and that wind turbines ruin the view that so many flocking to Wyoming crave.

"They look like crosses, no?" There is a church near their home in Casper that has three large crosses like sentries posted outside their building. When they first drove by it, Chitra and Rajah had thought they were drying clothes on one of them, as purple cloth was draped on the arms like shawls.

Chitra squints out the window. She sees a pumping jack. "And that fellow then looks like he is bowing to Allah!" Prayers abound on the prairie for them.

They continue on their drive. The pumping jack pulls up more oil.

*

When Richard Larson asks if he can wear a sari, Nancy Larson leaves the room with a handful of quilts in her arms like a shield.

"You want to see a sari?" Chitra is not sure what to make of his request.

Richard Larson laughs nervously. "I'd like to try one on... if that's okay." He has lost the bluster she has seen in the office. He looks at his cowboy boots, which are ostrich and stippled like a pimply face.

"You mean Nancy wants to try one on?" Chitra is still confused, and wondering if this is a kind of trick. She wonders if this has something to do with Rajah at work.

Richard Larson is embarrassed. But then he gains back the same bravado she has heard when he calls their house looking for *the Senator.*

"It's like those people you talked about in India? At the Christmas Party?"

Chitra thinks back to the holiday party. She remembers the white elephant, drinking glasses of wine the color of rose water. But she doesn't catch his drift. And then she remembers her talk about hijras, and how she found them happy, while Rajah found them a nuisance.

"Chitra, I am going to show you something." He pronounces her name Chee-tra.

She follows him into the basement, past a pool table and more deer watching them in a solemn line. He takes her into a room with wood-paneled walls. The floor is concrete. In the room are several large safes—or what Chitra thinks are safes.

"This is where I keep my guns," he says pointing to a safe. "Kids. I told the Senator if he takes up hunting, he needs to get something like this. You don't want Harry there getting into guns." Nancy and Richard have one other child besides Luke. A girl named Gretchen Larson. She is in the army and stationed in Germany.

There is a narrow door with a lone padlock on it in the room. Richard Larson takes a ring of keys from his pocket and opens the lock. It is a small room, meant at one time as a kind of pantry. Inside is a little vanity with an oval mirror. A bench is tucked neatly in the middle. On the surface of the table is a wide array of makeup. Compacts, eyeshadows that look like an artist's palette, brushes of all sorts of sizes, lipsticks lined up like bullets. There is a full-length mirror next to the vanity. It is also oval, and swivels on its wooden base. A stained-glass floor lamp stands in the other corner. Next to it is another plush chair. But unlike the cloud chairs from the living room, this one has a Victorian feel. It is an elegant chair. Light mauve with a kind of paisley pattern. It is not a Nancy Larson chair. There are framed paintings on the wall—and again they are different. They are of flowers, English cottages with thatched roofs.

But the thing in the room that delights her the most is a metal bookcase. Lined up are mannequin heads, all in a row. On each of their heads sits a blonde wig in various hairstyles: a straight bob, a curly bob, long Rapunzel-like hair, and a cut with layers framing the face. The mannequins line up and look like the deer heads they passed on the way into the room. Watching and taking it all in.

Chitra does not say anything, because she is genuinely unsure of what to say. This is a condition she felt a lot in Toronto. But since being in Wyoming, she has lost this to some degree. She appreciates not having anyone ask her why Hari was losing his Bengali, why she now cooked burgers, and didn't she know that Japanese cars were the way to go?

Richard Larson walks back into the room with the safes and turns the dial of one. Chitra half expects he is going to show her his guns as if they are similar to the display of makeup. But when Richard Larson opens the heavy door of the gun safe, it is like he has opened a closet. Inside is a rack of dresses. They are beautiful. They are the kind of dresses she has seen on TV. The kind of dresses as a little girl in India she thought American women wore. Her biggest disappointment since arriving in Wyoming is seeing how sloppy women are. In the grocery store she marvels and the loose sweatpants and stained winter coats most women wear. She has to give it to Nancy Larson—she is matchy, but dresses well.

There are dresses with sequins that look like silver fishes. There are taffeta dresses in which the fabric whorls in discreet patterns. There is a suit with Native American beadwork making out flowers. There are slips like valentines hanging on padded hangers.

Richard Larson, who has for the most part been quiet, says this: "I am not gay and I love my wife."

Chitra nods.

"Nancy has known about this since before we got married. That's twenty-four years now. And she's okay with it. You have to know I am not gay. I just like to put these things on. It's not like your country. People don't consider it lucky."

Chitra touches a pink satin dress. It is strapless and has a large bow on the waist. Along the hem is lace. She wants to explain the complexities of hijras, their place. But instead she strokes the dress.

"Okay," she answers.

Richard Larson sees her face. "Would you like to try it on?"

*

When they arrive at the graduation, they are late. They are unsure where to park, and end up walking in circles around the university campus. Chitra is wearing an orange sari and slip-on heels, so she struggles to keep up with Hari and Rajah who are both in sports coats, pressed pants, and ties.

"Do you want to go to school here?" she yells up to Hari.

Hari turns around and gives her a pained look. "Baba says I'll go to school in India. To IIT. Why would I go here?"

Chitra has no answer. She knows that school, Hari's schooling, should be her singular focus. That is why she has held off other children. Rajah wants more. She thinks of the IUD she had put in in Toronto. Her secret. Her own broken cartwheeling cross inside her uterus. It gave her a kind of power, a kind of energy.

When they find the stadium, they do not sit with the Larsons. Luke Larson is graduating in engineering. He will come back to Casper at the end of the summer and begin work at the same firm as Rajah and Richard. The Sens sit in hard-back seats and hold programs embossed with the logo of the university. Inside are row upon row of names. Hari plays a pocket video game. If the ceremony is having an influence on his future academic career, it does not show. Chitra and Rajah watch as speeches are given, a woman sings, and as the graduates file out onto the stadium floor it is just like a movie.

As they walk out, the graduates walk two by two. In their black gowns and tasseled hats, they look like walking lamps. Their faces beam. They look fresh-faced and ready for the future. Chitra finds she is strangely happy and excited for these young people. For their accomplishments. For the future that lies before them. She follows their names in the program; she takes pictures of graduates she does not know.

*

Chitra decided that day in the basement not to try on the dress. Instead, Richard Larson takes her back into the little room and shows her albums of him in various outfits. When he wears dresses, he likes to be called Clara. Clara, from what Chitra can tell, is demure. Everything Richard Larson is not. She imagines that Nancy Larson has taken these photos, as most of them have been taken in the wood-paneled safe room. There are pictures of Clara in suits, in dresses, even in a velour track suit.

The only sari Chitra has is the one she is wearing. And so until she can next come over, she gives Richard Larson a taste of what wearing a sari is like. When they go back upstairs, she picks up one of Nancy Larson's quilts. It is a Log Cabin quilt, all in shades of blues and greens. It is thick and awkward. But Chitra drapes the quilt around him in a faux sari.

"It will look like this," she laughs. And Richard laughs with her, as the weight and bulk of a quilt are nothing like a sari. She feels amazingly light for knowing this about Richard Larson. The secret moves inside her.

Nancy Larson does not appear again on that visit. Richard Larson shows Chitra out, and she promises to bring back the purple sari for him to try on. Richard Larson does not ask her not to tell Rajah about this request, but she knows not to. It is unspoken between them. This kind of thing can get you killed in Wyoming.

*

The ceremony is long, and when it is over, they meet at Luke Larson's apartment. It is near the University. The apartment is filled with other Larsons and with Nancy's family, who are Boyds. The Sens are one of the first to arrive and since they have never been to a graduation party, they all sit quietly in the corner until Richard and Nancy Larson arrive.

"Senator! Chee-tra! Harry!" Richard Larson exclaims their names when he arrives. He is wearing a kind of suit with the same cowboy boots he wears most days. Around his throat is a lariat with a turquoise stone. He has a large elk tooth ring on his finger. Nancy Larson is wearing a flowered dress. She smiles a thin smile at the Sens.

It is Rajah who speaks for them. "You must be proud of Luke! Such a lot of graduates! What a sight!" He is genuinely happy for Luke Larson and wishes his wife would also show more spirit.

"Yes, yes, now you all get some food now," says Richard. He doesn't look at Chitra, which disappoints her. She has picked the orange sari because she knows Richard Larson will appreciate it. Western women just seem to notice a sari's color. But Richard Larson notices the intricacies of a sari. The weave, the fabric, the zari work. In fact, Richard Larson is the only person who has asked her anything beyond, "Are they hard to wear?"

*

When Chitra goes back to the Larsons, she brings a suitcase of saris. She has the purple one from the Christmas party, but she also packs a variety of saris. For fun, she puts in a salwaar kameez and a box of jewelry, which she has removed from the small safe they keep in a cupboard in their bedroom. It also holds their passports and visas.

Nancy Larson lets her in, and again, they have coffee alone. They eat lemon bars. Chitra finds herself driving the conversation. They do not mention the purpose of her visit.

"You must be missing Gretchen? So far away?" she asks.

"Yes. But we e-mail." The clock's ticking punctuates her sentences. Nancy Larson is not a talker.

Richard appears as they are finishing their coffee. This time, Rajah is in Cheyenne, but will be back later that night.

"How do you like this weather?" he asks. It had been snowing on and off for a few days, and now the streets are a slushy mess. Chitra is still new at driving, and Richard Larson knows this.

"I have to get a big broom to clean the car. And wear boots!" Chitra lifts up her sari to reveal a new pair of brown leather boots. She had put on a sari especially for the visit, but had spent the week in sweats and jeans—she suddenly understood the women at the grocery store.

Chitra motions to the suitcase. "I have brought many choices." She walks over and opens the suitcase, and begins to spread the saris out on the same chair where Nancy showed her the quilts. She unfolds the saris to show the pallus—which are rich in decoration. She has a *Kanchipuram* silk sari, handloom sari, a blocked printed sari—saris with fake crystals affixed in patterns like stars. She likes showing someone her clothes. In Toronto she worried her saris weren't fancy enough, but here, spread out across the upholstery, they look sumptuous, like wealth.

Richard Larson takes them all in. He runs his hands over the silks, the cottons, even the rayons. He is quiet. It is Nancy Larson who breaks the silence.

"I could make a nice quilt with these," she says.

                                    *

The party is a tedious one. The first wave of family has been replaced by a second wave of Luke's friends. They are polite and well dressed and dig into the food with glee. Nancy Larson has bought trays of cut-up vegetables and cheese from Wal-Mart. She has made plates of lemon bars and cookies. She has a slow cooker filled with little sausages. Next to the cooker is a small crystal glass brimming with toothpicks.

Rajah and Chitra fill their plates with crackers and pieces of carrot. No one from the party talks to them, except the occasional person en route to the buffet.

"What a pretty (costume) (dress) (outfit) (thing) you have on! And what a color! Is it hard to wear?" Chitra answers politely and for a moment longs for the Indian parties of Toronto.

Chitra is annoyed and cannot bear Rajah's stubbornness. She has told him that it was just tea with Nancy, that Richard came in hardly at all. That they didn't drink any alcohol (but she suspects Rajah thinks she did). But she knows that Richard Larson has become nervous. He cannot gauge her ability to keep a secret, and so stupidly has been silent and awkward at work. Poor Rajah! He cannot imagine what his wife might have said. He worries that he might never get a promotion.

*

The difficulty with Richard Larson wanting to wear a sari is that all of Chitra's choli blouses are too small for him. So instead she tells him to wear a t-shirt underneath the sari. But all of Richard Larson's t-shirts are walking advertisements—for races run, political candidates, for places they have traveled. And although his shirt advertising Sombrero Mike's in Cancun is a similar purple to her sari, it will not do.

Chitra hands him the slip worn under a sari and tells Richard Larson to tie it tight.

"Tight, tight, almost like you can't breath!" she instructs.

And a few minutes later, he comes into the safe room in her cotton slip and a white undershirt. It is as if he is naked, and for the first time, he seems embarrassed.

Chitra cannot ever remember being told or shown how to wear a sari. Perhaps she watched her mother and grandmother so many times it imprinted into her very being. Richard Larson does not just want to wear a sari; he wants to learn how to put one on. And so Chitra shows him.

"First you make a knot like this, and tuck it in," she said while tucking the end of the silk into his waistband. It is the first time beyond a handshake that she has touched Richard Larson. Somehow feeling the soft give of his belly and seeing the paleness of his arms, she feels protective of him. She senses his vulnerability.

She turns him around and adjusts the pallu over his shoulder. She pleats the fabric. Richard Larson, as an engineer, is meticulous, and carefully folds the pleats into even amounts.

"It isn't heavy at all," he says.

"No, but walk carefully." Chitra takes out two large pins and discreetly pins the sari at the shoulder and at the pleats.

"Even I do this sometimes," she lies.

When she is done, she takes a long look at Richard Larson. It is as if he is no longer Richard Larson, but Clara. He stands very still almost as if he is taking something in.

"I think I'll just go do my makeup," he says to Chitra, and she nods.

Richard Larson takes small steps to the little door, to his secret room, and then stops just as he crosses the doorway. He turns around and looks at Chitra.

"Do you think Rajah would think this looks nice?" It is the first time Chitra has heard him call her husband anything but the Senator.

"I think he would think you wear it very well," she says and means it.

*

It is when a series of toasts have begun that Chitra leans to Rajah. Hari, who has spent the entire party either eating cookies or playing his video game, sits quietly in a corner lost in his own world.

"They like me. I wasn't rude. Look, all is well!" she says.

Rajah says nothing, but pretends to laugh at the toasts.

"Stop this. I am telling you. It was just tea. Why can't you understand?" Chitra feels shrill and wonders if the one glass of champagne she drank at the insistence of Mr. Boyd has gone to her head. She thinks she shouldn't drink, but it is hard not to with his co-workers.

"Fine," says Rajah. "Then promise you'll go again if they invite you—that you'll invite them over!" He seems like he is going to say more, but then Nancy Larson comes over to them and asks Rajah if he will take some group photos of the family. Rajah hates it that his wife doesn't have to work so hard to fit in, and takes it all so lightly.

*

When Richard Larson emerges from his little room, he has put on a full face of makeup and is wearing the long blond wig. He doesn't look Indian—but he also does not look like himself. Chitra also thinks he is better looking than most hijras she has ever seen. When he is Richard Larson in his big boots, his aggressive nature is more like a hijra then. As Clara, he seems turned down in volume. He doesn't say anything but stands waiting for her approval.

"You are looking very nice. Now just a few more things." Chitra digs through her suitcase and pulls out a flat box. Inside is part of her wedding set. Gold-dipped and not 24-carat. The earrings have thick posts and so they are out. But Chitra affixes a heavy gold chain around Clara's neck. Her bangles are all for her small wrists, so instead she wraps another necklace around his wrist.

"And now, for the perfect end," Chitra says. She lifts the folded paper to which a row of colored bindis are attached to a clear piece of plastic. She chooses a purple bindi with a small diamond in the middle.

"There," she says. "You are done."

Clara looks at herself in the mirror through the open door. And then begins to yell.

"Nancy! Nancy! Get down here, quick! Bring the camera!" he bellows up the basement stairs.

*

Rajah takes a series of photos of Luke Larson. Poor Luke poses with the Larsons, the Boyds, and then his friends. Rajah directs Nancy, Richard, Luke, and Gretchen Larson in a series of poses. One is next to his graduation cake, another outside the apartment, by a late-flowering crab apple tree. Richard Larson jokes.

"It's not every day you have a Senator taking your picture!" and "Don't tax us for the photos!"

Rajah says little. And when the photo shoot is done, he hands Nancy Larson back her camera.

"Don't you want to see what you've taken?" she asks and hands the camera back to him. "Just press this to review the photos," she says sweetly pointing to a small silver button.

And Rajah takes the camera.

*

When Nancy Larson appears downstairs, she is holding a camera. She walks past Chitra and goes straight for Clara. She takes his hand and strokes his hair, she fingers the bindi on his forehead, and she runs her hand over the purple silk. She then turns to Chitra.

"Thank you. He looks, I mean Clara, looks beautiful."

Chitra feels like she is once again in a world she doesn't know. And while Nancy Larson begins to take pictures, to talk to Clara in a low voice, Chitra excuses herself to the bathroom.

When she comes back, she sees that Nancy is looking through her saris. She is holding a simple handloom that is also purple.

"Would you like to try it on?" Chitra rummages around for a choli and slip.

Nancy Larson looks like she is going to say no, but she looks at Clara, who now is sitting in her chair in the little room. She looks again to the sari.

"Yes," she says. "I would like that very much."

Once Nancy Larson is in her sari, it is Chitra who takes photos of the two of them against the pine wall. She instructs them to fold their hands in Namaste, which they do. They pose with their arms around each other, and Chitra is glad she has pinned them both into their saris.

It is when the photo session is over that Clara/Richard Larson turns to his gun safe and spins open the combination. He pulls out the pink dress that Chitra had held on her last visit.

"You have to try this on," he says. Without pausing, Chitra takes the hanger with the pink satin dress, she takes a short blonde wig. She heads into the little room. The temptation is too great. And when she comes out, she feels like she is part of something for the first time. She poses with Clara, and then with Nancy, and then they use the timer to take a shot of them all. They all laugh as the

Larsons' saris fall off the shoulder, as they pool to the ground like a swirl of cream.

*

When Rajah Sen begins to review the photos of the graduation, he continues to go back, back, back. He examines a series of pictures of Nancy Larson's latest quilt in progress. It is the Ohio Star pattern and the fabrics she has picked are very nice indeed.

*

Once all the saris are packed up, Chitra keeps out two saris. They are cheap ones. One is rayon and the other a kind of fabric that looks like, but is not, silk.

"For you," she says and hands them to Nancy and Richard Larson. Nancy Larson in turn gives her a plate of lemon bars. She hands Richard Larson a packet of bindis. He has tried to give her the pink dress, but she doesn't want it. It would be hard to explain, and she cannot imagine wearing such a dress out in public. The very immodesty of it surprised her when she put it on. She doesn't need it to feel American.

They will not ask her to come again, and she imagines they will not talk of this. That in several months there will be another white elephant party where the only elephant in the room will be this day. Chitra will know to buy a joke, a laugh at someone else's expense. She will tell another story of India, this one with a tiger, or how at her wedding they had 600 guests, which was considered not a big wedding at all.

As she leaves the Larsons' house, she is almost blown over by the wind. Their house is sparsely landscaped with no mature trees. She feels the wind deep in her bones.

*

Chitra sees Rajah with the camera in hand, and comes over and puts her hand on his. He has gone back, but not far enough.

"Did you take good pictures?" she asks and takes the camera. Rajah has been studying the star quilt with intensity.

"Okay," says Rajah. He repeats what Nancy Larson said months ago. "Your saris would make a nice quilt."

"Are you an idiot? I would never cut them!" Chitra laughs. "But I'd cut your mother's." Chitra's mother-in-law has given her a series of bland old lady saris.

Rajah laughs, as he hates his mother's taste. Chitra pulls a wrapped Waterman pen set from her bag.

"I bought Luke some pens. Engraved."

And Rajah is touched by his wife's thoughtfulness. Although the day has not enchanted Hari, he is happy to see that seemingly all is fine between the Larsons and Chitra. That the day has gone on without a hitch.

The Sens say goodbye to the Larsons and begin the trip home. She is once again given a plate of lemon bars for the road.

They drive. They are near Como Bluffs, and Hari has spent the last half-hour talking of dinosaurs. It is not the graduation that has caught his attention, it is the idea that just beyond the hills is a graveyard of bones. He tells them theories of extinction, facts about the size and speed of these creatures that roamed the earth before humans ever existed. He tells them that there are wagon ruts from the Oregon Trail not far away. That pioneers crossed this way.

They stop again at the same convenience store in Medicine Bow and they take turns using the bathroom. When Chitra comes

out, the clerk eyes her with suspicion. Hari is already outside, comb-
ing the parking lot gravel for fossil finds.

"You have to buy something to use the bathroom," the clerk
says.

Rajah scans the shelves of beef jerky and cigarettes, soda and
hot dogs.

"We're not hungry," he says pleasantly. "My son, he needed to
use the toilet."

The clerk sighs, "You have to buy something."

Chitra thinks Rajah is going to bend, to buy a pack of gum or
postcard. He pauses at a postcard of a prairie dog proclaiming that
Someone in Wyoming Loves You!

It is Chitra who moves in front of him. "Don't you know," she
says to the clerk. "He is a Senator. A King. He can do whatever he
wants, whatever he pleases."

"I didn't know that," says the clerk and snorts. And then she
goes back to arranging matchbooks in a small display on the counter.

Chitra takes hold of Rajah's hand. Her skin is dry and his hand
is warm. He opens the door and walks into the sun, into the wind.

When I Make Love to the Bug Man

Laura Benedict

Bug Man, Bug Man, who came to save me from the spiders.

It didn't seem fair that there should be so many spiders in one house. Wolf spiders, jumping spiders, daddy and granddaddy longlegs, cave cricket spiders (sure they're a kind of cricket, but just take a look at one and tell me you don't think, *that's the ugliest spider I've ever seen*), orb spiders, brown recluse spiders. If I turned a lamp on in a dark room, I didn't have to wait long to notice one fleeing for the threshold, or crouching motionless in the light, playing dead.

Oh, yes, I saw them. I heard them, too, as I lay in bed at night beside my husband, Robert. Robert pretended not to hear, but I'm not ashamed to say I heard them knocking softly, messaging each other.

"Are you there?"

"Yes, I am here."

Fact: you are never any farther than three feet from a spider. Fact: Wolf spiders—the females are the ones you'll see—look furry, but that's not fur on their backs. It's their young. Hundreds of them. Mama carries them around with her as she explores her territory. Fact: You'll rarely see a female brown recluse unless you rip into walls and crevices. They hide like reluctant royalty, hatching their young away from the light. Fact: Those are males crawling out of the guest bedroom pillow or the electric socket. There's something about cardboard boxes that attracts them too, like perfect camouflage, their compact, angular bodies and bent legs gliding across the boxes' bone-dry walls as though the walls were made of ice. Fact: Spiders have no capacity for vocal sound. Thus, the knocking. Not many spiders can communicate this way, but some do.

I know these are Facts because the Bug Man whispers them to me when I'm in his embrace. The Bug Man has no reason to lie.

I am in love with the Bug Man. I cannot leave him.

I fled my cheerful, shiny family for the Bug Man. Fit, grinning children with summer tans, good teeth, and stunning green eyes the color of new grass. Relentlessly healthy children. Blonde, enviable children. They greet each day with terrifying vigor: water guns and war games, barefoot races and soccer tournaments. Robert and I have raised them in the light. They attack the world, ready to rule it.

They are a product of me, but mostly of Robert. He will be an excellent father and mother to them. He will miss me, and he will miss the sex. Will I miss it? Or him? That remains to be seen.

You might think I was dissatisfied with Robert. No. Robert was more than satisfactory. Maybe even too satisfactory. Too good.

Even our sex was aggressively superior, like an Olympic relay event. Brisk foreplay in the kitchen because he liked the way

I leaned, naked, against the counter as he told me about his day. A sprint down the hall past our children's bedrooms, his dignified button-down shirt sliding from his body as he approached our room, with me close behind, trying to keep up. It was his energy—yes—his enthusiasm that first attracted me. What woman doesn't want her man to be ready to go when he gets home? In the darkened bedroom, he would hand off the shirt to me, and take a quick detour to the bathroom, pinching my breast playfully as he passed. He returned, newly erect, efficient in his desire. Never stumbling, he settled me at the foot of the bed so he could test my readiness. And I was, and am, easily ready. Sometimes I needed only the sound of his key in the front door lock, leading him to wonder, *Naughty girl, what were you doing before I got home?* But I never told him. I only smiled. It was all the encouragement he needed, and we were down to business, the part where our breath was short and my mind never wandered, and we could see our common goal, like a glittering trophy.

Where were the shining, remarkable children whose rooms we passed in such haste? Does it really matter? You're worried about them, I know, thinking that no child should have to witness their parents in mutual bestial pursuit. Their mother naked in the kitchen where there are so many concerns about sanitation, not to mention that their MOTHER was NAKED in the daylight, IN THE KITCHEN. Their father in slavering worship of that fertile, naked body. Feel free to think of them as being at Scouts, or at a neighbor's house, or even behind their bedroom doors, stupefied with a few drops of *shhhh!* rum in their afternoon juice. No, it doesn't really matter. You will be relieved to know that they weren't anywhere near the first time I made love to the Bug Man.

*

When Robert saw the Bug Man's estimate for the treatment of the house, he called me into the study. "Where'd you find these people?" he said. He handled all the bills. There wasn't a penny I spent that he didn't see, first.

"Someone recommended them," I said, keeping it casual. "I don't remember who it was." In fact, I did remember, but I didn't say. Leeza had left her husband without explanation weeks earlier, and Robert didn't like to be reminded. When he first heard, he shook his head and said, "She had it so good. I just don't understand." Robert has never thought deeply about other peoples' lives. Robert has an endless capacity for optimism, but is not a deep thinker.

"Damned expensive," Robert said. "But I bet we don't see any more spiders. They have a money-back guarantee."

He was right. There would be no more spiders, but it didn't matter by then because I already knew the Bug Man was my hero.

*

You wouldn't call the Bug Man handsome. Hair steely gray, push broom mustache, mature belly straining confidently against the fifth button of his tidy uniform shirt. He's the barber, the shoe salesman, the produce guy at the grocery store. Polite. Not a professional man, but someone who knows a day's work. His eyes are clear and dark and steady. Infinitely calm. *I never act rashly, or ask for more than I need*, they say. His uniform agrees: Above his neatly pressed black pants, his starched white shirt (nobody uses starch anymore) bears a logo with a spider emerging from a cave. Below it is his name in machine-perfect script: *Darrin*. (No one is named Darrin anymore either.) My daddy wore a uniform when he was in the U.S. Army, and ended up a sergeant. He never earned any serious medals. The Bug Man has a single medal: a bright, gold-plated rectangle that he wears on the pocket opposite the logo side of his shirt. *25 Years. Pest Control Excellence.* The Bug Man takes everything seriously.

I was fully dressed the day he showed up at the house, in case you're wondering. I didn't wander around the house naked as a regular thing. But I confess that when I saw him, I sucked in my stomach as much as I could without holding my breath, and quickly checked my front teeth for lipstick or errant food. They were gestures I was barely conscious of making. (Watch a woman and her reflection walk by a store window sometime. See the way she smoothes her hand over her abdomen, as though it will make her look more slender. See her nervous smile of approval, or moue of disapproval, depending on how she's feeling that day.) I wanted the Bug Man to approve of me even before I met him.

As he inspected the house, I boldly followed him—barefoot— from room to room.

"Has anyone been bitten?" he asked, shining his flashlight up the narrow attic stairway. The beam exposed an empty web strung between a stud and unfinished wallboard about halfway to the top.

I was momentarily embarrassed about my poor housekeeping. It was probably what had led to the infestation in the first place.

"*Steatoda*," he said.

My hand wandered to the small lump of a bite that had appeared overnight on my upper right thigh. It itched like hell.

"No worries," he said, turning back to give me a reassuring smile. "They stay in their webs. No threat to humans."

The Bug Man had an herbal smell, like sage. The sage was in bloom everywhere in the neighborhood, including my garden, its purple shafts smothered with pollen-drunk honey bees. If I hadn't been so nervous, I might have gotten close to him to better take in his scent. I couldn't see him well in the shadows behind the flashlight, but how he looked didn't matter.

In the basement, the Bug Man told me about the wolf spider living in his laundry room.

"Two years old," he said. "My wife tried to kill her with a shoe."

I hadn't thought to look for a wedding ring on the Bug Man's hand. I glanced at his ring finger. Nothing. But so many men go without their rings. His job entailed a certain amount of physical danger, didn't it? Poking blindly into dark corners and attic eaves. If he were bitten, his hand might swell and the ring would strangle the finger of blood before it could be saved. Not wearing a ring seemed like the sensible thing to do.

As if sensing my curiosity he said, "That's not a problem anymore, though."

Uncertain about his meaning, I felt myself blush.

"You've got a lot of damp down here. I would recommend a dehumidifier, and more caulk around those windows. That's where your cave crickets are coming from. They love the damp."

*

The kids swam all afternoon at the hotel. Robert and I took turns sitting in one of the rubbery white sling chairs pushed up against the walls, watching them splash one another and kick water onto the soaked tile floor. When they were showered and dry, Robert suggested pizza at a restaurant in an adjacent shopping mall, and miniature golf. He was in a holiday mood. If it hadn't been for the kids, I'm sure he would've suggested some vigorous hotel sex to pass the time. He had that look in his eye.

"How about it?" he said. "We'll do the tough eighteen holes, with the spinning waterfall. The kids will sleep like puppies." Hopeful.

The hotel was our home for twenty-four hours while the Bug Man and his people got rid of the creatures in our house. I had left a key under a flower pot at the back door. The Bug Man had told me not to worry, that they—along with every bug—would be gone in the morning.

Ever since the Bug Man had first visited my house, I'd been gripped by a kind of madness. I had wanted to follow his dented white truck to his workplace, his house—anywhere he was going. Madness, yes! I felt it then, and I know it, now.

"I'll catch up with you at the golf place, okay? I'm running by the house for just a few minutes," I said. "Someone should check."

Robert shook his head. "They won't even be done with the spraying and dusting. You don't need to be around that crap."

"Daddy said, 'crap!'" The youngest child, my only girl, threw herself to the floor in a melodramatic fit of laughter. "Crap! Crap! Crap!"

"What the hell are you teaching these kids?" Robert said, pointing at her. "Who lets their kids talk like that?" He could barely hide his smile.

It was all I could do not to give him a playful kick, but I settled for kissing him on the cheek and squeezing the tiny amount of flesh at his waist. "You're such a smart ass," I said. I swept everything that the youngest had pulled out of my purse back into its place, and headed for the door.

"Mommy doesn't love us any more, kids," Robert said, after me. "You're a bad mommy, Mommy!"

Down at his feet, our daughter was still laughing. It had turned forced and more than a little creepy, but she is often silly that way.

*

It wasn't quite seven o'clock, and wouldn't be dark for a couple of hours. Most of our neighbors would be eating dinner. No one saw me park a few doors down from the house—and if they did, so what? It was *my* neighborhood. *My* house. I was the one other women called for news. I couldn't *be* the news.

I had expected to see several trucks in my driveway, but there was only one. The way the Bug Man had explained it, the bombing of the house was like a complicated military exercise. I was confused. Maybe they weren't starting until morning. No, that didn't make sense. He had said we could come home at ten the following morning.

"It's better if you leave for the night," he had said. "You don't want to take any kind of chances with your little ones. The government says it's safe to go inside four hours after treatment, but don't you believe it."

Where were the other trucks? Where was the Bug Man?

I watched and waited for almost an hour, concerned that he was inside, hurt and alone. Maybe even injured by his own poison. Or was he going through our things? We didn't have much in the way of silver, only a pair of candlesticks and a carving set left to us by Robert's great aunt. No guns or impressive electronics. Robert had his laptop with him, and I shared a five-year-old PC with the kids. The two televisions together with my pathetic stash of jewelry were probably only worth a few hundred bucks. Still, the thought of him touching our things, *my* things, filled me with a desire that melted between my thighs.

Finally, I couldn't bear the torture of waiting, and I got out of the car.

*

I felt like a drugged-up criminal, sneaking into my own house.

Once inside the basement door, I listened. Footsteps passed back and forth above me with quiet, irregular speed, as though someone were slowly wandering from room to room. When something tickled my bare leg, I startled and almost cried out, certain that it was a cave cricket. "They can't see worth a darn," the Bug Man had told me. "When they're afraid, they jump. If you're in the way, it's too bad." But when I brushed at my leg and looked around, I saw no sign of the spidery cricket bastards. Not even around the water heater, where I knew they liked to hang out. My heart was beating so that it was hard to breathe.

I found the Bug Man, alone, in the living room. He didn't hear me come in, and this is why:

He stood facing the wall behind the couch, his left arm outstretched, the palm of his hand flat against the wall, a small black box at his feet. The lights were off, but in the waning sunlight I could tell his eyes were closed. He wore such an air of peace and calm that I was tempted to walk across the room and touch him. He was so masculine, so interesting. Not arrogant. Not intimidating. I could never be afraid of him.

The sound began so quietly, it might have been going on for several minutes before I noticed it. It was a sort of music, a humming with a range of only a couple of notes. It filled my comfortable living room like incoming waves of the warmest, purest water.

I floated on those waves, letting them carry me to him. He didn't move, even when my cheek was close enough to feel the warmth of his back through his starched white shirt.

I worry that you will sneer at our first lovemaking, it was so strange. At least it was strange to me. I don't even know that I would call it making love in the traditional sense. I was naked, yes, there on my living room carpet. The curtains had been drawn, but I don't remember how.

The Bug Man stood over me and removed his own clothes with slow deliberation. He laid his shirt over the back of Robert's favorite armchair, the medal facing up, but dull in the darkened room. The belly that had pushed so firmly against the Bug Man's buttoned shirt was now free and surprisingly taut. After loosing his pants, he sat down on the chair to take them off.

The music, the humming had stopped, but I still couldn't look away from him. No, he wasn't handsome. God, he was certainly not even half as good-looking as Robert. The scent of him was stronger, and I could feel it working inside me. As I watched him he touched himself, while watching me.

"Are you there?" he said.

"I am here," I told him.

He laid himself down on top of me. Drowsy with the scent of him as I was, I recoiled from the prickliness of the hair on his legs and abdomen. In response, he held me closer. His kiss was harsh and thirsty, as though he would suck my body dry. I found myself responding, not minding that he was consuming me.

I tried to guide him inside of me, but he gently pushed my hand away and put his hand on himself once again. Another woman, another time, might have been insecure about what was happening. I've always been one to leave myself open to possibilities. Or maybe I just wasn't thinking straight.

Yes, I wanted him in the worst way. But I sensed that this affair—if that's what it was—was going to have different rules.

When he came, he buried his rough face in my neck, silent. I won't tell you what he did, next. Not yet.

*

Sometimes I think about my three children, and Robert. But I am more needed here. I am truly wanted here.

*

Robert was watching television and the children were sprawled over the second bed, their limbs tangled in the crisp white hotel sheets and around one another. Tow-headed angels.

I had left my phone in the car while I was in the house, but Robert hadn't called. He never imagined that he couldn't trust me.

I took a shower, marveling at the tingling abrasion of my abdomen and between my legs.

Please don't judge me. This situation with the Bug Man...it's not like me. It's not like me at all. I'm the mom who teaches Sunday School and never complains. I'm the mom who remembers teachers' birthdays and Grandparents Day and tips the waitress at Chili's a minimum of twenty percent. I know which of my kids doesn't like fabric softener on his clothes, and what kind of dental floss Robert prefers. At least, I was that kind of person. I can't help it that I've lost those feelings. I've lost my compassion for everyone but the Bug Man.

Some nights I hear Leeza and the Bug Man together, the way that Leeza must hear me with him. I hear her scolding the Little Ones when they're too insistent and greedy. Sometimes I hear her weeping when she is back in her room, gestating or just resting. Waiting.

I saw Leeza's husband in the grocery before I, too, came to the Bug Man. Their twelve-year-old daughter was pushing the grocery cart while her father chose cans of soup from the shelf. Of course, I didn't know then where Leeza was, but after making love with the Bug Man, I had come to suspect. Her husband didn't look so unhappy. Truth be told, Leeza had never been a very good wife. She took a lot of getaway weekends with girlfriends, leaving her family to fend for themselves. Plus, she drank a lot of wine.

After a few days, the abrasions went away, and I stopped putting Robert off when he wanted to have sex.

I couldn't stop thinking about the Bug Man. I called the pest control company for his address, pretending that I wanted to send him a thank you note for the excellent job he'd done. They insisted that they would get it to him if I sent it to their post office box. I wondered how many other women had called with the same request. They wouldn't even tell me his last name.

If he wanted to be with me, if he wanted me at all, wouldn't he have given me his number?

"What's up with you?" Robert asked. "You seem so angry all the time. Do you want to tell me? You're scaring the kids."

After two weeks, my clothes were loose on my body. I couldn't eat. The kids were sullen around me, preferring to cling to Robert when he was home. When Robert and I had sex, it hurt deep inside. I tried to hide it, but he could see the pain on my face, I know.

I cried with relief when I found the Bug Man's note on my windshield.

Did I know that when I kissed my children goodbye before leaving them at my mother's house that it would be for the last time? No. I swear.

The Bug Man met me in the lot of a playground I'd never been to before. I parked the minivan beside his white work truck. He smiled and touched the bill of his white, logoed baseball cap in greeting. I felt suddenly shy.

The playground was abandoned, but there was the scent of honeysuckle in the air.

Did I know it would be the last time I might smell something so pure, so lovely? Definitely not.

When I started out of the car with my purse, the Bug Man said, simply, "Leave it."

The Bug Man's house isn't hidden away, as you might think. It's in a cul-de-sac, on the edge of a large development, and isn't any different from the tidy, traditional houses on either side of it. The yard is always trimmed, and at night it's generously lighted with blazing flood lamps.

You might wonder why the Bug Man doesn't hide in the darkness, but it makes perfect sense if you think about it. Bugs are drawn to the light. A thousand moths beat themselves against the broad faces of the floods, June bugs scatter like marbles on the slats of the porch. They are there for the collecting.

Inside, the Bug Man asked me if I was hungry, but I was too nervous to eat. "A drink?" he said.

I took the amber glass he offered and we toasted. He looked at me with hesitation in his eyes, or maybe regret? He had loosened the top button of his shirt, which was not so vivid inside the house. There were fleshy circles beneath his eyes, and a skin tag at the corner of his right eyelid that I hadn't noticed before. I reached out and touched the patch of stiff hairs in the V of his shirt. Painful as they were, they were a part of coupling with him—and coupling was why I was there. In that place I had no other purpose or desire.

The Bug Man's bedroom was as luxurious a room as I had ever seen. Does this surprise you? Like me, maybe you thought that an exterminator would sleep in a tidy, plain room, a reflection of the neat efficiency of his uniform. I wasn't prepared for the plush nest of snowy-white comforters and pillows on the bed, or the silken net surrounding it, hung from the ceiling by a delicate brass hoop. The shades at the window filtered the sunlight, casting a warm glow throughout the room. The other furniture was simple: a tall armoire of Art Deco design, and a pair of beige leather chairs with a long table in between. In the middle of the table sat the box he had had with him at my house.

Was it a music box? As I approached it, I could hear the same humming that had filled my living room. When I reached out to open the lid, the Bug Man stayed my hand. Smiling, he gently steered me over to the bed, and secured the netting around us.

I have made you wait, I know. Now I will tell you, and yet I'm afraid it won't be the most shocking thing I'm going to share with you.

I hinted that the Bug Man did not penetrate me that first time—but that isn't quite the truth.

He did. He penetrated me with his hand, which held a soft white ball of his jism. Afterward, he gave me the kind of pleasure—orgasm after orgasm—that a subject might give a queen. Even Robert could learn from him.

*

I woke, startled from a dream in which I was training dogs for a shabby carnival. Opening my eyes, I saw the Bug Man, outlined by the harsh light from the outdoor floods, standing between the chairs at the other side of the room. I had slept until evening.

"What are you doing? What time is it?" I said. My jaw was stiff, my mouth clouded with the effect of all the honey mead I'd drunk.

"Come and see," the Bug Man said.

I tiptoed naked and unashamed across the inches-deep carpet.

Another woman might have been terrified to see what my lover had in that box. But I was filled with whatever strange fruit that had come from my lover's loins. I was filled with happiness, and the kind of curiosity that comes with new love.

The music from the box was nothing more than the sound of a thousand insects and spiders thrumming. They moved, but none were escaping over the edges of the box. Even the cave crickets seemed hobbled, stumbling blindly over the slow-moving caterpillars and fat beetles. Feeling my lover's delight, I shoved the revulsion I felt down into my gut, telling myself that they weren't so bad. People had worse hobbies. How strange, though, that he spent his days exterminating the same creatures that he now smiled over.

I remembered the transcendent look on his face that evening at my house, the way the box had hummed. There had been no chemicals, no cloud of poison that had rid my house of the creatures that I was so afraid of. It had been the Bug Man himself who had called them out. He had called them out and carried them away. How strange and wonderful!

I was about to put my arms around his waist in silent affection when I saw the things that he had really meant me to see. They were crawling across the table in a disorganized group, the tiniest lagging a couple of feet behind.

"Little Ones," he said.

Little Ones.

Calling them anything but an abomination—a word that implies I'm judging them, yes! I am judging them, and thus my lover—sent my mind into a frenzy. They were tiny monsters!

Of the dozen, the largest was as big as my lover's fist, its eight leathery legs the size of a toddler's slender fingers. But the legs were curved and bent like a crab's, each ending in a point much like a fingernail, so that they made a busy clicking sound as they hurried across the table. The furry brown body those legs carried was shaped into three parts, the rear large and bulbous, the center more oval, and the third...I am used to the Little Ones, now, but that first time I saw them, I felt like the end of the world had come, and I was the only sane witness left.

You've guessed, I'm sure. You understand that each Little One bears a perfect human head at its front, a head that is as human as yours or mine.

Beside me, the Bug Man stood over his brood, beaming with love. It was a look I'd never seen on his face before, and I knew I was nothing to him.

These *things* that were deftly climbing the sides the box, kicking back at their siblings to be the first to attack the feast inside, were his only love. They were his—God help me—children.

Yet I couldn't look away. The first, the largest, dove into the box and used its hand-like pedipalps to quickly grind the body of a cave cricket to a pulp before latching onto it with his pale pink lips.

I ran from the room wanting out! Out! Out! I could only think of getting beyond the front door, naked or not. It didn't matter what or who was waiting for me. Nothing could come close to the horror in that room.

And there was Leeza—or the woman who had once been Leeza—blocking my way to the front door. Leeza, looking tall and immovable. Her shining blonde hair had faded to a parched silver and her skin had turned the color of newsprint. Leeza of the expensive spray tan and the many bracelets. Leeza who drank wine spritzers and flirted with Robert thinking he would never dare to tell me. Leeza with the impish blue eyes. Leeza who had laid a hand on my arm in the grocery store as I reached for the organic bug spray. "Let me give you the name of my bug man," she said. "He's like magic." Had she been with him even before she saw me? I don't think so, but I might be wrong. She might have been lying in wait there in the cleaning chemicals aisle for me, or just someone like me. I haven't asked her because we don't often speak. We are too busy. Too worn. I don't think Leeza will live much longer.

The Bug Man was too occupied with his Little Ones to come after me. What did he care? Even if I had run away, who would have believed me?

"It's too late," Leeza said. She didn't sneer at me, or look angry. Her face was composed, and her eyes, bright and febrile, offered me pity. If she had glanced down at my belly or touched me, I might have screamed. Even in my panic, I knew she was right.

I had a friend who used to say that you can't rape the willing. I made the choice to follow my lover and sacrifice my old life. I try to be philosophical about it.

After Leeza gave me honeyed tea and calmed me down that night, she helped me into a comfortable set of clothes she brought from her own large collection in her room. Our lover isn't stingy. He tells me often how much he appreciates me, how he appreciates my sacrifice. He is anxious for the children we will have together. I've learned not to snap at him when he calls the Little Ones *children*.

My belly hasn't swelled, but I can feel my own Little Ones growing inside me. Leeza has told me how it will be: the tiny egg sacs fighting their way out of my body as though it were a battle for life and death, how a few are born with minuscule fangs and try to bite their way out. I think of my children by Robert, who were expelled from my womb without a fight and straight into the capable hands of a clinic-trained midwife. My children who are not helpless. They have Robert.

I watch Leeza when we are together during the day, the Little Ones clinging to her chest and neck. They make pleasing noises when they aren't fighting to be the one who is allowed to rest in the hollow of her collarbone.

"What would they do without me?" she says.

At night the Bug Man separates us, giving us each a chaste kiss before closing us in our well-furnished rooms. He takes the Little Ones downstairs, alone, unless he wants one of us along to watch the Little Ones feed.

If one of us is not wanted, we lie in our separate beds in our separate rooms, waiting.

If we're lonesome, we tap on the wall to each another.

"Are you there?"

"Yes, I am here."

Rooey

Kelly Luce

Since Rooey died, I'm no longer myself. Foods I've hated my entire life, I crave. Different things are funny. I've stopped wearing a bra. I bet they're thinking about firing me here at work, but they must feel bad, my brother so recently dead and all. Plus, I'm cheap labor, fresh out of college. And let's face it, the *Sweetwater Weekly* doesn't have the most demanding readership or publishing standards.

You can tell they're trying to be sensitive: along with the police blotter and wedding announcements, I'd covered obituaries; afterwards they gave the obituaries to Ryan the intern so I wouldn't have to think about death all day. I do anyway. Bloody violent death, wakes and funerals and the way a person's eyes look right before they die, how when you try to close them they don't stay closed like in the movies—they pop back open.

I've started adding things to the blotter, things that never happened but that he'd find funny, and the chimp wedding announcement I slipped in—photo included—didn't get caught until right before press.

A few days ago I tried logging into Rooey's email and got the password on the first guess. (It was "Miyazaki," his favorite animator. Rooey was obsessed with Japan. When we tagged our suitcases for Hawaii, he'd spelled his name "Rui." He'd even figured how to write his name in Japanese using the characters for "drifting" and "majesty.") Now I check his email all the time. I've just logged in when Myra, the assistant editor, comes by my cubicle. She's wearing the same man's button-down shirt as always.

"Hi, hon." Even when she smiles she keeps her lips pressed tightly together. I've never seen her teeth.

"Hi."

She opens her mouth and closes it like she's changed her mind about something. "Maxine, how are you *doing*?"

"Oh, you know. It's good to keep busy with real challenging tasks at work, like typing up wedding announcements."

She sighs and looks at me pityingly. "I wanted to talk to you about that."

I stare at the screen.

She lowers her voice. "I got your point with the monkey thing, okay? I thought it would be best to lighten your workload, but obviously that's not working. So, Maxine, how about a cover story?"

"Great." I empty Rooey's spam folder. The screen looks clean and expectant.

"Really?"

"Sure." My phone chimes, announcing the arrival of a text message.

She nods harder than necessary and says, "Well, great then! Why don't you think it over this week and we can chat about it on Friday. I'm sure you're full of ideas. Sound good?"

"Sounds great, thank you," I say, because that's what the old Maxine would've said. But now I guess I've just lost interest.

Here's a story: two people are in trouble and the wrong one dies. There's been a cosmic mix-up, but there's nothing anyone can do about it, and they all live sadly ever after. The end.

I snap open my phone and read Felix's message. It says "Uijoljoh pg zpv."

He's used this code before. The trick is that each letter is really the one before it. It says "thinking of you."

I write back "V 3" for "U 2," close the phone, and go back to my email.

*

I walk to Felix's after work. He rents a garden apartment which means he lives half-underground and there's not much light, but it's cheap. When we save enough we're supposed to get a place together, somewhere up high.

Back before Rooey started high school our family lived near here, across from the tracks on Burlington in a house with an aboveground pool and a pop-up camper that never moved from the backyard. Mom said she and Dad had used it all the time and that I'd taken a few trips in it too, but I don't remember them and by the time Rooey came along, Dad was gone and I didn't remember him, either.

There was a small door we could use to squeeze into the camper even when it wasn't popped up and we'd take turns locking one another inside. The object was to see how long we could stay in before getting scared and knocking to come out. We called the game Coffin. It was pitch-black inside the camper and the air was stuffy and smelled of hot wool.

I was five years older and generally humane, but once—I think I was mad because Mom had let Rooey get away with something, again—I didn't let him out when he gave the triple-knock. He tried again. There was a moment of silence that I took to be him getting pissed, and I laughed.

Then he started pounding, and after few seconds, screaming. I fumbled with the lock while the door shuddered. *"LEEEET MEEEE OOUUUUT!"*

"Hang *on*!"

When the door finally swung open my little brother fell out onto his side, his face white save for two spots of color on his cheeks. He stared at me in disbelief, his brown eyes watery.

When he stood and came at me, I didn't fight back. I let him flail his fists and scream himself hoarse. Eventually we played something else. He didn't tell Mom—he never did. That was the last time we played Coffin.

There are six stairs leading down to Felix's door. When I get to the bottom I'm always aware of how much of me is below ground. It's like a very wide grave, this apartment. Recently I've had to fight the urge to turn around and go back up.

Felix is cooking with his back to the door and doesn't hear me I come in. He's got his khakis on from work and no shirt. He has what he calls a "techie tan," which means he is white like recycled paper. He works at an Internet dating company fixing the employees' computers. He finds it exciting. He finds almost anything exciting. It's probably why I like him.

I watch his papery back at the stove and think, he is biodegradable. Then I think that his body mirrors the apartment, the bottom buried and the top exposed to light.

He turns and sees me and sings, "Ma-a-a-axine! You don't have to put on the red light!" He takes my face in his hands and kisses me loudly.

We have pesto for dinner and he talks about how he managed to solve three peoples' problems without even showing up at their cubicles.

"If people would just *troubleshoot*, it would save so much time. A simple logical process, that's all it takes!"

Since Rooey died, Felix has become even more enthusiastic, maybe to make up for my silences.

I tell him about the cover story. He wants to celebrate so we get in bed and drink a bottle of champagne under the covers.

"I'm feeling better."

"Yeah?"

"About Rooey."

"Good!"

"I think I'm getting over it. I think I'm done crying."

"Wow! Well. You know. Take your time. There's no time limit." He looks at me solemnly and I notice his pores. When did they get so big? On his nightstand, turned upside-down, is a book: *When a Loved One Grieves.*

"Have you thought any more about trying therapy?" he asks.

"Mm. Not my thing."

"I know you believe that, but how can you know if you don't try?"

"I'd rather not talk about this stuff right now." I slip my hand in his boxers. I could care less about sex with Felix lately and now is no different, but at least it will shut him up.

I wonder how he'll react if I tell him to fuck me, so I whisper it—"I want you to fuck me"—and he blushes; we've never used this word before and I realize he doesn't necessarily know how it differs from what we usually do, what he always refers to as "making love." But he gives it a shot. He gets on top of me, sticks it in, and buries his face in my neck, biting me, I think, though I can't be sure.

"Harder," I tell him, squirming a bit, and he tries to pin my arms over my head while holding himself up with one hand, but he loses balance and folds down on top of me.

His face finds my armpit for a second and his nose wrinkles up.

I sniff under my arm. "Whew. Kind of manly, I know."

"No big deal."

"I've been using Rooey's deodorant."

"Oh." He pauses, traces my bellybutton with his middle finger. "Why?"

"Works better. And it doesn't smell like flowers."

"What's wrong with flowers?"

I shrug. "They're so *girly*."

We fall asleep. I dream I'm alone, bobbing in a black sea. I don't know which way to swim and the bottom's miles below. A fin appears in the distance. I swim away from it, but it catches up and as it gets closer I see it's Rooey, and I see in his eyes that he hates me. I watch helplessly as he speeds closer, teeth and gums bared, and when he finally reaches me there's a flare of heat in my neck, and afterwards a sensation like dissolving. Only when I give in, do I wake up. That giving in is a release so powerful I find myself sitting up in bed, heaving. That giving in is the saddest feeling in the world.

*

It's been three months and three days. Mom hasn't touched up her strawberry blonde dye job since the attack and the dark roots are like a measuring stick: her grief is lengthening. She sleeps all morning and spends her afternoons shopping and preparing elaborate dinners. She cooks things Rooey liked—curry pork, eggplant parmesan. I've come to find comfort in this and, for once in my life, I eat everything on my plate. Mom is the opposite. Once, after filling our plates with salmon ragout, she sat down and stared at the table's empty seats, two of them now, as if she were expecting guests who were running late. I had no words to offer up; I shoveled down the over-salted food and sat there as long as I could stand it, then stood and cleared her untouched plate.

While Rooey looked just like dad, I resemble no one. My face is a little of this, little of that, like a meal thrown together last-minute. When we ran into old friends of my parents', they would make a fuss over Rooey. "A carbon copy of Dean," Mom would say, mussing my brother's blonde, moppy curls. Then they'd turn to me and joke about the milkman.

School was my redemption. In high school I was a member of the National Honor Society, Vice-President of the Ecology Club, and a varsity swimmer. When Rooey and mom came to my swim meets they'd always sit in the same place, at the top of the bleachers, laughing and eating Reese's Pieces. Tearing through the water on the final leg of a race, I would think of them watching me and swim harder, muscles screaming, knowing that if I won, I would for a moment be the focus; I would fill that tiny space between them.

At the wake, I talked about taking Rooey for driving practice last Christmas. For a kid who liked cars so much, he was a horrible driver. He made a joke out of it. Before leaving the house he'd preface everything with, "Allah willing." It was an expression he picked up from a movie. "When we come back from driving, Allah willing, let's get Mom to take us to Culver's." "Allah willing, I'm gonna parallel-park this baby, *hard*." It was a testament to Rooey's good nature that he was able to mock himself, I said; even more than that, though, he never seemed to get discouraged. He had confidence in life; he never whined. The part about "Allah willing" got a laugh.

What I didn't talk about was how mad I'd been when Mom told me I'd have to give Rooey my car when I moved out. The Nissan had been a hand-me-down from my grandparents, and I'd had it less than a year. I never had a car when I was his age, I argued. It wasn't *fair*.

But Rooey solved the problem—he didn't want my car. He wanted an old Thunderbird and he got a job helping Roger, a Buddhist hippie guy who lived down the block, in his metalwork shop to earn the money for it. He was a hard kid to resent, and for that, I have to admit, I resented him even more.

*

Rooey's door has been closed since I got back from Hawaii. Mom's not ready to open it yet. "It's too much of him at once," she told me, crying at the mere mention of his name. But me, I can't get enough. I've been coming in here every night. I lay in bed and wait until the sleeping pills I stole from Mom kick in, then creep over the cracked parquet to his room, my feet instinctively avoiding the creaky spots that, when we were little, would give us away as we snuck into the kitchen after brushing our teeth for a handful of Reese's Pieces from the green jar.

The room is stuffy and smells vaguely of peanut butter. When he was in grade school, Rooey had insisted on painting his walls to look like outer space; I had painted Jupiter and Neptune, and Rooey'd done the rest, except Earth, which Mom did, and after the paint dried Rooey etched our tiny trio in ballpoint pen where he approximated Indiana to be. There's a tiny chip of paint missing where my head once was.

I flop down onto his bed and try to imagine what it was like to be him.

Rooey'd had something of a girlfriend, though we never called her that; she was just "his friend." Lily. Her parents came here from Japan right before she was born, and gave her a name neither of them could pronounce. Once I walked in on Rooey and her together, in bed. Or rather *on* the bed—they lay belly-up beside one another, Lily's arms at her sides, the hand nearest Rooey touching both her leg and his. Rooey's hands were folded atop his stomach. They both stared at the ceiling.

She was a strange-looking girl, with a tiny pucker of a mouth and hair to her waist. Her eyes and nose were just little pinches too, and you wondered how her head didn't tip back under the weight of all that hair. She had braces—maybe that helped balance things out. At the funeral she cried and covered not her eyes but her mouth.

The entire night passes this way, me, flat on his bed as if afloat, my mind full of details, all the questions I'd never thought to ask him: what was happening with Lily, and whether he had a clue what he was doing; how his job was going at the metalworking shop; was he any good at the work?

The stucco swirls above me, lit by the half moon outside. Then that spot of ceiling, that personal place where the eyes rest when you're thinking in the dark, whispers answers:

Things with Lily were slow moving, excruciating, thrilling; they'd French-kissed once after school and it tasted salty; if he were still alive, he'd take her to see a movie when he got his T-Bird. When things got serious, he'd make her something in the metal shop, a figurine of some kind, and give it to her for her birthday. He was good at transferring the molds and pouring and measuring and scraping, all the intricate business of making casts. He had the patience for it.

When the first gray light struggles into the room I open my eyes, or maybe it just feels like I'm opening them, since I haven't really slept. I wouldn't call what I do in this room at night "sleep." It's more like a nocturnal hypnosis that only clears when the sun comes snapping its fingers.

I stand up and go to the closet. CD album covers shingle the door and partially obscure the mirror hanging there. At eye level is the cover for the Vapor's "Turning Japanese" single I gave Rooey for Christmas last year.

I pull the door open and cool, sour-smelling air drifts out. Rooey's favorite T-shirt hangs crooked on a wooden hanger. The shirt is gray and is noticeably shorter than the other shirts that hang there. The turquoise lettering on the front says POCARI SWEAT. He'd come home from school late one day, having stopped and bought it at Teed Off, the T-shirt place downtown. He said he'd looked online—he was always looking up something online—and read that Pocari Sweat was like Japanese Gatorade, and when he called Lily and told her about it she'd laughed and laughed; Rooey held the phone away from his ear and I could hear her from across the room.

I yank the shirt from its hanger and put it on. Then I lie on the bed and slide two fingers under the waist of my panties.

I don't fantasize anymore when I masturbate. It's just a lot of furious rubbing, no imagination required, though sometimes towards the end an image of Lily, sunbathing naked, pops into my mind. Before Rooey died, my orgasms had come in sweet, rolling waves. Now they're like squalls, the pleasure almost violent.

Afterwards I think about my cover story. There was a time, I realize, when I fantasized about this opportunity—my name on the front page, a color photo illustrating my words—but the ideas I used to toss around aren't appealing anymore. Profile piece on the owner of Ambrosia, the green grocer? A report on the solar-powered nunnery out in Teastown? When did I ever find *that* interesting? For a moment I think it'd be cool to write something on the guy in town with the Porsche Carrera GT. A half-million dollar car in this town—now *that's* news.

I close my eyes and imagine I'm driving an incredibly fast car on a circular track, around and around, on the brink of losing control.

*

The trip to Hawaii had been a graduation gift from my grandma. I'd taken classes over the previous two summers in order to graduate early and hadn't left the Midwest since I could remember. I'd chosen to bring Rooey over Felix because, as I saw it, Rooey and I were at the end of our shared childhood. Soon I'd be moving out for good, leaving him for the real world. I wanted to hang on to that life just a little longer.

They tell me I did the right thing, swimming ashore and yelling for help, but I don't remember this. I remember sounds: a scream, a moan, then the sloshing of water like kids in a bathtub; I could hear children calling to one another on the sand, a game of Red Rover, while Rooey's head went under and his forearm drifted away from blonde hair that clung to the surface; the fingers that had reached up from the bottom bunk brushed my abdomen while I watched ragged strips of tissue jet blood. I remember turning and swimming away. That I headed for the shore was purely coincidence.

*

I must have dozed off, because when I open my eyes a few hours have passed and I'm thinking of Lily. Her long dark hair, and the way she locks eyes with you when she laughs. My chest aches, and I realize: I miss her.

It's a weird feeling, missing someone I barely know, yet when I think about it seems odd that I'd feel any other way. Why don't I go for a visit? I look around the room for something to bring her. I look down and—that's it—I'll give her shirt—the shirt she'd found so funny!

I walk there, swinging the CVS bag that holds the T-shirt. I'm walking quickly, looking up at the clouds as I go, wondering what Lily will have to say, and whether she'll be glad to see me. A car horn blasts. I jump back and a woman in a Jeep waves me across the street I'd been about to step into. I hustle across, blushing. I'm glad to have an excuse to rush, and I jog the last block to Lily's house.

Mrs. Mizukami answers the door. She's wearing bright orange slippers. Her mouth drops open at the sight of me, and she keeps a hand on the doorknob as I remind her who I am, though of course we've met before. I hold up the bag, full of nervous energy. She ushers me into a dim living room full of ferns, and looks at me with sad eyes. I want to say, don't be sad! Things are going to be fine, really!

Mrs. Mizukami leads me into the kitchen, where Lily is seated at the table, doing homework.

She scoots her chair back when she sees me and stands up. I can tell she's surprised, and I say so.

"Yeah!" she says, taking me in. "But, you know, in a good way." She doesn't say anything else.

Mrs. Mizukami sets a glass of iced tea and a plate of cookies on the table. "Please, sit," she says, and we do. She shuffles out the room.

"I'm sorry I interrupted your homework," I say. "I should have called."

"Nah, it's okay." Lily pushes an open textbook away and leans both elbows on the table. "Math sucks anyway."

I ask her about school. I watch her mouth move as she answers, then follow the smooth line of her hair down, over her small breasts, to where it puddles in her lap, like a waterfall. I want to touch it.

"Are you okay?" She leans back.

"Yeah, sorry." I blush, and fish for something an older sister would say. "Your hair's great. I wish I could grow mine that long."

She makes a face and bats her hair back, then picks up a pair of red-handled scissors from the table. "I think I'm gonna chop it."

"What? No! It—it's so pretty."

"Whatever. It's been long my whole life." She gathers a fistful. "Time for something new."

She slides the scissors open, brings the blades to her hair. "Very funny," I say.

She's watching me, eyes wide, and then snaps the scissors shut. I lurch out of my chair to stop her, but she moves the blades at the last second.

"I made you pretty nervous," she says, grinning.

"You had me for a second. Well, maybe a half-second."

"Well, I still might do it." She pulls a few strands forward and really does snip them off. We watch them float to the ground. She says, "It could be like...an offering."

"But—wouldn't he want you to keep it?"

She shrugs. "He's not here to ask."

I look at the hair on the floor and am seized by a desire to pinch it up and hold onto it forever. Then I remember the shirt. I grab for the bag and dump out the T-shirt in front of her. "So, I brought this for you. I thought you might like to have it."

She stares at the balled-up fabric and bites her lip. She blinks back tears, and I lean over and hug her tight. I close my eyes. We rock together, her head on my shoulder and my face in her hair. It feels wonderful. I move my hand on her back, hold her tighter.

"Can I—" Mrs. Mizukami slippers back into the kitchen. Lily and I spring apart like two kids caught necking.

"Beg your pardon," Mrs. Mizukami says, bowing slightly and backing out of the room. "I just wondered if I could give you more food."

"No, Mom," Lily says.

"No thank you," I say as she leaves, and though I haven't touched them I call, "The cookies are delicious, though."

Lily and I look at each other. She looks at her lap.

"I should get going," I say.

"Thank you," she says, standing up, grasping the shirt with one fist.

At the front door, I put my shoes on and say goodbye to Mrs. Mizukami. Lily steps outside with me.

"It's nice to see you," she says. "Just, you know, a surprise. Sorry I'm all crying and stuff. I mean, he was *your* brother."

"It's good to see you too. Someone he was close to, who he really liked. He was *very* picky about people, you know." We laugh; she sniffles and catches my eye.

"I dunno, this is weird, but when you walked in, I thought it was him. I could've sworn it. Isn't that messed up?"

"I think I see him all the time."

She touches her hair. "I just…miss him."

I think of them lying on the narrow bed together, touching without acknowledging it, and think of me lying there with her instead, what that might feel like. I want to tell her this, but what would I say?

She's looking at me again, really focusing, like she's looking for something she dropped. She takes a deep breath and hands me the shirt.

"You should really keep this."

I say no and reach for it anyway.

"Really, I'm definitely sure." Her eyes are watering, her tiny nose pink, as she backs into the door. It's shut, and she fumbles for the handle while keeping her eyes on me.

"Thanks again." She turns the handle and takes a step backwards, into the shadows. "I'll see you around."

"Yeah," I say, and force a grin, a wave with the shirt. "Allah willing!"

I walk home slowly. It's only September, but the sidewalk's already full of leaves that crunch underfoot. It seems like the leaves are always falling. I don't know how the trees keep up.

*

It's Friday. My meeting with Myra is not going well.

"I'm not saying the story on Metalfest is a bad idea," she's saying. "At all. Just not right for our *readership*."

I can tell she's not wearing a bra under her light blue blouse. I wonder what her nipples look like.

"How about the comic book convention?"

"Well, I mean, it *could* work, my only concern is that, well, it raises the same issue as the music festival. Japanese comic books are certainly popular these days, but for most of our subscribers..." She licks her lips, slowly. Her tongue is plump and pink and her lips shine.

"You know," she continues when I don't respond, "didn't you mention something once about a profile of that lady who owns Ambrosia?"

Something is happening inside me, a wild building energy like a wave.

The AP report had read like a Mad Libs:

"Died of blood loss." Nope: Cardiac arrest.

"Swimming alone." Wrong: It could've been me.

"The victim was sixteen years old." Wrong again: he was fifteen. If he'd been sixteen, he probably would've stayed home, peeling around corners with his friends in his Thunderbird. He'd be a different person. He'd be alive.

"Oh, fuck it," I say. "Fuck journalism."

Myra jerks back in her chair.

"I don't give a shit," I say. I get up and walk away, all the way to the door, and out into the blinding afternoon sunlight.

*

On the drive home I get a text from Felix. "rinned ta iva lebla?" it says. I've been avoiding Felix since our awkward night in bed and whatever the message means—probably an invitation of some sort—I'm not in the mood to figure it out. "Call u later," I respond.

When I get home, Mom's not there. I go to Rooey's room, the only place that really feels like my own anymore.

The shelves are lined with Japanese comics and language learning manuals. I slide one of the thin books from the shelf. In the cover illustration a blue-haired, starry-eyed girl holding a red ball reaches out to a boy swathed in tentacles. The boy's teeth are clenched; his face fierce. The girl is saying, "Swallow this orb to reverse the spell!" The title is *101 Japanese Phrases You'll Never Use.*

My phone rings: Myra. I don't pick up and she leaves a voice-mail suggesting that I take a week off, "to think things over." She wants me to know that I am in everyone's prayers. As soon as I'm done listening to her message, Felix beeps in and I answer without thinking.

"Hey," he says. "You didn't call."

"Oh yeah. Sorry. I got sidetracked."

He's silent for a second, then says, "Did you figure out my text?"

"Oh. No, I forgot."

"Aw. Well I was suggesting dinner at Via Bella. We haven't been there since our anniversary. I'm going through withdrawal." He laughs.

"Ah."

"It was an anagram," he adds.

I pick up Rooey's guitar, a red electric with frets worn down past the grain.

"Can I call you back in a few minutes?"

"Sure, babe."

I hang up and cradle the guitar. Despite all my accomplishments in school, music has always eluded me. Band's the only activity I've ever quit.

But Rooey's guitar feels right. Its slim weight against my chest is a comfort and the curved wood nestles into my thigh. The neck is thin and the strings soft. I know no chords but find it soothing to close my eyes and let my hands wander, the smooth wood grain cradling my fingertips, and occasionally I hit upon a combination of strings that sounds like a choir.

When it gets too late to have dinner Felix texts me, *Are you okay?* I pick up *101 Japanese Phrases You'll Never Use*, open it to a random page, and respond back with the first sentence I see: *Ebi wa dashi ni yuukan na tatakaimasu ne!*

It means: How valiantly the shrimp struggle in the broth!

*

They'd held Mass at my grandparents' church. While the deacon said things like, "The Lord takes first whom he loves best," and "To die young is a blessing," images of that day slideshowed through my mind—Rooey's head, just above water, snapping back on his neck, Rooey's eyes wide and black as he had looked at me that last time, while I treaded water a few feet away. I wondered if he knew he was dying, that when he closed his eyes on the pain, they would never reopen. I thought of this as the deacon droned, as my mother's pale jaw clenched and unclenched, her eyes like ice—she had not cried yet—and I stood up in the pew and whispered, "Bullshit."

My voice rang through the church. I began to sob, and the sound echoed off the rafters and the stained glass window where

Jesus hung on the cross with a trickle of blood on his palm and a serene smile on his face.

Him, not me, though I was just ten feet away. Him, not me, though it had been my idea to swim out that far in a race we both knew I'd win. Not me, though I'd been on my period that day. It doesn't take much blood to draw a shark.

I stood there, shaking, everything in slow motion, while the deacon wrapped up the homily, in his calm gravelly voice, and I only began to move when he descended from the podium. He never looked in our direction. When I sat down, my mother shed her first tear.

*

I'm still playing the guitar when there's a knock on the front door. I go to answer it: Felix. He looks worried.

"Hey," he says. What's going on?"

I shrug.

"Can I come in?"

I let him in and lead him into Rooey's room. We sit on the bed and he looks around. His gaze stops on me. I don't meet his eyes. It's not a comfortable silence, but it's not uncomfortable, either.

"I've never been in here before."

"I like it here."

"I realized that message was in Japanese, Romanized, so I translated it but I don't know if I got the words all right because sometimes there are a few different meanings for the same word."

"Good job," I say, and pick up the guitar. I strum indiscriminately and he starts rubbing my back. Then he gives me a series of small pats, like I'm a baby he's burping.

Finally I say, "I saw Lily today."

"Oh yeah? Where at?"

"Her house."

"You went over there? That was nice. How is she?"

Cute, I want to say. Crazy cute and wonderful. Instead I say, "I can see the attraction."

"That's good, I guess. Did you talk much about Rooey?"

"A little."

"She misses him too. It's good to talk about it."

He takes my hand, kisses it. Then I'm crying, sobbing into my palms. "She's going to cut off all her hair." I sniffle.

"Who is?"

"Lil-Lily."

"I see." He hugs me tighter. "Let it all out."

"I don't want to move in together."

We sit in silence after that. After a while I notice he's crying, too.

"It's not your fault," I say.

"No, no. You're confused right now," he said. "This *is* my fault, I shouldn't have tried to be so cheery. I'm going to find some help for you. A therapist, or a group or something."

"I feel sick," I say, and I do.

"Do you want something to drink?"

"I think I'll just lie down. I'll give you a call later on."

"You want me to go?"

I nod. "I'll call you."

"If it's what you really want. Is it?"

I nod, yes, yes. He's barely out the door when I start to gag. I run to the bathroom, where I empty my stomach of water and some half-chewed bread. It feels good to do that, to cleanse myself of the unnecessary. Afterwards I call Lily, but there's no answer. I leave a message: Thanks for today. If you ever need to talk, or want company, please give me a call. I really hope you will.

*

The cotton of this shirt is worn so thin it's silky. I catch a glimpse of myself in the mirror. Lily was right. I do resemble him.

My hair has gotten lighter. From being out in the sun, Felix says. It's also developed a wave for the first time in my life.

I remember something Felix told me, something out of his book: "Grieving and healing go hand-in-hand. Cut yourself a wide swath. Things *will* get better."

"Fuck that," I say to the mirror. "I don't give a flying fuck if I get *better*." I like that, "a flying fuck." Rooey used to say that.

"*Fuck* getting better. The sooner I get better, the sooner someone else is going to die."

It could've been me, and maybe it should've. After all, it was my scent in the water. It was my idea to race. It was my graduation trip.

Could've been me, should've been me. Hell—maybe it *was* me. I look in the mirror. Are my eyes getting darker? I lean in close to the mirror. Brown speckles the blue.

I sink to the floor. The boards creak.

True: I have not had my period since the attack.

True: I haven't slept in days.

True: I no longer desire anything. Well, no, that's not exactly true. I am horny as hell.

From the floor I can see under the bed. There are so few things under there, I can count them. Seven—eight, if you count each hockey skate. Two shoeboxes, a sock, an orange peel, a measuring tape, an unopened bottle of Corona.

I reach my foot under the bed and nudge the big shoebox toward me, the one that had originally housed the hockey skates. It's heavy. Stuff clinks around inside. Tools, maybe.

I lift the lid, feeling ceremonious.

The box is filled to the brim with figurines. The ones Roger makes in the metal shop, little Buddhist statues about an inch tall—what are they called again?

(Jizo)

Juzu? Something like that?

(Jizo)

I close my eyes and the explanation comes: *They're called jizo. Like a combination of Jesus and Bozo.*

Jizo.

I pick one up and examine its face. Two crescents arch across the smooth metal face to form eyes. The ears are overlong; the earlobe grows out of the jaw.

I think they have something to do with Buddhism, but beyond that, I have no idea. I set the figurine down and fetch my laptop.

The online encyclopedia tells me that translated from Japanese, *jizo* means "earth treasury" or "earth womb." "Traditionally," says the article, "jizo are seen as the guardians of travelers, firefighters, and children."

Children. I should bring one to Lily. Lily would like one.

I read on: "In particular, jizo are said to tend to the souls of miscarried or aborted fetuses, or any child who precedes his parents in death. It is said that children who die in this manner are not allowed to cross the sacred river to heaven as penance for the pain they have caused their parents."

If I focus all my willpower I can bring him back, I think, staring at the jizo's sleepy face. I just have to want it enough.

I focus on the statue's face so long it begins to move. It wriggles in my palm and the lips move to speak but before I hear the words, Mom's voice cuts in. She is standing in the doorway. What she says is, "Hi, sweetie."

"Look," I whisper, holding out the statue. "Did you know? He's the guardian of children."

Without a word she crosses the room, wraps her arms around me from behind, and begins sobbing into my hair. In the mirror I watch as she clutches at my hair, pulling and twisting, and each time she releases a handful it is blonder and wavier than before.

I close my eyes. I'm kicking through clear, warm waves, my throat and nose stinging from salt water. I'm already a few lengths behind her. Then I feel a sudden, massive presence beneath me, its skin like sandpaper as it shoots past my leg. Dark stripes. The pain in my shoulder like a star exploding. I open my eyes and my vision is blurry, like that of a newborn. For a second I smell the hot wool of the old camper.

"Oh, Rooey," she says. "What are we going to do without her?"

I hug her back without turning away from the mirror. I gaze at our reflection, her arms around the figure in the gray T-shirt.

"It's okay," I whisper. "I'm not going anywhere. I'm going to stay right here."

Author Bios

Laura Benedict is the author of five novels of dark suspense, including *Charlotte's Story* and *Bliss House*, the first books of the Bliss House trilogy. Her work has also appeared in *Ellery Queen Mystery Magazine, PANK*, and numerous anthologies like *Thrillers: 100 Must-Reads*. With Pinckney Benedict, she originated and edited the *Surreal South* anthology series. She lives with her family in Southern Illinois. Visit laurabenedict.com to learn more.

Paula Bomer is the author of the novel *Nine Months* of which *Library Journal* warns, "Mommy Lit Lovers will be horrified" and the collection, *Baby and Other Stories* (Word Riot Press, 2010), which received a starred review in *Publisher's Weekly*. *O Magazine* put it as number one in their "Titles to Pick Up Now" calling it a "brilliant, brutally raw debut collection." Her most recent collection, *Inside Madeleine*, came out in 2014. She grew up in South Bend, Indiana and now lives in New York. Find out more about her at paulabomer.com.

Karen Brown is the author of a novel, *The Longings of Wayward Girls,* and two collections of stories—*Little Sinners and Other Stories*, which was named a Best Book of 2012 by *Publishers Weekly*, and *Pins and Needles: Stories*, which was the recipient of AWP's Grace Paley Prize for Short Fiction. Her work has been featured in *The PEN/O. Henry Prize Stories*, *Best American Short Stories*, *The New York Times*, and *Good Housekeeping*. She teaches creative writing and literature at the University of South Florida.

Shannon Cain's short stories have been awarded the O. Henry Prize, twice the Pushcart Prize, and a fellowship from the NEA. Her short story collection, *The Necessity of Certain Behaviors*, won the 2011 Drue Heinz Literature Prize. She lives in Paris.

Kim Chinquee is the author of the collections *Oh Baby* and *Pretty*, and the chapbook *Pistol*. Her work has been published in *NOON, The Pushcart Prize XXXI: Best of the Small Presses, The Nation, The Huffington Post, Conjunctions, Denver Quarterly, Fiction, Mississippi Review, Best of the Web 2010*, *Ploughshares, StoryQuarterly, Indiana Review*, and several other places. She is an associate professor of English at Buffalo State College, and an associate editor for *New World Writing*. Her website is www.kimchinquee.com.

Monica Drake is the author of the novels *Clown Girl* and *The Stud Book* and a story collection, *The Folly of Loving Life* (Future Tense Books). Her stories and essays have been published in *Spork, Oregon Humanities Magazine, Northwest Review, Beloit Fiction Journal* and other publications. She currently teaches at the Pacific NW College of Art in Portland, Oregon.

Kathy Fish's stories have been published in *Guernica, Indiana Review, The Denver Quarterly*, and elsewhere. She guest edited Dzanc Books' *Best of the Web 2010* and has published three collections of short fiction: *A Chapbook in A Peculiar Feeling of Restlessness: Four Chapbooks of Short Short Fiction by Four Women* (Rose Metal Press, 2008), *Wild Life* (Matter Press, 2011), and *Together We Can Bury It* (The Lit Pub, 2013). She blogs at kathy-fish.com.

Amina Gautier is the author of the short story collections *At-Risk, Now We Will Be Happy, and The Loss of All Lost Things*. *At-Risk* was awarded the Flannery O'Connor Award; *Now We Will Be Happy* was awarded the Prairie Schooner Book Prize in Fiction, and *The Loss of All Lost Things* was awarded the Elixir

Press Fiction Award. Gautier teaches in the Department of English at the University of Miami.

Tina May Hall lives in upstate New York where she teaches creative writing at Hamilton College. Her collection *The Physics of Imaginary Objects* won the 2010 Drue Heinz Literature Prize and was published by the University of Pittsburgh Press. Her stories have appeared in *Quarterly West, Black Warrior Review, The Collagist, Fourth River,* and other literary magazines.

Nancy Hightower's short fiction and poetry has been published in *Strange Horizons, Word Riot, storySouth, Gargoyle, Interfictions, Prick of the Spindle,* and *A cappella Zoo,* among others. Her debut novel *Elementarí Rising* came out with Pink Narcissus Press in 2013. Her short story collection *Kinds of Leaving* was shortlisted for the Flann O'Brien Award for Innovative Fiction in 2014, and two stories from that collection won first place and honorable mention in *Prick of the Spindle's* Open Fiction Competition. She currently reviews science fiction and fantasy for *The Washington Post.* You can see more of her work at Nancyhightower.com

Jessica Hollander's story collection *In These Times the Home is a Tired Place* won the 2013 Katherine Anne Porter Prize and was published by the University of North Texas Press. Her stories have appeared in many journals, including *The Cincinnati Review, The Normal School, The Journal,* and *Sonora Review* and most recently the *Georgia Review, Redivider, Bat City Review,* and *Hotel Amerika.* She received her MFA from the University of Alabama and teaches at the University of Nebraska at Kearney. Visit her at jessicahollanderwriter.com.

Holly Goddard Jones is the author of a novel, *The Next Time You See Me,* and a story collection, *Girl Trouble.* She teaches in the MFA program at UNC Greensboro.

Stacey Levine is the author of four books of fiction. Her story collection *The Girl With Brown Fur,* which was long-listed for The Story Prize, was also short-listed for the Washington State Book Award in 2012. Her novel *Frances Johnson* was short-listed for the Washington State Book Award in

2005. Her first collection, *My Horse and Other Stories*, won a PEN/West Fiction Award. Her work received a Stranger Genius Literature award in 2009. A Pushcart Prize nominee, her fiction has appeared in the *Denver Quarterly*, *Fence*, *Tin House*, *The Fairy Tale Review*, *The Iowa Review*, *The Notre Dame Review*, *Yeti*, and other venues.

Kelly Luce's story collection, *Three Scenarios in Which Hana Sasaki Grows a Tail*, won the 2013 Foreword Review's Editors Choice Prize in Fiction. Her work has appeared in *O Magazine*, *The Chicago Tribune*, *Salon*, *Electric Literature*, *The Southern Review*, and other magazines. She's the editorial assistant for the O. Henry Prize anthology and editor-in-chief of *Bat City Review*. Her debut novel, *Pull Me Under*, is forthcoming from Farrar, Straus, and Giroux. She hails from Illinois and lives in Santa Cruz, California.

Nina McConigley was born in Singapore and grew up in Wyoming. She is the author of the story collection *Cowboys and East Indians*, winner of the 2014 PEN Open Book Award and a High Plains Book Award. Her work has appeared in *The New York Times*, *The Virginia Quarterly Review*, *American Short Fiction*, *Salon*, *Slice*, *Asian American Literary Review*, *Puerto del Sol*, and others. She teaches at the University of Wyoming.

Janet Mitchell's debut collection, *The Creepy Girl and Other Stories*, won the 5th annual Starcherone Prize, as chosen by Lance Olsen. She garnered her Master of Fine Arts in Fiction from Columbia University, where she was the Bingham Scholarship recipient. She won the Hob Broun Prize for her fiction, and her short stories have appeared in such literary journals as *Gargoyle Magazine*, *The Brooklyn Rail*, and *The Quarterly*, and have been optioned by Lifetime Television and independent producers. She earned her Master of Fine Arts in Film Production at USC. Here she won the John Huston Award for her directing and a Paramount Pictures Fellowship for her writing. Her work as a writer-director includes the award-winning short "How Does Anyone Get Old?" starring Mark Ruffalo, Mina Badie, Gregg Rainwater and Melissa Lechner.

Alissa Nutting's debut novel, *Tampa*, was published by Ecco/HarperCollins in 2013. She is also the author of the short story collection, *Unclean Jobs for Women and Girls* (Starcherone/Dzanc 2010), which won the Starcherone Prize for Innovative Fiction judged by Ben Marcus. Her fiction has or will appear in publications such as *The Norton Introduction to Literature, Tin House, Bomb,* and *Conduit*; her essays have appeared in *Fence, The New York Times, O: The Oprah Magazine,* and other venues.

Ethel Rohan's debut novel, *The Kingdom Keeper,* will be published by St. Martin's Press in early 2017. She is also the author of two story collections, *Goodnight Nobody* and *Cut Through the Bone,* the former longlisted for The Edge Hill Prize, and the latter named a Notable Story Collection by The Story Prize. Winner of the Bryan MacMahon Short Story Award and shortlisted for several other awards, her work has or will appear in *The New York Times, World Literature Today, PEN America, Tin House Online, BREVITY Magazine,* and *The Rumpus,* among many others. Born in Ireland, she lives in San Francisco.

Richard Thomas is the award-winning author of seven books—*Disintegration* and *Breaker* (Random House Alibi), *Transubstantiate, Staring Into the Abyss, Herniated Roots, Tribulations,* and *The Soul Standard* (Dzanc Books). His over 100 stories in print include *Cemetery Dance, PANK, storySouth, Gargoyle, Weird Fiction Review, Midwestern Gothic, Arcadia, Qualia Nous, Chiral Mad 2,* and *Shivers VI.* He is also the editor of four anthologies: *The New Black* and *Exigencies* (Dark House Press), *The Lineup* (Black Lawrence Press) and the Bram Stoker-nominated *Burnt Tongues* (Medallion Press) with Chuck Palahniuk. In his spare time he writes for LitReactor and is Editor-in-Chief at Dark House Press. For more information visit www.whatdoesnotkillme.com or contact Paula Munier at Talcott Notch.

Karin Tidbeck is the award-winning author of *Jagannath: Stories* and the novel *Amatka.* She lives and works in Malmö, Sweden, where she makes a living as a freelance writer. She writes in Swedish and English, and has published work in *Weird Tales, Tor.com, Words Without Borders* and the anthologies *Steampunk Revolution* and *The Time-Travelers Almanac.*

Damien Angelica Walters' work has appeared or is forthcoming in various anthologies and magazines, including *The Year's Best Dark Fantasy & Horror 2015, Year's Best Weird Fiction: Volume One, The Mammoth Book of Cthulhu: New Lovecraftian Fiction, Nightmare Magazine, Black Static,* and *Apex Magazine*. She was a finalist for a Bram Stoker Award for "The Floating Girls: A Documentary," originally published in *Jamais Vu. Sing Me Your Scars,* a collection of short fiction, was released in 2015 from Apex Publications, and *Paper Tigers,* a novel, is forthcoming in 2016 from Dark House Press.

Claire Vaye Watkins was born in Death Valley and raised in the Nevada desert. She has been named one of the National Book Foundation's "Five Under 35" fiction writers of 2012. Her work has appeared in *Granta, The Paris Review, The Hopkins Review, Hobart, One Story, Ploughshares,* and *Las Vegas Weekly*. She is an assistant professor at Bucknell University in Lewisburg, Pennsylvania.

100 Women to Watch

Why did some women get into the collection and others only make this list? Well, first, I had to draw the line someplace, right? Also, I wanted to focus on emerging authors, so in order to whittle the list down I looked for a couple of things. First, if an author had already "emerged" in my opinion, then they were too "big" to make the final 20. (Of course a lot has happened since this anthology was started.) Second, I wanted the final 20 to have some meat on the bone, material that you, the reader, could find if you fell in love with their work (as I'm sure you have by now). So I wanted authors that had AT LEAST one novel or short story collection out. Many of the authors on this list do not—yet (or not when we started this project). I also wanted to focus on short fiction, so women that write only novels, or non-fiction, or poetry, I didn't consider for the final 20 authors. And beyond that, it was really just my familiarity with their work, and whether they moved me—strictly a subjective and personal opinion, no doubt.

—RT

A

Abbott, Megan—*Dare Me* and *The Fever*, novels

Avasthi, Su—"Greedy, Greedy" in *Men Undressed*

B

Baylee, Eden—*Fall Into Winter*, novellas

Becker, Lauren—*If I Would Leave Myself Behind*, stories

Ben-Oni, Rosebud—"A Way Out of the Colonia" in *Camera Obscura*

Beukes, Lauren—*The Shining Girls* and *Broken Monsters*, novels

Blau, Jessica Anya—*Drinking Closer to Home*, novel

Bryant, Rae—*The Indefinite State of Imaginary Morals*, short stories

Burke, Cheysa—*Let's Play White*, short stories

C

Cain, Chelsea—The Gretchen Lowell Series, novels

Campbell, Bonnie Jo—*Once Upon a River* and *American Salvage*, novels

Chadburn, Melissa—"Plans to be Loved," at *Word Riot*

Chase, Katie—"Man and Wife," in *The Missouri Review*

Chase, Victorya—"Anti-Theft," in *Cemetery Dance*

Christle, Heather—*The Difficult Farm*, poetry

Collins, Myfawny—*Echolocation*, novel

Crane, Antonia—*Spent*, memoir

D

Davidson, Hilary—*The Next One to Fall* and *Damage Done*, novels

Davis, Amanda C.—"Drift," in *Shock Totem*

Duffey, Barbara—"And All Night Long We Have Not Stirred," in
    Exigencies

E

Ehrhardt, Pia Z.—*Famous Fathers and Other Stories*, short stories

Elliott, Franki—*Piano Rats*, short stories

Engel, Patricia—*Vida*, short stories

Etter, Sarah Rose—*Tongue Party*, short stories

F

Fallon, Siobhan—*You Know When the Men Are Gone*, novel

Farrell, Jenn—*The Devil You Know* and *Sugar Bush*, short stories

Faust, Christa—*Choke Hold* and *Money Shot*, novels

Faust, Gabrielle—Eternal Vigilance Series, novels

Fitzgerald, Erin—"This Morning Will Be Different," in *Shut Up / Look Pretty*

Fouquet, Kristin—*Twenty Stories*, short stories

Foster, Heather—"Armadillo" in *Exigencies*

Fowler, Heather—*Suspended Heart*, short stories

Frangello, Gina—*Slut Lullabies*, short stories

G

Gardner, Faith—"My Mother's Condition," in *Exigencies*

Gaudry, Molly—*We Take Me Apart*, novella

Gowen, Rose—"He's a Porketarian and I Love Him," at *McSweeney's Internet Tendency*

Gowin, Amanda—*Radium Girls*, stories

Gran, Sara—*Come Closer* and *Dope*, novels

Gay, Roxane—*Bad Feminist*, essays

Gray, Amelia—*THREATS*, novel

Guerlain, Nikki—"Sick Ticket," in *In Search of a City: Los Angeles in 1,000 Words*

H

Hamilton, Mary—*We Know What We Are*, short stories

Hinton, Frank—*I Don't Respect Female Expression*, short stories

Hoang, Lily—*Changing*, novel

Hunter, Lindsay—*Daddy's* and *DON'T KISS ME*, short stories

I

Irby, Samantha—*Meaty*, essays

J

Jemc, Jac—*A Different Bed Every Time*, short stories

Jones-Howe, Rebecca—*Vile Men*, stories

K

Krilanovich, Grace—*The Orange Eats Creeps*, novel
Knickerbocker, Alyssa—*Your Rightful Home*, novella

L

LaSart, C. W.—*Ad Nauseam*, short stories
Laskowski, Tara—"The Etiquette of Homicide," in *Barrelhouse*
Lepucki, Edan—*California*, novel
Lewis, Lauryn Allison—*The Beauties*, short stories
Link, Kelly—*Magic for Beginners* and *Pretty Monsters*, short stories
Lippmann, Sara—"Queen of Hearts," at *Metazen*
Logan, Kirsty—"Local God," in *Shut Up / Look Pretty*

M

McDonnell, Madeline—*There Is Something Inside, It Wants to Get Out*, stories
McKibbins, Rachel—*Pink Elephant*, poetry
McNett, Molly—*One Dog Happy*, short stories
Miller, Mary—*Big World*, short stories
Morrissette, Micaela—"The Familiars," in *The Weird*

N

Nelson, H.L.—"Dirtman" in *Nightmare Magazine*

O

Ostlund, Lori—*The Bigness of the World*, short stories

P

Parkison, Aimee—*Woman with Dark Horses*, short stories
Percy, Jen—*Demon Camp*, non-fiction
Petrosino, Kiki—*Fort Red Border*, poetry
Pokrass, Meg—*Damn Sure Right*, short stories

R

Read, Sarah—"Golden Avery," in *Black Static*

Reale, Michelle—"What Passes For Normal," in *Shut Up / Look Pretty*

Renek, Nava—"Mating in Captivity," in *Men Undressed*

Rooney, Kathleen—*For You, For You I Am Trilling These Songs*, essays

Rubio, Marytza—"Brujeria for Beginners," in *Exigencies*

Ryder, Pamela—*A Tendency to Be Gone*, short stories

S

Scott, Laura Ellen—*Death Wishing*, novel, and *Curio*, short stories

Sefton, Meg—"Ash" at *Dark Sky Magazine*

Sellers, Heather—*You Don't Look Like Anyone I Know*, memoir

Solomon, Susan—"Chicks With Two First Names," in *Men Undressed*

Sneed, Christine—*Portraits of a Few of the People I've Made Cry*, short stories

Spiegel, Jennifer—*The Freak Chronicles* and *Love Slave*, novels

Sparks, Amber—*May We Shed These Human Bodies*, short stories

Stark, Kio—*Follow Me Down*, novel

Stielstra, Megan—*Once I Was Cool*, essays

Straub, Emma—*Laura Lamont's Life in Pictures*, novel

Svoboda, Terese—*Bohemian Girl* and *Pirate Talk or Mermalade*, novels

T

Towell, Gayle—"Paper," in *Burnt Tongues*

Trent, Letitia—*Echo Lake*, novel

Tuite, Meg—*Domestic Apparition*, novel

U

Unferth, Deb Olin—*Minor Robberies*, short stories, and *Vacation*, novel

V

VanProoyen, Laura—*Inkblot and Altar*, poetry

Veselka, Vanessa—*Zazen*, novel

W

Wells, Brandi—*Please Don't Be Upset*, short stories
West, Dawn—"George Sand," at *PANK*
Wong, Alyssa—"The Fisher Queen" in *Fantasy & Science Fiction*

X

xTx—*Normally Special*, short stories

Y

Yskamp, Amanda—"Long Division," in *Caketrain*
Yuknavitch, Lidia—*The Chronology of Water*, memoir and *Dora*, novel

Z

Zambreno, Kate—*Green Girl*, novel
ZoBell, Bonnie—"Serial," at *Necessary Fiction*
Zolbrod, Zoe—*Currency*, novel

Acknowledgments

Black Lawrence Press and Richard Thomas would like to thank the journals and presses that originally published these stories. We'd also like to thank the authors for granting us the permission to reprint their work in this anthology.

"Parts" by Holly Goddard Jones, *The Hudson Review*

"See You Later, Fry-O-Lator" by Monica Drake, *Spork Press*

"The Creepy Girl Story" by Janet Mitchell, *The Brooklyn Rail*

"This Is How It Starts" by Shannon Cain, *The Massachusetts Review*

"Mereá" by Nancy Hightower, *Bourbon Penn*

"Shot Girls" by Kim Chinquee, *Mississippi Review*

"Blooms" by Kathy Fish, *Indiana Review*

"Jagannath" by Karin Tidbeck, *Weird Tales*

"A Galloping Infection" by Paula Bomer, *Word Riot*

"The World of Barry" by Stacey Levine, *The Notre Dame Review*

"Push" by Amina Gautier, *The Southern Review*

"They Make of You a Monster" by Damien Angelica Walters, *Beneath Ceaseless Skies*

"Rondine al Nido" by Claire Vaye Watkins, *Printer's Row*

"Pomp and Circumstances" by Nina McConigley, *Slice*

"When I Make Love to the Bug Man" by Laura Benedict, *PANK*

"Rooey" by Kelly Luce, *The Literary Review*

"Lifelike" by Ethel Rohan first published in *Keyhole Magazine* and collected in the book *Cut Through the Bone* (Dark Sky Books, 2010).

"Like Falling Down and Laughing," first published in *The Cincinnati Review* and collected in the book, *In These Times the Home Is a Tired Place* (University of North Texas Press, 2013). Copyright 2011 Jessica Hollander.

"Rodine al Nido," from *Battleborn* by Claire Vaye Watkins, copyright © 2012 by Claire Vaye Watkins. Used by permission of Riverhead Books, an imprint of Penguin Group (USA) Inc.

"Skinny Girls' Constitution and Bylaws" by Tina May Hall, *The Physics of Imaginary Objects* (University of Pittsburgh Press, 2010).

"Stillborn" by Karen Brown, *Little Sinners and Other Stories* (University of Nebraska Press, 2012).